"Araminta,"

It was the first time [he had used] her name, and a stra[nge]... "Araminta," he mur[mured], curiously impassioned, "for your own sake do I tell you this, I swear: Do not wed Judd Hobart. He is not the man for you."

"So you keep saying. But you give me no real reason why I should not marry him, General," Araminta rejoined breathlessly, mesmerized by his dark, hot eyes. She wished he were not standing so close to her.

"You are too stubborn for your own good, *señorita*. Very well, then. You shall have a reason!" He moved suddenly and swiftly, pinioning her arms behind her back, forcing her up against him. Then, his eyes darkening with passion, Rigo crushed his mouth savagely down on hers. She had been kissed before, but not like this, never like this . . .

———————

Also by Rebecca Brandewyne

Across a Starlit Sea
And Gold Was Ours
Desire in Disguise
Forever My Love
Heartland
Love, Cherish Me
No Gentle Love
The Outlaw Hearts
Rainbow's End
Rose of Rapture
Upon a Moon-Dark Moor

Published by
WARNER BOOKS

REBECCA BRANDEWYNE

DESPERADO

WARNER BOOKS

A Time Warner Company

WARNER BOOKS EDITION

Cover illustration by Greg Gulbronson
Cover lettering by Carl Dellacroce
Cover design by Jackie Merri Meyer

Warner Books, Inc.
1271 Avenue of the Americas
New York, NY 10020

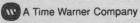 A Time Warner Company

Printed in the United States of America

First Printing: November, 1992

10 9 8 7 6 5 4 3 2 1

For my readers,
my constant joy and inspiration.
With much affection and deepest appreciation.

Special thanks to Ozzie, Bill, and Robert,
for understanding about a writer's deadlines
and going above and beyond the call of duty
to keep my computers up and running!

The Players

IN TEXAS:

Noble Winthrop, a rancher

His granddaughter:

Araminta

Frank Hobart, a rancher
Elizabeth Hobart, wife to Frank

Their children:

Judd
Velvet

IN MEXICO:

Rigo del Castillo, a Revolutionary
Pancho Villa, a Revolutionary

Contents

PROLOGUE
To Kidnap a Gringa Bride
1

BOOK ONE
Desperado
17

BOOK TWO
Silken Ties that Bind
169

BOOK THREE
The Villistas
275

EPILOGUE
Lovers Entwine, and Hearts Enfold
357

Desperado

A desperado went a-raidin', and he did ride, olé, sí, sí,
O'er the Rio Grande so muddy and wide, olé, sí, sí;
A knife and a pistol by his side,
He rode to kidnap a gringa bride.
¡Olé, sí, sí, olé!

A desperado went a-courtin', and he did find, olé, sí, sí,
Sweet are the silken ties that bind, olé, sí, sí;
Around the body and heart, they wind
To drive a man clean out of his mind.
¡Olé, sí, sí, olé!

A desperado went a-warrin', and he did fight, olé, sí, sí,
Through many a long and wearying night, olé, sí, sí;
He and Villa would turn all wrong to right,
While la gringa danced by a campfire light.
¡Olé, sí, sí, olé!

A desperado went a-seekin', and he did hold, olé, sí, sí,
A green-eyed gringa with hair of gold, olé, sí, sí;
She was gentle, and he was bold.
Lovers entwine, and hearts enfold.
¡Olé, sí, sí, olé!*

*The ballad of General Rigo del Castillo and his woman, la gringa.
Sung by the Villistas to the tune of "Mr. Froggie Went-A-Courtin'."

Prologue

To Kidnap a Gringa Bride

The High Sierra, Texas, 1913

They mistook the shots for fireworks, at first.

It was a natural mistake, Araminta was to think later, much later, when her initial shock had passed, leaving in its wake a deep fury and a fear darker than her wedding night—which the fireworks celebrated. But in the beginning, her head aching, her senses dulled by heartbreak and too much champagne, she, like everyone else gathered at her grandfather Noble Winthrop's ranch, the High Sierra, had paid little heed to the brilliant explosions that set the night sky ablaze. Her polite, artificial smile—worn throughout the long ceremony held in the courtyard, beneath a white canopy that had provided scant protection against the blistering rays of the summer sun; throughout the boisterous barbecue that had followed, lasting until the heat had at last driven the ladies to retire to cool, stuccoed bedrooms to loosen stays and lie down, the gentlemen to seek the shade of wide porticoes, where drinks and cigars were plentiful; and throughout the evening of promenading, dancing, and merrymaking—now felt permanently engraved upon her face. Araminta, not a happy bride, was exhausted and yearned intensely for the interminable day to end, for a bath, and for bed. But still, she continued her brittle pretense of gaiety to postpone as long as possible the moment when she must go upstairs with her husband, for the thought of what was still to come this night dismayed her utterly. For an instant, her smile faltered before she forced it back to her lips, once more masking her true emotions, while silently, fervently, she prayed for a miracle to spare her from her husband's unwanted attentions. Yet when the miracle came, so swiftly and unexpectedly, she was as stricken as she had expected to be by the wedding night she had dreaded so long.

For the sounds that split the night air were no longer the detonation of fireworks, but of guns and grenades. That much was made clear when the Mexican manservant burst without warning into the opulent ballroom. There, the wedding guests from far and wide had repaired for the cotillion and to watch—from the portico that ran the length of one beautifully papered wall lined with open French doors—the fireworks that, even as the manservant babbled in fright, sputtered and died. Disturbed in the midst of playing a waltz, the orchestra discordantly lapsed into stillness; and in some confusion, the guests who had not yet seen or heard the agitated manservant glanced about inquiringly, wondering what was the matter. Several people—doubtless more inebriated than the rest and not realizing that aught was amiss—shrugged off the unwelcome, untimely interruption. Someone cracked a loud, drunken joke, and spurts of conversation and laughter broke out again here and there. Somebody else demanded that the orchestra resume playing, and then Noble Winthrop's raised voice called authoritatively for attention as he made his way to the dais where the orchestra was assembled. But before he could make any announcement, a shower of bullets bombarded the long row of colonnades outside on the portico, chipping and pitting them, spraying the ballroom and guests with shards of adobe and lead. At that, the remaining sounds of revelry within turned to screams of terror, and panic erupted as the crème de la crème of Texas society metamorphosed into beasts brutally shoving and trampling one another to flee from the menace that threatened from the darkness beyond the ballroom.

Stunned and disbelieving, Araminta was slow to accept that the wedding night she had dreamed about with more than mere maidenly apprehension had suddenly become a different nightmare. She stood rooted to the center of the ballroom floor—callously deserted by her unchivalrous partner—while, like a wild blue norther whipping and whining about a lone tree, chaos swirled around her. Everything occurred so quickly that she could not seem to reconcile what was taking place with the fact that, to her, all appeared strangely to move in slow motion, the edges of the mad scene blurred like those of a vignette. This could not be happening, she thought dumbly. The nineteenth century, with its savage Indian raids, marauding outlaws, professional gunslingers, and turbulent range wars, was past. It was 1913. Nobody attacked ranches anymore—especially not the High Sierra. This could not be real. Yet somehow, it was. Awareness of her peril abruptly penetrated as she was violently jostled this way and that, and then swept terrifyingly into the path of the mindless stampede from the ballroom.

Only dimly did Araminta register now what were plainly the persistent reports of guns and grenades, the answering shots from the rifles and carbines of her grandfather's men as they belatedly began to fire, the pounding of booted feet and jingle of Mexican spurs as shadowy forms raced across the courtyard toward the portico and ballroom, and the urgent shouts and shrieks of pain and dread that echoed on the night wind. As she spied the intruders, Araminta's mind was consumed with fear, cotton-tasting in her mouth; sweat oozed from her every pore, seeping through the elaborately embroidered fabric of her champagne-gold bridal gown. The yards of flowing material that swathed her from the waist down twined sinuously about her legs, hindering her flight. With a tearing sound, the heel of one slipper caught in her hem. She tripped and, as she lost her balance, was knocked to her knees by the onrushing mass of guests. Her heart leaped to her throat, choking off her horrified gasp. In moments, she would be crushed underfoot! Futilely, she raised her arms to try to protect herself from the barrage of bodies that bore down on her.

Above the cacophony of the riot, a voice cried her name sharply, "Araminta!" Then a large, powerful hand thrust its way through the crowd to close like an iron manacle about her wrist and jerk her up from the floor. Flooded with a deep sense of relief at her narrow escape, Araminta scarcely felt the pain when her arm was nearly wrenched from its socket and her rib cage bruised as her husband flung her unceremoniously over his brawny shoulder. His fists and elbows drove a wedge through the mob as he rapidly propelled his way across the ballroom, carrying Araminta as easily as though she weighed no more than a fifty-pound sack of flour. For the first time that day, she was thankful for her husband's bullish size and strength.

Through the snarl of her long blond hair, tumbled loose from its pins in the uproar, she witnessed a horde of unfamiliar men—Mexican *bandoleros*—bursting now through the open French doors, bristling with an array of weapons—rifles, carbines, shotguns, pistols, machetes, knives, and cartridge-filled bandoliers. To her horror, the desperadoes, on gaining entrance, opened fire on the ballroom, shooting—much to Araminta's gratitude but complete incomprehension—over the heads of the guests and increasing the panic and pandemonium. No one was killed, but plaster and glass rained down everywhere as the ceiling and the two massive crystal chandeliers, alight with a thousand candles, were riddled by bullets. Shortly afterward, one of the heavy silk cords from which each of the chandeliers was suspended was shot in half, and the chandelier crashed to the floor, where it shattered, slinging glass and candles in every direction. Mercifully, nobody was beneath the chandelier when it hurtled to its doom. But several of the burning candles, rolling here and there and kicked on by heedless feet across the floor, came to rest along the wall bordering the portico, igniting the brocade draperies that hung like gilded waterfalls on either side of each set of French doors. Within moments, the whole ballroom resembled an inferno, the tongues of flame licking their way up the draperies endlessly reflected in the mirrors that lined the opposite wall—until the guns of the *bandoleros* spat again and yet again, and the mirrors rived and splintered, fragments spilling like molten fire upon the highly polished floor. Fearing that the blaze would spread through the entire house, several of the braver guests and servants ran under the cover of the acrid smoke permeating the ballroom to yank the draperies down and stamp on them, smothering the flames.

Araminta's head reeled. The ballroom seemed to spin crazily before her tearful green eyes as, like a rag doll, she dangled upside down against her husband's back, trying with her hands to shield her nose and mouth from the smoke. She closed her eyes against the sting of the smoke, coughing and gagging, her stomach roiling. With relief, she gulped fresh air when, finally, her husband strode from the ballroom into the grand entry hall that ran the width of the imposing, two-story adobe hacienda.

Here, now that the fire had been extinguished, the female guests were frantically scrambling up the sweeping staircase to the safety of their bedrooms above, while the males were seizing the weapons and boxes of ammunition being hastily passed out from the gun cases in Noble Winthrop's study by the ranch's foreman, Clem McCabe, and several other ranch hands. Her grandfather himself, Araminta dazedly observed, was standing in the great hall, outraged, cursing and issuing orders right and left at the top of his lungs. With scarcely a glance at her to assure himself of her well-being, Araminta's husband deposited her roughly at the foot of the steps.

"Get upstairs to your bedroom," he commanded curtly. "Lock yourself in, and don't open your door to anybody but me."

She nodded numbly, her face ashen, her eyes wide with trepidation. She longed for some word of encouragement, a comforting gesture; but taking her obedience and mettle for granted, her husband had already turned away, a rifle now in hand. She was the bride of one of the most important men in Texas; he expected her to behave as such. When she last saw him, he was heading outside through the huge, ornately carved wooden front doors of the hacienda, all thoughts of her, she felt sure, driven from his mind by his desire for vengeance. This attack upon the High Sierra—on his wedding day at that—he would view as an arrogant affront to be answered as speedily and harshly as possible. Knowing the cruelty of which her husband was capable, Araminta shuddered for an instant with more than just fear of the desperadoes who had dared to assault her grandfather's kingly domain. Then, gathering up her skirts, she hurried upstairs, pausing to knock on the closed doors all along the corridor as, tardily recollecting her obligations to the guests, she checked to be sure that the ladies, at least, were securely barricaded in their bedrooms.

Once in her own bedroom, Araminta shut the stout door firmly and turned the key in the lock. For a moment, she leaned weakly against the door, trembling and trying to catch her breath, grateful for the concealing darkness of the room, brightened only by the silver moonlight streaming in through the open French doors that led to her balcony beyond. Then, hearing the escalating shots and explosions outside, she ran to peer over the rough-hewn timber balustrade of the balcony.

Below, the night was alive with turmoil and violence. The flames of the myriad torches lighted in honor of her wedding celebration flickered in the wind, erratically casting into relief and shadow the *bandoleros* and her grandfather's men as they exchanged fire and lobbed grenades from the shelter of the porticoes and outbuildings. Blazes ignited during the battle further illuminated the darkness, and as the caustic smoke billowed and drifted on the wind, Araminta could see that bodies lay sprawled on the ground and that wounded men slowly but desperately crawled for cover. She shivered at the sight, wondering how many of them would not survive.

Calmer now in the relative safety of her bedroom, she pondered the reason for the onslaught upon the High Sierra. Most of the Mexicans who raided across the border were bandits and cattle rustlers, and unlikely to wage such a direct and predatory attack upon the ranch. Still, like her husband, her grandfather was a rich, powerful man with many rancorous foes. It was entirely possible that the desperadoes were mercenaries hired by someone whose animosity her grandfather—or even her husband—had, rightly or wrongly, earned over the years. But why should retaliation come now, tonight of all nights, with her wedding celebration in progress and the house full of guests, many of whom were men as wealthy and influential as her grandfather and her husband?

A hail of bullets whizzed by Araminta, hazardously near, wrenching her from her reverie as she abruptly recognized how exposed she was on the balcony. How foolish of her to have stepped outside! Quickly, she retreated into her bedroom, pulling the French doors closed and, with difficulty, sliding the brass bolt into place, alarmed as the muntined panes in the doors suddenly began to rattle furiously, as though the whole house were quaking, about to collapse. She could hear the repeated hammering of wood against wood coming from downstairs and realized that the *bandoleros* must be battering a ram against the front doors. She wondered why. The desperadoes already had access through the ballroom; they might even now be roaming the corridors of the house, committing murder and mayhem.

Araminta was no coward. But as she huddled in her bedroom, she had never been more aware of her femininity and her vulnerability. Fearful of being raped and killed, she yearned for a gun or even a knife. But nothing was nearer at hand than a heavy brass candlestick, which would have to serve. Taking up the improvised weapon, she slowly removed the key from the lock of her bedroom door and knelt to press one eye to the keyhole. The hall beyond appeared to be empty, but still, anxiety gnawed at her, and she dared not open the door. Silently, sternly, she chastised herself, attempting to work up her courage. What if someone needed help?

Strangely, Araminta felt no anxiety for either her grandfather or husband. The awe in which both men were held in Texas was such that they might have been invincible. The idea that either of them would be struck down was simply inconceivable. But there were the guests and servants to consider, and until she took up residence at her husband's ranch, Araminta was still the lady of her grandfather's house. It was her duty, she told herself, to look after those for whom she was responsible.

Araminta was so absorbed in her inner conflict that she had not heard the stealthy tread of boots upon her balcony. Now, one of the panes in the French doors was suddenly smashed, the blow sounding as loud as a bomb. Gasping, she whirled on her knees to spy two Mexican *bandoleros* standing outside on her balcony. With the butt of his pistol, one of the men was knocking out shards of glass so he could reach inside and unbolt the doors. Within moments, the desperadoes would be in her bedroom! Dully, Araminta realized that her candlestick would not offer much protection against them. With all her might, she hurled it at the French doors, hitting the hand of the man fumbling at the bolt. Growling an oath, he snatched his injured hand back, glaring at her malevolently through the glass. She did not wait to see more, but turned back to the bedroom door. The key! Where was the key? She had taken it out and laid it down. . . . Frenziedly, she scrabbled on the floor for the key, as, behind her, the bolt on the French doors slid back with a loud snap. Her fingers closed over the key just as the *bandoleros* burst into her bedroom. Crying out with terror, Araminta jerked up the key, jammed it into the lock, and twisted hard. Then, springing to her feet, she wrested open the bedroom door and ran.

Behind her, she could hear the thudding of booted feet and the jingle of Mexican spurs as the two men gave chase down the corridor. She could almost feel the heat of their labored breathing—mingling with her own hard rasps—against her nape as they raced after her. She knew, with a sinking heart, that she had little chance of eluding them, especially trammeled by her skirts as she was. Tears streamed down her face. She did not even have breath enough to scream for help.

Somehow, Araminta managed to reach the main staircase. Panting, shaking, she stumbled down the steps, only to stop short on the landing halfway down as the front doors finally yielded to the battering ram of the desperadoes outside and, whooping victoriously, they surged into the great hall, cutting off her only avenue of escape. Hard on their heels through the arched portal came a magnificent black stallion flecked white with foam and ridden by a bold, handsome man as dark as his mount. For an instant, man and beast poised on the threshold, the man momentarily fighting to retain control of the high-spirited animal amid the hand-to-hand combat taking place all about them, the horse whinnying and snorting, rearing and prancing, shod hooves ringing sharply on the terra-cotta tiles of the great hall. Then, shouting to the *bandoleros*, his rifle raised high in triumph, the man spurred the stallion into the melee.

After casually dispatching three would-be attackers, he paused and glanced up the staircase to where Araminta was still standing, petrified. From beneath the wide, upturned brim of the black, silver-trimmed sombrero that shadowed his face, his glittering, dark-brown eyes pierced her own huge, frightened green ones; and in that moment, all about her seemed to fade into nothingness, her senses to narrow, to focus acutely on the man as, suddenly, she at last grasped the purpose of the desperadoes' barbarous assault upon the High Sierra. A slow, sardonic smile that sent an icy shiver up her spine curved the man's sensual mouth as he observed her face drain of color. Then, with a fierce cry, he roweled the stallion forward. Scrabbling for purchase, the horse plunged up the steps toward Araminta. In desperation, she turned to flee, but the *bandoleros* who had broken into her bedroom waited behind her at the top of the staircase, blocking her path to freedom. She was cut off. There was nowhere to go, nothing, even, with which to try to defend herself. She could only stand there helplessly on the landing, while man and beast came on.

As the man bent to swoop her up, Araminta thought that his hard, mocking face gentled with a trace of admiration and regret; but the look was fleeting, and she concluded that she must have imagined it, that it must have been a trick of the candlelight and shadows, after all, for he was not deterred from his objective. His left arm tightened like a steel band about her slender waist, pulling her up and settling her firmly before him on the saddle, though she fought him wildly, blindly, pummeling him about the head and shoulders until the pressure of his arm increased around her, shutting off her breath and ending her futile struggles. He murmured something in Spanish— she did not understand the words—then laughed softly in her ear, his warm breath making her tingle with fear and a queer excitement that made her feel sick and ashamed.

"*¡Vámonos!*" he yelled hoarsely to his men, waving his rifle peremptorily. "*¡Vámonos, compadres! ¡Montad vuestros caballos! ¡Cabalguemos!*" Let's go! Let's go, comrades! Mount your horses! Let's ride!

Moments later, they were galloping out into the darkness, down the hard-baked road that led away from the High Sierra, Araminta's tears mingling with the cool night wind sweeping through her wildly streaming blond hair. The desperado's arm gripped her tightly, pressing her against him familiarly, in ominous promise of further intimacy, as they left the ranch far behind. Above, a falling star streaked like a silver bullet across the gunpowder-black sky, an ill omen Araminta already understood.

She was to spend her wedding night with her husband's bitterest enemy.

Book One

Desperado

Chapter One

The Plains, Texas, 1912

As she gazed out the window of the private coach at the rolling plains beyond, Araminta Winthrop, lately of New York City, didn't know whether to be glad or sorry that the train on which she was traveling was heading west instead of east. She was still not sure she had made the right decision regarding her grandfather's cable. For the hundredth time, it seemed, since she had begun her journey, she withdrew from her reticule the plain envelope she had saved and read again the single sheet of paper inside. It was as cordial as was possible for a cable—in which verbosity could not be expected—and her grandfather's reasons for wanting her to join him in Texas were certainly plausible. But still, Araminta could not rid herself of the niggling doubt that plagued her.

Noble Winthrop, her grandfather, was a land baron and cattle king, one of the richest and most powerful men in the state of Texas, and his influence extended even as far as the nation's capital. When last she had seen him, she had still been a child—and numb with heartbreak, so she only vaguely recalled him. Even so, the fear and loathing that her dim memories engendered were so stark and real as to be almost palpable. She remembered him as a towering figure, with a bald pate surrounded by a fringe of short-cropped white hair, and with bushy white brows and mustache, a hooked nose, and dark-gray eyes like gunmetal, so fierce and piercing that their stare was uncannily eaglelike. He had never been fond of children, although a grandson would undoubtedly have won his attention and perhaps even his affection. But his granddaughter—whenever he had been reminded of her—had earned only his contemptuous dismissal. Araminta had been grateful he had scarcely paid her any heed, and knowing how irascible his disposition was, she had taken care to keep out of his way.

Her most vivid recollection of him was of the day when he and his only son, Preston, her father, quarreled for the last time. Araminta, only seven years old at the time, did not comprehend the terrible argument she inadvertently overheard. She knew only that, afterward, Papa packed up her and Mama and stormed from the High Sierra, vowing never to return. Only many years later did Araminta finally understand the acrimonious words exchanged between father and son that pivotal day and grasp the fact that her mother had not been able to have any more children, thereby extinguishing Noble Winthrop's fervent hope of founding a dynasty through his son. Even now, as she closed her eyes tiredly, Araminta could hear the hideous dispute between father and son ringing in her ears, making her cringe as though she were a child again.

"Should have put your unproductive mother away or divorced her when I learned she couldn't have any more children, Preston—damn all whey-faced, narrow-hipped females! Useless for breeding! I tried to tell you that when you married Katherine, but you wouldn't listen to me—no, sir! Thought you knew it all!" and "Don't make the same mistake I did, son. Don't martyr yourself for a woman. They only despise you for it in the end," and "For Christ's sake! All cats are gray in the dark, you fool!" were just some of the abusive statements Noble roared at his son that day. But Preston Winthrop loved his wife, and he adamantly refused to set her aside, preferring instead to be banished from the High Sierra forever and cut off without a cent for thwarting his domineering father.

Knowing that Noble's vindictive arm had a long reach, Preston took his small family as far away as possible from Texas, to New York City. He possessed an inheritance from his dead mother, of which his father could not legally deprive him, and his background was such that doors that would have remained firmly closed to another opened easily to him. He was not without his father's shrewdness, and over time, Preston prospered through numerous investments and holdings in various enterprises, eventually making his own fortune, which he lovingly lavished on his wife and daughter. So the family, although made uneasy by the occasional thought of Noble's plotting to seek retribution on his son, was nevertheless affluent, happy, and close. Then, without warning, tragedy struck. Gaily departing from a party one evening, Araminta's parents plunged to their deaths in an elevator accident, leaving Araminta a twelve-year-old orphan. But as though the blow she had suffered were not enough, she soon discovered from her grandfather and the phalanx of other gentlemen and their agents who came to New York City that the majority of her father's assets were pledged as collateral against several business loans, which were promptly called at his death. When all of Preston Winthrop's affairs were sorted out to the satisfaction of the bankers, the investors, the stockholders, the lawyers, and the accountants, Araminta was left virtually penniless, dependent for her livelihood upon her grandfather, who had become her legal guardian.

Beset by shock and sorrow, she felt a deep sense of relief when, rather than insisting that Araminta accompany him back to the High Sierra, Noble instead enrolled her in Miss Standish's Female Academy, an elite boarding school in upstate New York. Despite his gruff but benign treatment of her, she still found him frightening. In addition, Araminta could not help holding him responsible for the deaths of her parents. She hated him and never wanted to see or hear from him again.

Her wish was partially granted, for her grandfather

never visited her once during all the years she spent at the academy, although appropriate presents, no doubt selected by his efficient secretary, Mr. Gideon, dutifully arrived for her each birthday and Christmas. Other than this, her grandfather displayed, to Araminta's knowledge, no real interest in her, for which she was mostly thankful. She did not know that per his orders, regular, detailed reports about her were made to him each quarter by her teachers and his agents. Still, despite herself, she could not help now and then but think heatedly, especially at holidays, that he ought to take some notice of her, however small; for no matter how horrid he was, he was still her only living relative, and she was lonely and unpopular at the boarding school.

Now that her graduation was behind her, Araminta could see that she herself was responsible for much of her misery at the academy. In her initial grief and forlornness at the deaths of her parents, she had retreated inward, walling herself off from the girls who tried to befriend her. Later, though she was not without backbone, she was also naturally shy and reticent, and she hesitated to push herself forward, unsure how to combat the reputation she had by then unjustly acquired of being a cold and aloof snob. Angered and hurt by her classmates' scorn and ridicule, their spiteful rejection of her tentative overtures, she proudly withdrew into herself again, applied herself to her studies, and received the highest marks in her class— which, unhappily, only served to alienate her even further from the other girls. She told herself fiercely that she did not care. But as a result, upon graduation,

Araminta departed with heartfelt gladness from Miss Standish's Female Academy to take up residence in New York City, the only place she had ever truly thought of as home.

Hers was a laudable but foolhardy decision for a young woman hardly turned eighteen, and she made it without her grandfather's knowledge, approval, or support, ardently determined to sever forever the connection between them rather than to obey his arrogantly delivered behest that, after graduation, she return to the High Sierra. She was an adult, Araminta assured herself. He had done his duty by her. Now he owed her nothing—and she wanted nothing from him. Like her father, she would make her own way in the world. Writing and sketching had been her fortes at the boarding school, and she was resolved to put these skills to use as a journalist, to establish a name and career for herself. But in 1912, in an era in which any lady worthy of the title neither toiled nor spun, women who did so were taken gross advantage of—in more ways than one—by the pragmatic, conscienceless men who controlled the nation's industries, including its wire services, newspapers, and magazines.

Araminta's sex, beauty, and youth were against her from the start. Alone, unprotected, desperate for a job, she was an easy mark for villains—and New York City had more than its share of these. If Miss Winthrop would care to step into the back room, some mutually beneficial agreement could no doubt be reached? Naively, the first time she applied for a position, Araminta swallowed this deceitful line. For the majority of her young life, she had for all practical purposes been sheltered from the harsh realities of the world—first by her parents and then by her teachers at the boarding school—and taught to believe and to trust in the innate honesty, goodness, and kindness of her fellow man. Her grandfather, whenever she thought of him, she labeled an anomaly, a freak of nature, soured by some unknown element and, if she were charitable and God-fearing, to be pitied and forgiven instead of despised. She had not as yet been cruelly disillusioned, only wounded in ways that, while grievous, had eventually healed, leaving her ultimately merely a little sad and bewildered when she dwelled on the scars. This was not often, however, for Araminta possessed the natural resiliency of youth, and her inherent faith and quiet courage sustained her, bolstering her conviction that in the end, good always triumphed over evil.

She scarcely escaped—from that first back room on Newspaper Row—with her virtue intact. She was sickened and horrified by the lascivious advances forcibly thrust upon her; but still, after her initial revulsion, outrage, and dread had passed, she continued her quest, stubbornly undeterred. The man who had assaulted her had been a blackguard, a scoundrel, lacking morals and decency. She would not encounter his ilk again. Weeks later, she knew, bitterly, that all like promises of employment were equally mendacious; no man would take her seriously as a reporter. The groping hands, bold propositions, crude insults, sly leers, and, rarely, well-meant but dispiriting counsel she endured in her search for work at last convinced her of that—and of the inborn base and unscrupulous nature of all men.

New York City itself, also, contributed to the removal of the blinders from Araminta's eyes. It was not at all the city she had seen as a child from the secure, resplendent confines of the impressive mansion and elegant carriage her father had owned, but a teeming, terrifying place of menace, hardship, poverty, and starvation. Though Araminta had hoarded every dime of the pocket money her grandfather had sent to her each quarter at the academy, her savings depleted at an alarming rate as she pressed on with her search for legitimate work.

Finally, she was reduced to accepting a post as a clerk at a small daily newspaper, the *Record*, whose publisher and editor, a bighearted Irishman by the name of Liam O'Grady, took pity on her and hired her to do such menial tasks as running errands, fetching coffee, and sharpening pencils. Sometimes, she doubled as a classified-ad taker and proofreader. Once in a great while, after she had been at the *Record* for over three months, Liam permitted her to indulge her dream of becoming a proper journalist by writing short, genteel articles on fashion, food, and general "fluff" for the women's page, which appeared twice weekly. For all this, Araminta was paid seven dollars a week— which was all that Liam could afford—and in an age when the average man earned less than fifteen dollars a week for sixty hours' worth of work and many people were unemployed, she felt herself lucky to get it. Still, it was sometimes not enough to cover even her meager expenses, and then she was forced to dip into what little remained of her savings, a circumstance that panicked her.

She lived in a room smaller than the closet that had once held her clothes in her father's mansion, in a dilapidated tenement owned by a slum lord who moved, ironically, in the same circles of society as Preston and Katherine Winthrop had; and though Araminta shrank from violence, she nevertheless learned early on, of dire necessity, how to defend herself, both verbally and physically, from the riffraff who haunted the mean streets of New York City. She carried in her reticule at all times a heavy paperweight and a sturdy umbrella to ward off any rogue who dared to accost her; and after she had, with her weighty purse, fearfully but determinedly whacked two knaves and, with her sharp-tipped umbrella, jabbed another, most of the men in her own neighborhood, at least, steered clear of her. She made the most of the plain, serviceable garments her grandfather had deemed fitting for a young lady at Miss Standish's Female Academy, emphasizing their unattractiveness and playing down her looks by pinning her long blond hair up severely, wearing an old, shabby, wide-brimmed hat over her head, and keeping her face modestly cast down when she rode the streetcar that ferried her to and from Printing House Square, at the north end of Park Row, where most of the city's newspapers were located. These precautions further ensured that she was seldom bothered by anyone—with the exception of the inevitable beggars on every street corner, even more destitute than she; for although New York City was home to some of the richest, most powerful men in the nation, it also, as she now knew, swarmed with masses of the downtrodden and the derelict. The vast majority of these were immigrants worse off in America, land of freedom and opportunity, than they had been in the countries from whose afflictions they had so desperately fled, and Negroes the North had freed shortly over a half a century previous and then callously abandoned to their ignorance and own means, however inadequate.

So careful was Araminta about not attracting attention to herself or approaching for assistance any of her parents' old friends that it took Noble Winthrop's agents several months to locate her—months in which, fuming, he alternately cursed her vehemently and worried that she was dead, lost to him forever, and that his most cherished hope was once more dust in the wind. Because he had always perceived women as subservient to men, put on earth solely to gratify men's desires and breed heirs, he had, after the break with his son, in truth, forgotten Araminta's existence. However, it had struck Noble most compellingly upon seeing her again when making the arrangements for her parents' funerals and her own future that at twelve years of age, she held promise of blossoming into a breathtaking beauty; and for the first time, it had occurred to him that she might be of some use to him, after all. His godson, Judd Hobart, would in a few years be in need of a wife; and by then, if Noble's budding scheme bore fruit, Araminta would be ripe for the plucking and, dowered with the promise of his considerable fortune, a prize any man with an ounce of red blood in his veins and greed in his soul would covet. Through his godson and his granddaughter would Noble's dream of founding a dynasty at long last be realized. He need do nothing but wait until Araminta was grown and, in the meanwhile, drop a subtle hint now and then to the Hobart family and plan.

That Araminta would have the nerve to defy him, to disregard his instructions about traveling to Texas after her graduation from Miss Standish's Female Academy, and to run away before the arrival in New York of the two hirelings he had dispatched to the boarding school to fetch her home, never once occurred to Noble. But he was not without a certain grudging admiration for his granddaughter's gumption and grit, and his interest in her increased. So, like her father, she dared to rebel against him, did she? The thought did not wholly displease him, for his godson, Judd, liked his fillies spirited rather than docile. Still, Araminta must learn that no matter how hard she struggled, she would be bridled, saddled, mastered, and— sooner or later—ridden, just like any other female.

Yet when his agents finally tracked his granddaughter down and reported her whereabouts and activities, Noble astutely recognized the fact that his command that she come home and his taking her compliance for granted had impelled her to flight. Her love and loyalty lay with her dead parents. Because of that, if nothing else, she would never return to the High Sierra of her own free will unless all other avenues were closed to her. Intolerant of defeat, Noble instantly set about to eliminate her alternatives. If Araminta desired to

challenge him, she would soon discover he was a
worthy opponent.

A thorough investigation into Liam O'Grady's
background and affairs was conducted. Then, late one
evening shortly after all the delving deemed necessary
was concluded, Liam himself was called upon by Noble's agents, during which visit it was politely suggested to the publisher/editor that the *Record* would
be better off without Araminta Winthrop on its staff.
Information about Liam's heavy drinking, numerous
gambling debts, indiscretions with assorted and sundry
whores, and friendships with certain unsavory charac-
ters was casually mentioned. It was hinted that it would
not only be an embarrassment to the editor, but also
disastrous to his newspaper were his advertisers to
learn of his highly "colorful" private life; for armed
with such knowledge, they would surely prudently
decide to take their business elsewhere, lest they unintentionally become embroiled in some scandal. Liam
was outraged. He felt bad for Araminta. But he was
not a fool, and he had a wife and four children to
support, besides. Unable to meet Araminta's eyes, he
handed her her walking papers the following morning,
his mumbled criticism of her "unsatisfactory work"
and "suffragette's attitude" sounding lame even to
him. He only hoped that she would someday find it in
her heart to forgive him.

Araminta was devastated. She had looked upon
Liam not only as a fatherly benefactor, but also as her
friend. She could not understand the sudden reversal
of his good opinion of her, what she had done to earn
his displeasure. But she soon realized that no amount

of arguing or pleading would move him to change his mind. In a daze, she slowly gathered her belongings and stumbled outside. For hours, she roamed the streets of the city aimlessly before at last making her way to the tenement in which she lived. There, the manager presently appeared at Araminta's door to inform her that her rent was being raised. The weekly sum that would henceforth be required from her was so exorbitant that she gasped, stricken, not knowing how she would have paid it even had she still had a job.

She was cast into the depths of despair at the day's awful turn of events. She knew there was little hope of her obtaining a position at another newspaper. A governess's post would entail service in the very circles of society she had sought to avoid, and she was mortified by the thought of being reduced to begging for charity from her parents' friends and acquaintances. Thus all that realistically was left to her were the factories, the sweatshops where women labored for twelve hours a day or more, six days a week, grew old before their time, and died shortly after their youth had fled. Either the unsanitary working conditions polluted their lungs and sapped their strength, or the monstrous machines they operated ensnared hair, limbs, or skirts and dragged the hapless victim into a crushing mass of pounding rods and grinding gears. Araminta did not want even to think about the women who daily sold themselves in brothels or on street corners, exposing themselves to all sorts of brutality and disease.

Several days later, just as she was on the verge of

being evicted from the tenement, her grandfather's cable arrived. He was disappointed that she had evidently preferred New York to Texas, she read. He was an old man, and lonely. Each was the other's only living relative. It was not right that they should not be a family. It was time to bury the past. Should Araminta wish to reconsider her earlier decision not to make the High Sierra her home, Noble would welcome her with open arms. In the faint hope that she would come, he had arranged for her to draw a draft upon his bank account in New York City. The sum would more than cover the cost of hiring a private coach on the train, any incidental traveling expenses, and all other attendant necessities. At the time, her grandfather's cable seemed like a godsend to Araminta.

Now, in the private coach of the train bearing her steadily westward, she wondered again how her grandfather had known where she was, and she pondered the strange coincidence of her loss of employment and the increase in her rent's being followed so soon by his cable. Clearly, her grandfather must have hired agents to locate her. Had he guessed she would not voluntarily return to the High Sierra and engineered her firing from the *Record* and the raising of her rent to compel her to concede to his wishes? She remembered the way Liam had carefully studied his shoes— as though lying and ashamed of himself—when he had told her she simply wasn't "working out" at the newspaper. Had he somehow been coerced into letting her go? And the tenement . . . she knew from talking to others in the building that hers had apparently been the only rent increase ordered. Further, it had not escaped Araminta's notice that her grandfather had not offered to support her financially so long as she continued to reside in New York City, that his largess was dependent upon her joining him in Texas. But why should he care what happened to her?

It was true that after the deaths of her parents, he had not shirked his duty to her. But even so, he had made no effort to get to know her over the years. His few notes to her at birthdays and Christmases had been terse, stilted, containing no word of love or affection. To suspect, then, that he was responsible for the dire straits in which she had suddenly found herself seemed senseless, crazy. What possible motive could he have that would have driven him to such lengths to secure her presence at the High Sierra? None, really, Araminta thought. He was an old man. Perhaps, in truth, he wanted only to make amends for the past, to ensure that when he died, he could stand with a clear conscience before his Maker. The timing of his cable, however odd, must have been nothing more than a quirk of fate. Perhaps she was, as she half believed, letting her imagination run away with her, seeing shadows where none existed.

Her months in New York City had taken their toll on her, Araminta knew. Often hungry, she had lost weight, and mauve crescents of exhaustion darkened her eyes, for she had never really slept easily at the tenement. Despite her reservations about her grandfather, if she were honest with herself, she was forced to admit that, right now, the thought of being well fed, looked after by a household of servants, and safe in her bed at night held a certain undeniable appeal. Were it not for the fact that she had failed miserably in her bid for independence and felt as though she were somehow betraying the memory of her parents by going back to the High Sierra, Araminta knew deep down that she would be glad not to be rising at four o'clock tomorrow morning to prepare herself for another long, grueling day in New York City.

Sighing heavily, she abandoned her reverie and her contemplation of the rolling plains. It was all of a piece now. However it had come about, she had made her decision, and there was no turning back. Soon, the train would come to a halt at the depot in El Paso, where her grandfather would be waiting.

Chapter Two

Shuddering and screeching, the westbound train on which Araminta traveled drew slowly to a halt at the depot in El Paso. For a moment, however, she did not rise, but continued to gaze out the window, trying to still the sudden racing of her heart. Her long journey was finally at an end—yet she could not help but feel that her future was just beginning. The prospect both excited and unsettled her. She had not felt this way even after graduation and leaving the academy for New York City. Indeed, her short months of independence now seemed unreal and like a nightmare. At last, gathering her belongings, she disembarked from the private coach on to the platform, glancing around expectantly for her grandfather. But she did not see him. Instead, striding toward her was his secretary,

Mr. Gideon, whom she recalled as having accompanied her grandfather to New York City when her parents had died. Araminta did not know whether to be relieved or indignant that her grandfather had not come himself to meet her. Had he cared at all for her, he would surely have been here! But, no, she must not be too quick to judge him, she reminded herself firmly. She wanted their relationship to start off on the right foot, and perhaps he had good reason for his absence. Still, she had steeled herself to face him, and now that the moment was postponed, she would have to sustain her courage somehow during the long drive to the High Sierra.

"How do you do, Mr. Gideon." Araminta extended her gloved hand to the secretary.

"Miss Winthrop, how nice of you to remember me," he greeted her, obviously flattered and pleased, as he shook her hand.

Noble Winthrop had employed Mr. Gideon for many years; yet she did not even know if Gideon was the secretary's first or last name. Her grandfather always called him simply Gideon. He was a quiet, dapper, but otherwise undistinguished man, in his early forties, she judged. However, despite his unprepossessing mien, his blue eyes twinkled not only with kindness, but also with intelligence; and she knew that her grandfather valued him highly. She pointed out to him her leather-bound trunks, which had been unloaded from the train and now sat upon the platform; and after Mr. Gideon had hired a porter to carry her baggage, they made their way to the street, where he had parked her grandfather's long, low-slung motorcar, its top down, its black body shining like jet in the sun. As the porter loaded her trunks in back, the secretary assisted her into the front seat, where she tucked the lap robe securely about her to guard against dust. Presently, they were under way.

El Paso sprawled at the foot of Mount Franklin in the distance, below the narrow pass from which the Rio Grande emerged from the stark, southernmost spurs of the Rockies and which had given the town its name, El Paso del Norte—now known simply as El Paso. With a population of over ten thousand and, since 1881, four railways, the town was crowded and rowdy. The wide, dusty streets were thronged with automobiles, horses, and carriages; the sidewalks were alive with a multitude of whites, Mexicans, and Indians mostly, although Araminta also spied an occasional Negro. Despite this mélange of races and cultures, however, the flavor of El Paso itself was distinctly Mexican. Almost all the edifices were adobe, in a style resembling that of the equally close-packed buildings of Ciudad Juárez, El Paso's sister city, which lay directly across the Rio Grande. The great river was the U.S.-Mexican border and, over the years, as a result of its meanderings, had proved a source of heated border disputes.

It was sienna colored and sluggish with mud. Still, as she caught glimpses of it through the trees and structures, Araminta thought the river looked inviting, and she envied the brown-skinned children who splashed and waded at its edge. An Indian-summer sun blazed overhead in the boundless turquoise sky, so the day was hot; and although the air was dry rather than humid, her traveling costume was damp with perspiration, making her feel uncomfortably warm and sticky. Because of this, even though it meant a further delay in seeing her grandfather, she was glad when Mr. Gideon informed her that per her grandfather's instructions, he had made arrangements for her to freshen up and have lunch at a local hotel before undertaking the drive to the High Sierra, Noble Winthrop's vast ranch southeast of El Paso. Raising her parasol against the glare of the bright yellow sun, Araminta continued her interested perusal of the town as Mr. Gideon deftly guided the motorcar along the teeming streets, occasionally honking the horn at a slow-moving donkey or wagon as he pointed out the sights to her. She hardly remembered the town from her childhood, so it was as though she were viewing it for the first time. It was quite different from New York City and all to which she was accustomed, its Mexican architecture and culture giving it a foreignness that both intrigued her and made her feel as though she had stepped into another world.

They reached the hotel at last, a small but elegant two-story edifice of whitewashed adobe with a wide, shady portico, ornate black wrought-iron balconies, and a red-tiled roof. Inside was a spacious lobby with white walls and a dark, hardwood floor polished with beeswax to a burnished glow and scattered with colorful Mexican rugs. White-globed chandeliers of brass hung from the ceiling. A grand, sweeping staircase that ascended to the second floor dominated the center of the lobby, around which were intimate groups of sofas and chairs upholstered in tapestry fabric, and tables filled with plants in brass pots and willow baskets. While Mr. Gideon approached the front desk to request the key to her suite, Araminta closed her parasol, stripped off her gloves, and wandered idly about the lobby, surveying her surroundings.

The hotel was evidently a popular one, with guests coming and going, many through the archway that led to the restaurant, from which wafted the appetizing smells of steaming tortillas and *frijoles*. To her surprise, the aromas made Araminta's throat tighten with emotion as she recalled herself as a child, sitting in the kitchen of the High Sierra, while plump, kindly Teresa, the cook, smiling and singing as she worked, deftly prepared hot, tasty enchiladas and other Mexican dishes. Sometimes, she had let Araminta lend a hand in kneading the masa dough or stirring the spicy salsa. Unexpectedly, at the memory Araminta found herself actually longing to be back at her grandfather's ranch—where she had not felt wholly unloved or miserable, she now realized. She had had happy times there, with her parents and Teresa and some of the other servants, despite the long shadow her grandfather had cast. At least the High Sierra was familiar, a place where Araminta had once belonged. She could never really have called New York City home. She had not lived, but only existed there, her future as bleak, in truth, as that of the poor women who had labored in the sweatshops or prostituted themselves, with no hope of raising themselves any higher in life.

Laying her gloves down upon an elaborately carved table that stood before a large, gilt-framed mirror, Araminta studied her reflection critically for a moment. She had not realized until now just how thin she had actually grown, how pinched and wan her face was beneath the veil of her hat, her sloe green eyes standing out startlingly against her pale skin, her high cheekbones sharply defined. The healthy rose bloom in her cheeks—born of fresh air and exercise at the boarding school—had vanished. Perpetually tired in New York City, she had paid scant attention to her appearance. Now it dismayed her, for more than anything it would demonstrate to her grandfather how wretchedly she had failed in her bid for independence, what a godsend his cable had, in fact, proved; and she had hoped to conceal that knowledge from him, determined to begin their relationship, as much as was possible, on an equal footing. After adjusting her hat and patting a few stray strands of her hair back into place, efforts that did little to improve her weary image, she turned away from the mirror, biting her lower lip hard to still its sudden trembling.

Above all, her grandfather despised timidity and weakness, she reminded herself sternly. It would never do to appear a faded, shrinking violet before him. Yet, abruptly, the task of continuing to bolster her courage seemed insurmountable.

"Your gloves, *señorita*." At first, lost in her troubled thoughts, Araminta did not hear the low, silky voice that addressed her. It was only when the man spoke a second time that she became aware of him. "*¿Señorita?*"

Involuntarily, her breath caught in her throat; for he was undoubtedly the handsomest man she had ever

seen, tall—standing a couple of inches over six feet—
and lithe but powerfully built, like a panther, his body
rippling with the same savage, supple grace when he
moved and exuding the same animal magnetism and
menace. His broad shoulders tapered to a firm, flat
belly and thighs corded with muscle, all emphasized
rather than concealed by the clinging cut of his expen-
sive, elegant black suit tailored in the Spanish fashion—with a bolero rather than a long jacket—and
exquisite white cambric shirt with its froth of lace at
the throat and cuffs. He wore little jewelry—a signet
ring and a watch chain adorned with a single fob and
seal—but it was solid silver and of superior design.
His entire appearance bespoke refinement and riches.

His hair was as black and gleaming as obsidian,
swept back in shaggy waves from his dark-bronze,
hawkish visage that was hard and impassive, as though
it had been chiseled from stone. Not only the color of
his skin, but also his aquiline nose, with its fine, flaring
nostrils, and his high cheekbones revealed his Spanish
blood, obviously little diluted by that of the Indians
so many of the Spanish settlers had married over the
years. He looked every inch the grandee, lord of the
hacienda, master of all he surveyed. His carnal, cynical mouth hinted at a dissolute and jaded existence,
while his proud, aristocratic bearing and the imperi-
ous, self-assured thrust of his jaw proclaimed him as
a man accustomed to demanding—and getting—what
he wanted. Unwittingly, Araminta shivered at the
thought. She suspected he possessed that backbone
of steel that is inbred rather than acquired, and thus

infinitely stronger, more implacable than its developed counterpart. He would be a dangerous, even deadly man to cross, she sensed instinctively.

But most of all, it was his eyes that riveted her where she stood. Deep-set beneath swooping black brows and spiked with thick black lashes, his eyes shone as dark brown as smoky quartz and were just as fathomless. From beneath his hooded lids, they raked her lingeringly, in a bold, thoroughly cavalier fashion that brought a crimson blush to her cheeks and made her heart flutter alarmingly in her breast. Why, he was staring at her as though—as though he knew what she looked like stark naked! It was indecent, mortifying. How dare he? The gall of the man! He reminded her of those offensive men in Newspaper Row, and Araminta half readied herself to do physical battle with him. Yet something told her that should she act on the impulse, he would not only easily fend off her assault, but also find it distinctly amusing. The notion further infuriated her. She would have turned on her heel and stalked indignantly away had she not at last realized that the man was holding her gloves in his outstretched hand. Of course. She had laid them down on the table before the mirror and, in her distress, had forgotten to retrieve them.

Angry, flustered, Araminta practically snatched the gloves from his grasp. As her hand brushed his, a sudden, inexplicable tremor shot through her, as though she had been struck by a bolt of lightning. His skin was startlingly warm, electric. His fingers, though long and slender, flexed with the strength of a tempered-steel Toledo sword. The notion made her uncomfortably aware of her own fragility in comparison. Damn the man! Why must he keep on staring at her in that horribly brazen, unnerving fashion? Her green eyes flashing sparks, Araminta lifted her chin and stiffened her spine resolutely. She would not permit this arrogant man to intimidate her.

"Gracias, señor," she uttered coolly. The Spanish words she remembered from her childhood came of their own volition to her lips as she nodded curtly, a gesture both of thanks and dismissal. Unconsciously, though, the way in which she twisted and crushed her gloves as she spoke revealed her agitation, something the man's appraising glance did not miss.

A mocking smile curved his mouth, as though at some private joke. To her humiliation, Araminta felt the flames upon her cheeks grow even hotter. She could not understand why he should be having such an unsettling effect upon her. It was irrational. He was a total stranger and clearly not someone with whom she wished to become acquainted. This thought was further reinforced by the appearance of Mr. Gideon, who scowled blackly, perceiving her flushed face and the man who was the cause of it. With a terse nod in the man's direction, the secretary acknowledged him, then turned to her and spoke.

"My apologies for having kept you waiting, Miss Winthrop. Unfortunately, there was a slight delay at the front desk, a small mix-up regarding your suite, which it was necessary for me to remedy. I do hope you have not been . . . inconvenienced as a result?"

"No. This . . . gentleman was just returning my gloves, which I had carelessly mislaid." It had not escaped Araminta's notice that Mr. Gideon had neither identified the man nor introduced him to her. Tension stretched between the two men; plainly, they knew each other, and the relationship was not a cordial one. "Well, thank you again, *señor*," she murmured hurriedly, wishing to avoid any possible trouble. "And now, Mr. Gideon, since I am both tired and hungry, I would appreciate your showing me to my room. I would like very much to freshen up and then have that lunch you promised."

"Yes, of course, Miss Winthrop. This way, if you please." Nodding again shortly in the other man's direction, the secretary took her arm politely.

Briefly, frighteningly, Araminta glimpsed the glitter of something hard and dangerous in the other man's eyes before he once more smiled at her sardonically, clicking his heels together in a smart, military fashion and executing a small, courtly bow to her as she was led away. Somehow, she knew, even without looking down over the banister, that he was still staring at her and Mr. Gideon as they ascended the staircase that rose from the heart of the lobby.

"Miss Winthrop," Mr. Gideon said when they reached the second-floor landing and proceeded along a narrow corridor to her suite, "normally, I should not presume to render to you any unsolicited advice; however, in this instance, I feel I must. It would be best if you . . . er, ahem . . . do not mention to your grandfather your encounter with General del Castillo in the lobby—"

"*General* del Castillo?" Araminta interrupted, startled; for she had thought the man, in his early thirties, too young, surely, to hold such a high rank. "He is an army officer, then?"

"No, he's a *guerrilla*, a Revolutionary—and as such, he is no better than a *bandolero*, a desperado, in rebellion against the official government of his country and its army, the Federales. Further, he is—for reasons to which I have never been privy and about which I therefore cannot enlighten you—a bitter enemy of both your grandfather and the Hobarts. You may recall them as being your grandfather's closest friends and owning the Chaparral, the nearest neighboring ranch to the High Sierra. All this is why I caution you against speaking to your grandfather about your meeting with the general. Rigo del Castillo is *not* a proper person for you to know, and your grandfather would doubtless be angered by the general's accosting you, however innocently and by chance."

"I understand, and I appreciate your warning, Mr. Gideon. I shouldn't like to upset Grandfather, especially straight off, so I won't say anything to him, I promise."

By now, they had reached Araminta's suite. Inserting the key in the lock, the secretary opened the door for her and stepped back to allow her to precede him into the spacious sitting room, elegantly furnished in the Mexican style. Crossing to the double doors that led to the equally commodious bedchamber, Mr. Gideon opened them as well. Then, having checked to be certain that Araminta's trunks had been brought upstairs and a bath readied for her, he left her, saying he would return in an hour or so to escort her to lunch in the hotel's restaurant.

After he had gone, Araminta wasted little time in stripping off her garments—dusty from travel across the arid plains of west Texas—and sinking gratefully into the steaming-hot water that filled the porcelain bathtub nearly to overflowing. With a bar of gardenia-scented soap, she began to lather herself generously, reveling in the luxurious feeling that pervaded her body. It was ages since she had had a proper bath, for she had been forced to make do with nothing more than an old, cracked porcelain basin at the tenement in which she had lived in New York City. Perhaps because of that, however, she also felt awed and even slightly ashamed by her grandfather's authorizing Mr. Gideon to rent a hotel suite for her for no more than an afternoon, simply so she might freshen up and nap a while after her long journey. It seemed both wasteful and extravagant, the height of sinful indulgence enjoyed only by the very wealthy. But then, her grandfather *was* rich, one of the richest men in Texas, perhaps even the entire country, his power and influence extending far and wide. This alone was enough to imbue him with an air of formidability. Combined with his fierce appearance and forceful personality, it made him a man even his peers hesitated to cross.

Yet Rigo del Castillo—who must have guessed, both from her name and her being in the company of Mr. Gideon, her relationship to Noble Winthrop—had not seemed in the least daunted at the prospect of incurring her grandfather's wrath. Closing her eyes, Araminta slowly submerged herself ever farther beneath the bathwater's surface as, at the memory of the general's lazy gaze roaming over her insolently, her whole body suffused hotly with color. Really! He was no gentleman, she thought. Mr. Gideon had been quite right not to introduce him to her; he was, indeed, not the sort of man with whom any decent female would willingly claim acquaintance. Yet as his tall, dark, handsome image came, unbidden, into her mind, she felt again that odd, incomprehensible shudder that had coursed through her when her hand had touched his; and she was beset by bewilderment. She could not understand why such a disagreeable and disreputable man should have such a strange, unsettling effect upon her. She must be more exhausted from her journey than she had realized. Perhaps her grandfather had foreseen that she would be, and that was why he had arranged for her to have lunch and rest before continuing on to the High Sierra. If so, it represented a kindness and thoughtfulness she would not have associated with him. Maybe he *had* changed, had mellowed in his old age. But surely, if that were true, Mr. Gideon would not have felt it necessary to advise her against telling her grandfather about her encounter with Rigo del Castillo.

Curious, Araminta wondered why there was such enmity between the two men; and as she remembered the general's demeanor, the determined set of his jaw, the steeliness of his fingers, she trembled. No, Rigo del Castillo was not a man who would cower with fear before her grandfather; he was, in fact, she suspected, just the opposite—a man who would take great satisfaction in attacking and besting his opponent. Perhaps, Araminta thought, he had known her identity even before he had spoken to her. If so, perhaps he had had some ulterior motive for approaching her, and her gloves had provided nothing more than a convenient excuse. By surveying her in that brazen manner, he might actually have hoped to provoke her in some way, to force a confrontation with her grandfather.

She would be true to her promise to Mr. Gideon and say nothing, she decided. There was no point in starting off on the wrong foot with her grandfather— and besides, she had no desire to be used as a pawn by Rigo del Castillo in whatever game he might be playing. Thus resolved, Araminta finished her bath and vigorously toweled herself dry, feeling much rejuvenated. After changing into clean clothes, she brushed her long blond hair until it shone like gold, then securely pinned it up again in her customary, demure chignon. A light dusting of powder upon her face and a few subtle drops of gardenia perfume behind her ears and upon her wrists completed her toilette. By then, Mr. Gideon had arrived to escort her to lunch.

As they were strolling down the hall toward the staircase to the lobby, Araminta heard the door to another suite open behind them and glanced back. There stood Rigo del Castillo, in passionate embrace with a young brunet woman whose features Araminta could not clearly discern, and he was kissing her deeply. Araminta's cheeks stained scarlet at the sight, and she hastily turned away—but, unfortunately, not before the general broke off the kiss and, looking up, saw her staring at him and the unknown woman, who now had her face buried against his chest. Over the top of the woman's head, he smiled slowly, tauntingly, at Araminta, then deliberately bent to kiss the woman thoroughly once more, his eyes still locked upon Araminta's own. Her heart hammering in her breast, Araminta strode so swiftly on down the corridor that she stumbled. As she righted herself awkwardly, Rigo del Castillo's low, derisive laughter echoed in her ears.

Chapter Three

After a hot, savory lunch in the hotel restaurant, during which Araminta had discovered that her palate had lost none of its appreciation for Mexican cuisine, she had returned to her suite for the siesta hour, indulging herself in a restful nap. The combination of her nervousness, excitement, and the clatter of the train's wheels upon the railroad tracks had prevented her from sleeping well during her long journey from New York to Texas. So, worn out, she had fallen into a deep slumber within moments of loosing her stays and lying down upon the soft feather bed in her bedchamber. The cool breeze that had wafted in from the Rio Grande through the open windows and the muted sounds that had drifted up from the street below had proved a soothing lullaby. Only the knocking of Mr.

Gideon upon her door a few hours later had roused her.

Now, she once more sat beside him in her grandfather's automobile, her eyes eagerly drinking in the countryside along the rough road that led to the High Sierra. She had forgotten how vast and sweeping the land actually was, with its wide-open spaces stretching endlessly to the bluffs and mountains in the distance, so different from New York City, with its densely packed buildings. Mile after mile, the rolling plains of west Texas spread out, uninterrupted, before her, a blend not only of sand and clay in hues ranging from palest ocher to deepest umber, but also of coarse, dry prairie grass, its earlier green now bleached as gold as wheat by the Indian-summer sun. Here and there, hardy cacti clung defiantly to long expanses of dunes: the sharp-spined barrel cactus with its roughly defined ridges and tiny flowers that ranged in color from bright yellow to deepest purple; the cholla; the fishhook; the hedgehog; the woolly living rock with its almost thornless rosettes and blossoms of white, cream, yellow, and magenta; the night-blooming moon cactus; the fuzzy old man; and the proliferate prickly pear. Agaves with pulpy green spike leaves squatted upon the ground. Their cousins, the taller, crowned yuccas, stood proudly, like soldiers marching out to do battle, against the stark, barren horizon. Scrubs of many-branched sagebrush with wedge-shaped foliage glinted silvery gray amid patches of thorny paloverde, tangled chaparral, and tarry creosote bushes that sprang up in haphazard profusion. An odd tumbleweed or two lay brown and lifeless where the dying prairie winds had scattered them earlier that spring. The narrow olive leaflets of the shrubby mesquite trees curled brittlely at their edges, their dense catkins of cream-colored blooms wilted, their clusters of long, narrow, pale-yellow beans hanging limply in the heat, though the sun had slipped from its zenith in the heavens and begun its slow descent in the west. Even the few silver-barked cottonwoods that nestled forlornly upon the banks of torpid rivers and muddy streams drooped with thirst.

This harsh, savage land, Araminta mused, was the making of some and the breaking of far too many others. Here, only the strong survived, and even they must struggle to overcome. As she gazed at the land stretching out forever in all directions, she felt small in comparison—small and humble. Even so, the sight gladdened her heart, filled it with joy; for, unlike New York City, this was land in which a man could breathe, where he could stand wild and free beneath the infinite sky and feel as though he stood in the very hollow of God's palm. It appealed to something vital and earthy inside her; and for the first time, she wondered how her father had ever forsaken it. She began to feel as though she were indeed truly coming home, a feeling that increased as, some moments later, the hacienda that was the nucleus of the High Sierra's one hundred and fifty thousand acres came into view.

It was a magnificent, sprawling, two-story structure built of whitewashed adobe that gleamed like mother-of-pearl in the sun, a perfect jewel for the wild setting that encompassed it. Its tile roof was the color of moist red clay, and its heavy timber doors, shutters, and balconies were the shade of the sienna rivers. All around it, her grandfather's ranch spread as far as the eye could see. In the distance, the mountains rose like sentinels keeping watch over his kingly domain. Unconsciously, Araminta leaned forward to get a better look at the hacienda through the clouds of dust churned up by the wheels of the motorcar as it sped on down the road toward its destination. In one hand, she gripped her open parasol; with the other, she clutched the top of the windshield to steady herself against the jolting as the automobile struck a rock or pothole in the rough road carved out over the years by horses, wagons, herds of cattle, and, more recently, motorcars. She had been a mere child when she had left the ranch; she was returning as a woman grown. She had changed, and now she wondered how the ranch had altered, as well, in the intervening years; for she did not deceive herself that time had stood still here, though the house itself looked just as she remembered it.

Presently, Mr. Gideon brought the automobile to a halt before the front doors; and a beaming Teresa stood there, as plump and kindly as ever, her teeth shining white in her familiar brown face, her arms outstretched to welcome Araminta home. Araminta flung open the door of the motorcar and, crying "Teresa! Teresa!", flew into the waiting embrace.

"Oh, Miss Araminta, I can hardly believe it's you!" Teresa declared, shaking her head with affection as she studied the woman who had taken the place of the child she remembered. "You were just *muchacha* when last I see you, and now, you all grown up—and fine lady *muy bonita*, too. Aiee! How you will turn the heads of the ranch hands! Welcome home, welcome home. Come inside the hacienda. I make the *sopaipas*, your favorite, no? And I just now take them from the stove, so they are still fresh and piping hot. Oh, Miss Araminta, is so good to have you back. You been away far too long!''

Continuing both to praise and scold her fondly, Teresa led Araminta inside; and there, at long last, was her grandfather. Appearing at the doorway of his study, which opened onto the grand entry hall, he surveyed the scene before him critically for a moment, his fierce, bushy white eyebrows drawn together in a forbidding frown. Then, leaning more heavily on his ornate malacca cane than she recalled, he stumped toward Araminta.

He harrumphed gruffly in greeting. ''So you're the cause of all the ruckus, are you? And high time you got here, too! I was beginning to think Gideon had run that newfangled car of mine off the road into a ditch or something. A pony and trap's more his speed. Ain't that right, Gideon?''

''Quite right, Mr. Winthrop,'' the secretary murmured affably. It was his habit, Araminta observed, always to agree with her cantankerous grandfather's insults, particularly as these were seldom intended personally; Noble Winthrop's practice was to disparage everyone equally.

''Well, let's have a look at you, gal,'' her grandfather continued, ignoring Mr. Gideon as though he had not spoken. ''You're as pale as a pussy willow, and just about as frail. But I guess that's to be expected, what with your living up there in New York City, where all the buildings are jammed so close together that a body can't get a proper breath of fresh air or ray of sunshine. Good thing you decided to come back to Texas—where a man don't spit out his back door and hit his neighbor's front stoop in the process. Not much meat on your bones, either. But then, I imagine Teresa will fatten you up soon enough. Ought to have her feeding my damned cattle; they'd be ready for market in half the time it takes now. She's been in the kitchen, cooking, for the past three days—but do you think I've got a bite to eat around here? No, siree, bob. If you hadn't got here, gal, I reckon I might have starved to death," he declared acidly, giving Teresa a withering glance.

Then, finally reaching Araminta's side, her grandfather grasped her hand awkwardly; and to her surprise, she realized that in some ways he was as nervous as she about their meeting—not that he would ever have admitted it. Leaning forward, she impulsively bestowed a quick peck upon his weathered cheek. He was startled, she could tell, for his dark-gray eyes widened and he glowered at her even more fiercely than before.

"You don't much look like a man a strong wind would blow away, Grandfather," she observed dryly, knowing that any attempt to humor him would only enrage him. "In fact, all things considered, I'd say you appear pretty fit and feisty."

This was no less than the truth, for though troubled by gout, which necessitated his using a cane, Noble

Winthrop was in all other respects a hardy specimen for a man of his advanced years. Though stooped now with age, he was still taller than the average man and powerfully built, with broad shoulders, a massive chest and arms, and long, sinewy legs. Some people declared that in his youth he had been able with one punch to poleax a steer. Studying him now, Araminta had no reason to doubt the claim. His large hand was like an iron band encircling her own smaller one. It was all she could do not to wince at the pressure, a fact, she suspected, of which her grandfather was well aware; for he squeezed her fingers even harder before at last releasing them, giving a terse snort of surprise and grudging approval at her having passed his initial test. That there would be others, however, she did not doubt. Noble Winthrop believed strongly in people's proving their mettle—and he had no use for those who did not measure up to his exacting standards.

"Well, why are we all standing around here like a bunch of tree stumps?" he barked abruptly. "Teresa, didn't I hear mention of a stove full of *sopaipas*?"

"*Sí, patrón.*"

"Well, go 'n' fetch 'em, then. Bring 'em into my study, along with a pot of hot coffee—and mind that it's strong and black, none of that sugar-'n'-cream mess favored by women. My granddaughter's a Winthrop, and she'll drink her coffee like one, won't you, Araminta?" Not giving her a chance to reply, he held out his arm, indicating that she should take it. Then he ushered her toward his study. "This way, gal. You and I have got a lot of catching up to do and matters

to be settled, and there ain't no time like the present
to get started. A man don't get ahead in this world by
wasting daylight. You remember that now, you hear?''

Araminta nodded, carefully measuring her step to
match his own slower one as they crossed the great
hall. Despite the passage of the years, the appearance
of her grandfather's study had not changed since last
she had seen it. The furniture was still upholstered
in the rich wine leathers and multicolored tapestry
fabrics she recollected, and Noble Winthrop's massive oak desk and swivel chair still dominated the
room. Above the fireplace hung a huge portrait of
her grandmother, Victoria, long dead now but forever captured on canvas as she had looked as a young
woman. Seeing the picture again after all this time,
Araminta realized suddenly that she was the image of
her grandmother.

''You resemble her a great deal,'' her grandfather
remarked, as though he had read her mind. ''Victoria
was as beautiful as a rose—but unfortunately, she had
a rose's flaws, too. She lacked stamina, and she just
withered and faded away out here in west Texas. We
must hope that despite your looks, you're made of
sterner stuff than that, gal. You and I are the last of
the Winthrops, and though my enemies swear I'm too
mean to die, I won't live forever. Not much time left
to me now, I expect. Nevertheless, I don't fear death;
I've lived with it too long for that. Back when I first
came to west Texas, this land was still as wild and
dangerous as a bronco, and sudden death was an every-
day occurrence. I fought off Indians, Mexicans, scor-
pions, and rattlers as big around as my arm, blue

northers and creek risings, diseases and wounds that would have made you faint just to see 'em. Many was the time I drank juice from a cactus or water from a muddy hoofprint and was glad to get it, I'll tell you, because back then, a man who didn't learn to watch his step and make do with what he had out here was soon buzzard bait, his bones picked clean. I started with nothing, and with sweat and blood and guts, I founded the High Sierra and built it into what it is today, one of the biggest damned cattle ranches in the entire state of Texas—hell, the whole blasted country. I'd hoped to have a parcel of fine, strong sons to leave it all to, to carry on the Winthrop name and heritage and the labor of a lifetime. But . . . things didn't work out the way I planned; and now, all I've got is you, a wisp of a young woman still wet behind the ears and who don't yet know manure from *menudo* about life.''

''I don't agree with that assessment of me, Grandfather,'' Araminta dared to say, returning his penetrating stare steadily and ignoring his blunt language, which she suspected he had used to shock her. ''I, too, have known hardship, suffering, and death—and New York City was in its own way as wild and dangerous as west Texas. But I survived.''

''Hmph!'' he snorted, as though he knew better. Then, as Teresa appeared, bearing a sterling-silver tray laden with the *sopaipas*, a sterling-silver coffeepot, and two Sevres china teacups, saucers, plates, and linen napkins, he motioned for Araminta to be seated on the chesterfield, before which stood an elaborately carved satinwood tea table. ''You'll do the honors, of course,'' he said matter-of-factly to her.

"If you wish, Grandfather," she replied serenely, with more confidence than she felt.

Obediently, she poured the coffee and put two *so-paipas* on each plate, then rose to serve her grandfather, who had seated himself in a comfortable wing chair across from her. Then she resumed her position on the chesterfield, relieved that although her hands had trembled, she had managed to perform gracefully and without disaster the duties of a hostess.

"Well, I see they taught you something of the womanly arts at least at that boarding school you attended." With relish, for he had a sweet tooth, her grandfather bit into one of the honeyed fritters, then, blowing on his coffee to cool it, took a generous sip. "I'm delighted to know that the money it cost me to send you there was well spent. I can't abide waste; it's foolish and invariably leads to want and, ultimately, ruin." He paused for a moment, then went on brusquely. "But enough of this chitchat. Let's you and me get acquainted, Araminta; for despite our being family, we are in many ways strangers to each other—not that I'm denying that much of the blame for that is mine. I never was much good with children; and frankly, after your parents died, I figured you'd be better off at the academy, under the care and guidance of other females, rather than being reared by an old cowpuncher like me. Besides, it struck me that you didn't much like me, gal; and perhaps in your mind, you had good cause for that, seeing as how your father and I had parted on such ill terms and never managed to reconcile our differences. Still, we need try to put the past behind us now and concentrate on our future together. We've no one else in this world; and no matter what, blood's always thicker than water in the end. Had he lived, your father would have understood that, eventually.''

The next hour in her grandfather's company passed fairly amicably. But at the end of it, Araminta's feelings toward him were no less conflicted than before. She understood him better, she thought, but she could not make up her mind about whether she really liked him. She admired him for what he had managed to accomplish in his lifetime. Yet it was clear to her that during his long climb up the ladder to success, he had callously stepped upon others, even brutally knocked them from the rungs in order to get ahead. Despite his fame and fortune, he was an embittered, lonely old man, she felt sure. Although it seemed he had at this late date developed not only a conscience, but also a love for her and a desire to mend fences, she doubted it.

It had not escaped her notice that he had not welcomed her to the High Sierra. Nor, despite his talk of their having no one save each other, had he expressed any real affection toward her. Yet he had allotted to her a liberal sum of pin money, to be paid monthly, and had generously insisted upon replacing her entire wardrobe—''for those plain, schoolgirlish duds you are wearing will never do if you want to make a mark in west-Texas society.'' He had also said that she might choose from the stables any mount she wished, with the exception, naturally, of his own horse. She was, of course, to look upon the High Sierra as her home and need only inform him or the servants if there was anything else she desired.

However, when she had dared to mention pursuing her career as journalist, he had, with an upraised hand, cut her off abruptly, stating flatly that no granddaughter of his was going to act in so common and unladylike a fashion as to take a job and to mix herself in a man's business. Debutante, society hostess, wife, mother, and do-gooder for church and charities were the only appropriate roles for a woman of her station, and she was not to disgrace the Winthrop good name by behaving otherwise. As he had made this pronouncement, her grandfather's demeanor had been so stern that Araminta had forborne to argue with him, sensing instinctively that it would only anger him and avail her nothing. Inwardly, however, she had resolved that she would not meekly bow to his rigid demands and expectations, that she would find some way of achieving her dreams.

Still, despite her determination, even she was forced to admit that she did not see how this was currently possible. Perhaps, however unlikely it appeared, she could in time change her grandfather's mind. If not, she would simply have to search for some other answer. Meanwhile, getting settled in at the ranch, learning to know her grandfather better, and resting and regaining her strength seemed more than enough challenge.

In fact, now that she need no longer worry about her physical safety, Araminta found herself experiencing the total letdown that follows a period of stress and strain, when body and mind have been compelled to function beyond the limit of their natural reserves; and after supper, pleading exhaustion from her long day, she retired to her bedroom. Her grandfather escorted her upstairs, since he, too, was ready to turn in, no longer able to keep the late hours he had of old. When they reached her suite, Araminta recognized that she had been installed in her old suite, the one she had been given when, at the age of six, she had left the nursery. Like everything else at the High Sierra, her sitting room and bedroom looked the same as they had when she had gone away. It was as though with the departure of his only son, her grandfather had lost interest in the hacienda itself, not bothering to bestir himself to modernize it with even the installation of gas or electric lights, which he could easily have afforded, or even to redecorate it—although she guessed from his acquisition of an automobile that she would not find this to be the case with the remainder of the ranch. Now, however, as Noble himself glanced about Araminta's suite, it must have dawned on him how girlish and unsophisticated the decor was, for with something akin to embarrassment, he cleared his throat and spoke.

"I reckon you'll want to redo these rooms, gal, furnish 'em more to your taste 'n' liking. Hell! I expect the whole damned place could use some sprucing up, for that matter. I haven't done much entertaining lately. But now that you're here, I want to see that you're launched proper into west-Texas society . . . throw a real fancy shindig that'll make folks so green with envy that their eyes'll pop clean out of their heads. And what with all the beaux I imagine will be buzzing like bees in a hive around here once all the eligible bachelors from the Rio Grande to the Sabine River get a gander at you, why, we'll soon be receiving invites to so many barbecues and card parties and wingdings that it'll make your head spin—and naturally, we'll have to reciprocate. I'll talk to Gideon first thing tomorrow morning. He'll know what we need, and all the best stores to take you to and to order from if the shops in El Paso don't suit. And mind, don't spare the expense, Araminta. I won't have it said that the Winthrops are cheap; and I don't mind standing the bills, just so long as I get my money's worth. So do things up right now, you hear?''

At that, not waiting for her to respond, her grandfather nodded good night and left her, stumping his way down the hall to the master suite. For a moment, lost in thought, Araminta stared after him. Then, quietly, she closed her door. Her trunks had been brought upstairs and unpacked, she discovered as she began to get ready for bed. Her clothes, showing signs of having been recently pressed, hung in the armoire; her lingerie was neatly folded in the drawers of the chest, and the silver-backed mirror, brush, and ivory comb she had inherited from her mother lay upon the dresser. Her small collection of treasured books, most of which had belonged to her father, sat upon the nightstand. Perched in the rocking chair was her favorite childhood doll. It was worn with use and age, but somehow, Araminta had never been able to bring herself to throw it away. As she looked at her few possessions, she realized suddenly that they reflected the entire sum of her life to this point. Abruptly, tears welled in her eyes at the thought. She had had such high hopes when she had left the boarding school. That they had amounted to nothing was indeed a bitter pill to swallow—particularly as she considered the future her grandfather had mapped out for her. Plainly, he intended that she should acquire a husband from among the scions of the wealthy land barons and cattle kings who composed west-Texas society. No doubt, he already had one or more suitable candidates in mind.

Araminta shuddered at the notion. She had nothing against marriage; in fact, part of her longed for a husband and children. It was the way in which her grandfather appeared bent on proceeding with his scheme that she found both disturbing and distasteful—as though she were a prize heifer to be auctioned off to the highest bidder. Obviously, her grandfather viewed marriage as he did a business merger, a view that she not only could not share, but also was repelled by. Her parents had loved each other passionately, so much so that to stay together, they had sacrificed everything they had ever known, including the High Sierra, Preston Winthrop's birthright. Having grown up surrounded by that deep, abiding love, Araminta knew in her heart that she herself could never be happy settling for less when it came to a husband and marriage. But to her dismay, her grandfather had not once asked her feelings about his plan; clearly, these were of no consequence to him, and he expected her to follow his dictates. The idea that this might extend to her wedding a man she did not and could not love was both alarming and appalling, as was the knowledge

that her grandfather had never hesitated to use his rank
and riches as a weapon against those who thwarted
him, including his own son. So why should she prove
any exception?

At last, however, Araminta realized she was letting
her imagination run away with her, envisioning the
worst about her grandfather, marriage, and the future—when she hadn't even as yet met any men who
could be considered as potential beaux. But even as
that thought occurred to her, she remembered Rigo del
Castillo, his low, mocking laughter and the sensation
of his skin against hers, as electric as the crackle of her
hair as she brushed it vigorously, then deftly plaited it
into the bedtime braid she wore to prevent her long
blond tresses from tangling while she slept. At the
memory of the general, she frowned at her reflection
in the dressing-table mirror, annoyed that although
their encounter had lasted no more than a few minutes,
he kept intruding into her mind. He *was* handsome, she
grudgingly admitted, in a dark, dangerous, devilish
fashion that appealed on some primitive, earthy level.
She could understand why despite his reputation as
both a rake and a rebel—perhaps even because of it—
certain women, like that brunet at the hotel, would
find him attractive. Not that she herself did, of course,
Araminta reassured herself. It was the fact that for
whatever unknown reasons, he and her grandfather
were such bitter enemies that intrigued her, made her
curious in spite of herself about the general, she told
herself. Knowledge was power, and it would be interesting to learn what sort of a man had crossed her
grandfather—and prospered afterward—for she did

not think there were many men who had done so. Even her father had feared the long, vengeful reach of Noble Winthrop's arm—and with good cause, she thought.

Her grandfather was as hubristic and autocratic as ever. After her conversation with him today, she felt sure that it was not love, but pride and vanity that had prompted him to ask her to return to the ranch. He was a king without an heir, save for her. She was the last of the Winthrops, the last of his blood. Egomaniacal, he could not bear to think he should not live on long after his death, through her and the High Sierra. Still, Araminta was compelled to admit that inheriting the ranch, and thus all the money she would ever need, was not an unpleasant prospect, especially after the poverty she had experienced in New York City. It would certainly be more than enough to tempt any other young female into humoring her grandfather and accepting the future he had outlined to her, a future that was, in fact, exactly what most women wanted. What was wrong with her, Araminta wondered, that she should aspire to more than that? Recalling the glow of love that had seemed to radiate like sunshine between her parents, she knew the answer to her question and, too, that her grandfather would never comprehend her wistful yearnings, indeed would label them romantic nonsense and insist that she put such foolish notions from her head.

With a sigh, she bent and blew out the lamp, slipped into the beautiful mansion bed that dominated the center of the room, and drew the covers up about her. Through the open French doors that led to the balcony beyond, the night wind, cool and welcome after the

hot day, drifted in, billowing the long curtains gently.
Lying there in the familiar room, the familiar bed,
Araminta felt herself a child again; and as she mused
about her parents and the unhappy turns her life had
taken, a great tide of depression and aloneness engulfed her. In the distance, an owl hooted, a hawk
screamed, and a lone wolf or coyote bayed at the
moon, a haunting, forlorn wail that seemed to echo
her own feelings of solitariness and heartache. *Ah-
ooooo. Yip-yip-yip. Ah-ooooo.* Sudden tears stung her
eyes, and, burying her face in her pillow to muffle her
sobs, she cried herself to sleep.

Chapter Four

Araminta's days soon settled into such a busy pattern that she had little opportunity to dwell further on the distressing thoughts that had plagued her that first night at the High Sierra. She had chosen a horse from the stables, a pretty roan mare, Desert Rose, with a long, cream-colored mane and tail; and although rising early was no longer a necessity, she was still up every morning at the crack of dawn, when she rode, exploring the sweeping expanse of the ranch. The more she saw of the land, the more she was drawn to it, felt a oneness with it, as though it were bred into her bones and blood; and from it, she derived strength and solace, a quiet, inner peace she had never before known. She began to understand what had attracted her grandfather to the rugged terrain, what had led him to endure its harshness and hardships. It was beautiful in a stark, savage way that appealed to something deep and atavistic inside her. It was a land to be claimed and conquered—but never tamed—a land where the sun blazed too bright and hot in the endless turquoise sky; where the rain burst fast and furious from the dark, roiling clouds that massed as though from nowhere on the horizon, shot through with lightning and a peculiar blue fire that danced between the horns of the cattle; and where fierce winds whipped down from the north to set biting dust devils awhirl. Araminta felt herself challenged, exhilarated by it. She was certain there was nothing in the world quite like the feeling of galloping wild and free over the wide, rolling plains, with the unbridled wind upon her face and streaming through her hair. It was as close to flying as one could get and still be earthbound, she thought.

Still, she never forgot the dangers of the land, carrying with her at all times both the rifle and pistol her grandfather had given her and insisted that she learn how to shoot. She had a good eye and steady hand, and with practice, she soon became proficient with the weapons. Her tools of choice, however, were her sketchbooks and canvases, her charcoal pencils and watercolors and oils, which she invariably tucked into her saddlebags. Often, she paused to dismount and rest upon some grassy knoll or rocky outcrop and take out the wooden box that contained her artist's implements to lose herself in drawing or painting, hardly aware of how time passed. With skillful strokes of her pencil or brush, mountains and bluffs, plateaus and plains came alive on paper or canvas. Gradually,

she added pictures of the herds of cattle that roamed
the land, and the ranch hands at their work in the
corrals and on the range; and then she penned words
alongside, and the story of the High Sierra, of the
West itself, started to emerge. But this was Araminta's
secret, kept locked in her artist's box, just as she kept
her dream of being a journalist locked in her heart.

Following her daily excursion, she returned to the
hacienda for breakfast with her grandfather, who noted
with approval not only that she was no lazy slugabed,
but also that the exercise gained from her rides had
fortified her and put the healthy rose bloom back into
her cheeks. For this, Noble was thankful; he had
thought his granddaughter looked so plain and peaked
upon her arrival at the High Sierra that he had de-
spaired of her attracting the eye of his godson, Judd
Hobart.

After she had finished breakfast, Araminta joined
Mr. Gideon in the morning room, where he not only
advised her about what was needed to refurbish the
house, but also about what she herself would require
in a wardrobe for the functions she would be hostessing
or attending in the weeks to come. Once she and the
secretary had developed several extensive lists, Mr.
Gideon drove her into El Paso, where he escorted her
to all the best stores. What could not be acquired
locally was ordered from as far away as St. Louis,
Chicago, and New York City, and even from Europe,
if necessary. By means of fashion dolls, Araminta
selected fancy frocks and ball gowns from no less
than Worth in Paris. During their sessions and forays
together, she marveled at the extent of Mr. Gideon's

knowledge on such diverse subjects as fabrics and furniture, gowns and jewels. This very knack of gathering information, she realized, had made him invaluable to her grandfather.

Then, finally, there came the day when the last painting was hung on the wall, the last dress was hung in Araminta's armoire, and her grandfather deemed both the hacienda and her ready for west-Texas society. Invitations were sent out far and wide; arrangements were made with caterers, florists, and musicians, and the ballroom was lavishly bedecked for her debut ball or fandango, as it was more commonly called in the Southwest. Knowing that white drained her of color, Araminta chose to wear for the event a silk gown that was the deep pink of a Texas sunrise and made her fair skin, now gilded from the sun, glow like roses and gold. The dress had short, elaborate, off-the-shoulder sleeves and a heart-shaped décolletage, above which her full, ripe breasts swelled enticingly. From the sash at her waist, the skirt swept down like a bell into a deeply flounced hem. Carmen, her maid, pinned Araminta's long blond hair up in a cascade of ringlets threaded with pink silk ribands and tiny pink silk roses. A fringed pink shawl and matching gloves, reticule, and slippers completed her ensemble. Diamonds, a gift from her grandfather, glittered at her ears, throat, and upon one wrist. Now, as she gazed at her reflection in the cheval mirror that stood in one corner of her bedroom, Araminta knew she was beautiful. Had it not been for the thought that her grandfather's sole aim in holding the fandango was to introduce her to every eligible bachelor in west

Texas, she would have been excited about the evening's forthcoming affair. As it was, she could only hope her grandfather would demonstrate a modicum of restraint and discretion about her being a spinster rather than bluntly announcing it to one and all, as she felt uncomfortably certain he was quite capable of doing.

As Araminta joined him at the foot of the stairs in the great hall, Noble beamed with approval at her appearance—an expression that, unfortunately, contrived to make him look as crafty and gleeful as someone who had got away with a crime.

"Gal, you look as handsome as that prize mare of mine you chose for your own from the stables—not to mention how you fixed the hacienda up as fine as a palace. Never thought the place could look so damned good, 'n' that's a fact." Noble nodded with satisfaction as he glanced around the tastefully decorated great hall, which, like the rest of the house, Araminta—with her artist's talent for patterns and colors—had done in rich, desert shades of sandy gold and cactus green, turquoise blue and dusty rose, accented with deeper hues of ocher, umber, and sienna. "You've got class, Araminta, class and style. There ain't a filly in the whole blasted state to compare to you, even if I do say so myself. Man'd be a fool not to see it. Why, if the young bucks hereabouts don't come to blows over you before the evening's out, I'll be mighty disappointed!" Rubbing his hands together, he cackled with delight at the prospect, in such high spirits that Araminta would not have been surprised if he had suddenly tossed aside his malacca cane and danced a jig.

"Thank you, Grandfather," she said, pleased despite herself, though she could only be anxious at the thought of a brawl's ensuing over her. Further, she knew enough by now about her grandfather to know that his admiration of her was, in truth, a form of self-flattery, that he was really complimenting himself that she had proved herself a credit to him, the Winthrop name, and the High Sierra. Doubtless, he felt himself entirely responsible for both her and the hacienda's improved appearances, as though she herself had had nothing whatsoever to do with either.

The clatter of automobiles and horses and carriages on the drive out front drew Araminta from her reverie as she realized abruptly that the guests had begun to arrive. As though from nowhere, Sanchez, the butler, had quietly materialized in the great hall and moved toward the front doors, which he now opened wide; and from the back of the house drifted the voices of the other servants as they hurried to finish their preparations and the strains of music as the orchestra completed the tuning of their instruments, then started to play a lively, melodious tune.

The whitewashed walls of the hacienda glistened like mother-of-pearl in the silver moonlight and red flames of the flickering torches outside. Through the lead-glass, muntined panes of the casement windows streamed the light of a multitude of oil lamps and the hundreds of candles burning in the crystal chandeliers. And now, as the guests started to make their way inside the great hall, to the drawing room, where green-bast card tables had been erected, and to the ballroom, the house rang with talk and laughter and music. Through

the ballroom's open French doors that led to the colon-
nade-lined portico beyond, the sounds of the revelry
wafted into the darkness to mingle harmoniously with
the plaintive calls of the night creatures—the distant
baying of wolves and coyotes, the faraway cries of
night birds. Inside, the gentle clink of the punch-bowl
ladle and liquor bottles as they filled and refilled crystal
glasses with lemonade and other, more potent libations
was accompanied by the voices of the Mexican servants as they made certain that the guests wanted for
nothing.

Long, white-linen-covered tables at the ballroom
end of the great hall groaned under the weight of their
heavy burdens: ornate silver platters piled high with
beef, ham, and chicken, all of which had been slowly
barbecued earlier, and catfish *a la minuta*; enchiladas,
tamales, *frijoles*, and other Mexican fare kept warm by
kerosene wicks lighted beneath elegant silver chafing
dishes; a large silver tureen filled with still-simmering
chili con carne; crystal bowls of assorted vegetables
and salads, salsa, corn relish, and other condiments;
pans of spoon bread so hot that butter just melted on
it, and plates of steaming tortillas. There were all
manner of desserts, too. Tantalizing chocolate and
yellow cakes perched on crystal stands alongside shallow dishes of crisp peach cobbler and lattice-crusted
apple pie sprinkled with cinnamon. An array of *sopaipas*, tarts, and cookies surrounded a solidly frozen
basin of vanilla ice cream.

Doors swung smoothly on oiled hinges as the cease-
less procession of servants moved to and from the
kitchen, bearing trays heavily laden, some heaped with

hors d'oeuvres and other mouth-watering edibles to replace those already eaten, others stacked high with dirty dishes. Not once was even so much as a drop of liquor spilled or a guest on the dance floor jostled; for Noble Winthrop's high and unyielding standards were legendary, and those servants and ranch hands who could not meet them did not last long at the High Sierra.

Carrying a silver tray on which squat glasses of whiskey and mescal sat neatly, one of the servants made his way unobtrusively toward the blue clouds of tobacco smoke that drifted from the open doors of the drawing room. There, several gentlemen too jaded for dancing or otherwise mingling with the fairer sex had congregated at the green-bast card tables, and games of faro and poker, accompanied by the clinking of the chips that had been distributed, were in progress. Other knots of gentlemen, also smoking fine Havana cigars and with glasses of spirits in hand, were assembled on the portico, discussing subjects not fit for ladies' ears. In one corner of the ballroom, a group of matrons sat, patiently waving away the smoke that wafted inside from both the drawing room and the portico, and avidly exchanging the latest news and gossip.

Among the women, recipes and fashions, births and deaths, and courtships and escapades were popular topics of conversation. Among the men, it was war. The United States had dispatched its Marines to Honduras, Cuba, and Nicaragua to protect American interests there, and the Mexican Revolution was being fought in many cases close to Texas. As Noble and

Araminta finished greeting the last of the arriving guests and began to move through the throng, she heard snatches of dialogue that fascinated her, references to Mexican horse and cattle raids upon not only the High Sierra, but also its neighboring ranches all along the Rio Grande. Someone remarked that there was a fortune to be made from the brutal civil war south of the border, from gunrunning and other means she thought sounded at best nefarious and at worst actually illegal. More than once, she heard Rigo del Castillo's name mentioned in connection with both the rustling and the arms trading, and, curious, she wondered if these activities had anything to do with her grandfather's quarrel with the general. Her grandfather would not take lightly the theft of his horses and cattle, Araminta knew.

Before she could learn more, however, Noble propelled her into the ballroom, where she was instantly enveloped by a cluster of eager young men desirous of adding their names to her program. She was just as suddenly rescued from the crush when the boldest and handsomest of the crowd, her grandfather's godson, Judd Hobart, arrogantly elbowed the others aside and swept her away without permission onto the dance floor.

"I don't believe I had the pleasure of hearing your invitation to dance, Mr. Hobart," she snapped tartly, her green eyes flashing sparks, for she found him as provoking as she had Rigo del Castillo, and she was angered by his presumption in not bothering to request her consent before leading her out. Judd, however, only grinned.

"That's because I didn't ask you, Araminta, as well you know. When I decide to cut a pretty little filly out of the herd and put my brand on her, I dig my spurs in and throw my rope around her neck. I don't stand around like some sapheaded tinhorn, waiting for the other ranch hands to make their move, 'cause if there's one thing I've learned in life, it's that it just don't pay to shilly-shally around. Quick on the draw . . . those are the kind of men who survive and prosper out here in the West. Yes, siree. A man's got to take what he wants in this world—before some other fellow beats him to it!"

The implication was that he wanted her. Araminta gasped with shock at his effrontery, the unmistakably possessive tenor of his words. How did he dare? Why, she hardly even knew him!

"I didn't give you permission to address me by my first name, either, Mr. Hobart." Her own words were clipped with outrage at his audacity. But instead of his being properly quelled, as she had intended, Judd merely laughed at her infuriatingly.

"Now, Araminta, don't tell me that you mean for us to stand on ceremony, especially when I've known you since you were knee high to a grasshopper—even if I haven't laid eyes on you for over a decade, much to my regret, I do assure you." His gaze raked her lewdly, making her flush and tremble and cast her eyes down before his.

Uncertain how to handle his advances, Araminta bit her lower lip. It *was* true that she had known Judd in her childhood. But not very well, for even then, he had been a man grown, fifteen years older than she;

and so they had had nothing in common, and certainly, with her being barely out of the nursery, had never socialized together. Still, upon their meeting in the receiving line, she had remembered him. He was not only a man hard to forget, but also had been embroiled in some notorious scandal, she vaguely recalled, something to do with a woman, she thought, an affair the Hobarts had been quick and powerful enough to hush up, however, so the truth was never learned.

Judd's physical size alone was exceptional. He towered over most other men and weighed well over two hundred pounds—all of it big, strong bones and solid muscle, not fat. His neck and shoulders and chest were as powerful and massive as those of a beefy bull. His thick, leonine mane of tobacco-brown hair was streaked as golden as the Indian-summer sun, neatly slicked back from a tanned, weathered face that showed unmistakable signs of his profligate lifestyle. Beneath his sun-bleached brows, his eyes were the clear, deep turquoise of the southwestern sky and spiked with brown lashes gilded at the tips. As hard as the stones they resembled, those eyes glinted from beneath his shuttered lids, continuing to roam over Araminta speculatively, assessing her finer points as though she were up for sale and he were a prospective buyer. It was even more insulting, if that was possible, than the manner in which Rigo del Castillo had surveyed her, she reflected indignantly, longing to slap the lazy, self-assured smile from Judd's sensual, fleshy mouth.

As though he had read her mind, the nostrils of his chiseled Roman nose flared, and the pugnacious set of his square jaw grew even more pronounced. Tightening his arm around her, he pulled her uncomfortably close to him, as though deliberately to agitate her still further as he expertly waltzed her about the ballroom. Had she been able, Araminta would have broken away from him and rudely left him standing on the dance floor. But his grip was like a shackle, imprisoning her; and she sensed instinctively that any attempt to wrest free of him would not only prove fruitless, but also amuse him. So she suffered his unwanted attention in frosty silence, which he blithely ignored, that maddening grin still curving his lips. She prayed for the music to end swiftly.

Araminta's relief when the orchestra at last finished the piece they were playing was short-lived, however; for instead of releasing her, Judd tucked her arm securely in his and proceeded to promenade her outside along the portico. Short of causing a scene, she did not know how to escape from him. She had not thought to have need at the High Sierra of a heavy paperweight in her reticule. But now she yearned for the defense she had employed on the mean streets of New York City and, with a great deal of relish, imagined herself delivering a resounding whack to Judd's skull and knocking him senseless. The vision of his heavily crumpling to his knees, like a poleaxed steer, made her smile inwardly with satisfaction. She wagered that he would not be so brazen and conceited then.

Still, she could not refrain from sighing at the unpleasant realization that the men in Texas were no different from those in the back rooms of Newspaper

Row in New York City, simply less sly, more forth-right in their crudity. To think that her grandfather actually intended for her to marry one of these crass Texas men made her heart sink. She had little in com-mon with any of the men who had surrounded her this evening, Judd least of all. He was everything she despised in a man—boorish and domineering, taking for granted that she would be attracted to him and flattered by his notice, uncaring of her own thoughts and feelings, clearly believing, just as her grandfather did, that a woman's proper place was firmly under a man's booted heel. The idea of being wed to Judd, of being compelled to submit to him, made Araminta shudder; for both her childhood memories and her current impression of him led her to believe that he would not hesitate to ride roughshod over anyone, including his own wife. As though it might offer some protection against him, she drew her fringed shawl more closely about her.

"Cold?" Judd inquired, lifting one brow.

"A little. If you don't mind, I'd like to return to the ballroom now."

"But I *do* mind, Araminta. A crowded ballroom is hardly the place to renew our acquaintance, don't you agree?" The question was purely rhetorical, for with-out waiting for her to respond, he went on. "Besides, if we go back inside, all those fellows in there'll be circling around you in moments, like wolves around a lamb prime for slaughter; and then I might be forced to break a few of their heads to protect you—not that I'd mind doing it, of course. In fact, I'd purely enjoy it. But it sure as hell would raise a ruckus that would be bound to ruin your fine fandango, and somehow, I just don't believe you'd like that at all, Araminta.''

Judd smiled as he spoke, but it was a smile that did not quite reach his narrowed eyes; and Araminta perceived an iron threat behind his velvet words. She did not doubt that he was entirely capable, out of sheer perversity, if nothing else, of instigating such a fray; and since she felt sure that a single punch thrown amid the rowdy and, doubtless, by now liquored-up young bucks inside would indeed set off one of the fierce, unbridled brawls for which Texas was infamous, she reluctantly shook her head in agreement, her mouth thinning with vexation.

''No, you're right, I wouldn't like that—and neither would my grandfather.'' Her implication was plain. If Judd wished to duel with her, he would soon learn she was no spineless opponent.

''I wouldn't be too sure about that, if I were you,'' he rejoined affably, not in the least cowed by the notion that he would incur her grandfather's wrath by starting a fracas. ''Noble likes a good fight as much as any red-blooded man with an ounce of grit; and since, naturally, I'd be defending his granddaughter's honor, I don't reckon he'd take too much exception to a round of fisticuffs. You see, Noble's right partial to me, what with my being his godson and all, and because of that, the High Sierra is like a second home to me. I come and go here pretty much as I please, and you know what? Somehow, I get the feeling I'm going to be calling here a lot more often in the future than I have in the past, if you get my drift.'' His eyes held hers intently.

"It seems to me that you are taking a great deal for granted, Mr. Hobart,'' Araminta retorted stiffly, attempting without success to withdraw her hand from his.

"Judd. All my friends call me Judd—and I knew from the moment I saw you standing there in the High Sierra's great hall that you and I were going to become the best of friends, Araminta. I've waited a long time for that, a long time for you to grow up and come home; and now that you finally have, well, hell! You can't blame me if I'm a trifle impatient, can you?''

Araminta supposed she should feel complimented by his words, but somehow, they just didn't ring true. Judd had never paid any attention to her when she was a child. Nor had he ever once visited or even written to her during all the years she had lived in New York. Thus, surely, his sudden interest in her had more to do with his desiring the High Sierra than wanting her. She would be a foolish romantic, she realized, to hope that a man would be drawn to her for herself alone— and not because of her grandfather's rank and riches.

Undeterred by her unresponsiveness, Judd calmly ignored Araminta's icy, stilted replies to his comments as he conducted her into the lavish gardens. They had been carefully cultivated and irrigated in the courtyard, and were broken here and there by discreet arbors with whitewashed adobe benches and white wooden lattices, upon which climbing flowers abounded. The trees rustled gently in the cool night wind, scenting

the air with a sweet, green fragrance rivaled only by
the perfume of the profusion of late-blooming blossoms that filled the courtyard. The gardens had been
planted years ago by first Noble's wife, Victoria, and
then his daughter-in-law, Katherine. Araminta marveled that her grandfather had ordered the gardens'
upkeep, for he did not strike her as the sort of man
either to indulge such an extravagant fancy or to continue it. She was glad he had, however, for since
returning to the ranch, she had spent many an hour
here in the courtyard, tending the trees and flowers,
sketching and painting and sitting in the shade, sheltered from the hot afternoon sun.

The noise and music from the ballroom faded into
the background as she and Judd walked on into the
darkness illuminated by the moonlight and torchlight;
and now, the sounds peculiar to the night could be
heard—the call of the wild creatures stalking the plains
and skittering through the brush, the chirrup of toads
and locusts and crickets, the sigh of the wind that
always spoke with a different voice, somehow, after
sundown. Among the bushes bordering the long, low,
whitewashed adobe wall that bounded the far end of
the courtyard, fireflies flashed; and a solitary woman
stood at the black, wrought-iron Spanish gate, gazing
at the distant horizon, where the sky glowed crimson
and pink and gold from lightning, and thunder rum-
bled. There was something familiar about the shadowed woman, about the tilt of her brunet head. . . .
And then Araminta remembered where she had seen
her and realized that this was the woman who had been

locked in Rigo del Castillo's arms at the hotel in El Paso.

"Velvet!" Judd's voice was sharp, both its tone and the name he had spoken startling Araminta; for she knew then, even before the woman whirled abruptly and her lovely countenance was cast into the moonlight, that it was Judd's younger sister who stood alone at the ornate gate. "What are you doing out here?"

"It was so hot inside that I came out for a breath of fresh air. I was just coming in to get you. I heard guns, Judd, and look, there's a fire out there! Oh, Judd, it's the Chaparral!" Velvet's heavily lashed eyes, as turquoise as her brother's, were huge and scared in her ashen face.

It was not lightning that brightened the sky, Araminta understood then. The Chaparral was burning, and it was gunfire, not thunder, that echoed ominously on the soughing night wind.

Chapter Five

"You tell Pa about the fire, Velvet"—Judd's face was grim and angry as he stared into the distance at the Chaparral—"and let him know I'm on my way home now to check things out. The sky's lighted up like the Fourth of July, but I don't think it's too serious a fire. If it were, Ty Danner would already have sent word. Since he hasn't, it's probably just an outbuilding or something burning, not the house itself or, God forbid, the land. As dry as it's been all summer, a range fire would be the worst kind of disaster."

Young as she had been when her parents had taken her away from Texas, Araminta knew that Judd spoke the truth. Baked by the sun, the prairie grass, if ignited, would catch flame like tinder, growing quickly into a wildfire that could consume miles of land before being brought under control. She hoped Judd was right, that the fire was a minor one. Still, even if it *were* only an outbuilding that was ablaze, the ranch hands fighting the fire would undoubtedly require treatment for burns, cuts, and scrapes, and would be hungry and thirsty, too, after their work was done. Perhaps she could help.

"I'll go with you," she offered to Judd as he strode so swiftly toward the hacienda that she and Velvet were practically running to keep up with him. "All of us at boarding school had to take turns helping in the infirmary, so I have some knowledge of first aid."

"Thanks. We may need it," he replied.

Nothing in his manner now toward Araminta even hinted of his earlier high-handed treatment of her. He was all business—cool, levelheaded, and purposeful, a man who could be counted on during a crisis, she realized, somewhat surprised. She had been ready to dismiss Judd as little more than an obnoxious blow-hard. Now she saw that there was more to him than had first met her eye. Could it be that if, as she suspected, he favored Judd as a husband for her, her grandfather had her best interests at heart? Perhaps her judgment of both men was too severe and needed revising.

Inside the ballroom, Noble, after learning of the fire at the Chaparral, supported Araminta's decision to accompany Judd. Although the fandango was being held in her honor, the current crisis at the Chaparral naturally took precedence. Noble agreed that Araminta should lend Judd a helping hand if she could. Should Judd discover that the situation at the Chaparral was worse than he suspected, he would send word back to his father and Noble at the party at once. It was the consensus of the three that in the meantime, there was no point in disrupting the fandango, which was in full swing, and spoiling the guests' gaiety over what would probably turn out to be little more than an outbuilding ablaze. Such incidents had occurred several times before and were suspected to be the work of Mexican *bandoleros* under the direction of the disreputable General Rigo del Castillo.

Judd's sleek, shiny red automobile, its top down, was brought around out front, and after he made certain Araminta was securely tucked in her seat, he climbed in beside her and stepped on the accelerator. The motorcar's churning wheels sent dust and pebbles flying as it surged forward to the main road and continued on toward the Chaparral at a breakneck speed. Araminta found it as exhilarating as when she was flying on horseback across the range. As the cool night wind whipped her hair into disarray and her cheeks flushed with a becoming pink glow, Judd was intensely aware of her disheveled beauty, and he thought to himself that so would she look after being made love to by him—for, the moment he had seen her standing in the great hall of the High Sierra, he had made up his mind that she would belong to him and no other. Not only was she a desirable woman, but also the heiress apparent to the High Sierra. Noble Winthrop would not have summoned her home otherwise.

For years now, Judd had counted on inheriting not only the Chaparral, but also, as Noble's godson, the

High Sierra; and he had planned how he would combine the two ranches into the single biggest spread in all the country. He had envisioned himself not just as a land baron and cattle king, but as an omnipotent master, a virtual deity over his vast domain. He was not about to permit that dream to slip from his grasp because Noble had evidently suddenly gone soft in his old age and developed an unexpected, sentimental attachment to Araminta. Had she been as disagreeable, ugly, and fat as a mean, bristly sow, Judd would nevertheless have married her in order to get his hands on the High Sierra. That she was classically lovely and temptingly voluptuous was an added bonus. Both ravishing and reserved, she was the epitome of the proverbial ice maiden, he mused, waiting to be thawed, melted by the heat of a virile man—and he was determined he would be that man. Only the danger of the Chaparral's burning to the ground prevented him from driving her out to some isolated spot to claim her as his by seduction or force, if necessary—not that she would have resisted for long, Judd reflected smugly. She would have had no choice but to wed him afterward. That she would instead have denounced and exposed him, he did not even consider. Her shame at his hands would have kept her silent and submissive, as it had others before her. They had made him suitable, dutiful mistresses, just as Araminta would make him a suitable, dutiful wife.

Blissfully unaware of Judd's thoughts, Araminta sat quietly beside him, taking simple pleasure in the windy ride while, at the same time, her mind raced ahead to the situation at the Chaparral and the possible injuries of the ranch hands, which would require medical treatment. She hoped there would not be any wounds too serious in nature, for she did not feel herself equipped to deal with those. Thankfully, however, upon arriving at the Chaparral, she saw that it was just as Judd had supposed: nothing more than a minor outbuilding was ablaze. The primary purpose of the fire had apparently been to serve as a distraction while desperadoes escaped with several of the ranch's corralled horses. It was the ranch hands' shooting at the *bandoleros* that Araminta had heard in the distance. But the band of Mexicans was gone now. Shouting and discharging their pistols, they had galloped away into the darkness, chousing before them some of the Chaparral's prime breeding stock.

Despite herself, Araminta could not help but admire how calmly and authoritatively Judd took charge of the situation, consulting first with the Chaparral's foreman, Ty Danner, and then issuing commands right and left, effectively bringing order to chaos. Hasty and uncoordinated efforts already under way to contain the flames were quickly organized, and the women of the hacienda placed under Araminta's direction.

Amid the billowing smoke and flying cinders, three of the ranch hands were attempting to rescue a man pinned under a burning beam that had fallen from the roof of the outbuilding. Seeing them struggling with the timber, Judd cursed mightily under his breath. Damned fools! They were wasting valuable time, messing around with the beam instead of chasing after the desperadoes and recovering the stolen horses fast. Each horse was of far more worth and importance than a thirty-dollar-a-month ranch hand! With angry impatience, he roughly elbowed the three men out of his way. Alone, grunting from the effort, he lifted and heaved the beam aside, freeing the trapped man. Watching Judd, Araminta marveled at his strength, his risking his life to save the helpless man. She would not have attributed such selflessness to Judd had she not witnessed it with her own eyes. She could not lightly discount what she had seen. Clearly, her poor opinion of him was undeserved! Impulsively, she raced to his side.

"Oh, Judd, are you all right?" she asked anxiously as he vigorously slapped and rubbed his arms. The sleeves of his jacket were smoldering from where the flaming timber had momentarily rested upon them, she realized. His skin was probably burned underneath. "Take off your jacket, and let me see if you're hurt."

"No, I'm okay, just a little red and raw from the charring, I expect—and I'll be damned if a few blisters can slow me down when there's work to be done," Judd insisted as he brushed the last of the embers from his jacket. "I've got to get this fire put out and the horses back—and no doubt there are others here with wounds more serious than mine, Araminta. Tend to them for me, will you? I sure as hell don't have time to play nursemaid, too!"

"All right . . . if you're sure . . . ?"

"I'm sure." He smiled at her encouragingly. "But I appreciate your concern."

"Of course I'm concerned. Why, you might have been killed!" she exclaimed. "It was a very brave and noble thing you did, saving that man's life at the risk of your own!''

"Aw, it was nothing, really," Judd declared with what he hoped was just the right amount of humility. "Just all in a day's work. Sam's a good hand, and so I'd sure hate to lose him." In reality, Judd thought that Sam was the worst kind of fool, standing around like a tinhorn while a burning beam collapsed on him. "I hope he's not hurt."

Touched by Judd's solicitousness, Araminta turned her attention to the freed ranch hand. Sam's shin was badly bruised, she discovered, but she felt certain that the bone was not broken. With medical supplies from the hacienda, she and several of the other women dressed his wound, then treated burns, cuts, and scrapes suffered by other ranch hands, while the remaining servants prepared food and drink for the men battling the blaze.

The fire was soon extinguished by means of both a trench hurriedly dug around the outbuilding to prevent the flames from spreading and the bucket brigade that had been formed to douse the blaze with water. As the charred adobe shell and timber of the outbuilding sizzled and smoldered, Judd took stock of the situation. Though an unnecessary loss, the outbuilding could, of course, be replaced. The missing horses, however, were another matter entirely. Prime breeding stock was obviously not so easily come by as adobe bricks and lumber. Assembling several of the best ranch hands, Ty Danner at their fore, Judd instructed them to arm and provision themselves to set out after the *bandoleros* and the horses purloined from the corral. By this time, Judd thought acidly, there was probably little hope that the ranch hands would catch up with the desperadoes, who were doubtless already south of the border by now; nevertheless, the effort to recover the stolen stock must be made.

"Damn those Mexican bandits!" Judd's face was dark with rage in the moonlight. "They've hit the Chaparral half a dozen times in twice as many months. It's uncanny how the greaser pigs always seem to know just when to strike. I'm beginning to believe that Del Castillo must have spies even among my own men—though I've never had cause to question the loyalty of any of them before."

"The general really is responsible for all these attacks on the ranches along the border, then? But if you and all the other ranchers know that, Judd, then why don't you press charges against him? Why isn't he arrested?" Araminta asked as she slowly rewound a roll of gauze bandage she had not needed to use.

"We've no real proof as yet, only suspicions. The bastard's clever, I'll give him that. But sooner or later, he's bound to slip up, and then we'll get him." Clearly, Judd relished the prospect, as his next words confirmed. "How I look forward to that day. Still, even hanging's too good for the likes of him. Why, he's nothing more than a peasant, a thief, and a murderer—even if he does manage these days to pass himself off as an aristocrat, a respectable Spanish grandee. It's only because Del Castillo is reputed to have a fortune as large as a king's ransom—all of it ill-gotten, I'm willing to wager—that he is welcomed into some of the best drawing rooms in Mexico and Texas both.''

''Do you really consider him a murderer? Killing is what soldiers do, isn't it? You could call them all criminals by that standard.''

Briefly, Judd's mouth thinned with annoyance at her pointing out this fact, as though she had in some way contradicted him. ''Right,'' he said. ''But shooting your enemies during a war's one thing. Murdering your wife in cold blood is quite another; and *that* is what Del Castillo is rumored to have done—a charge, I might add, that he's never bothered to deny, so I can only suppose it to be true.''

Involuntarily, Araminta shuddered at this announcement. Truly, Rigo del Castillo deserved his wicked reputation. That such a man roamed freely to wreak havoc upon industrious ranchers like her grandfather and the Hobarts appalled her; and if the general had indeed killed his wife, how could any woman feel safe in his presence, wish to entertain him in those drawing rooms of which Judd had spoken? Surely, then, she was mistaken in thinking that it was Velvet Hobart she had seen with Rigo del Castillo. Because of her sudden confusion and uncertainty regarding the identity of the woman at the hotel in El Paso, Araminta did not mention the matter to Judd. Velvet was his sister. He would not take lightly such a terrible accusation about her, and besides, Araminta had no desire to start trouble over something that was really none of her business in the first place.

''We made quite a team this evening, you and I, even if I do say so myself.'' Judd smoothly changed the topic of conversation as he walked Araminta to his automobile and assisted her inside. "I like a woman who can keep a cool head in a crisis."

"I'm glad I could help," Araminta responded. Somehow, having seen Judd single-handedly rescue the ranch hand and take control in a dangerous situation had altered her previous opinion of him.

On their return to the High Sierra, she hurried upstairs to change her smudged and stained gown. With her maid Carmen's deft assistance, Araminta was swiftly presentable again and arrived back downstairs just in time for the late supper being served in the dining room. Judd was waiting at the foot of the steps to escort her inside. Though she shook her head at him ruefully, she still could not repress a smile.

"Don't you think you've monopolized me enough tonight, Mr. Hobart?" she asked lightly.

"So . . . we're back to 'Mr. Hobart,' are we?" He made a gentle clicking sound of regret with his mouth. "And here I thought we were well on our way to becoming the best of friends. Hell's bells, Araminta! If there's some other man here you'd care to go into supper with, just let me know, and I'll clear off. Otherwise, I'd be mighty pleased to do the honors."

When he put his invitation that way, she didn't see how she could refuse. Besides, much against her better judgment and no matter how she fought it, she *was* flattered. She had never been courted before. Taking his proffered arm, Araminta allowed Judd to lead her into the dining room, feeling that perhaps she might come to like at least one Texas man, after all.

Chapter Six

If there had been some other man interested in her, a man who had also interested her, Araminta knew he would not have stood a chance against Judd's relentless, determined pursuit of her. After the night of her fandango, hardly a week went by without his calling upon her several times, even if for no more than a short ride on horseback across the range. While her grandfather greeted Judd's visits with obvious approval, Araminta's own feelings toward him continued to be mixed. She was not without her share of feminine vanity, as well as a secret, intense longing to be loved and accepted; and so for these reasons, she increasingly welcomed Judd's attentions. He both flirted with and flattered her outrageously, making her laugh despite her blushes at his brassiness. But although undeniably a braggart, Judd was no fool. His boldness was born of an authority and acumen in business that rivaled Noble Winthrop's own. Yet Araminta could not rid herself of the niggling suspicion that, like her grandfather, Judd possessed a hard, ruthless, vengeful core that could make him a deadly and implacable foe. It did not escape her notice that the respect Judd commanded in west Texas was tinged with fear, lending credence to rumors about his hot temper and his being quick with his fists to settle a dispute. Often, she heard him referred to as a ''chip off the old block,'' and it was not long before she recognized that the ''block'' was not Judd's father, Frank Hobart, but her grandfather, Judd's godfather. She discovered that when his own son, Preston, had proved loath to follow in Noble Winthrop's footsteps, Judd had willingly stepped into Preston's shoes. Nor was Araminta slow to grasp that were the High Sierra and the Chaparral to be combined, the result would be the largest, richest ranch in the entire country, a prospect that a man like Judd would scarcely ignore. More than once, she wondered if Judd would be so persistent a suitor if she were not Noble Winthrop's only living relative and heiress apparent; and she was deeply hurt to think that the answer to her question was no.

So, although she did not turn down his invitations, neither did Araminta permit Judd to sweep her off her feet, as he so clearly intended, but resolutely held him at arm's length, thereby unwittingly maddening him and fueling the mounting flames of his desire for her. With a word dropped here and there, he had let it be known that he considered Araminta his and would not look kindly upon any of his cohorts calling on her; and although there were one or two who might have been tempted to do so—if for no other reason than to put a burr under Judd's saddle—Noble himself, with a few dry, well-chosen words, had made it plain that he didn't approve of any of them as a prospective husband for his granddaughter. Thus did Judd gain a clear field, only to find himself thwarted by Araminta herself from attaining his goal of winning her. Frustrated, he would have seduced or forced himself on her had it not been for Noble's stern admonition that he expected Judd to conduct a proper courtship of Araminta.

"I'll have no scandal attached to either the Winthrop name or my granddaughter's skirts, Judd," Noble had warned as he had poured brandy from a decanter into a pair of crystal balloon glasses one evening at the High Sierra.

The two men had retired to Noble's study for drinks and a smoke following a late supper, at which Judd had been the only guest. At Noble's warning, Judd, who could stare down most men, had lowered his gaze uncomfortably, appearing to focus his attention on the cigar he had been lighting. Shaking the flame from the match, he had dragged deeply on the cigar, then exhaled, blowing a cloud of blue smoke into the air.

"I'm sure I don't know what you mean, Noble." His tone had been carefully casual; still, it had not deceived his godfather.

"Hmph!" Noble had snorted, handing him one of the snifters. "Don't you dare to talk to me as though I were some tinhorn idiot! It ain't just Frank who's had to pay over the years to hush up your escapades with women and keep your ass out of jail—not to mention your neck from being stretched by a rope—and don't you ever forget that again, boy, you hear?''

"Yes, sir."

"You'd damned well better." Scowling darkly, Noble had paused, sipping his brandy, then continued. "Hell, Judd! I ain't got nothing against your sowing your wild oats; any right-thinking, red-blooded male's got needs, after all. I understand that. But . . . for Christ's sake! If you want to play rough, get rid of some of that healthy animal lust you got burning inside you, do it with servants and whores, boy. They're paid to take that kind of crap; they expect it—hell, half of 'em even enjoy it—and ain't nobody who gives a good goddamn about what happens to 'em, anyhow. If I've told you once, I've told you a hundred times, Judd: Don't mess around with the ladies. You do, and one of these days, some man who don't like the idea of learning a fox has been having a heyday in his chicken coop is going to shoot you and cut off your tail for a trophy.''

Now, recalling these words, Judd sighed heavily and signaled the waiter to bring him another whiskey. Who would have thought that Noble would turn out at this late date to have a conscience—at least where his granddaughter was concerned? For that matter, why should Noble have got such a maggot in his brain as to send for her in the first place? Noble must surely be getting soft in his old age. For years, Judd had counted on Noble's willing the High Sierra to him. Now, with Araminta's arrival on the scene, there seemed little chance of that unless Judd got her wedded and bedded as soon as possible. The longer she remained single, the greater the likelihood that she might have her head turned by some other man and that the High Sierra would slip through Judd's fingers. That wouldn't suit him one bit. He had not endured Noble's choleric temper and mulish freaks all these years to be done out of the ranch by a mere slip of a woman, no matter how beautiful and desirable she might be. That Araminta should stubbornly persist in resisting his advances was a blow to both his pride and vanity. With the greatest of difficulty, he held his wrath in check as he studied her across the table of the café to which he had brought her for lunch in El Paso this afternoon.

Because of the heat, Araminta had elected to sit outside beneath the shade of the café's portico; and despite his surly reverie, Judd was compelled to admit that she looked quite fetching. Had he possessed a romantic nature, he might have likened her to a dewy rose; for over the passing weeks, her fair skin had been dusted pink and gold by the sun, and now, a fine sheen of perspiration glistened upon her face. Despite this evidence of the sultry temperature's effect upon her, Judd thought she nevertheless appeared as cool and remote as the ice maiden he had mentally christened her; and he yearned more than ever to melt her, to discover whether fire lay beneath her icy exterior. In his mind, he tore the flowered hat from her head and stripped her of her pale, mint-green gown, imagined her naked, struggling and straining beneath him, her long blond hair loose and disheveled, her head thrown back, her full, ripe breasts heaving with each gasp;

and it was all he could do to prevent himself from dragging her down the street to the nearest hotel and having his way with her. He did not in the least mind marrying her, especially when it meant getting his hands on the High Sierra. What he *did* resent was being led on and kept dangling and made to look as foolish as a schoolboy mooning after a schoolgirl, which was the game he felt that Araminta played with him.

She herself would have been surprised and shocked to learn Judd's thoughts, for they were not her own and, indeed, were the farthest thing from her mind. In truth, despite its plainly being her grandfather's wish that she wed Judd, Araminta wanted to be sure in her heart that he was the right man for her before committing herself to him for the rest of her life; and she simply did not see how that was possible when she had been courted by no other beaux save him. That Judd and her grandfather had conspired to keep any other man from wooing her, she had no doubt; and the notion angered her, although she had as yet met no one else she had hoped would, in fact, call on her. She just resented having her freedom to choose taken away from her and her mind made up for her, with no regard for her own feelings in the matter. She would not be dragged to the altar; she would go willingly—or not at all.

Despite all of her grandfather's querulous claims that he might at any moment be summoned by his Maker, Araminta suspected that there was a good deal of life left in him yet, and so she was in no hurry to give herself into Judd's keeping. Indeed, whenever he pressured her, he reminded her so vividly and unpleasantly of the blackguards on Newspaper Row in New York City that sometimes she felt as though she actually hated him. Then, guiltily, she would think how unfair this was to him, that he was really no worse than any other man in west Texas, including her grandfather; and she would try harder to be more receptive to Judd. This, she was unaware, gave her the appearance of blowing hot and cold; and because she had such limited experience with men, she did not realize how this both enraged and inflamed him. She sensed only how his emotions roiled inside him, even as her own did, bewildering her. Only twelve years old when her parents had died, she clung fiercely to her memory of their fairy-tale romance, of the love that had leaped between them like lightning between the heavens and the earth. As a result, she yearned deeply for more than what Judd offered. Despite the ardent words he sometimes whispered to her on a moonlit garden path, the feverish kisses he pressed upon her before she broke away from him, trembling with longing and turmoil, he did not love her. He only wanted her, just as he wanted the High Sierra. This, Araminta knew instinctively; and therein lay the crux of her reluctance to become his wife.

Stifling a sigh at the dispiriting turn of her thoughts, she rose to her feet. Earlier, she had told Judd that she had some shopping to do after lunch—a convenient lie she had used because she had known shopping held no interest for him and she did not want him to come along and learn the true nature of her errand in El Paso, which she felt certain he would oppose as vehemently as her grandfather would have. As she had hoped and expected, Judd had replied that he had some business affairs to attend to. Now, after arranging to meet him in an hour back at the café, Araminta forced herself to walk away as calmly as though she indeed had nothing more important planned than a shopping excursion; she even paused deliberately before a store window as though to examine a dress on display. Once she was sure she was safely out of Judd's view, however, she abandoned all pretense of a nonchalant stroll and hurried toward the post office, her real destination. She was in such a rush, and glancing back so anxiously over her shoulder to be certain Judd did not spy her, that she did not see the man going into the post office until it was too late and she had run right into him.

Startled, she stumbled back from the impact, dropping the black leather portfolio and white kid gloves she carried and losing her balance. Only the man's powerful arms shooting out swiftly to grab hold of her prevented her from falling. For a moment, she was enfolded tight against his broad chest. Instantly she felt as though an electric current were passing through her, prickling the fine hairs on her nape and making her heart beat fast. The man's body was warm and lithe and hard with muscle, his fine white, ruffled cambric shirt crisp with fresh starch, the smell of which mingled pleasantly with the other fragrances emanating subtly from his smooth, dark skin—sandalwood, cheroot smoke, mescal, and his own masculine scent. His hands gripped her firmly, their long fingers slender but strong. When the man slowly put her from him and she was able finally to look up at him, her eyes widened with shock and sudden confusion as they met his own. Her breath caught sharply in her throat.

"Señorita Winthrop, we meet again," Rigo del Castillo drawled in his low, throaty, Spanish-accented voice. He still held her, making it impossible for her to escape. "What a delightful surprise. But . . . I am forgetting my manners, am I not? We have not yet been formally introduced. Rigo del Castillo, at your service." As he had before, he clicked his heels together smartly, military fashion, and sketched her a bow, his fingers, as they slid down her arm to clasp her right hand and gallantly raise it to his lips, sending another queer, inexplicable quiver through her as his mouth brushed her skin. She had the impulse to snatch her hand from his grasp, but as though he sensed her thought, his fingers tightened around hers, so she could not withdraw her hand from his. "I trust you have suffered no injury from our unexpected encounter?"

"N-n-no, not at all," she stammered in a rush, blushing at how like a flustered schoolgirl she sounded. Damn the man! Why must he be so handsome? It was not right that a man so notorious should be so attractive. "I'm—I'm fine, thank you."

"I am glad to hear it." Releasing her at last, the general bent to retrieve her belongings. "You seem to have a habit of losing your gloves," he observed as he handed them to her, along with her portfolio, which Araminta tucked tightly under her arm. "Where is your redoubtable watchdog, Mr. Gideon, to look after you? Did he not accompany you into town today?"

"No, he did not—and he is hardly my 'watchdog,' besides." She was amused by the notion. "I am perfectly capable of fending for myself, I assure you."

"Indeed?" One brow lifted demoniacally. "Then you are alone in El Paso?"

"No," she replied shortly, without elaboration.

"In that case, I must not detain you." Del Castillo had hooded his eyes against her gaze, so she could not read his thoughts. Nevertheless, it seemed to her that her answer had in some way angered him, for his jaw was set and the smile he flashed her sardonic. Opening the door to the post office, he said, "After you, Señorita Winthrop."

Araminta was only too glad to precede him into the building. She had not wanted to continue standing on the street, talking to the general, where Judd might at any moment have spied them and, given his hot temper and bitter animosity toward Del Castillo, surely have caused trouble. Nor, remembering Mr. Gideon's warning to her, had Araminta wished some passerby to see them and remark upon her chance meeting with the general to her grandfather.

"Good afternoon, General." She nodded to him politely but did not extend her hand, a deliberate oversight that did not elude his notice. Briefly, his eyes hardened, his nostrils flared, and his mouth tightened, making her shiver involuntarily at the menace he exuded.

"Señorita." His tone made a mockery of the word.

Forcing herself to turn her back on him, Araminta approached the counter, where she withdrew from the portfolio she had bought just a few days ago the package she had carefully prepared last evening in the privacy of her bedroom. In it was an article she had written about life at the High Sierra, along with three charcoal sketches she had drawn. She had not referred to the ranch by name, but, rather, worded the story in such a way that it was a generalized account of ranch life, for she did not want her grandfather to learn of her attempt to establish herself as a journalist and to sabotage her career before it even got off the ground. To that end, she had written the article under the pen name of A. K. Munroe, which were the initials of her first and middle names, Araminta Katherine, and her mother's maiden name. She had addressed the parcel to Liam O'Grady at the *Record* in New York City and had enclosed a short cover letter to him, making no mention of the fact that she and A. K. Munroe were one and the same, although she felt that Liam might guess as much.

Now, from the reticule looped about her left wrist, Araminta withdrew the necessary money to pay for postage and, acutely conscious of Rigo del Castillo's proximity, quietly informed the clerk that she also wished to acquire a post-office box under the name of A. K. Munroe. Since the clerk—like everyone else in west Texas—was well aware of her identity, that she was Noble Winthrop's granddaughter, Araminta could not help but flush nervously as she spoke, as though she were guilty of some crime and about to be apprehended. Nor were matters improved by the clerk's staring at her curiously and with obvious disapproval over the tops of his silver, wire-rimmed spectacles. She felt sure he knew the post-office box was for her.

"A. K. Munroe. Don't know anybody by that name hereabouts. Is that a friend of yours, Miss Winthrop?" the clerk, a small, withered stick of a man with a voice to match his appearance, inquired a bit too eagerly.

"I don't really think that's any of your business. Do you, Pimby?" Rigo del Castillo spoke softly, but there was an unmistakable hard edge to his tone, all the same. Overhearing her conversation with the clerk, the general had moved to stand beside Araminta. He made no apology for his interference in her affairs, but leaned against the counter, his eyes fixed intently on the clerk, Pimby. At this, Pimby blanched and swallowed hard, running his fingers around the inside of his white, stiffly starched collar, as though it were too tight for his neck. "You've got a customer here who wants a post-office box for A. K. Munroe. Now, you give her one, *pronto*, no questions asked, no tales told. *¿Comprende?*"

"Yes, General. Right away, General."

Without further ado, the clerk assigned a post-office box to Araminta, under the fictitious name she had given. She was relieved that the matter had been taken care of with a minimum of fuss and that Pimby's silence should apparently be assured. But she was also dismayed that she should be beholden to Rigo del Castillo; for it was clear to her that without his intervention, she would not have got the post-office box so easily, perhaps even not at all—and this after she had insulted him outside by refusing to offer him her hand. Why had he spoken up on her behalf, she wondered, especially after she had treated him so rudely? Plainly, he must have suspected that she was doing something that would displease her grandfather greatly and had wished to help her thwart him. Still, even if the general's assistance had sprung from a less-than-noble fount, Araminta felt uncomfortably that she owed him her gratitude.

"I—I want to thank you," she said to him after he had finished transacting his own business at the post office and turned away from the counter.

"Por nada." Del Castillo shrugged casually. "It is the way of a man, always to come to the aid of a damsel in distress, no? Only, I admit I *am* curious as to why you wished to acquire a post-office box under an alias, Señorita Winthrop."

"Oh, dear, was it that obvious?" Her voice was rueful. "I was afraid of that. I—I assure you that it is for nothing more nefarious than that I have—I have submitted for publication a newspaper article I have written, and I—I did not wish my grandfather to learn of it," Araminta explained, then could have bitten off her tongue for her honesty. Still, it seemed extremely unlikely that the general would report this information to her grandfather.

"Ah . . . I see. *Sí*, it is indeed doubtful that Noble Winthrop would approve of his granddaughter's being more than just a lily of the field."

"Who neither toils nor spins?"

"You are as quick-witted as you are beautiful, *señorita*. It is most refreshing to meet a woman of your quality. They are few and far between, I promise you." His voice was warm and smooth, melting like molasses in her ears. His eyes held hers hypnotically, their dark-brown depths seductive, fathomless; she felt peculiarly as though she were drowning in them.

How could he be so attractive, so charming, and yet so lethal? Araminta wondered. Had he really murdered his wife? Surely not. Surely, the stories told of him must be lies. But why else would Pimby have been so quick to acquiesce to the general's wishes? It was fright she had seen upon Pimby's prune face; it was as though he had been confronted by a savage, unpredictable mountain cat instead of a man. The same kind of look she'd noticed on the faces of those who quailed before her grandfather's ire. Yet unlike her grandfather, who bellowed and shook his fist when in a rage, Rigo del Castillo had not raised his voice, had made not a single threatening gesture toward the clerk. The general's infamous reputation alone was enough to inspire fear, it appeared. Surely, then, the stories about him must have substance, must be deserved. Unwittingly, Araminta shuddered at the thought. She dare not let her strange fascination with this man take hold of her. If gossip were to be believed, he was an unrepentant criminal, a man who had slain his own wife in cold blood and attacked every ranch along the Rio Grande, stealing, looting, burning, and killing. She must not let herself forget that, no matter how Del Castillo flattered and, however much against her will, attracted her.

"I—I must go," she uttered breathlessly, as though she had run a long way. "Thanks again." Then, without waiting for his response, she hurried from the post office, sensing somehow that he remained standing there, gazing after her until she disappeared from sight.

That night, Araminta dreamed, and in her dream, a devil on horseback appeared from out of a dust storm to swoop her up and carry her away to his home in hell—and when she looked upon his face, it was the face of Rigo del Castillo.

Chapter Seven

The long Indian summer had at last begun to give way
to autumn, and the days to cool, the blistering heat
mellowing to a golden warmth that, being bearable,
was welcome. Now, when the wind swept down from
the mountains across the range, it brought with it the
coolness of high altitudes rather than the hot breath of
the plains and deserts, and it was moist and tangy with
the scent of the Rio Grande. Fall wildflowers burst
into bloom amid the tall grasses that carpeted the
range, and the leaves of the trees turned the shades
of the bluffs in the distance. Only the sky remained
unchanged, as turquoise as the stones that the Indians
called pieces of sky.

Although Araminta knew better, the romantic legend of the turquoise stones' having fallen to earth from

the heavens appealed to her fancy, and she worked hard to get the blue hue just right on the canvas she was painting. She had chosen this morning to use oils instead of watercolors, so she was able to take her time, even to correct her mistakes, though her art teacher at the academy had frowned on this and Araminta herself, accustomed to the swifter pace working with watercolors demanded, made few errors. She usually preferred watercolors, because they were lighter and much more delicate, ethereal; but the scene she envisioned in her mind's eye seemed to require the richness of oils.

Because Judd monopolized so many of her hours, Araminta had continued her habit of riding at dawn, to ensure that she had some time alone. Although her grandfather had at first insisted that one of the ranch hands accompany her, she somehow always managed to slip away without one, preferring solitude; and Noble had reluctantly resigned himself to her waywardness. To ease his mind, Araminta always left behind a note at the ranch, indicating in which direction she had ridden, so that if she did not return within a reasonable length of time, her grandfather would have a starting point for a search party. Still, he fretted about her safety, to the point of being overly protective, she thought. But she was uncertain if this was because he disliked her independent ways or had come to care for her. She preferred to think that it was the latter. Even so, it did not lessen her feeling sometimes that she would suffocate and die if she could not have a few hours to herself, to paint, to think, to dream.

She was accustomed to solitude, required it as the

flowers did rain. At the ranch, it seemed that she was never alone. Even when her grandfather and Judd were not there, the servants, all Mexicans, hovered perpetually in the background, alert to her every need. With her limited Spanish, she could not make them understand that they need not wait upon her hand and foot, as though she were royalty. In their eyes, she *was* royalty—or as near to it as one could get in west Texas—and many of them, like Teresa, had a fondness for her from the old days, when she had been a child at the High Sierra. To request that they leave her alone would have hurt and confused them, Araminta knew. So she endured the servants, knowing that their attentions stemmed from love and kindness and a desire to please, and how churlish and ungrateful she would appear by rejecting what they offered.

Thus, now, she reveled in her aloneness, unaware of passing time or even of her surroundings, except that what she captured on the canvas she surveyed with an adept and critical eye from every angle where it stood upon her easel. The painting was good, perhaps the best work she had ever done, she thought. It showed dawn breaking on the eastern horizon, shades of rose and gold streaking into blues that faded into the changing colors of the cottonwood and mesquite trees that lined the creek bank upon which she stood. The rays of the sun glinted through the branches of the trees, dappling the water, as though its surface were scattered with a multitude of precious gemstones. The prairie stretched away behind, the tall, yellowed grasses touched also by the sun, as though they were aflame. She had done the dawn first, to capture it as closely as possible, so the rest of the painting still needed work. But now that she had the essence of the scene on canvas, she could finish the remainder at her leisure. Araminta decided that she would take a break and eat the simple alfresco breakfast she had packed in a basket before departing from the hacienda.

Humming to herself under her breath, she laid aside her brush and palette, then bent to wash her face and hands in the creek. The water was cool and felt good against her skin as she splashed herself liberally, scrubbing her lower left arm hard to remove the oil paint inadvertently smeared on it from her palette. When she finally rose, wiping the water from her eyes, there was Rigo del Castillo on the opposite bank of the creek, mounted on a huge black stallion and looking like Satan himself! She was startled by the sight of him, for she had not heard him approach. She wondered if he intended to harm her. After all, he was the hated foe of both her grandfather and Judd. Her first instinct was to run from him, but as she was afoot and he was on horseback, he could easily ride her down if he chose. There was no escaping him—at least for the moment—though Araminta stepped back from him warily, beginning to edge subtly toward her mare.

"What are you doing here? Where did you come from?" she asked sharply.

He laughed. "My dear Señorita Winthrop, you are looking at me as though I had horns and a pointed tail. I am aware that I *do* have something of a reputation as a devil, but do you really believe that my powers are such that I simply materialized out of thin air?"

"No, of course not," she retorted, angered that he should ridicule her, as though he had read her mind and sought to prey upon her apprehension. "You merely frightened me for a moment, that's all. I did not see you ride up."

"Perhaps because you were intent on your washing?" he suggested, nudging his stallion forward into the creek. When the beast had waded across and stood dripping between Araminta and her mare, effectively cutting off her avenue of escape, the general casually dismounted, a smile still curving his mouth. "My apologies for scaring you, *señorita*. That was not my intent, I assure you. Like you, I, too, enjoy an early morning ride. I chanced to spy you here and took the liberty of joining you."

"Uninvited, and on High Sierra land, as well? You are trespassing, you know. Are you always given to such presumption, General?"

"Strictly speaking, I was not on High Sierra land until I crossed the creek, which marks the boundary between your grandfather's ranch . . . and mine. My own ranch, Casa Blanca, is not so large as the High Sierra, of course; nevertheless, when I am here in Texas, I call it home. But, *sí*, to answer your question, I am, when it pleases me, given to a certain amount of presumption, as no doubt you will by now have heard."

Araminta had not anticipated such frankness. From a man of Del Castillo's sordid reputation, she had expected if not deceit, at least dissembling. She was as surprised by his honesty as she was by the fact that the land adjoining her grandfather's belonged to the

general, for no one had made mention of this to her
before. Still, despite Del Castillo's truthfulness and
apparent friendliness, she dare not lower her guard
against him.

"And how do you know I enjoy riding in the morning?" she inquired tartly.

"I make it my business to know everything about
my enemies."

Unlike his others, this answer alarmed her. For the
first time, she cursed her own willfulness in not obey-
ing her grandfather and taking along a ranch hand for
protection during her rides. Now she understood her
folly. She and the general were totally alone together,
isolated on the plains. If he should suddenly attack
her, no one would hear her screams. She would be at
his utter mercy. Her rifle was tucked into its scabbard
on her saddle, and her pistol was in her gun belt, which
she had taken off earlier and looped around the saddle
horn. As Del Castillo continued to stand between her
and her mare, it seemed unlikely that she would be
able to reach the horse before he set upon her. Thus,
the nearest defense at hand was no more than the
small, blunt putty knife she employed when oil painting—hardly a deadly weapon, she thought. Until his
reference to his "enemies," she had not really thought
he would harm her. Despite all that she had heard
about him, Araminta still somehow could not believe
he would actually assault her, perhaps even kill her.
But now she felt a frisson of fear.

"You—you rank me among your enemies, then?"
she asked hesitantly.

"Not at the moment, no. But come now, *señorita*.

Surely, you cannot have lived at the High Sierra these past months without learning of the ill will that both your grandfather and particularly Judd Hobart bear me. They would gladly see me hanged.''

"And what else would you expect?" Even as she spoke the bold words, Araminta silently damned both her unruly tongue and foolish bravado. It was definitely not wise to provoke a man such as he, especially when she was virtually helpless against him. "Don't you rustle their horses and cattle, loot and burn their outbuildings—"

"And in your eyes, those are terrible crimes, are they not?" the general interrupted tersely, neither confirming nor denying her accusations. "But what of your grandfather and others like him, men such as Frank and Judd Hobart, who grow rich and fat off the very life's blood of Mexico, eh? Or is that a crime to which you turn a blind eye, *señorita*, because it pays for the fancy clothes on your back and the good food in your mouth? Answer me that, then, if you can."

"I—I don't know what you mean—" Araminta stammered, shrinking from him.

"Don't you?" His voice shook with anger. Then, strangely, after a moment, it gentled. His sudden rage seemed to drain away, though it was obvious his emotions still roiled inside him. "No. No, perhaps you do not." He indicated her painting on the easel. "It is a very pretty picture, *señorita*. Had you more insight, it might even have been a masterpiece, like the works of Corot. You are familiar with his oil sketches and paintings, perhaps?" he asked, his knowledge of art surprising her. "They are very highly regarded for their freedom and clear color, such as you yourself have employed in your own work. But alas, *señorita*, your vision is as narrow as that of a horse with blinders. You see only the beauty of the land, not its inherent ugliness.'' He bent and scooped up a handful of mud from the creek bank. Then, before Araminta realized what he intended, he grabbed her and forcibly pressed the wet earth into her hands, making her tremble both with fear and a peculiar, perverse excitement at his strength. ''There is what lies beneath the surface of the land, Señorita Winthrop. Open your eyes so you can see it! Muck! The muck of poverty, starvation, disease, and a hundred other adversities that plague the poor, common people of Mexico. But of course, what would a wealthy, genteel *gringa* like you know of these things?'' He sneered at her as he released her. Swallowing hard, she knelt once more to rinse her hands until they were clean, as though she could wash away not only the mud, but also the highly charged feel of his hands upon hers. ''As little as you know about the power inherent in a brilliant painting, as little as you profess to know of the unconscionable activities of your grandfather and the Hobarts and others of their ilk.''

''And what activities are those?'' Araminta tossed her head proudly, hurt and outraged that he should not only interrupt her solitude, but also insult her, especially when she had done nothing to earn his contempt.

Determining that she would not give him the satisfaction of seeing how he had wounded her, she stood and deliberately turned her back on him, although it took every ounce of her courage to do so. Perhaps if she ignored him, he would go away—for, if he had meant to do her some injury, he would already have done so, surely. Forcing herself to remain outwardly calm, she began to unpack her alfresco breakfast, first laying out upon the grass the red-checkered tablecloth folded on top of the basket's contents. Still, her hands shook as she worked, and her movements were clumsy as she set out the food and drink she had prepared earlier that morning. To her dismay, however, Del Castillo did not take the hint and leave.

"Your grandfather, the Hobarts, and several others are, among other things, running guns and supplies to the Federales and the Rurales, guns with which the army and the police are murdering the people of Mexico, *señorita*, people who have little but their hope to sustain them and their desperation to defend them. But as I said, what would you know about being poor and hungry?"

"Much more than you know about me, obviously, since I have in my time been both." Her voice was filled with quiet dignity. "Your means of gathering information must need a good deal of improvement if you don't already know that, General. So why should I believe your stories about my grandfather? And even if they *are* true"—Araminta recalled uncomfortably the snippets of information she had overheard at her fandango—"the Federales and the Rurales represent the legitimate government of Mexico, and therefore, aiding and abetting them can hardly be considered a crime. It is your Revolutionaries—your Maderistas, Zapatistas, Orozquistas, Vazquistas, and all the rest—

who started your civil war and who are thus ultimately responsible for the death of your people."

"Come, come, *señorita*," Del Castillo chided, gracefully lowering himself to sit beside her on the red-checkered tablecloth, "as a budding journalist, you of all people should know better than to believe what you read in the newspapers. They are filled with lies and half-truths, all slanted to reflect the views held by their publishers, their editors, and their prominent advertisers, *¿es verdad?*" Raising one brow, he awaited her denial, which did not come, for she knew in her heart that he was right. In fact, that was one of the main reasons she wanted to become a journalist: She wished to write the truth, not the falsehoods that were the current vogue in publishing. "Porfirio Díaz was a dictator, who cared nothing for the common people," the general continued, "and now that he has overthrown Díaz and taken his place, Francisco Madero chooses to forget the common people, as well. There is a saying in Ciudad de México, *señorita:* *'Fuera de México, todo es Cuautitlán.'* 'Outside Mexico City, it's all Cuautitlán.' You see, in Mexico, if one is not of the capital, but of the provinces, one is nothing at all." Del Castillo paused for a moment, gazing at the alfresco breakfast she had spread upon the tablecloth. Then, with a sweeping motion of one hand, he went on. "All this food and drink, only for yourself, *señorita*. Do you know that on all this, a peasant family in Mexico could live for days, perhaps even a week?"

As she glanced down at the appetizing fare before her, Araminta was suddenly stricken. She had not realized, until just now, that she had packed so very much. In her haste to be gone from the hacienda, and thinking she might not return before lunch, she had simply gathered whatever was at hand and tossed it into the basket. Now it looked to her as though there were enough spread upon the tablecloth to feed an army: a stack of tortillas, a sizable chunk each of meat and cheese, an array of fruits, a portion of *frijoles*, a couple of *sopaipas*, a dab of butter and the inevitable salsa, and a jug of fresh milk. Her eyes had certainly been larger than her stomach this morning, she thought, dismayed. Was it any wonder that the general stared at her so scornfully? He must think her either a glutton or a wastrel.

"Plainly, I do indeed have more than I alone can eat," she admitted, flushing and wishing, now, that she had not opened the basket in his presence. Not knowing what else to do, she tentatively inquired, "Would you—would you care to join me for breakfast, General?"

"Rigo. All my friends call me Rigo."

"But I thought—I thought that because of my grandfather, you saw me as your foe."

"Is that your desire, *señorita?*"

"No. I should think that you would be a . . . most formidable adversary, General."

"*Sí*, and so I am. But do not worry, for if ever I should become yours, I myself will be the first to tell you. This, I swear." He spoke so intently that Araminta could not doubt his honesty—and she shivered at the thought that, someday, he might proclaim himself her enemy.

It was the strangest, frightening, and yet somehow the most exciting morning Araminta had ever spent in her life, despite that she felt she flirted with danger every single moment of it. Over and over, she told herself that she should not be alone with this man, particularly in this secluded place. She knew that Rigo was a Revolutionary and, in all likelihood, a *bandolero*, a desperado, as well. Possibly, he had even murdered his wife in cold blood—she did not dare to ask. Yet in his company, she found it increasingly difficult to credit these tales. As they talked, she discovered that his mind was fine, his wit sharp, his knowledge obviously broadened by his travels. For the first time since leaving boarding school, Araminta was able to converse at a level that matched her own intelligence, cleverness, and education; and despite her constant guilt that her grandfather would surely suffer a stroke if ever he somehow learned of this morning, she could not seem to tear herself away from Rigo. He reminded her of a panther basking in the sun as he lounged upon the tablecloth, long and lean, dark and beautiful, sinewy and unpredictable, purring one moment, growling the next. He was elegant, suave, charming, and sophisticated. But despite all that, he was also hard, arrogant, jaded, and cynical—and no gentleman, although he appeared for the moment content to play the part of one.

"You . . . puzzle me, General," Araminta remarked, still self-conscious about increasing the intimacy of their situation by using his Christian name.

"In what way?"

"Well, in every way, actually. Your speech, your

manner, your dress, your erudition . . ." She shook her head. "Somehow, despite the fact that your sympathies clearly lie with them, I just cannot see you as having sprung from the common people of Mexico."

"Oh, but I did, I assure you, *señorita*. I am the bastard son of a rich *hacendado*, who had other, legitimate sons, and so had no use for me—or *mi madre*, either, after he had repeatedly, and forcibly, taken what he wanted from her and then, eventually, wearied of her." Araminta gave a small, choked gasp at the monstrous revelation Rigo had so casually voiced, and a mocking smile twisted his lips. "You are horribly shocked, are you not? For such things do not happen in your world, *señorita*, do they? Unfortunately, they are all too common in mine. I took my name from the hacienda of *mi padre, del castillo*—from the castle— because that is what all of us who worked the land of *mi padre* thought his great house resembled. No, do not feel sorry for me—you've an easy face to read, do you know?—for I do not want your pity."

"What *do* you want, then?" she asked, still baffled by him but at least beginning, she believed, to get a glimpse of the boy who had become the man.

"This morning? No more than I have received," he rejoined enigmatically. "I cannot remember when I last so enjoyed a breakfast. *Muchas gracias*." With that, much to her surprise and odd disappointment, he stood. Moving to his stallion, which grazed nearby, he gathered the reins and swung up into the saddle. Tossing its head, the high-spirited horse danced a few steps before being brought under its master's control. From the animal's back, Rigo gazed down at Araminta intently for a moment, his eyes narrowed and shuttered, so she could not read his thoughts. "Before I go, a word of . . . friendly advice, if you will, *señorita:* Regardless of what either your grandfather or the Hobarts may think to the contrary, Judd Hobart is not the man for you. You would be wise not to encourage his calling upon you."

Then, before she could respond, he set his silver Mexican spurs to his stallion's sides and was gone.

Chapter Eight

Araminta was perplexed and not a little angered by Rigo's cryptic parting remark to her. She did not know why he should be interested in who courted her—even if it were Judd, whom he hated. It was none of the general's business whom she spent her time with, she thought hotly, and he certainly had no right to interfere in her life. She conveniently thrust to the back of her mind the fact that she had been grateful for his intervention at the post office. Besides, she told herself, he had helped her with Pimby, the postal clerk, only to thrust a spoke into her grandfather's wheel—hardly a recommendation for Rigo's character, which she knew to be reprehensible, in any event. The man was a Revolutionary, a thief, perhaps even, if rumor were correct, a murderer, though Araminta did not want to believe this last about him. That his miserable childhood had done much to shape his nature was understandable but, still, no excuse for his behavior. Although he had scorned her pity, she felt sorry for the general—yet she wasn't sure she even liked him. His handsomeness and the magnetism he exuded were as frightening as they were exciting. They made her think of him as a sleek, beguiling predator who, for all his magnificence and allure, might turn on her and attack her at any moment, although, to be fair, he had never made the least threatening gesture toward her. Indeed, although, blushing at her wanton thoughts, she had sometimes wondered what it would feel like to have his arms wrapped around her, to be kissed by him, he had touched her rarely, and then only briefly. Still, Araminta did not forget his notorious reputation or that he was her grandfather's enemy—and might someday be hers.

Yet against her will, Rigo continued to fascinate her, and that early morning encounter became only the first of many meetings. Despite herself, she felt a strange affinity for him that she had never felt for anyone else. Unexpectedly, they had much in common, from their love of literature, music, and art to their interest in travel and foreign cultures to their concern with worldly affairs, of news and politics, in all of which matters he was knowledgeable and well educated, even more so than she herself was. Araminta could not seem to put him from her thoughts. If she were honest with herself, she must admit that his manner thrilled her, that his conversation enthralled her, for he talked to her as an equal and challenged

her to think for herself, a refreshing change from the
way both her grandfather and Judd treated her, as
though her mind should not be taxed by anything more
serious than planning a menu or picking out a gown.
Her grandfather, knowing of her desire to become a
journalist, had even prohibited her from reading any
of the local newspapers, stating firmly that their contents were not fit for a lady's perusal. As a result,
Araminta was compelled to sneak a peek at the newspapers whenever her grandfather was absent from the
house.

Like sudden, fierce thunderstorms, the outbreaks of
violence south of the border continued to escalate as
the year wore on, she read. By now, because of her
unwilling preoccupation with Rigo, Araminta had
learned much about the Mexican Revolution—including the fact that despite the general's bitterness in this
regard, and while it might have been, in his words,
"unconscionable," there was nothing illegal about
Americans' supplying guns to the Federales and the
Rurales of Mexico, which represented the legitimate
government of the country. However, a joint resolu-
tion by Congress had empowered President Taft to
prohibit all other arms shipments to Mexico so long
as civil unrest prevailed. This decision represented a
serious setback to the Revolutionaries, who had, as a
result, increasingly begun to stir up anti-American
sentiments. Had the Revolutionaries, like the Federales and the Rurales, been armed with American guns,
they would have been on an equal footing with the
government against which they were in revolt. As it
was, this was just one of several obstacles they were

compelled to overcome however they could. As she started to grasp the bigger picture, Araminta no longer felt so certain that the fact that these means included raids across the border could so easily be condemned. Perhaps she, too, would have been driven to such desperate measures, however wrong, had she been cruelly oppressed and fighting for her very life, she reflected.

Still, it was not right that her grandfather, the Hobarts, and the other Texas ranchers should suffer, either, for their prosperity and for what was not their war. But if the ranchers north of the border were, in fact, running guns and other supplies to the Federales and the Rurales, Araminta could understand why the Revolutionaries should see her grandfather and the rest as legitimate targets. It was a difficult situation, and there were no easy answers. Her grandfather, when she questioned him about the matter, claimed that business was business, that there was profit to be made from the civil unrest in Mexico, and that he was doing nothing illegal. His conscience was not in the least perturbed by the moral aspects of the affair—the arming of one side but not the other, the elitist and repressive regime in power in Mexico, the injustices suffered by the poor, common people. Previously, Araminta had paid little or no heed to the war. But the more she saw of Rigo, the less able she was to ignore the violence south of the border and the contributions of the Texas ranchers to it.

Torn, she told herself that her meetings with the general were dangerous and wrong and should cease. Ultimately, they could lead to naught but trouble.

Regardless of the fact that he always behaved like a gentleman toward her, if he truly were a *bandolero*, a murderer, she placed herself in peril every time she saw him—and surely, he had some as yet unknown motive in seeking her out, a motive connected to the animosity he felt toward her grandfather and Judd. Yet despite Araminta's resolve to have nothing more to do with Rigo, temptation was sometimes impossible to resist; and now and then, she found herself riding of an early morning toward the creek where they had shared breakfast and where, more often than not, Rigo would be waiting. If she were bedeviled by him, it seemed he was equally and reluctantly bewitched by her.

"You are not at all what I expected Noble Winthrop's granddaughter to be," he said to her once, a muscle working tensely in his jaw, as though he were angry with her for this. His next words confirmed her thought. "I do not like that you should be as you are."

"Oh? And why is that?" Araminta inquired, although she suspected she already knew the answer. He would have preferred her to be ugly, stupid, vain, and silly. Then they would have had nothing in common, no peculiar but undeniable attraction to each other, muddying the otherwise crystal-clear course of their lives.

"It would be easier if you were no different from every other *gringa* of your class in Texas."

"Easier? In what way? And how am I different?"

"You . . . disturb me, *señorita*. You are stubborn, willful, and discontented, and when you care, you care deeply, I think, a combination I fear may prove devastating for you one day. Texas, Mexico . . . they are not lands that are kind to their inhabitants, and those who endure are strong and hard; they have learned to do whatever is necessary in order to survive.''

''And you think I won't?'' she asked, disconcerted that he should have such insight into her character, as though he could see into her heart and mind.

For a moment, Rigo was so still that Araminta believed he was not going to answer. But then, at last, he rejoined slowly:

''No, for there is within you a quiet strength and courage, I think. But I am afraid you may find the learning process . . . painful, *señorita*, and for some strange reason, the thought of that . . . troubles me.''

He had an odd, faraway look in his eyes when he spoke, as though he could see into her future and knew that it was not a happy one. At the unsettling notion, Araminta felt a chill creep down her spine. Still, however much she pressed him, he would not elaborate on his disquieting, enigmatic pronouncement, but abruptly stood and tersely took his leave of her, bewildering her and hurting her feelings so, she thought once more that, in truth, she despised him. Mounting her mare, she rode home, furious at Rigo and even more furious at herself that she should be so drawn to him nevertheless. She would not see him again, she told herself sternly. Doing so was a betrayal of both her grandfather and Judd, as well as of her own good breeding. Ladies did not sneak off alone to rendezvous with a notorious man, and certainly, she had been reared better. She did not understand what was wrong

with her that she should behave so wantonly, so recklessly, so heedless of her own reputation and physical
well-being. She must rid herself of this strange enchantment with Rigo before it was too late.

If her grandfather or Judd should ever find out
about her meeting the general—Araminta shuddered
violently at the notion—their rage would know no
bounds. Judd had such a fierce temper and had grown
increasingly so possessive of her that he might even
kill Rigo. More and more, Judd was pressuring her to
marry him, and though even she must admit that it
seemed the ideal plan—that Noble Winthrop's granddaughter should wed his godson, and the High Sierra
and the Chaparral be combined—still, Araminta hesitated.

Common sense told her that even if her inheriting
the High Sierra were not dependent upon her marrying
and her grandfather willed her the ranch outright, she
would never be able to run it alone, not without a
husband—or at least a strong, capable foreman at her
side, one who respected and believed in her. It was
not that she lacked the intelligence or the ability to
operate a huge spread; if need be, she could surely
learn and diligently apply herself to the job. Even so,
no man would take her seriously as the owner of the
High Sierra, she knew. It would be difficult, if not
impossible, for her not only to retain experienced
ranch hands, but also to enforce her authority, especially when she lacked any real practical knowledge
about running a ranch. There was no chore, large or
small, at the High Sierra that her grandfather himself
had not done in the past. Unfortunately, she could not

say the same. If she were to take over the spread tomorrow, she would be as ignorant as a tinhorn, getting her education on the job and becoming an easy target for any unscrupulous man who wished to take advantage of her. Her grandfather could have eliminated at least this problem by training her himself in the management of the ranch, but on the few occasions when Araminta dared to broach the subject to him, he merely snorted.

"If God had intended women to mix themselves in business, he would have given 'em brains, gal—instead of bodies for keeping men happy and bearing children. So why don't you quit worrying about putting on a shirt and pair of britches and concentrate on picking out a wedding gown instead? Judd's getting mighty damned impatient, dangling on your string, and I can't say as how I blame him none. What's wrong with you, Araminta, shilly-shallying around like some coy chit just out of a schoolroom? You ain't gonna find a man better 'n Judd to take care of you and the High Sierra both when I'm pushing up daisies."

"I—I just don't . . . love him, Grandfather, and he doesn't love me."

"Love!" Noble spat contemptuously. "Why, that's nothing but a fool's notion—and you ain't struck me as no fool, gal! Let me tell you something, Araminta: Once the fire burning inside you's been quenched, love goes out the window soon enough, and then what you've got left—if you're lucky—is liking, companionship, contentment, a shared past, and common goals. You don't hate Judd, do you?" he asked sharply.

"Well, no, but—"

"And you'd be content here on the ranch with him, wouldn't you?"

"Well, I—I . . . guess I could be," she conceded reluctantly.

"Then, hell's bells! What's the problem, gal?" His eyes narrowed with sudden suspicion. "You ain't found some other man you've got a hankering for, have you?"

"No." She shook her head, then flushed slightly and glanced away, unable to go on meeting her grandfather's penetrating gaze as, without warning, Rigo's image rose, unbidden, in her mind. Of course, he was nothing to her—or she to him, she told herself, vexed. Why she should even think of him now—or at all—she did not know. Her chin came up resolutely. "No, Grandfather, there's no one else," she stated firmly, looking him square in the eye. "It's just that I don't understand why you and Judd should keep making such a fuss, should be in such a rush for me to marry him. I know that you think highly of him, but I—I need more time, Grandfather. I've only known him, really, for a short while, and I'm—I'm just not sure . . ." Her voice trailed away, and she bit her lower lip, knowing how childish and petulant she sounded.

"A lot of damned fool nonsense, I say! There's no need for you to be sure. I never knew a blessed female who could make the right decision about anything, anyway. *I'm* sure that Judd's the man for you—if I weren't, do you think I'd favor him for you? As to pushing you to make up your mind, Araminta, well, I'm no spring chicken. I don't have too many years left. I haven't told you before because I didn't want to worry you, but I've been feeling mighty poorly lately; and frankly, it'd be a help to have Judd here to take over the day-to-day management of the ranch. I'd like to retire, enjoy the fruits of my labor while I still can, and live long enough to dandle my great-grandchildren on my knee—'' Noble broke off abruptly, seized by a violent fit of coughing. Dropping his cane and clawing at his chest, he doubled over.

"Grandfather!" Horrified, Araminta rushed to his side, assisting him into the big swivel chair behind the desk in his study and loosening his collar. "Hold on. I'll get you some water."

"No . . . a—a shot of—of . . . whiskey," he managed to choke out between spasms.

Given the circumstances, she did not think that liquor could possibly be good for him. But fearing to anger him otherwise and thereby worsen his condition, she raced obediently to the bar that stood to one side of his desk and, unstoppering one of the crystal decanters, splashed some of its dark-gold contents into a glass. Then she hurried back to his side, helping him to steady the glass as he lifted it to drink. Once he had downed the alcohol, he seemed to recover. Leaning back in his chair, his eyes closing, he wordlessly extended the glass to Araminta, indicating that he wanted it refilled.

"Grandfather, are you all right? Have you suffered an attack like this before? Perhaps I should summon your physician—"

"No, no, this isn't the first time this has happened. The pain will pass in a minute. It always does. I'm just getting on in years, gal, and there ain't nothing any doctor can do to cure that.''

Araminta, however, was not convinced that her grandfather's abrupt paroxysm was merely the result of old age; and her brow was knitted with worry as she reluctantly returned to the bar, pouring another shot of whiskey from the decanter into the glass. Until today, she had not even suspected that there might be something wrong with her grandfather's health. The thought alarmed her. Despite her reservations about him, she had developed a certain affection for her cantankerous grandfather. He was her only living relative, after all, and he had treated her kindly, in his crusty fashion. Further, although he had made clear to her that his bequeathing her the High Sierra was contingent upon her being wed, she had no idea what would become of the ranch if she was unmarried at his death. Even Judd did not know, which was probably why he kept badgering Araminta to tie the knot. She believed, however, that were she still a spinster at the time of her grandfather's demise, she would not inherit the High Sierra—and then what would become of her? She could not even be certain of a monetary legacy from her grandfather, and she had no funds of her own and little means of earning any. She had as yet received no reply from Liam O'Grady to the letter she had sent him, so she did not know whether her article had been accepted for publication in the *Record*, if there was any hope of her ever returning to her job at the newspaper in New York City. If her grandfather were to die tomorrow, she would be as destitute as she had been before coming to Texas, cast out again on life's mean streets. The thought was terrifying—and the prospect of wedding Judd suddenly seemed a lot more appealing.

At least he was feared, respected, and knowledgeable about running a large spread. No one would dare to challenge *his* authority at the High Sierra, to slack off under his management, or to attempt to cheat him. As his wife, Araminta's future would be secure and any children she might have would be well provided for. Frank and Elizabeth Hobart would, with open arms, welcome her into their family; and even Velvet, who, for some obscure reason, had been oddly distant toward her, might eventually become, if not as close and dear as a sister, at least the best friend for whom Araminta had often longingly wished.

All this, Noble felt sure she was contemplating as he glanced at her slyly from beneath half-closed lids. He chortled silently with glee, delighted at the sudden inspiration he had had to deceive her into thinking he was on his last legs. Now, surely, she would forget her silly, romantic notions, quit her missish hem-hawing around, and marry Judd. Had Araminta glimpsed her grandfather's expression in that moment, she would instantly have grown suspicious. But unfortunately, standing at the bar, she had her back to him; and when she once more turned around to deliver to him the second glass of whiskey, Noble's face was suitably composed in a grimace of pain as a low moan emanated from his throat. It did not occur to her to notice that his skin definitely lacked the pallor of someone who was ill; nor was he the slightest bit blue about the lips.

"Grandfather, are you certain you don't want me to send for your doctor?"

"Quite certain. I'll be fine in a minute, so don't you fret now, you hear?"

But despite his words of assurance, his voice quavered, and his hands, wrapped around the glass of whiskey, trembled. As a result, Araminta's anxiety did not dissipate, but planted itself like a poisonous seed in her brain and began to grow.

Chapter Nine

Christmas in Texas was not at all the same as Christmas in New York, Araminta discovered as the short, cool autumn days gave way at last to winter, and the holiday season drew near. There was no thick, bushy fir tree bedecked with old, treasured Victorian ornaments and new, peppermint candy canes such as had been raised in her father's house and at the academy in years gone by. Instead, in the great hall of the High Sierra, there stood what Araminta considered a rather poor, spindly, scraggly pine tree, but that Noble proudly informed her was the best to be found for miles in every direction, a statement that, given the vegetation of the region, she thought was probably true. The tree was hung with, among other unfamiliar adornments, strings of dried chili peppers so pungent that they made her eyes smart when the candles on the tree lighted each evening slowly heated them. Two customs indigenous to the Southwest and that Araminta remembered with delight, however, were the suspending of a gaily colored *piñata*—this year a bright burro—from one of the timbered beams of the great hall's ceiling and the lining of the hacienda's winding drive with *luminarias*—small, translucent paper bags weighted with sand, into which a single candle was placed, making the sacks glow like angel fire at night, when the candles were set ablaze. Once or twice, when no one was looking, Araminta could not resist taking up the long, stout stick used expressly for smashing open the *piñata* on Christmas Day and giving the burro a few tentative pokes. She forced herself to refrain from doing this, however, after Teresa, smiling and shaking her head at Araminta's antics, caught her at it.

"Aiee, that just what you did when you *muchacha, señorita*. And, oh, *el patrón*, he get so angry once when you accidentally bust the *piñata* before Christmas—so hard that the toys and candy inside go everywhere. Your mama and me, we busy in kitchen and not hear the *piñata* break, so you have plenty time to unwrap everything, make big mess all over room and eat so much candy that you sick, sick, sick!"

At Teresa's words, Araminta laughed, even as she flushed with embarrassment and guilt; she had forgotten all about the incident Teresa had described. But now, Araminta recalled it vividly, how, upon seeing her handiwork, her grandfather had shouted at her, scaring her so badly that, already nauseated from the candy she had consumed, she had thrown up on the floor, rendering him speechless with rage. It was a wonder he hadn't suffered an apoplectic fit then and there, she mused wryly. Then, her humor vanishing, she frowned with worry as she thought of his recent ill health. Since that day in his study, he had experienced several similar seizures. Despite this, however, he had continued steadfastly to insist that there was nothing more wrong with him than the effects of old age and had belligerently refused to permit Araminta to send for the doctor. She feared that if she ignored him and summoned his physician anyway, her grandfather might grow so furious that he would have a stroke or heart attack and die. It was alarming how the prominent blue vein in his forehead swelled and throbbed when he was irate, as though it would burst open. No less frightening, however, was the way in which he staggered and grabbed at his throat when stricken by the fits of coughing that came upon him so suddenly and violently.

Araminta wished fervently that she had someone to turn to, to advise her about the matter. But there was no one. Judd was certain to fret and fume and press her all the harder to marry him; and although her reluctance to commit herself into his keeping was definitely wavering, she still did not feel ready to become his wife. His sister, Velvet, had she proved more amicable, would have been a natural confidant, given her and Araminta's closeness in age. But despite Araminta's overtures, Velvet had so far shown little interest in pursuing a friendship with her. Nor, for all their amiability, did Araminta feel that she could approach Frank or Elizabeth Hobart, or even Mr. Gideon, about her grandfather; for if he had wanted them to know about his attacks, he would have told them himself, and they would surely confront him about his health. The servants, Araminta did not even consider. As kind as they were, they were bound to worry and gossip among themselves, and then her grandfather was certain to learn she had discussed his personal problems with those he staunchly believed were his inferiors. The best that Araminta could do, she thought, was to speak to the doctor herself in a generalized way and to hope he would take the hint and, of his own volition, call on her grandfather. She would seek out the physician today, she decided. Judd was taking her to El Paso so she could do some Christmas shopping.

The drive into town passed pleasantly, Judd regaling her with the latest news and his morning at the Chaparral. As the automobile sped over the road, it occurred to Araminta that she and Judd might already have been married, she had come to know him so well, to grow so accustomed to him. Startled, she realized she had actually come to depend on him, even to take for granted the fact that he would be there when she needed him, as he was this afternoon. For the first time, she thought to consider what her life would be like if she lost not only her grandfather, but also Judd. The prospect was daunting. She would be utterly alone in a world that did not treat its women kindly—especially when they had no man to protect them. Remembering her life in New York City, she shuddered.

Despite the independence she had enjoyed, if she were honest with herself, she must admit that she had not been happy there. Her days had been long and grueling, full of more drudgery than excitement. She had had no social life, no beaux, no hope of marrying, of having children. Now it seemed that there was no chance of her having the career to which she aspired. Which was worse, Araminta wondered, being alone or being dependent? The problem was that she didn't want to be either; she was shameless and greedy to want it all, to hope that perhaps Judd would prove more amenable than her grandfather about her wanting to be a journalist.

Why, she was actually contemplating wedding Judd, Araminta recognized. Well, and why not? He had a great deal to recommend him. Maybe her grandfather was right; maybe her romantic notions *were* foolish. Maybe she *could* be happy with Judd if she just gave their relationship half a chance.

Unexpectedly, this feeling was reinforced as, after maneuvering down the main street of El Paso, Judd parked his sleek red motorcar in an empty space. Nearby on the sidewalk, a group of children were taunting unmercifully a Mexican boy far smaller than they; and as Judd drew to a halt beside them, Araminta could see that the obviously frightened boy was both bruised and sobbing. Even as she watched, one of the older youngsters spat a mean remark and shoved the little boy hard, knocking him down.

"Oh no, Judd, look! How cruel!" she exclaimed. "Why don't those horrible bullies pick on somebody their own size? Why doesn't somebody do something? Why hasn't anybody made them stop tormenting that poor boy?"

Even as she spoke, Araminta was fumbling with the handle, trying to get the automobile door open so she could go to the boy's assistance. Judd, however, was faster. Not bothering with his own door, he simply vaulted from the motorcar and in moments was pushing his way through the mob of children to pluck the Mexican boy from their midst. Of course, Araminta should have known she could count on Judd to intervene; hadn't he risked his life to save the ranch hand trapped under the burning beam during the fire at the Chaparral? Judd was always to be depended upon in a crisis, she realized.

"Here, you kids! What do you think you're doing? Beating up somebody half your size! You want to go a few rounds with me? No, I didn't think so." His voice was loud and sharp, both it and his size making even the boldest of the youngsters step back from him warily. "Why aren't you all in school, where you belong? You'd best get along now, all of you, before I call the truant officer—or, worse, a policeman and have you all clapped in jail for disturbing the peace!" The unruly youngsters didn't wait to hear any more, but raced away, leaving Judd holding the Mexican boy. "Here, you." He gave the youngster a small shake. "Stop all that squawking! You don't want some farmer to come along and mistake you for a chicken, do you? He might do worse than just pluck your tail feathers. *¿Comprende?*" Evidently, the child did, in fact, understand, for presently, he ceased his sniveling. At that, Judd reached into his pocket and withdrew a shiny nickel. "Here." He handed the coin to the boy. "Go buy yourself a peppermint stick. I'll bet that'll make you feel better, *¿es verdad?*"

"*Sí, señor. Gracias.*" Clutching the nickel in his grubby fist, the youngster scampered away.

"Cute kid," Judd commented as he turned to help Araminta out of the motorcar.

"Yes, he was," she agreed. "Thanks for stepping in to help him, Judd."

"It was my pleasure. Frankly, I like kids. I hope to have a whole herd of 'em someday, and I wouldn't want 'em mistreated by a pack of brats like that. Kids like that, now, they lack the proper guidance, don't have the benefit of a decent upbringing, a good education, and the basic necessities that money can buy. A woman ought to take a hard look at a man before she marries him, make sure he can provide for her and their children, take care of 'em right, give 'em the best life has to offer. You know what I'm saying?"

"Yes, I do."

Araminta's face was pensive, and shrewdly, Judd said nothing more, aware that he had made his point. In truth, while he wished for sons to prove his virility and carry on his name, children annoyed him, and he disliked having to bother with them. Had he been alone when he had driven into El Paso this afternoon, he would have ignored the youngsters bullying the Mexican boy. Certainly, it would never have occurred to him to intervene on the boy's behalf. But Judd was clever, and when he had spied Araminta's outrage at the scene unfolding on the sidewalk, he had quickly perceived an opportunity to cast himself in a favorable light in her eyes, and he had promptly seized it, using it to his advantage. Clearly, Araminta had a soft heart where children were concerned. She would not want any of her own reared by an unfit father, an ineffectual provider. Judd had given her food for thought, he hoped, and perhaps after she had ruminated upon it, she would consent to wed him at last.

For her part, Araminta was indeed contemplating what she had seen and heard. She had not really considered Judd as a father before; now it was impossible not to. She knew now that he felt as she did and would do whatever was necessary to ensure the well-being of any children she might have. The kind of advantages Judd had described he could provide as a husband and father. More and more, it seemed that he had much to recommend him, that her grandfather had, in fact, chosen wisely for her; and perhaps, in his own fashion, that Judd truly did care for her, as he claimed. Maybe it was just that tender emotions were difficult for a man such as he to express.

These thoughts stayed with her while she shopped for Christmas presents, selecting an ornately carved cane for her grandfather to add to his collection, three white linen handkerchiefs for Mr. Gideon, a beautiful *rebozo* for Teresa, and small gifts for the rest of the servants, as well. She also bought presents for the Hobarts, including a lovely silk shawl for Velvet, hoping to win the friendship of Judd's aloof sister. Over Judd's gift, Araminta pondered longest of all, lingering at counters, wanting to get something more special than she had previously had in mind. She finally settled on an elaborate brass inkwell and pen.

She stopped at the doctor's office, but much to her disappointment, he wasn't in. So she went away without leaving her name. A glance at the pendant watch she wore told her that she still had time to stop at the post office before meeting Judd, who had had business in El Paso. Her arms loaded with boxes and bags, Araminta hurried down the street toward her destination. When she peeked anxiously through the tiny window of her post-office box, her heart leaped with anticipation; there was an envelope inside! It was the first time that her post-office box had actually contained anything. Hardly daring to believe that a reply had come from Liam O'Grady at last, she set her packages down on the floor. Then, with trembling hands, she fished her little brass key from her reticule, unlocked the small, square door of the box, and removed its contents.

After ripping open the envelope, she unfolded the letter inside, startled as two crisp one-dollar bills and a newspaper clipping fluttered to the floor. As she bent to retrieve them, she could have laughed aloud with joy. She had sold her article and sketches to the *Record!* Liam had liked her story; his readers had liked it! Araminta was thrilled to her toes as she reread the note she held in her shaking hand. It was true; her work had been published in the *Record*—and not on the women's page, either. Tears stung her eyes as she read the enclosed newspaper clipping, a column and a half of her words, with her pseudonymous byline at the top

e had felt was her best charcoal sketch
ongside. She suspected from his letter that
had deduced her true identity, though he had not
ded to it. Still, even if he alone knew who A. K.
Munroe really was, even if she had earned only two
dollars, scarcely a living, she had made her first sale
as a serious journalist!

She was so excited that she nearly walked off and
left her parcels scattered on the post-office floor. Only
as an afterthought did she gather them up, Liam's
missive still clutched in her hand. In a daze, she exited
the post office, bursting to share her good news with
someone. But she dared not tell even Judd, Araminta
realized slowly—at least, not until they were married
and she felt sure he would support her against her
grandfather in the matter. Why, yes, of course, if she
were Judd's wife, he would have to stand up for her,
defend her, make her grandfather understand just how
important her work was to her, so she could continue
it openly and not have to worry about her grandfather's
finding out and putting a stop to it. Carefully, she
folded up Liam's letter, along with the dollar bills and
the newspaper clipping, and tucked them back into
the envelope. Then she slipped the envelope into her
reticule.

It was on the way home to the High Sierra that
Araminta, her heart singing, told Judd she would
marry him. At her words, Judd drew the motorcar to
a screeching halt and turned to her, his turquoise eyes
searching her own green ones earnestly.

"Do you mean that, Araminta?"

"Y-y-yes. Yes, I do."

"Well, hell's bells! It's about time!" he growled fiercely.

Then he took her in his arms and his mouth claimed hers, his tongue shooting deep between her lips, ravishing her mouth until she was breathless and trembling with the tumult of emotions inside her. When, finally, he released her, Judd's eyes were lazy and triumphant, and as they surveyed her leisurely, Araminta felt an unexpected shiver of apprehension tingle up her spine. She *had* made the right decision, hadn't she? Of course she had. She mustn't let her vivid imagination run wild again, her silly, childish, romantic notions once more take hold of her. Like any woman who had just become engaged, she was simply nervous and excited, that was all. Still, she could not repress another involuntary shudder as Judd, his hands deliberately caressing her, lingering over the task, tucked the lap robe more securely about her. Then, at last, stepping on the accelerator, he sent the automobile hurtling forward over the frost-rimed road, toward the wintry gray clouds that massed on the far horizon.

Chapter Ten

Araminta had come to say good-bye. This, Rigo knew in his heart, as surely as he knew that she intended to marry his bitter enemy, Judd Hobart. She and Judd had on Christmas Day announced their engagement, and within hours, Rigo himself had through his myriad sources of information learned the news; for ever since Araminta had arrived in Texas and he had become aware of her relationship to Noble Winthrop and then Judd Hobart, Rigo had made it his business to know everything about her—what she did, where she went, whom she saw. In the beginning, he had set his spies upon her because he had learned over the years that knowledge was power and so it behooved him to know everything he could about his adversaries. But then, more and more, it was Araminta herself who had intrigued him.

He should never have let himself be drawn to her! Rigo told himself, infuriated, as he watched her cloaked figure gallop toward him, her golden hair glinting with silvery highlights in the pale glow of the wintry sunrise. He had known that no good would come of it, and still, though he had tried to fight his strange attraction to her, he had sought her out. If only she had proved as haughty and shallow and vain as Velvet, throwing herself at him, knowing he was forbidden to her and, so, perversely excited by his infamous reputation and hot Spanish blood. It would have been easy to harden his heart against Araminta then, to use her, to despise her. But she was not like Velvet or any of the other women of Texas society—the self-centered or the self-righteous, those who looked down upon him and, in his presence, drew their skirts close, lest he should accidentally brush against them and taint them—and therein lay the difficulty. Araminta was different; she challenged and captivated him, and he had not been able to resist meeting her by the creek where he had happened upon her that first morning.

And now, she had come to say good-bye.

She was going to marry Judd Hobart, Rigo thought again, his fists clenching so tightly with fury that his nails dug into his palms. A muscle pulsated in his taut jaw. Why could not Judd's bride have been any woman but Araminta? Or Araminta herself been other than what she was? Rigo had waited so many years— too many—to gain his revenge upon his foe; and now, for the first time, he doubted his ability to carry out his plan. But he must! For over a decade, it had been as much a part of him as his heart, his mind, his soul. It had consumed him; he had lived and breathed it. To discard it now, unfulfilled, would be like cutting off his arm or leg, a disloyalty to everything for which he had worked so hard and so long, an unspeakable betrayal of the memory that haunted him ceaselessly, that drove him in all he did. The thought of that memory sustained him now. His lids hooded his eyes, and his face became as impassive as a mask as he watched Araminta slowly dismount from her mare and begin to walk toward him.

"General," she greeted him, for despite all the time that had passed since their first encounter, she somehow still could not bring herself to say his name, "I—I hoped that you would choose to ride this way this morning. I especially wanted to—to see you, for I have news I—I fear that you—that you will find . . . displeasing." Araminta was nervous and flushed as she stammered out the words, unable to meet his shuttered gaze.

Rigo looked unusually forbidding this morning, she thought, dismayed, as though he were already angry about something, and she felt that the tidings she had come to impart to him would prove like fuel to a fire, inflaming his temper. Despite the strange, unfathomable rapport they had come to share, she had never quite banished the sense of uneasiness he evoked in her, the guilt she endured over meeting him. She had never lost sight of the fact that he was a dangerous man, capable of violence, with doubtless some hidden agenda behind his interest in her, an agenda that had

to do with the enmity he felt toward her grandfather
and Judd. Rigo had never again, since that first morning, repeated his warning to her about marrying Judd,
but Araminta had not forgotten it, and so she was
apprehensive about his reaction to the news. Yet she
had felt that she had to come, to see Rigo one last
time. She had felt, oddly, that she owed him that,
although he was neither friend nor lover, but, rather,
a mysterious, shadowy figure in an interlude out of
time, a dark, faceless man from a mazelike, mist-
edged dream, unknown, forbidden. Perhaps because
of the clandestine nature of their rendezvous, she had
been someone else with Rigo del Castillo—not Noble
Winthrop's granddaughter, not Judd Hobart's belle,
not even the Araminta Winthrop she showed to the
rest of the world, but the woman she was in her mind
and heart. It was perhaps this, more than anything,
that had led her to ride more than once along the creek
that, as the Rio Grande divided Texas and Mexico,
separated the High Sierra and the Casa Blanca. And
now, those rides must end. Bad enough that she had
dared to undertake them when she was single; as
Judd's bride, she knew that she must not see Rigo
again.

"You intend to wed Judd Hobart," he said, his
voice low and harsh with emotion, his dark-brown
eyes hard and gleaming like the smoky quartz they
resembled.

It was a statement, not a question. Araminta knew
then that he had already learned of her engagement,
and her heart fluttered with fright—and, to her surprise, a peculiar, inexplicable pain, as though she had

been struck a mortal blow. She had not thought to feel such an ache at parting from him. Yet he looked, suddenly, silhouetted against the gray dawn horizon, so proud, so alone, so strangely vulnerable—despite the grimness of his visage—as though she had hurt him somehow.

"Yes," she whispered. "I'm going to marry Judd."

Rigo was silent for a moment, as though he had expected, hoped that she would deny the truth of his words. When she said nothing more, he spoke again, his tone so soft and silky that its cold, contemptuous, cutting edge seemed all the more threatening somehow, making her shiver, making her wonder why she had, even for an instant, believed she had the ability to wound him. She meant nothing to him, as he meant nothing to her.

"Once before, I told you that Judd Hobart is not the man for you, *señorita*. Yet now, you choose to disregard my . . . advice. I had thought you wiser than that."

"Perhaps I did not consider your warning significant," Araminta replied tartly, stung. "After all, in all this time, when you must have known he was calling on me—for rumor has it that your spies are everywhere, that you know everything there is to know in Texas and Mexico both—you never mentioned his name to me again, General. You never gave me any reason why I should heed your counsel."

"Did I not?" Rigo stalked her slowly, like a panther its prey, the black poncho he wore billowing in the wind, his sinewy muscles rippling in his long, supple body, his eyes hypnotic, holding her still in place as he came to stand before her. He did not touch her, but his proximity alone was enough to unsettle her, for rarely did he ever come so close to her. "And if I gave you a reason, would it serve to deter you from your chosen course?"

"I—I suppose that it would depend on the—on the reason."

"*Sí*, of course. Even so, I do not think that you would truly like to hear it."

"No, p-p-perhaps not."

Trembling at his nearness, Araminta averted her gaze from his, no longer able to go on meeting his hooded eyes. They smoldered like twin embers as they deliberately assessed her, flustering and confusing her so, she suddenly wished she had not come. Such was the look of naked desire upon his hawkish bronze face that she could not mistake it, and her breath caught in her throat. She had never allowed herself to consider that Rigo might want her in that way. He had never given her any cause to believe that he did, and now, she did not know what to think. As she felt his warm breath against her skin, her heart began to hammer in her breast, and a slow, swooning sensation she had never before felt started at the very core of her being and spread like a feverish chill through her body, making her shiver with mingled fear and excitement. The pulse at the hollow of her throat raced erratically, and her mouth went dry. Her tongue darted forth to moisten her lips, an unintentionally provocative gesture that caused him to inhale sharply.

Without warning, her world contracted keenly to that place where they stood upon the creek bank. It was as though the morning had grown abruptly still, that the wind had died, like the peculiar lull before a storm, that the rustle of the prairie grass and the withered leaves upon the trees that lined the banks of the creek had faded, that even the water itself had ceased to ripple, leaving her senses focused acutely on Rigo. Araminta believed that if he touched her, she would shatter like the finest crystal; she felt suddenly so fragile and vulnerable, exposed to him as she had never felt herself exposed to him before—helplessly, utterly. Even that first day when he had chanced upon her at the creek, she had not felt like this.

Swallowing hard, she took a cautious step back from him. Her hands tightened upon the riding crop she held, as though it might offer some protection against him, however small; for she could not help but be aware of her weakness in comparison to his strength, that she was alone and powerless against him. She had been a fool to come here, she thought, to go on meeting him as she had. She had known what sort of man he was. She had heard the stories about him, and while he had never admitted their truth, he had never bothered to refute them, either—not even when she had, just once, dared to ask him about his dead wife.

"People say that you—that you . . . killed her, General," Araminta had said, unable to bring herself to use the word *murdered*, which had somehow seemed far uglier.

"*Sí*, that is what they say, *señorita*," he had replied casually, neither conceding nor denying the veracity of her statement.

But she had not missed the way his eyes had glittered darkly, how his nostrils had flared, how his mouth had tightened, and she had not dared to press him further. Still, despite everything she had heard about him, she could not believe in her heart that he was capable of cold-blooded murder. She had not *wanted* to believe it. Now, the accusation haunted her, as did the list of other crimes commonly attributed to him. Though he had invariably behaved as a gentleman toward her, she knew that it was only because it had pleased him to do so. Now, she glimpsed the savagery she had always sensed coiled inside him. Inwardly, Araminta quailed at the notion of his unleashing his wrath upon her, for she did not know what he might do to her, alone as they were. The thought of his forcing her down upon the frost-encrusted ground and raping her was uppermost in her mind, and she felt sick to think she had ever wondered what it would be like to be kissed and caressed by him. Still, she could not deny that, even now, she was perversely attracted and excited by the savage strength he exuded. She had no one but herself to blame for her predicament. Fear—and unwilling challenge—flickered in her wide green eyes as, inexorably, Rigo erased the short distance she had nervously put between them.

"Araminta," he uttered softly. It was the first time she had ever heard him speak her name, and despite her trepidation, a strange thrill tingled up her spine at the sound, for it was as mellifluous as warm, sweet honey flowing in her ears. He pronounced it in the Spanish fashion—*Ahr-ah-meen-tah*—accenting the third syllable and gently rolling the *r*, which was far more beautiful and romantic in cadence than the plainer English version—*Air-a-min-ta*—to which she was accustomed. "Araminta," he murmured again, his voice low and curiously impassioned, "for your own sake do I tell you this, I swear: Do not do this thing. Do not wed Judd Hobart. He is not the man for you."

"So you keep saying. But still, you—you give me no real reason why I—why I should not marry him, General," Araminta rejoined breathlessly, mesmerized by his dark, hot eyes, the muscle that throbbed in his cheek, as though it were only with the greatest of difficulty that he held his anger and desire in check, prevented himself from doing her some violence.

She felt somehow as though she had run a very long way and now could not get enough air into her lungs. She wished that Rigo were not standing so close to her, so close that she could feel the heat that emanated from his body, as though from a slow-burning fire— a peculiarly male characteristic—and smell the subtle scents of cheroot smoke and soap and sandalwood that wafted from his dark skin. More than anything, she feared his potent masculinity, even as, at the same time, because of it, she was drawn to him against her will. Perhaps if she kept him talking, played for time, she could escape from him. But at his reply, she knew that that hope was fruitless, that she had but goaded his temper to its breaking point.

"You are too stubborn for your own good, *señorita*.

You insist on persisting. Very well, then. Like it or not, you shall have a reason!''

He moved so suddenly and swiftly that even though Araminta was on her guard against him, it was only by instinct that her right hand, in which she now clutched her whip, came up defensively. With it— fueled by her terror and some other, darker, more primitive emotion she did not understand and could not have named—she would have slashed him across his handsome face. But as quick as a snake striking, his arm shot out; his steely hand closed around her wrist so hard that she knew she would have bruises there the next day. Desperate, she tried to wrench free of him, but effortlessly, with the merest flex of the muscles that corded his arm, he only tightened his grasp upon her. A half-smile twisted his carnal mouth but did not quite reach his narrowed eyes, which glinted as hard as nails as they raked her, ravished her.

"Let me go!" Araminta cried, wildly clawing at him with her free hand, but it, too, he caught in a punishing grip. Then, slowly, deliberately, as she twisted and turned in another vain attempt to escape from him, he pinioned her arms behind her back, forcing her up against him so that with her every breath, her heaving breasts brushed his chest and his thighs imprisoned hers, making her head spin, her body quiver, for no man had ever held her so intimately. She was painfully aware of how the hard, whipcord length of him rippled with muscle against her. She was certain he could feel the fierce pounding of her heart. With a low growl, Rigo jerked the riding crop from her hand so furiously that the leather-

wrapped handle burned her palm. Then, with the wide,
flat tip of the whip, he caressed her cheek lingeringly,
in a way that made her gasp and shudder and glance
away, before he slid the handle under her chin and
compelled her face back up to his. "Let me go, you
. . . you *brute!*" she demanded again, panting from
her futile struggles against him.

"Brute? Don't tell me that despite my reputation,
you expected better of me, perhaps?" he inquired
mockingly, raising one devilish brow. "What a pity,
then, *gringuita*, to disappoint you."

Then, his eyes darkening with passion, Rigo swept
her ruthlessly into his arms and crushed his mouth
savagely down on hers. His teeth grazed the tender
flesh of her lower lip, drawing blood that tasted cop-
pery and bittersweet upon her tongue. But she scarcely
felt the pain, for at his kiss, a wild, fearsome thrill
like nothing she had ever before felt, as though the
earth had abruptly dropped from beneath her feet,
sending her tumbling into an endless black void,
rushed through her like an atavistic storm. She had
been kissed before, but not like this, never like this.
In her wildest imaginings, she had not dreamed that
Rigo's kissing her would prove so shattering an experience, wakening within her feelings she had not known
existed, feelings that not only shocked and scared her,
but, inexplicably, so exhilarated her, too, that she
could not seem even to think. She was as dazed as
though, suddenly and violently, all her senses had
been scattered to the wind, leaving only primal instinct
behind—instinct that, of its own volition, leaped in
response to his virile maleness, the hot, hungry mouth

on hers, the sinuous, beguiling tongue that traced the outline of her lips before roughly compelling them to yield to his devastating onslaught upon her. His tongue shot deep into her mouth, searching out its innermost secret places, ravaging them, making her feel as though she were alternately burning with fever and shaking with chills. Her knees trembled so, she knew she would have fallen had he not held her so tightly. She felt as liquid as quicksilver in his embrace, as though all her bones were dissolving inside her, leaving her so weak and pliable that without difficulty he molded her body to his, determinedly bending her back as though he intended to break her in two.

Confused and terrified by her reaction to him, by the hard evidence of his desire for her that through her skirts she could feel pressed against her thighs, Araminta tried frantically once more to wrest free of him, to fight him—to no avail. Rigo was far stronger than she; resistance was useless. She had no hope of prevailing over him; his grasp on her was secure and relentless, and he subdued her easily by flinging away her riding crop and laying one hand at her throat, tightening his grip upon the slender, swanlike length until she ceased her exertions and stood acquiescent in his arms. She could not even turn her head aside to elude his encroaching, demanding lips, for now, his fingers slid up to snatch the pins from her upswept hair and, holding her captive, binding her to him, wrapped themselves in the silky golden tresses that tumbled loose, cascading to her waist. And all the while, his insistent mouth and tongue continued to invade and plunder her lips, leaving her dizzy and breathless in their determined wake. A low moan emanated from her throat; and of their own will, her own hands, now free, crept up to twine about his neck, pulling him even nearer as, to her horror and shame, Araminta realized she was kissing him back, reveling in his kisses, his caresses, his barbarous assault upon her. Rigo's lips left hers then, slanting ravenously across her cheek to her temple and the strands of her hair before trailing down her throat to her breasts. Her woolen cape had fallen open, and beneath the fabric of her riding habit, she could feel her nipples pucker, harden into twin peaks as his mouth devoured her, setting her aflame, so she no longer felt the chill of the wintry day, but was as hot as though she stood before a newly stoked fire.

In some dark corner of her brain, she thought dimly that in moments Rigo would be forcing her down upon the ground to have his way with her, even as he now forced her body to respond to him, despite her mind's protest at this thwarting of its dominion. She wanted to die a thousand deaths, for despite her fear and humiliation that he should dare to touch her so, as no gentleman ought, something vital and electric was coursing through her veins, some hitherto unknown thing deep inside her, now stirred and wakened by his lips and hands; and some dark, treacherous part of her longed for it to burgeon fully to life. But instead, without warning, Rigo swore and released her so suddenly that Araminta stumbled and nearly fell. Recovering her balance, some semblance of her sanity returning, she stared at him, as stricken as though he had hit her, her face ashen, her eyes huge, and her breath coming far too quickly and shallowly. Rigo's own eyes blazed with both passion and anger as he stared back at her, struggling visibly to regain command of himself and his emotions. He had not realized how much the kisses and caresses he had so brutally taken from her would affect him, how much he desired her. As his burning gaze flickered over her, taking in her enticing state of dishevelment, her loose, tangled hair, her tremulously parted mouth, swollen and bruised from his own exacting lips, he wanted her so badly that it was all he could do to refrain from finishing what he had started.

Instead, he abruptly strode to his stallion and, gathering the reins, swung up into the saddle, momentarily fighting for control of the mettlesome mount, which, tossing its head and snorting, pranced and sidestepped a little before obediently responding to its master.

"I made you a promise once, *señorita*, and now I keep it," Rigo grated as he looked down at Araminta, his dark-brown eyes seeming to pierce her very soul. "I warn you: On the day that you become the wife of Judd Hobart, you become *my* enemy!"

Then he set his spurs sharply to his horse's sides and galloped off. Upon the creek bank where she stood gazing after his disappearing figure, Araminta sank slowly to her knees, sobbing suddenly and shaking from her inner turmoil, her conflicting emotions. She buried her face in her hands, so stunned, so bewildered by his behavior toward her that she did not know what to think or do. Why had he kissed her? Why had he not raped her? Certainly, she had been helpless to prevent his doing so. She didn't understand any of it at all. Did he want her, or did he not? If he did not, then why had he acted as though he did? Why had he warned her not to marry Judd? Why had Rigo warned her that on her wedding day she would become his enemy? He had spoken no word of love or caring or even desire to her. He had not asked her to wed *him* instead. So what was she to make of his conduct? She did not know. She knew only that when Rigo had kissed her, she had felt something she had never felt in Judd's arms; and to her deep shame, despite her fear that Rigo would fling her down upon the ground and have his will of her, some tiny, traitorous part of her had half hoped he actually would.

Araminta was mortified by the realization. Surely, she must be a wanton or mad, she thought—and doubtless, she appeared so, too. She could not return to the hacienda looking as she did. Bending over the creek, she vigorously splashed some of its frigid water upon her face, then critically studied her reflection in its crystal surface. Somehow, she had expected to find herself altered after Rigo's savage kisses. But she was not. Except for her hair's resembling a tangle of tumbleweeds and her mouth's being as red and lush as a full-blown rose, she saw no change. How could that be? she wondered. For she *was* different, and somehow, she sensed she would never again be the same as she had been before Rigo had kissed her. Even now, there was inside her a haunting ache, an indescribable longing she had not felt before.

Tentatively, Araminta traced with her index finger the outline of her mouth, as Rigo had traced it with his tongue. Then she touched the tiny cut his teeth had made upon her lower lip, her cheeks burning, her body quivering as she remembered the feel of his hard, rapacious mouth on hers. Biting her lower lip to still its trembling, she ran her fingers through her snarled hair, trying to comb it into some semblance of order. Then she searched the ground for her hairpins, knowing she would not find them all, but even a few would suffice. After that, she twisted the entire mass of her hair around and around down its length, then wound it up at her nape into a chignon. One hand holding the heavy knot securely in place, she pushed into her tresses the hairpins she had recovered. Feeling more composed then, she rose and retrieved her whip.

Despite herself, as she glanced about the creek bank, where she had shared so many moments with Rigo, Araminta felt a sharp and unexpected pang at the understanding that she would not ride this way again, that especially after this morning, she dared not. She had worried what her grandfather and Judd would do if ever they learned of her meetings with Rigo; she did not want even to contemplate their actions if ever they discovered how he had kissed her here today. They would kill him, she thought bleakly. Well, thank God that they would never find out, that no one would—for she would never see Rigo del Castillo again.

Book Two

Silken Ties that Bind

Chapter Eleven

The Rio Grande, Mexico, 1913

On the day that you become the wife of Judd Hobart, you become my *enemy!* With each beat of the horses' hooves that drummed in her ears, Rigo's words thrummed in Araminta's mind. *On the day that you become the wife of Judd Hobart, you become* my *enemy!*

She had not believed him; she had not *wanted* to believe him, to think that he would actually turn against her, would strike out at her, intending her harm. She had decided after he had kissed her that morning at the creek bank that there must be some spark of caring for her in him, even though he had not told her so, and it was this she had ascribed to him as his reason for not wanting her to wed Judd—although common sense had dictated there must be more to it than that. But even if she *had* believed Rigo's warning to her, Araminta knew she would still have married Judd. There had been no other way to repay her grandfather for his kindness in giving her a home when she had so desperately needed one, no other way to lighten his heavy load in running the vast High Sierra, no other way to ensure her own future.

Yet trepidation had grown within her as her wedding day had approached, both because Rigo's warning preyed on her mind and because once Judd's engagement ring was on her finger, her fiancé had increasingly pressured her to celebrate their wedding night before the summer date they had set for their nuptials. The last time, he had thrown her down in an empty stall in the High Sierra's stables and nearly raped her. He had muttered hoarsely in her ear, coarse, vulgar descriptions of what he wanted to do to her, *would*, in fact, do to her when she was his bride; and he had actually appeared to derive a cruel enjoyment from her struggles against him as he had kissed and pawed her roughly, an enjoyment she had sensed was unnatural and by which she had therefore been instinctively terrified. If not for the unexpected entrance of one of the ranch hands, Araminta felt certain Judd would forcibly have taken her. She had been horrified, revolted by the obscene things he had said to her, by the loathsome feel of his mouth and hands upon her, and by the abhorrent thought of lying with him as his wife, knowing, now, that he would use her crudely, without caring or gentleness. She had remembered Rigo's kissing and caressing her that morning upon the creek bank. She had blushed with shame to think how he had compelled her to respond to him, how some part of her had actually desired him, and had compared her feeling then with the fright and disgust Judd's advances had awakened in her. Araminta had believed there must, in truth, be something wrong with her to feel so when Rigo was nothing more than a common bandit, perhaps even a cold-blooded killer, while Judd was a gentleman born and bred, scion of one of the most prominent ranches in the entire country.

Confused by her inexplicable emotions, worried about her grandfather's suffering a relapse when he had seemed lately, since the announcement of her engagement, to be in such improved health and spirits, she had said nothing to him of her increasing uneasiness about marrying Judd. Whatever Rigo del Castillo had aroused in her was as low and indecent as he was; she should die of mortification even to recall it! What had happened between them ought never to have taken place—*would* never have done so had she not encouraged him as shamelessly as any hussy by continuing to meet him when she had known how wrong it was. Her present feelings toward her fiancé were nothing more than the natural fears of a chaste bride, Araminta had assured herself. The sooner she was wedded and bedded, the better. As her husband, Judd would ease the ache Rigo had somehow instilled in her. So she had ignored the wisdom of her heart and married Judd.

But it was not in her husband's arms that she would lie on this, her wedding night, Araminta thought with a sinking heart as Rigo's demonic black stallion carried her farther and farther away from the High Sierra. Still, despite the fear escalating within her at every passing mile, she did not implore him to let her go; that would have been futile. He would not have violently attacked the High Sierra and kidnapped her, only to release her within a few hours of her capture. Nor did she expect or beg for mercy, for that, too, would prove useless. All the satisfying conversations they had shared, all the passion of that last encounter had vanished. She was his enemy now. She had become so the moment she had married Judd. True to his word, Rigo had warned her grimly about the consequences of that act, had he not? And she had not listened. What a fool she had been! She had known what he was— he had never made any attempt to mislead her about that—and still, against all her better judgment, she had believed better of him, somehow; she had *wanted* to believe better of him. Now—too late—she knew how misplaced her faith in him had been.

What would he do to her? Araminta wondered apprehensively, determinedly fighting back the hysteria that threatened to overcome her and shivering at the answer she felt in her bones. There was a significance in his abducting her on her wedding night—and a dark implication she did not dare to face.

"You are cold?" It was the first time Rigo had spoken to her since he had forcibly spirited her away from the High Sierra. His breath was warm and insufferably seductive against her ear, sending another involuntary chill down her spine. His low, velvety voice held a trace of mockery, as though he had guessed her thoughts and was amused by them. Compelling herself to gather the ragged remnants of her courage, Araminta resolutely stiffened her spine against him. She would rather die than let him know how frightened she was. But despite herself, she could not repress yet another shudder as his muscular arm tightened briefly around her; and as he laughed softly, mockingly, at her reaction to his steely embrace, she knew he was not deceived by her bravado. "You will be warm soon enough, *gringuita*. I will make certain of that, I assure you." His huskily uttered words held both a threat and a promise.

Araminta's worst fear was realized then. Her heart plummeted in her breast. Until this moment, she recognized that deep down inside, she had stupidly dared to hope that Rigo meant to do nothing more than to hold her for a sizable ransom from either her grandfather or Judd. Now she knew how foolish that hope had been. What Rigo desired from her was more precious than gold, a price too high and that only she could pay—with no guarantee of her freedom afterward, for even if he vowed to release her once he was done with her, she could not trust him, not now. Araminta trembled at the thought of his taking her, of her being forced to lie beneath him, his mouth and hands roaming where they willed; for she remembered how, despite herself, he had made her respond to him that day upon the creek bank, and she was afraid of the strange power he seemed to have over her, of how her treacherous young body had betrayed her at his touch. Yet, realistically, she knew she would not be able to prevent him from what he clearly intended. He was far bigger and stronger than she. No matter how hard she fought him, she would have not a prayer of prevailing over him. He would have what he wanted of her in the end—unless she was rescued or otherwise somehow managed to escape from him.

But after some hours of hard riding, this hope, too, grew dim and finally died. They should have reached Rigo's ranch, the Casa Blanca, by now. That they had not caused Araminta, numb with shock and despair, at last to understand that he was not taking her to his home in Texas, as she had mistakenly expected, but across the border, into Mexico. She was stricken by the realization; for even though she felt certain that by this time, her grandfather and Judd were aware of her kidnapping and had set out after her, Rigo and his *bandoleros* not only had a head start, but also, once they crossed the Rio Grande, would be much more familiar with the rugged countryside, cognizant of its every hiding place and defensible position. If the Federales and the Rurales of Mexico itself could not locate and penetrate these strongholds used by desperadoes and Revolutionaries alike, how could her grandfather and Judd possibly hope to? How could she, a lone woman, hope to escape, then survive the arduous terrain and the long trek across it to freedom and safety? She knew next to nothing about living off the land, and there would be other hazards far worse than the simple struggle to exist, to prevent her making her way back home to Texas, to the High Sierra.

Brutal soldiers, fierce guerrillas, cutthroat criminals, savage Yaqui Indians, and dangerous wild animals were all to be found in the craggy mountains and harsh deserts of Mexico. No region of the country was safe, especially the northern province of Chihuahua, into which Rigo was taking her; for at daybreak on February 9, Félix Díaz and Manuel Mondragón, two of the deposed President Porfirio Díaz's former generals, had, in the military zone of La Ciudadela, revolted against the Mexican government of President Francisco Madero. Madero had immediately sent one of his own generals, Victoriano Huerta, to quell the rebellion. But this, Huerta had only pretended to do, for he was, in reality, a traitor, in league with the rebels, as well as with the vice president, Piño Suárez. At the National Palace, Huerta had taken Madero prisoner and ordered him assassinated. But once Huerta had seized power, his government had been rejected by the Constitutionalists, led by Venustiano Carranza, who had called for a general uprising against the military dictatorship; and a month after Madero's murder, the *guerrilleros* who had made him president of Mexico were again on the move. One of these, Francisco "Pancho" Villa, had, on March 6, with eight other men, who were to become the origin of the renowned División del Norte, infiltrated the Sierra de Chihuahua, where Villa was even now gathering partisans and attacking the garrisons of the Federales. Thus, the fighting in Mexico was now more widespread and violent than ever.

All this, Rigo knew full well and surely counted on to prevent her from being recovered by her grandfather and Judd, or from running away, Araminta reflected bitterly, more dispirited and afraid than she had ever been in her life. Cool, clever, and as predatory and

unpredictable as a beast, Rigo would be neither easy
to catch nor to elude. Truly, she was at his utter mercy,
with only her wits to defend her. This realization
nearly proved the crowning blow to her dazed senses,
and it was only with the greatest of difficulty that she
restrained the hysteria churning inside her. Just as at
the creek bank, she had no one but herself to blame
for her plight, she told herself, deeply ashamed and
downcast at the thought. She had played the part of a
wanton, meeting Rigo as she had, as no lady ought,
kissing him . . . Was it any wonder that he thought
she was his for the taking, that he had proved brazen
enough to kidnap her? But if he wanted her so badly,
why had he waited until she had married Judd before
abducting her? It did not make sense—not if Rigo
cared for her, even a little. He must wish deliberately
to hurt her, then. But . . . why?

Araminta had no answers to her question; and finally, she forced herself to cease to reason, even to
think, allowing the terror and exhaustion that seeped
into the very marrow of her bones slowly to dull her
mind, her body, mitigating the sheer adrenaline that
was all that had sustained her, kept her from conceding
defeat to her captor. Tears slipping silently down her
cheeks, she at last slumped against Rigo wearily, her
head lolling listlessly against his shoulder. At that,
another low laugh emanated from his throat, and he
murmured something to her in Spanish. Her understanding of the language was limited, but "That's
better," she thought he said, and, out of pride if nothing else, would have resumed her rigid posture. But
all the strength seemed to have drained from her body,

and no matter how hard she tried, she could no longer summon either the will or the energy to remain upright. Besides, what difference did it make? she asked herself tiredly. She was doomed to her fate at his ruthless hands, anyway.

Still, regardless of how she quivered at the unbidden, unnerving image of his forcing himself on her, Araminta nevertheless welcomed the warmth that radiated from his lean, hard body, was perversely grateful for his strong arms that supported her, for she felt she would surely have fallen from the saddle otherwise. Never had she ridden at such a grueling pace for such an interminable length of time. As well accustomed as she was to the back of a horse, her muscles had begun to ache unbearably as they were pushed beyond the limits of their endurance. Her backside felt black and blue; it would probably be bruised and sore for a week, she thought. But at least some of the chill dissipated as her body was warmed by Rigo's. Almost, had she not been so scared, she might have slept, clasped securely in his embrace, with the rhythmic rocking of the saddle to lull her. No sooner had the thought crossed her mind, it seemed, than her eyelashes drooped shut, and she drifted into an uneasy slumber, only to lurch into wakefulness at the startling feel of frigid water lapping ominously at her lower limbs and dragging at her skirts. While she had dozed, the *bandoleros* had reached the Rio Grande, Araminta realized, and were now fording the river. In moments, she would be carried beyond the border into Mexico and certain imprisonment there, for as long as Rigo willed.

Dimly, she considered plunging from his arms into the dark, cold water. Under the cover of the night and with the current to sweep her away, perhaps she could escape from him! Death beneath the ripples that disrupted the river's surface might be preferable to what he had in store for her. But as though he had read her mind, his unyielding grip upon her increased, crushing her against his chest; and then his stallion was wading onto firm ground, snorting and shaking its soaked black coat of the water that clung to it, and her slim chance at eluding her devilish captor was lost.

"Drowning is a most unpleasant way to die, *gringuita*," Rigo muttered in her ear, a serrated edge to his voice, as though she had angered him. "Would you really have chosen it over me?"

"Y-y-yes," she whispered brokenly.

"How fortunate for us both, then, that I did not permit you to make such an unwise decision." The expression upon his face as he uttered the sharp, grating words was so murderous that for a moment Araminta was half afraid he would strike her, and instinctively she shrank from him.

It had not occurred to her previously that she had anything but rape to fear at his hands, that perhaps he would also beat her, torture her, maybe even kill her. He had murdered his own wife, hadn't he? Why, then, would he balk at slaying the *gringa* bride of his most hated enemy? For the first time, Araminta realized that not just her virtue, but also perhaps her very life was at stake. The last vestiges of her courage and control vanished at the thought, and the roiling hysteria she had earlier believed conquered suddenly swelled within her again, this time to erupt with a vengeance. Screaming and sobbing, she lashed out at Rigo blindly, twisting and turning like a wounded animal in his grasp, her arms flailing wildly, her fingers curled into claws that raked at him viciously. She felt a fierce exultation as she gouged his smooth-skinned face, leaving bloody streaks in her wake.

"*¡Dios mio!*" he swore as he grappled with her. "What a mountain cat you are at heart, and how I am going to enjoy taming you!"

Beneath them, agitated by their struggle, the high-spirited stallion pranced nervously, snorting and tossing its head. Hampered by her long, sodden skirts, Araminta could not effectively kick Rigo, and so hammered her heels into the shoulder of the horse, causing it to whinny and jump and dance sideways, forcing Rigo to turn his attention to restraining the mount. Jerking hard on the reins, he brought the skittish animal under control, then deftly slid from the saddle, hauling Araminta with him. To her great satisfaction, in the process she managed to land several punishing blows to his head and chest. But despite her struggles, she could not free herself from his iron grip, and as she hit the ground, she lost her footing and stumbled. Aware that she was hysterical, Rigo backhanded her smartly across the face, simultaneously releasing her, so she staggered back, sprawling headlong upon the earth. Stunned by the stinging slap, the wind knocked out of her from her fall, Araminta lay still, shaking and weeping. She made no effort to renew her battle against him, even when he bent over her and gathered her into his arms, rocking her gently and crooning to her in Spanish.

After a moment, he issued a sharp command in *pelado*, a harsh dialect of mixed Spanish and Indian, and one of the *bandoleros*, who had all assembled their horses in a protective circle about the pair on the ground, dismounted and approached, in his hand a bottle of clear liquid he had taken from his saddlebag. Taking the bottle, Rigo uncorked it with his teeth and, upending it, pressed it to Araminta's lips. As she inhaled the pungent aroma wafting from the bottle, she realized that it did not contain water. Turning her head, she tried to refuse the alcohol, but this he would not permit. Roughly wrapping his hand in her hair and yanking her head back, he forced her to drink from the bottle. She gagged and coughed as the raw, fiery liquor burned down her throat into her belly. Mescal. He had given her mescal; she was sure of it. For a minute, she was afraid she would be sick from the potent alcohol. Closing her eyes, she compelled herself to choke down her nausea; and presently, as a warm glow from the liquor spread through her, she discovered that she did, in fact, feel better. Slowly, her eyelashes fluttered open.

Rigo hunkered beside her, one arm supporting her, on his dark, handsome face, illuminated by the silver moonlight streaming down from the night sky, a combination of rage and concern and something else that Araminta could not define but that, inexplicably, made her heart beat fast, her breath come far too quickly and shallowly. She longed to turn away from him, but his fathomless, smoky-quartz eyes hypnotized her. Try as she might, she could not seem to tear her gaze from his. As he stared at her pale, frightened countenance, Rigo almost was moved to pity. Her long blond hair tumbled like tangled strands of silk about her, as golden as the deserts of Mexico. Her tearful eyes glowed as green as a saguaro cactus and were filled with a mixture of hatred and fear that somehow wounded him to see. But then a faint glimmer upon her slender left hand attracted his attention, and as he caught sight of her elaborate gold wedding ring encrusted with diamonds, his jaw set and his purpose hardened. She was the wife of his enemy, Judd Hobart. Rigo had cause not to forget that—not ever. Slowly, his hand moved to his face to stroke the deep furrows she had left there during her frenzied attack upon him.

"No man would have put his mark on me—and lived." He spoke the words evenly enough, but Araminta was not deceived. He would exact a price for those scratches, she knew, and as his next words confirmed. "But on you, *gringuita,* I shall take my revenge another way." His eyes roved over her boldly, making his meaning plain.

She cringed as he stretched out his hand to smooth back the hair from her face, to touch her cheek, which bore a faint redness from his slap. He regretted having to hit her, but he had not known how else to bring her to her senses. She was quiet enough now, he thought, and though she trembled at his feather-light caress, she did not attempt to do battle with him again. He was glad, for he did not want to hurt her any more than was necessary, though it was inevitable in the end that he *must* cause her pain. If only it had not been Araminta he had needed. If only there had been some other way . . . But there had not been. There *was* not. His mouth tightened purposefully as her diamond wedding band flashed once more in the moonlight. He yearned violently to snatch it from her finger, but he did not. It was a constant, grim reminder to him of his reason for kidnapping her. He must remember it; he must not permit himself to take pity on her and weaken in his resolve. Though shocked and frightened and silent at the moment, Araminta would eventually recover her wits and composure. Intelligent, resourceful, and possessing a brave heart, she would try to escape from him, to fight him again, perhaps even to kill him. He could not allow her to succeed at any of those things.

He barked another order in *pelado*, and with a sharp knife one of the desperadoes cut a short length of hemp from the coil of rope looped over his saddle horn, then handed it to Rigo. Before Araminta realized what he intended, he pulled her wrists to him and bound them securely, while, like a wounded animal, she stared up at him, fear and hatred flickering in the depths of her dull, glazed green eyes. Still, she did not protest, not even when he hauled her to her feet and led her toward his stallion, and she realized, disheartened, that the brief respite was ended, that the rest of the *bandoleros* were already mounting their own horses, that camp was not yet to be made this night. His hands strong and firm about her waist, Rigo lifted her into his saddle, then swung up behind her, one arm encircling her as before to hold her securely against him. In moments, they were under way again.

They rode forever, it seemed, though more slowly now than they had traveled in the beginning. But to Araminta, aching to the very marrow of every bone in her body, the plodding pace was no less tortuous than before. She felt so dazed and exhausted that she knew that even if a chance to escape arose, she would be unable to seize it, would be able to run no more than a few steps before Rigo caught her. Far worse, however, was the knowledge that not only was she too numb and sore and weary even to struggle against him when they finally did halt for the night, but also that she no longer cared. If he had meant to wear down her resistance to him, he had succeeded all too well. Now she only hoped that if raping her was truly his intent, he would take her quickly and be done with it—and if he killed her afterward, she would at least be out of her misery, dead to her disgrace. She was soaked to the skin and cold from the streams they had forded; and despite the poncho that, earlier, Rigo had unrolled from his saddle pack and given to her for warmth, she shivered, her teeth chattering. Only the heat from his body prevented her from freezing in the night air that grew progressively thinner and chillier as they wended their way steadily upward, through rocky, narrow canyons formed by bluffs and buttes, along twisting trails Araminta felt were fit only for a mountain goat.

Though, at first, she had cursed the darkness, for it had prevented her from discerning the direction in

which they journeyed, from observing any landmarks
that might be of use to her if she somehow managed
to gain her freedom, now she was glad of it, glad she
could not see how far below her were the bottoms of
the ravines that fell away from the steep cliffs along
which twined the rough tracks the desperadoes followed. Occasionally, a scattering of small stones was
dislodged by the horses' hooves to tumble down the
side of a gorge, and Araminta's heart leaped to her
throat as she heard the faraway splash of the pebbles
falling into the brook that sometimes trickled through
the chasm. Yet neither Rigo nor the other *bandoleros*
were deterred by the dangerous paths; they pressed on
relentlessly, pausing only to refill the canteens when
necessary, to eat tough strips of beef jerky, and to
water and rest the horses. She had no idea how far
they had traveled or where they were or even whether
her grandfather and Judd were hard on their heels, as
the punishing pace Rigo set would seem to indicate.
But perhaps it was only because he would not feel safe
until he had pushed deep into Mexico that he drove
himself and his men.

At last, he did stop, in a place where the path
widened into a rough-shaped half-circle, its convex
boundary formed by a shallow depression in the massive wall of rock that towered over them, a shelf of
stone cropping out to produce a protective overhang
above them. On either side, the stands of boulders that
made it impossible for more than one horse and rider
at a time to enter the natural shelter guarded against
an ambush. Along its far wall in an arroyo a stream
flowed, a source of cool, fresh water. By the light of

the moon reflected in the dark, silver-sheened surface of the creek, even Araminta, lurching into wakefulness as the jolting of the saddle ceased, could see that the small refuge was an ideal spot to make camp. But although she had prayed that their toilsome journey would soon end, she could not repress a shudder as she thought of what might happen to her here. Rigo dismounted, then helped her down after him. Had she been stronger, she might have tried impulsively to run from him. But she was so stiff and sore and weak that, immediately, her knees buckled beneath her, and she would have collapsed where she stood had he not supported her. Snarling a Spanish oath, he swept her up without warning into his arms then, as though she weighed no more than a rag doll, and strode swiftly beneath the overhang, where he sat her down so that her back was bolstered by the rock wall. Then, wordlessly, he turned away to take care of his stallion.

Araminta saw that the other desperadoes were already stripping their saddles and packs from their mounts, watering the horses, then hobbling them, placing feed bags on the animals' noses, and with saddle blankets rubbing their lathered coats down strenuously. Only when the beasts had been diligently attended to did the *bandoleros* move to spread their bedrolls upon the earth baked hard by the sun, to open their canteens and bottles of mescal and even-rawer pulque, and to prepare plates of cold *frijoles* and tortillas to go with the inevitable strips of dried meat.

Shaking in her wet garments and from the chilly wind that whined through the canyon, Araminta longed fervently for a fire, although she surmised that none would be built, that even here in this tiny haven, Rigo, as alert and watchful as a predator, would not trust that the flames would not be seen against the inky night sky. Even now, though he must be tired, too, she sensed that he was on his guard, his ears cocked intently, listening to every sound carried on the night wind, the far-off scream of a mountain lion, the mournful cry of some lone bird, the whispering skitter of some small creature in the clumps of brush that edged the stream. His dark-brown eyes searched the land constantly, missing nothing.

He was indeed an animal, Araminta thought. She had not seen him since that last day upon the creek bank that separated the High Sierra from the Casa Blanca, and it seemed that there was nothing in him now of the elegant, aristocratic *hacendado* with whom she had idled away so many lazy mornings. It was all too easy now to credit the wicked rumors she had heard about him, to believe that his notorious reputation was well-deserved. His hawkish Spanish face, in the moonlight, looked as though it had been chiseled from stone—hard, impassive, ruthless. His long, supple body rippled with the powerful muscles of a man who has lived hard and dangerously, relying on his own wits and instincts to survive. How had he come to be as he was? she wondered. He was the bastard son of a grandee who had given him nothing, not even a name, she knew. Was that why he had seemed to switch so effortlessly from the role of lord of the hacienda to that of brutal bandit, revealing now the dark, deadly side of himself that she had only sensed before—and shied away from? Araminta could no longer pretend that it did not exist, not when she was face-to-face with it and knew what it must mean for her.

As Rigo walked toward her, she shivered—and not from the cold. He squatted down beside her, a canteen slung over one shoulder and in his hands a bottle of mescal and two tin plates of *frijoles*, tortillas, and jerky, all of which he laid to one side to draw the sharp knife at his waist. With a single, swift motion, he sliced through the rope binding her wrists. She gasped with pain as the blood, which had been cut off by the tightly tied hemp, rushed to her hands; and to help restore her circulation, Rigo began to chafe her wrists vigorously, frowning at the marks the rope had left upon her. Then, handing her one of the plates, he indicated that she should eat. Still, although she was hungry, as she gazed down at the unappetizing fare— the dollop of cold, mushy beans and the single stale tortilla and strip of dried meat—Araminta's stomach churned. Shaking her head, she mutely refused the meal.

"What is the matter, *señora?*" Rigo's teeth flashed white against his dark skin in the moonlight as he gave a low, jeering laugh. "The food is not good enough for you, not what you are used to? My men are wolfing it down with gusto. They know that they are lucky to get it, you see, that many poor people in Mexico are not so fortunate as to have even so much as this." The derisive smile abruptly vanished from his face, and his voice hardened. "So you will eat what you are offered, *¿comprende?* Or I swear I will ram it down your throat! For I warn you: I will not permit you to starve yourself to death! Oh, no, *gringuita*. You shall not escape from me so easily as that, I promise you!''

Swallowing hard, remembering that Rigo had warned her that on her wedding day she would become his enemy, and knowing how he had kept that vow, Araminta reluctantly accepted the tin plate he now thrust toward her again. She did not want him to coerce her into eating, and she felt he was entirely capable of doing so. Picking up the fork stuck in the unpalatable glob of beans, she forced herself to take a bite and then another, somehow managing to choke them down. Breaking the tortilla in half, she ate it, too, and the jerky, finding, much to her surprise, that she actually did feel better after finishing the meager fare. When she was done, Rigo handed her the canteen, while he drank from the bottle of mescal. But observing that even within the folds of his poncho, Araminta shook from the cold, he insisted upon her having several sips of the mescal, as well, which he said would warm her. Recalling how he had forcibly poured the fiery alcohol down her throat earlier, she did not dare to protest— although her obedience did not, as she had half hoped, lull him into any false sense of security where she was concerned. The meal ended, Rigo retied her wrists and knotted the rope more loosely than before, for which she was grateful. Then, hauling her to her feet, he dragged her tired, stumbling body to the place where he had unrolled his blankets on the ground.

''No,'' she whimpered brokenly, driven now, despite her numbness and exhaustion, to resist. ''No, please. Oh, please, no.''

But he paid no heed to her entreaties. Still struggling

to free herself from his grasp, Araminta glanced around wildly, as though expecting one of the desperadoes to come to her aid. But except for the lone guard Rigo had posted on the boulders, which provided a clear view of the length of the gorge, the remainder of the *bandoleros* were already stretched out on their bedrolls, asleep. Well aware of where his duty lay, the sentry stood with his back to her, studiously ignoring her soft, imploring cries.

"Even if you scream, he will not help you, Araminta." Rigo's voice was low and insidious in her ear, her name melodious upon his lips. "None of them will. Like that of your grandfather at the High Sierra, here among my own men, my word is law, my authority supreme—as you will learn in time."

As you will learn in time. His words echoed ominously in her mind, for they suggested that she would be held prisoner for a long while. Previously, she had reckoned the length of her captivity in days. But perhaps Rigo meant to hold her for weeks, months, or even never to let her go, she thought wildly; or perhaps when he was done with her, had tired of her, he intended to share her with his men or to sell her as a whore to a bordello or worse here in Mexico. Hadn't she once overheard Judd and some of his friends saying that slavery was a common practice south of the border, particularly among bandits and Indians, that the *comancheros* who traded with the Mexicans, as well as with the Comanches, the Apaches, and other Indian tribes, earned as much as fifty pesos for every white woman they brought into Mexico and sold? That, especially in the border towns, a Mexican prostitute could literally be bought for as little as two American dollars—or even less? Ciudad Juárez, in fact, was frequently deliberately mispronounced as Ciudad "Whore-ez" by Judd and his cronies.

Never before had Rigo seemed so tall, so lithe, so muscular, so menacing—capable of anything. Araminta's mind now conjured whispered tales of atrocities, summoning forth fears that lurked deep inside every woman. Now, like invidious serpents poised to strike, they reared their ugly heads to terrify her. Fueled by her fear, she redoubled her efforts to escape from him. But her wrists were tied; she was weary to the bone and slightly drunk from the mescal, as well, and even had she not been, he was much too strong for her to combat. Easily, he yanked her down upon the blankets, and she felt with a shock the weight of his body on hers, one of his thickly corded legs flung over her to hold her still while he pinioned her bound wrists above her head and roughly clapped one hand over her mouth to muffle her sobs of fright.

"*¡Silencio!*" His voice was low and sharp in her ear. "Be silent, *bruja!* Witch! Or perhaps I will be tempted to cut out your tongue!"

Surely, he would not do such a dreadful thing to her, Araminta thought, her heart leaping uncontrollably in her breast at his threat; surely, he would not. But she did not know, and so, though her nerves crawled and screamed inside her, she forced herself to lie mute and still beneath him, miserably aware of how useless it was to defy him, how helpless she was against him. He could do anything he liked with her, *to* her, and she could not prevent it. Tears trickled from beneath her eyelashes as she attempted to prepare herself for what was to come.

"It is good that you learn quickly, *gringuita*," Rigo muttered, his dark eyes glittering in the moonlight, his warm breath fanning her face, "for I have no patience for histrionics and better uses for your tongue."

With that, he slid his hand from her lips to her throat. But before she could make a sound, his mouth claimed hers savagely, ravaging her; and when she tried to object, to clamp her lips shut against him, to turn her head from his onslaught, he tightened his fingers, in silent warning, about her throat, as he had done that day upon the creek bank. She would let him choke her before she submitted to him, the beast! she thought with reckless disregard for her tenuous position. But in the end, dizzy and breathless from the relentless pressure of his insistent mouth upon hers and his hand at her throat, she was compelled to acquiesce to his wordless demands, to soften her lips for him, to open them to his tongue's hot, searching invasion. Again and again, he plundered her mouth, his tongue questing, exploring every secret recess of the dark, dulcet cavity that yielded to him at last of its own accord as he tasted of its sweetness, licked its wine and nectar.

Araminta's blood rushed to her head and pounded there, making her feel flushed and dazed, powerless to resist the lips that went on devouring her hungrily, the hand that imprisoned her bound wrists and the other that first tangled in her unbound hair, then, roughly pushing aside the poncho she wore, swept over her trembling body, cupping her breasts through the rich brocade of her wedding gown, thumb flicking at the hard, taut nipples that strained against the fabric. Tears slipped down her face as his palm glided over the stiff little peaks, moving in a slow, light circular motion that made her gasp against his mouth as tingles of electric heat began to radiate through her breasts, spreading through her body; for this was far worse than what she had expected.

She had thought he would use her cruelly, more wickedly than Judd had tried to do. But Rigo seemed to know instinctively how to draw a response from her, no matter how unwilling, and she trembled as he kissed and caressed her, his tongue thrusting between her lips, twining with her own tongue, his fingers fondling her breasts; and then his hand moved lower still, over her belly and down her thighs, and his mouth was upon her nipples, his tongue rubbing the material of her bodice across them, taunting them, until they were smoldering embers bursting into flame. Although her teeth caught at her lower lip, she could not repress the low, animalistic moan that rose in her throat and that Rigo swallowed with his mouth as he clasped her to him. In moments, he would be shoving up her skirts to take his pleasure of her, she thought with fear and a terrible, insidious anticipation that made her feel sick and ashamed, that she should burn at the secret heart of her with an ache that begged to be eased by him, her captor, her tormentor.

But much to her bewilderment, instead of forcing himself on her as she had expected, he cradled her snugly against his chest, murmuring, "Go to sleep, Araminta. We ride again at dawn," as, with a surprising gentleness now, he stroked her hair and kissed the tears from her cheeks until the heat of his body enveloped hers; and giving in at last to the delicious warmth that seeped slowly through her, the exhaustion that inevitably overcame her, she slept like a child in his arms.

Chapter Twelve

It seemed to Araminta that she had hardly closed her eyes when Rigo shook her roughly awake. Dazed, disoriented at first, not knowing where she was or who was bending over her, she struggled frantically against him, crying out with terror. But as he had last night, he subdued her easily, and clapped his hand over her mouth to silence her screams. Despite herself, as she realized who restrained her, her body went limp with relief; for even if Rigo *had* abducted her and held her captive, he at least was familiar—and despite everything, she was grateful for that, for she knew her fate could have been worse. She could have been at the utter mercy of a total stranger—or an entire band of unknown *bandoleros* or *guerrilleros*.

So far at least, though he had forcibly pressed his

own advances upon her, Rigo had permitted none of the other desperadoes to touch her; and they had shown her nothing but respect, seldom looking at or speaking to her directly and addressing her as *señora* when they did. But if they pitied her, if any one of them would help her escape, they hid it well; and so she dared not approach any of them for assistance, knowing that if she chose wrongly, Rigo would instantly be informed of her attempt to suborn his men.

"Get up!" he now commanded curtly as he removed his hand from her lips. When, still groggy with sleep and aching all over from the hard ride just a few hours past and the equally hard ground upon which she lay, Araminta did not move, he growled a Spanish curse and, grabbing the rope knotted around her wrists, yanked her unceremoniously upright. Her body shrieking in protest at rising, she swayed on her feet, stretching out her hands to steady herself against the nearby rock wall. "When I give an order, I expect it to be obeyed—and quickly! *¿Comprende?*"

Wordlessly, Araminta nodded her head. This could not be happening to her, she told herself over and over. This was not real, but a nightmare from which she could not seem to awaken. This time yesterday, she had been standing in her bedroom at the High Sierra, trying on her wedding gown so last-minute adjustments could be made, preparing, however slowly and unenthusiastically, to become Judd's wife later that morning. How like a long-ago dream her wedding ceremony seemed now! And how enraged Judd must be at having been cheated of his wedding night, aware that his wife might even then be locked in the arms of his enemy.

Although Rigo had not yet taken her virginity, she had few illusions about his ultimate intentions toward her. It was only a matter of time before he acted on them, Araminta thought, dismayed. Even if he did not, no one, in light of his dark, handsome looks, his hot Spanish blood, his undeniable masculinity, and his notorious character, would believe him innocent of bedding her. Doubtless there would be many who would regard any accusations of rape as denials of the fact that she had readily lain with him. No matter what happened to her now, her reputation was irreparably ruined. Everybody who was anybody in Texas had been present at her wedding; her abduction must certainly be a statewide scandal by now. Even if she somehow managed to return home, she would never be able to hold her head high again. Decent people would undoubtedly shun her, and Judd . . . Judd would probably divorce her, so marrying him and everything she had suffered as a result would all be for naught!

With difficulty, Araminta stifled the sobs that threatened to erupt from her throat. She would *not* cry! Her eyes already hurt so badly, were so swollen and redrimmed from lack of sleep, that they felt as though they had been permanently sealed shut with sand. Her every muscle felt as stiff and strained as a taut thong. Even her joints seemed to groan and shriek in protest when she moved. Seeing how slow she was to stir, even after standing, Rigo felt a wholly unwelcome

twinge of guilt over kidnapping and using her so ruthlessly; almost, he regretted the deed. She was innocent, blameless of the heinous crime for which he
sought such equally monstrous revenge, and still, he
had abducted her and meant to claim what rightly
belonged to her husband. Rigo knew he had given her
just cause to hate him—and would give her even more
reason to despise him before all was said and done.
So, although he was determined not to be dissuaded
from his terrible purpose, when he again spoke, it was
more kindly.

"The pain will lessen shortly, *gringuita*, once you
are warm and moving. Here." He unknotted the rope
that imprisoned her wrists, chafing them as he had
before. Then he handed her a neatly tied bundle of
clothes. "I want you to put these on. It is going to be
very hot today, and your . . . wedding gown"—his
mouth tightened sourly on the words—"and corset
will be stifling. Since I don't want you to faint in the
saddle, you will, of course, dispense with both to
please me."

"Y-y-you mean you—you want me to—to undress? H-h-here? N-n-ow?"

"*Sí*, is that not what I just said?" Fearing that his
resolve to carry out his plan would weaken, Rigo
compelled himself to utter the words mockingly, his
mouth to curve in a derisive smile as, deliberately, he
let his eyes stray over her slowly, licentiously.

That part of his scheme, at least, was easy. For
another woman, he might have had to feign desire—
but not for Araminta. What he felt for her permeated
his entire being, making him constantly aware of her

and of the fact that as his captive, she was his for the taking at any moment he chose. She was so very beautiful, he thought. Her champagne-gold brocade wedding gown showed just the barest hint of her ripe, melon breasts. Its tight basque, adorned with a lacy gold sash draped from one shoulder to her knees, encompassed a waist so willowy that he could span it with his hands, and the yards of material that made up the full, sweeping skirt clung to narrow, slender hips, firm, round buttocks, and long, racy legs that gave her the appearance of being taller than she really was. Her fair, creamy skin had been turned to gold dust by the sun, and the high cheekbones of her piquant face glowed as peach-pink as the sunrise. Beneath delicately arched golden brows, her wide, sloe eyes, fringed with sooty lashes so thick and heavy that they seemed to pull her lids down at their slightly slanted corners, shone as green as emeralds in the early morning light. Her finely chiseled retroussé nose was set above generous, dusty-pink, rosebud lips that unwittingly invited a man's hard, hungry kisses. With her long, silky blond hair unbound, cascading down like a waterfall about her, she looked like a golden gypsy, wild and bewitching.

To Rigo, accustomed to the dark, black-haired women of his native Mexico, Araminta was the epitome of a culture and society that all too frequently scorned his bronze skin and Spanish blood. She enticed him, enchanted him; that her mind was as intelligent and intriguing as her face and body were exquisite made her irresistible to him. He had never before known her like and he never would again. If he were honest with himself, he must admit that it was not just to revenge himself on Judd Hobart that he had kidnapped her. He wanted her, had wanted her from the very beginning, when he had spied her standing in the lobby of the hotel in El Paso, looking as fragile and lovely as a rose amid thorns.

Now, as he waited expectantly for her to remove her garments, Rigo knew that he did not find the idea of watching her disrobe disagreeable; in fact, the thought of her standing naked and vulnerable before him made his loins tighten sharply with passion. He had often speculated about what she looked like unclothed, had imagined her lying beneath him, her head thrown back, her golden hair tumbled loose about her, her lush mouth parted for his own. Such was the picture he conjured even now in his mind, his memories of last night, when she had lain beneath his blankets and he had kissed and caressed her, that it was all he could do to prevent himself from ravishing her then and there. His nostrils flared; his heart hammered in his chest, and a sudden, unexpected tremor ran through him, making him quiver like a stallion in heat.

What was this strange power that she wielded over him? He had known many women over the years, so many that he had grown bored and jaded—and only for one other had he ever felt as he did now. That Araminta also should have this effect upon him puzzled and disturbed him. He should claim her as his and be done with it! he thought wrathfully; there was nothing to prevent his doing so—except the vow he had sworn to himself, that he would go slowly with her, that he would make her want him in the end as much as he did her, so that the pain she must endure at his hands would be not just bitter, but also sweet. That much, he could and *would* give her——although he did not ask himself why it was so important to him that it should be so. But before then, he would teach her the lessons a man taught a woman——and she would learn them well.

Araminta's eyes widened with alarm and confusion as she saw how Rigo looked at her, desire for her smoldering in the fathomless depths of his dark-brown eyes. Stricken, she abruptly came fully awake, her face flushing crimson with fear, fury, and embarrassment at the understanding that he expected her to undress not only in front of him, but also in front of all his men. But then, as she glanced around frantically, she saw that she and Rigo were totally alone in the sheltered place where they had camped——the rest of the *bandoleros* were gone; they had ridden out so quietly that she had not even heard them——and she grew even more afraid.

Perhaps now, Rigo intended to finish what he had started last night! Perhaps it was only some small shred of decency that had prevented him from taking her in front of his men, but now, there was no longer any reason for him to delay. Araminta knew there was nothing she could do to deter him from his purpose. Opposition was useless, as she had already learned last night, and flight was unrealistic. She was so tired and sore that she could not possibly manage more than a few steps at most before he caught her; and his nearby stallion, which she would have mounted and stolen without a qualm had she been able, was still hobbled, incapable of freedom of movement.

"Araminta . . ." Rigo's eyes gleamed in the pale dawn light slowly streaking the midnight-blue horizon with shades of rose and gold, and a sardonic smile that made her yearn fervently to do him some violence twisted his lips as he surveyed her. Plainly, he was deriving a malicious enjoyment from the notion of her undressing before him. Well, she would not do it; she would not! "I thought I gave you an order. Why do you delay? Can it be that you would like me forcibly to strip your clothes from you? Nothing would give me greater pleasure, I assure you, for I confess that the sight of you in your wedding gown displeases me."

He began slowly to stalk her, as though he did indeed mean to rip the garments from her back, and, panicked, Araminta stepped back from him hastily, resolutely stiffening her spine and clutching to her breast the bundle of clothing, as though it were a shield against him, however small and poor.

"I—I can change without—without your assistance," she choked out coldly, incensed at the widening of his mocking smile in response.

"Then do so . . . at once," he demanded softly when, still, she hesitated.

Fuming at her helplessness to defy him, trembling with agitation, and swallowing hard, Araminta deliberately turned her back on him and, laying down the bundle, slowly drew off over her head the fringed poncho that Rigo had given her to wear last evening and dropped it upon the ground. Then, with shaking hands, she reached behind her awkwardly to try to undo the long row of tiny hooks that fastened her wedding gown. In moments, Rigo stood behind her, his hands gliding sensuously across her quivering shoulders, pushing aside the mane of blond hair that hung down her back, draping it over her right shoulder so he could access the hooks.

"Since you have no lady's maid, permit me," he murmured.

His fingers moved deftly upon the fastenings, as though he had had much practice at disrobing a woman. Of course, he probably had, Araminta thought with an odd pang as she remembered the unknown woman he had kissed and embraced at the hotel in El Paso. The hot Spanish blood of his ancestors ran strong in his veins; his virility was so potent as to be almost tangible. Doubtless there were countless women in his past, women he had taken and discarded as easily as he would her once he was done with her. Her ruin at his hands would mean everything to her—and nothing to him, Araminta reflected bitterly, and a violent hatred for him welled up inside her. Yet her heart beat fast as the sleeves of her wedding gown slipped from her shoulders, and she hugged her bodice to her breast to keep the dress from falling off completely. She shuddered as she felt Rigo's hands push the wide straps of her camisole down, as well, baring her shoulders entirely. His breath was warm against her skin as, slowly, he lowered his mouth to the sensitive place where her nape joined her left shoulder, his fingers tightening on her arms to hold her still as he kissed her there, his tongue teasing and stabbing her with its electric heat, sending a wild, lightninglike thrill shooting through her whole body.

Her breath quickened with trepidation and a strange, inexplicable excitement that scared her even more than her fear of him. What was wrong with her that her traitorous body should respond so readily to the touch of a man who had kidnapped her and now held her prisoner—especially when Judd, her fiancé, had not evoked such feelings in her? Araminta did not know. Yet she could not repress a soft, involuntary cry as, after a moment, continuing to kiss her neck and shoulders, Rigo ever so gradually slid his hands inside the opened back of her wedding gown to cradle, through the soft, eyelet-lace cotton of her camisole, the full, ripe breasts that burgeoned above her ruffled corset, pulling her against the powerfully muscled length of his body as he did so, so that she could feel through her skirts the hard evidence of his desire for her. His palms lifted and squeezed her breasts possessively, and despite her apprehension, they soon grew heavy and swollen with passion as he fondled them, his thumbs taunting her nipples into tiny, firm buds furled tight against the fabric that constrained them.

Whimpering, Araminta tried to twist away from him, but Rigo refused to release her, went on kissing and caressing her instead. One hand was at her back now, skillful fingers unlacing the long ribands of her corset until, at last, her stays gave way and he was able to tug the corset from about her slender waist. Casting the ribbed garment upon the ground, he gently turned her around to face him, holding her captive in his arms. But, blushing and quaking with emotion, she would not look at him and clenched her bodice even more tightly to her breast, as though it would offer some defense against him. With a soft, seductive laugh, he pried her fingers from the material and deliberately eased her fallen sleeves from her arms, and her wedding gown tumbled into a heap upon the earth at her feet. Although she attempted to cover herself with her arms, he, with one hand, easily imprisoned them behind her back. She heard his sharp intake of breath as she stood before him, clad only in her underclothes. She felt his dark, glowing eyes upon her avidly, feasting on the breasts that heaved beneath her low-cut camisole, aching to burst forth, their taut, rosy nipples enticingly apparent beneath the translucent cotton they strained against. Slowly, he began one by one to undo the small buttons of her camisole.

"No, please, no . . ." Araminta whispered, her voice catching on a sob, tears starting in her eyes as she once more attempted to free herself, afraid and ashamed that he should make her feel as he did. But he had her wrists locked fast behind her back, and she was powerless to stop him. Closing her lashes, she buried her face against her shoulder, her tears spilling over. "Oh, don't, please, don't . . ."

But he paid no heed to her protests, his fingers expertly working the last button from its hole and then pushing back the edges of her camisole and sliding it down her arms to her wrists so she was left naked to the waist, her bare breasts exposed to his raking gaze. She shivered violently in his embrace, biting her lower lip to keep from crying out as her nipples puckered and grew even harder when the cool dawn wind and Rigo touched them, alternately grasping and kneading them with his fingers and gliding his palm across them in a slow, circular motion that sent warm ripples of pleasure coursing through her. Unwittingly, she moaned again, and his hand moved to the tearstained cheek she had turned away from him, hidden against her shoulder. Compelling her mouth up to his, he kissed her deeply, demandingly, his tongue tasting her tears as he forced her lips to part, invading and pillaging her as he returned to caressing her breasts, his thumb and forefinger capturing, stretching, and rubbing her nipples, heightening the intensity of the tantalizing sensations she experienced as he kissed and stroked her.

His hungry mouth left hers to travel hotly down her throat and the hollow between her breasts. Araminta gasped as his hand cupped one of the soft, engorged mounds, pressing it high, positioning it for his lips, which closed over her nipple greedily, as though he meant to devour it. Waves of rapture spread through her body as Rigo suckled her hard, catching the rigid little bud between his teeth, biting it gently and laving it with his tongue before feverishly searching out its twin and arousing it in the same manner. She could feel a honeyed moisture seeping between her thighs, a slow-burning heat that ached to erupt into fire, and she strained and writhed against him, instinctively seeking easement. But as there had been none last night, no assuagement was forthcoming now, either. Instead, muttering a Spanish profanity, Rigo abruptly released her, his eyes glowing like twin flames, his hands jerking the camisole from her wrists and crushing it spasmodically between his fingers, a muscle working tensely in his jaw.

Startled to her senses, Araminta began to shake and weep again, violently unnerved by this sensuous cat-and-mouse game he played with her. Why did he not just brutally rape her and have done with it? she wondered distraughtly, for she felt she could have borne even that far better than these erotic, loverlike attacks upon her senses. Crossing her arms over her bare breasts to conceal them, she turned away, deeply ashamed of her nakedness, of her seemingly uncontrollable response to him.

"Get dressed!" he ground out hoarsely. "Get dressed *pronto*, before I change my mind and take you here and now, out in the open, upon the hard ground!"

"Why do you not, then—and put an end to this?" she sobbed recklessly, hating him as, nevertheless driven by his threat, she knelt to retrieve the bundle of clothes he had given her earlier; with trembling fingers, she began to untie it.

"Because . . . because that would be too easy."

"I—I don't understand. Wh-wh-what do you mean?"

"Bodies are cheap, Araminta. A man can buy one for the price of a bottle of inferior wine—"

"Or take one by force?" she sniffled contemptuously as she saw to her surprise and wrath that the garments that spilled from the serape she had unwrapped were actually her own. Doubtless they had been stolen from her bedroom by the two desperadoes who had broken into it last night from her balcony and chased her down the corridor to the grand staircase in the great hall of her grandfather's hacienda, where Rigo, spurring his stallion up the steps, had grabbed her and flung her across his saddle.

"Or take one by force, *sí*," he agreed quietly, his gaze distant of a sudden, as though he were beset by some memory—and not a very pleasant one, she thought, curious, for his handsome face was anguished, his mouth grim. But when he again spoke, she felt what she had glimpsed must have been a trick of the early dawn light or of her imagination. He said nothing of whatever had caused his eyes momentarily to be haunted by such dark shadows, but issued a warning instead. "To possess the mind and the heart of a woman . . . well, that is another matter entirely—and those things I will have of you, Araminta, when I make you mine."

"You are mad!" she cried, stricken and more bewildered than ever, for he spoke of things that were given out of love—yet he did not speak of loving her, nor of her loving him; and he could not care for her, not even a little, else he would never have let her wed Judd, she thought. "How could you ever own my mind or heart? I loathe and despise you. And I shall never feel anything other than disgust for you, General! Not now . . . not ever!"

"Then you will be my captive for a very long time, *señora*," he assured her. His face was determined, and his eyes were hard as he stared at her. "I promise you I will not let you go until your betrayal of Judd Hobart is absolute!"

"My—my *betrayal*!" Araminta echoed, horrified, pausing as she drew forth her ruffled ecru silk blouse from the bundle of clothes heaped upon the ground. "Truly, you are indeed mad! No loving husband in his right mind would consider his wife's being abducted and—and *raped* an act of betrayal, General!"

"Rape?" One devilish black brow lifted with mock surprise, and his voice held a note of disdainful amusement that infuriated her. "Naturally, that is what you fear, is it not, *gringuita*? But you need not, for this I swear: When I *do* take you—as I assuredly will in the end—it shall be willingly that you lie in my arms. That is the cold dish of revenge I will serve up to your husband—and he shall find its taste bitter indeed!"

"Revenge? Is that the reason you have stooped so low as to kidnap me—a woman, innocent of the cause of your enmity for my husband and helpless against you—to use me as a pawn in some perverted plot against Judd?" Araminta's voice now dripped with venomous scorn. "Then, you have failed in your purpose, General, for you delude yourself if you think I shall ever willingly yield to you. I shall not! No, not even if you hold a knife to my throat and threaten to kill me will I ever submit to you, for I would rather die than lie with you . . . you—you *swine!* You filthy pig!"

His eyes blazed at that, and his nostrils flared, so she knew how she had enraged him with the invectives she had so rashly spat at him. As his fists tightened whitely on the camisole he still grasped between his fingers, Araminta, afraid that she had pushed him too

far, sprang to her feet and took a hasty step back
from him, her blouse held before her to hide her bare
breasts.

"You speak boldly for a woman at my utter mercy,
señora! You are lucky I do not beat you for those
insults! But you will pay for them later, I promise you.
Now, get dressed—and be quick about it! We have
delayed here overlong as it is."

"I—I need my camisole," she insisted.

"I, however, prefer that you do not wear it." He
smiled at her jeeringly, his eyes glittering as they
swept over her, making his meaning plain: He wanted
as little as possible between her and him.

"You—you *bastard!*" she hissed, not caring if he
did punish her for her insolence.

Deliberately, Araminta turned her back on him once
more and struggled into her blouse, her fingers fumbling at the tiny buttons. Such was her agitation, however, at the thought of his eyes upon her, the sense of
his growing impatience, and her apprehension that
he might decide to "assist" her again that she was
unaccustomedly clumsy at the task. She managed to
get only half the buttons fastened before finally giving
up in frustration and angrily tying the ends of her
blouse into a knot. She had never worn a blouse without her camisole and corset before; and now she was
all too aware of how the silk slid sensuously against
her naked skin, adhered to her body, molded itself
to her breasts, and, with her every movement, caressed
her nipples so that they stiffened and strained against
the soft, clinging fabric. The sensation was unset-
tlingly sinful, electrifying.

Not wanting to dwell on it, Araminta hurriedly divested herself of her layers of petticoats, her cheeks staining crimson at the knowledge that she now stood before Rigo, clad only in her blouse, pantalettes, stockings, and slippers. But then, what did it really matter? she asked herself bitterly. He had already stripped her bare to the waist and kissed and fondled her as no man ever had. Despite herself, her heart raced at the memory of his mouth and hands upon her breasts, of how her nipples had burgeoned beneath his tongue. He had no right to touch her so, she thought with despair, shivering both with fear and a horrible, perfidious excitement at the knowledge that he would do as much again, whenever and however it pleased him, and that there was nothing she could do to prevent it.

Kicking off her slippers, she snatched on the long, divided skirt of her rich brown riding habit, then shrugged into its short, Spanish-cut and -embroidered jacket. After that, she pulled on her leather boots, grateful that the *bandoleros* who had rifled her armoire and chest of drawers had also included her flat-crowned and -brimmed sombrero to protect her from the hot summer sun. The men had even taken her silver-backed hairbrush and comb, with which she rapidly worked the snarls from her hair, plaiting the thick tresses into a single braid and tying it off with one of the pieces of thong that had been knotted around the bundle of garments. Placing the sombrero on her head, she turned back to Rigo, who eyed her approvingly.

"You will be much more comfortable, I am sure, dressed as you are now, *gringuita*," he observed.

Collecting the petticoats and slippers she had shed, he folded them and her camisole and corset up tightly inside her wedding gown, binding the whole with more of the thong. This bundle he secured to the back of his saddle, along with his blanket roll, thereby dashing Araminta's faint hope that he would prove so careless as to leave her discarded clothes behind for her grandfather and Judd to find. She should have known that a man who appeared to have planned every detail of her kidnapping so meticulously, down to the theft of her riding habit and brush and comb, would not overlook something so obvious. Nor did Rigo neglect to retie her wrists before he tossed her, astride, into his saddle and, gathering the reins, mounted behind her.

Araminta shuddered as his arm encircled her body, pulling her close, so that her loose blouse rubbed against her unrestrained breasts, the silk fabric brushing and teasing her nipples. She tried to sit up straight, to stiffen her spine against him. But laughing softly, he simply drew her to him again, his hand beneath her short jacket, this time deliberately caressing her breasts—to chastise her for her small rebellion, she knew—as he set his spurs to his horse's sides, giving a low whistle as he did so. It must have been some sort of a signal, she realized, for in moments, three of his men joined them from behind, where they must have been posted as guards to watch the trail down from the north. Up ahead now, she could see the rest of the desperadoes moving in single file through the canyon, carefully picking their way along the narrow, wending path. The laborious journey was once more under way.

They rode endlessly, all day and half the night or more, and then, as they had before, started out again at dawn the following day—until the succeeding days and nights seemed to melt into one another, turning into a week, and then another, and Araminta lost all track of time, felt as though she had always been Rigo's prisoner. She began to believe that her grandfather and Judd had given up the chase and forsaken her, that she would never know any other life but that of Rigo's captive. Still, because she was young and alive and wanted to survive, she started slowly to adapt to the savage wilderness of Mexico, to the harsh, arid deserts that seemed to stretch to the ends of the earth, to the high, rugged mountains that were like massive spines ridging the land, to the long, grueling hours in the saddle, with the blistering sun beating down upon her relentlessly, and to the frigid nights, when the raw, wild wind blew down from the cold, thin altitudes of the mountains to whip and whine and wail unmercifully through the bluffs and buttes and canyons and across the soaring, sweeping mesas and flat desert plains.

Soon, she forgot what it was to be dry and warm instead of wet from the streams in the arroyos and either scorched by the sun or chilled by the night wind. She no longer remembered a time when she did not ache in every muscle and bone in her body, did not feel so sore and exhausted that she slept almost as soon as she lay down upon the coarse blankets spread upon ground baked as hard as adobe by the sun. She had lost not only all sense of time, but also of direction, and so had no idea where she even was. Sometimes, she believed that they traveled in circles; at others, she was certain that they plodded interminably southwest toward some mysterious destination of which only Rigo was aware.

Now and then, some of the *bandoleros*, in groups of two and three, slipped away, heading in a different direction entirely, as though to muddle and deceive anyone who might be following. Araminta, hopelessly lost and confused, did not see how her grandfather and Judd, if they sought her, could themselves be otherwise. Surely, Rigo and the desperadoes had long since shaken off any pursuit! Yet they continued to lay down false trails, backtrack, ride over rocks and in streams, brush away their tracks, and build no fires in the evening.

As the unremitting days passed, Araminta came to despise the taste of the tough, smoky jerky, though she ate it just the same, knowing that there would be nothing else forthcoming until long after sundown, when Rigo would at last permit them to make camp for the night. Often, before retiring, he would stand motionless in the night, his eyes scrutinizing sharply the moonlit plateaus and sweeping terrain below, his ears cocked, listening intently to the sounds of the night, his nostrils flaring as he inhaled the scents upon the wind. The *bandoleros* joked that he could smell the spoor of a mountain lion a mile away, but for all their laughter, Araminta noticed that they respected and heeded his sixth sense for danger, as though his uncanny instincts had kept them alive on more than one occasion.

Twice he bade them quietly but sharply to be silent,

and they heard in the distance the passing of men and horses—Federales or Rurales, Yaqui Indians, or some other danger; and so, although the travelers might conceivably have been her grandfather and Judd, Araminta did not dare to risk crying out, not only because she did not know who her screams would bring down upon her and the desperadoes, but also because Rigo clapped his hand over her mouth and actually held his knife to her throat to keep her still. He would slit her throat, she thought desperately, rather than allow her to endanger his men, who were wholeheartedly loyal to him—as she was not.

Deeply distressed by her shameless, wanton response to him, his diabolic means of revenging himself on Judd, she fought and resisted Rigo at every opportunity, fearing that, otherwise, she would surely in the end be utterly lost to him, as he intended. She had never in her life—not even in New York City—felt so helpless. She was dependent upon him for her every need, the food she ate, the clothes on her back, her safety and well-being, even her very life; and so, though she often told herself that she hated him, she discovered herself, as the weeks continued to slip by, sometimes actually forgetting that he was her captor, finding herself inexplicably but inexorably drawn to him as her protector instead. No more than she understood the irrepressible passion he aroused in her body did she understand the strange response he evoked in her mind. She did not know that she suffered from what, decades later, would be widely recognized as a classic syndrome born of being held hostage and strengthened by her unfathomable but undeniable fascination with him before the abduction. She knew only that, gradually, she grew accustomed to, accepting of, and—God help her—even longed for and welcomed the touch of Rigo's hands upon her, tying and untying the rope about her wrists, chafing them vigorously to restore their circulation, lifting her in and out of the saddle, holding and caressing her as they rode ceaselessly on day after day or when she lay next to him upon his blankets at night and he continued his ruthless, tantalizing onslaughts upon her body and senses.

It was indecent . . . what he did to her with his mouth and hands, she told herself over and over, as though trying to convince herself of that fact. He kissed her as though he meant to go on kissing her forever, to drain the very life and soul from her body and then pour it back in, his tongue tracing the outline of her lips before parting them and plunging deep to plunder relentlessly the dark, moist recesses, the sweetness and secrets within. And all the while, his hands moved on her, undoing one by one the buttons of her silk blouse, untying the knot in which she continued to secure the ends—because it was easier and more comfortable that way—and pushing aside the blouse's edges to reveal to him her naked breasts, which he fondled and suckled as though he were her lover, her husband, and it were his right. Unbuttoning his own shirt, he would draw her close against his bare chest, so she could feel the dark hair matted there, like velvet beneath her palms and against the sensitive tips of her breasts, and feel also the pounding of his heart against her own, a feeling so intimate that she was beset by longing and turmoil. Sometimes, he would compel her to press her mouth to his chest, to kiss his flesh salty with earthy sweat from the searing sun and the desert wind, and the taste of him was as heady as summer wine upon her tongue. It was as though he were the very elements themselves, she thought, fierce, merciless, crumbling her maidenly defenses against him as surely and savagely as the rushing mountain streams swept down from their snowcapped pinnacles to change and shape the land.

Years afterward, whenever Araminta remembered the bittersweet interlude of those endless days of summer in Mexico, she was never to see it clearly, only as though reflected by a smoky mirror, dark, diffused, and misty-edged. She seemed to live those days—and nights—in a perpetual daze, as though they were a dream from which she could not awaken and, finally, inevitably, did not want to awaken. Again and again, she told herself, and Rigo too, that she hated him—and in her heart, she hated him all the more for making her feel as though perhaps she did not really hate him at all, that, in truth, some terrible, treacherous part of her wanted him, had always wanted him and was destined, inescapably, to yield to him, as he intended. He had wakened her traitorous young body to passion, whetting her appetite and then deliberately, cruelly, refusing to satisfy her hunger, so that, sometimes, she believed she would grow mad from his sweet, savage torment of her. During drowsy, prolonged nights, he pulled her down beside him beneath his blankets and erotically teased and taunted her until, despite herself, she prayed for him to take her and sate her agonized yearning. Then there were the vibrant, feverish nights when, long after she had fallen asleep, he roused and excited her with brutal, insistent kisses, his hands roaming hotly, urgently, over her body as he lay atop her, his weight pressing her down upon the hard ground, torturing her with what he determinedly continued to deny her.

How Rigo kept himself in check, Araminta did not know; she could not even begin to imagine what it cost him to restrain himself when, more than anything, he coveted and craved her, wanted to take her and make her his. But true to his word, he did not—and worse, she knew that he would not until she asked him, begged him to possess her, body and soul, thereby betraying Judd, her husband, whom she had not loved, had not wanted, and whose face she sometimes now could scarcely even recall. Yet she was his wife; she had stood beneath a white canopy in the courtyard of the High Sierra and vowed to love, honor, and obey him; and if she had nothing more to give him than her loyalty, she owed him that much at least. She did not know what Judd had done to earn Rigo's enmity, so bitter and obsessive that it had driven him to the crimes he committed against her. This, Rigo refused to tell her, stilling with his lips and hands her questions, waiting for what he most wanted to hear, the words of surrender she would not speak. Her silence left them each aching, unfulfilled—and goaded Rigo into taking even further liberties with her body, heightening both her desire and shame.

Torpid with desire and lack of sleep, Araminta grew increasingly oblivious of all but Rigo. There was not a time when she was not painfully, passionately, aware of him, of how he watched her constantly, hungrily, a queer, eager, haunted expression in his smoky-quartz eyes when he thought she did not see, an expression that bewildered her, for no man had ever looked at her like that before. But when he spied her staring back at him, his eyelids invariably swept down to shutter his gaze, she could not guess his thoughts and was filled with an odd dismay that she could not. If only she knew what that expression meant, she felt strangely somehow that all would be changed between them. But then, as though he had read her mind, Rigo would rake her salaciously with his eyes, in a way that brought a blush to her cheeks and made her heart beat fast as she thought of what would happen later, when she lay in his arms. Then he would smile at her sardonically, so that her fingers itched to slap the smirk from his face, and she felt certain all over again that she hated him vehemently—and hated herself even more for ever having been such a fool as to believe him better than what he was.

Chapter Thirteen

Velvet Hobart was more frightened than she had ever been in her life. What had started out as a thrilling, dangerous escapade had, on her brother Judd's wedding night, suddenly turned deadly when the High Sierra had been attacked and Judd's bride, Araminta, had been abducted by the infamous General Rigo del Castillo. Velvet quaked in her slippers every time she dwelled on it, for if Judd ever learned what she had done, he would kill her. How she had repeatedly slipped away from the Chaparral to rendezvous with Rigo, her lover. How it had been from her own foolish, pouting lips, seductively plundered by Rigo, that the general had garnered much of his knowledge of the Texas ranchers upon whom he and his men preyed. And worst of all, how she had unthinkingly betrayed to him all the intimate details of the forthcoming wedding at the High Sierra, so that he had known exactly when, where, and how to strike.

Velvet had not known that Rigo planned to kidnap Araminta, and despite her fear that her affair with him would now somehow be exposed, she was more than annoyed that it *was* Araminta he had stolen instead of her—not that she had ever harbored any illusions about him. As marriage material, he had been wholly unacceptable, of course, a bastard and a brigand and far beneath her socially. He had never been anything more to her than an exciting challenge, a forbidden thrill, someone with whom she had amused and indulged herself to relieve the tedium of her days. Like Judd, Velvet relished walking on the wild side of life and deeply resented the freedoms that her brother enjoyed and that she, as a woman, was denied. She could run the Chaparral as well as Judd if she had a mind to—but was she to have any share in it? No, it was all to go to Judd! If she wanted anything out of life, she must get it from a husband. Meanwhile, Velvet chafed at the restraints placed upon her by both her family and society.

Rigo had not been her first lover—she had lost her virginity some time ago to Judd's best friend, her fiancé, Cole Parker, a selfish boor but quite rich, and a man whom she eventually did plan to wed. But Rigo *had* been a lover of extraordinary skill, even though he had treated her as casually and contemptuously as she had him, a novel experience for her, who was used to seeing men groveling at her feet. Of late, however, Rigo really had begun to pall, Velvet was forced to admit. He had spent less and less time with her, and when he had shown up, he had appeared curiously more interested in Judd and Araminta's romance than in her. Now, of course, Velvet knew why: He had been planning to abduct Judd's bride!

Velvet shuddered at the memory of her brother's violent rage that evening, when he had learned the purpose of the *bandoleros'* attack on the High Sierra. He had been angry enough to commit murder, and the thought of his finding out the part she had, however unwittingly, played in the debacle had stricken her to the core. She did not forget the time just a year and a half ago when she had accidentally lamed Judd's favorite horse by forcing it over a jump that had proved too high for it to clear safely. Upon spying her leading the limping stallion into the stables, Judd had grown so furious that he had grabbed her viciously and, placing his hands about her throat, choking her, had beaten her head so hard against the barn door that it was a wonder he had not killed her! She was certain that only the intervention of several of the ranch hands who had dragged him away from her had prevented him from throttling her or smashing in her skull.

Shocked and incensed by Judd's assault on her, she had thought she would even the score between them by having a fling with his worst enemy, Rigo, while all the time she was engaged to Judd's best friend, Cole. She had laughed up her sleeve at Judd, secretly delighting in how livid and horrified he would be if he ever found out how his sister had cuckolded his best friend!

The night of the fire at the Chaparral was when

Velvet had first uneasily started to suspect that Rigo's interest in her stemmed more from all the information he obtained from her than her own charms. She had not even been aware of how she was inadvertently assisting him in his forays upon the Texas ranchers. Now she knew for certain that Rigo had indeed used her, and for that reason, she bitterly regretted throwing herself at him as she had.

She had never dreamed that her revenge on her brother would result in the kidnapping of his wife; and now, despite the fact that deep down inside, she felt that it served him right, Velvet was terrified of his unearthing the truth. If Judd would commit such violence against her over his stallion, what might he do to her over his bride?

Beneath the brim of his western hat, Judd Hobart shaded his eyes against the glare of the sun to get a better look at the land spreading out before him and the rest of the mounted men who accompanied him and Noble Winthrop. It was hopeless, Judd thought; they were embarked upon a wild-goose chase. They had lost the trail days ago, and there was scant chance now of their picking it up again—thank God! he added to himself.

The deeper into Mexico they progressed, the more dangerous it grew, the more likely it became that they would be killed by *bandoleros* or Revolutionaries or even Federales or Rurales. The Federal irregulars, especially, known as the *colorados* because of their custom of riding with a red flag and because their hands were red with bloodshed, were spectacularly vicious.

Under General Pascual Orozco—who had turned traitor to the Revolution—they had swept through northern Mexico, burning, sacking, and looting from the poor. In Chihuahua, it was said that they had sliced the soles off the feet of a man and herded him a mile across the desert before he had finally died. It was claimed that a city of four thousand people was left with only five inhabitants still alive after the *colorados* had finished with it. When a *colorado* was captured by General Francisco "Pancho" Villa and his rapidly burgeoning army, he died at their hands.

All over Mexico, railroad and telegraph services were disrupted. In the north, in Sonora, Chihuahua, Coahuila, and Durango, not only the estates of the rich Mexican *hacendados* were gradually being seized by the Revolutionaries—many acting without authority from the División del Norte to do so, in Villa's name—but also the estates of the equally wealthy Americans who had settled in Mexico over the years. In the south, the Zapatistas continued to hold sway, fighting to advance toward the capital, Mexico City, and forcing the splitting of the government troops to battle ongoing assaults on two fronts. At the border, Americans were informed that if they dared to enter Mexico, they would be arrested, stood against a wall, and executed by a firing squad. Refugees crossing the border from Mexico into the United States were detained and checked by customs inspectors to be certain they were not smuggling contraband into the country, and many retreating Mexican troops and deserters were rounded up by American soldiers under the command of Colonel John Pershing, herded like cattle into a corral, and afterward incarcerated in a barbed-wire stockade at Fort Bliss, Texas.

Since the assassination of President Madero, anti-American sentiment in Mexico had grown by leaps and bounds, due in large part to the participation of Henry Lane Wilson, the American ambassador to Mexico, in the Pacto de la Embajada—the Embassy Pact—the agreement plotted between Huerta, Díaz, and Wilson to overthrow the Mexican government and seize power. Wilson had later denied any involvement in the scheme, calling his accusers "immature Mexicans" and the "emotional Latin race," which had only exacerbated the already strained relations between the United States and Mexico.

Anti-American ditties were sung everywhere, such as the two Judd had overheard just a few days ago being warbled by some peasants working in a field:

The gringos all are fools,
They've never been in Sonora,
And when they want to say: "Diez Reales,"
They call it "Dollar an' a quarta'. . . ."

and,

Yo tengo una pistola
Con mango de marfil
Para matar todos los gringos
Que vienen por ferrocarril!

(I have a pistol
With an ivory handle

With which to kill all the Americans
Who come by railroad!)

It was the height of foolhardiness, Judd thought angrily and apprehensively, that Noble had insisted they ford the Rio Grande into Mexico. Once they had seen where Del Castillo was headed, they should have turned back to the High Sierra. There, they could have waited comfortably for the ransom note to be delivered and, in El Paso, posted a reward for Araminta's safe return, as well as hired professional mercenaries to retrieve her—not that Judd hoped that any such actions, if taken, would prove fruitful.

But instead, after ordering half their men to ride to a nearby border town and directing them to obtain all provisions necessary for a prolonged trek, then catch up with the others, Noble had determinedly led the rest across the river. Fortunately, that wily, arrogant bastard Del Castillo had crossed into Mexico at a point where the border patrol on both sides was thinly scattered—and probably sleeping off the effects of too much pulque or sotol, besides, Judd had reflected with grim disgust.

Much as Araminta's abduction on their wedding night had infuriated and dishonored him, it had nevertheless been his opinion right from the start that his and Noble's chasing after her was a complete waste of time. It was indeed too bad about Araminta's fate, Judd had mused with a pang of regret for her loss and for the fact that he had been cheated of divesting her of her virginity; for that, he certainly intended to make Del Castillo pay sooner or later. But as for Araminta herself . . . well, after all the degradation she was sure to suffer at the hands of Del Castillo and the desperadoes who followed him, Judd just didn't see how he could be expected to welcome her back with wide-open arms. What man wanted a wife who had been thoroughly and shamefully used by a pack of filthy Mexican bandits—and that before he had even had her himself? No, it was just too much for any man—especially one of his riches and social standing—to swallow, Judd thought sourly.

But when he had tried in a roundabout way to make all this known to Noble, the older man had turned to him, mottled with rage and appearing to be seized by an apoplectic fit, so crazy had been the look in his eyes, the way in which spittle had flown from his lips when he had spoken.

"You shut your goddamned mouth right now, Judd!" Noble had spat. "And you keep it shut! We both know why that son of a bitch Del Castillo has kidnapped my granddaughter—and that you're to blame! And that's why, so help me God, you're going to take her back and stand behind her, no matter what that bastard's done to her, because if you don't, I'm warning you: I'll advise Araminta to divorce you, and I'll drag your name through the courts and the mud, and then I'll cut you off from the High Sierra. You may be my godson and your daddy may be my best friend, but I'll see you and the Chaparral ruined before I'm dead and gone, I swear! Do you get my drift, boy?"

"Loud and clear . . . sir," Judd had choked out, fuming.

How had Noble dared to speak to him so? He had

had no right, no right at all. And to insist upon Judd's holding his head up, pretending that a bunch of foul Mexican bandits hadn't lifted his wife's skirts and violated her in every sordid way possible . . . well, it was just too much to be borne—and he wasn't about to bear it! He wasn't about to don the horns of a cuckold for every other blueblooded young buck in Texas to smirk at and joke about behind his back! Before he let that happen, he would see Araminta dead.

Now, he turned in his saddle to Noble, eyeing with a certain amount of mean-spirited satisfaction the toll that their hard journey had taken on the older man. Noble was no longer young, and the endless days in the saddle had exacerbated his gout, crippling him so that at night, it took two ranch hands to maneuver him off his horse and assist him to a sitting position on the ground. Beneath his tan, his lined, weathered face was pale and drawn with pain. Judd did not think that Noble, no matter how stubborn, was in any physical shape to continue to argue with him about going home. Nor did Judd believe that, this time, the ranch hands would remain silent, refusing to back him up when he insisted upon returning to Texas. The trip had become much too dangerous; they were too far into Mexico to feel safe any longer.

"We've lost the trail, Noble"—Judd's face was set, his voice grim—"and we've no hope of finding it again. Del Castillo and his men have covered their tracks too well for that; and now that the *bandoleros* have begun to split up, we can't even be certain which way to go, even if there *were* signs enough for us to follow—which there just flat out ain't."

"Araminta's riding double with Del Castillo; we know that from his horse's hoofprints. . . ." Noble protested—but feebly, as though even he had finally realized that there was little hope of rescuing his granddaughter.

Frowning, Judd shook his head.

"We can't even be sure of that anymore. The son of a bitch is clever, I'll give him that. He might have traded mounts with two of his men, have them doubled up on his own horse just to confuse us, or maybe not—and what's more, you know it, Noble. You've got to face it: We're not going to recover Araminta this way. Our supplies are running low. We're liable to be ambushed and executed by Federales or Rurales or Revolutionaries at any moment. We've got to turn back. We've got to go home."

In the end, swayed by the sullen faces of the ranch hands, Judd's irrefutable logic, and his own growing pain, Noble was reluctantly forced to agree with his godson—though it galled him not to have succeeded in rescuing his granddaughter, to have to admit defeat at Del Castillo's hands. When Noble dwelled on what Araminta must endure, he was filled with fear and fury, for it was too much to hope that Del Castillo would play the part of a gentleman and that she would be returned to them as chaste as she had been when abducted.

Noble could feel his dream of founding a dynasty through his granddaughter and godson slipping, like sand in an hourglass, through his fingers. Judd did not want Araminta back—not now, Noble knew; the younger man had far too much hubris to take a sullied bride to his bed. He no longer cared if Araminta lived or died. If something were to happen to Noble, Judd would not lift a finger to retrieve her. It was up to Noble to ensure his granddaughter's safe deliverance. He realized uneasily, disliking the idea that he could no longer trust and depend on his godson and, from here on out, must be on his guard against him. Judd was not only unscrupulous, but also hotheaded, prone to permitting his temper to prevail over common sense.

Adding to Noble's worry was the fact that between the shock he had suffered over Araminta's kidnapping and the arduous journey he had undertaken in the attempt to reclaim her, he had recently begun to experience, in reality, the kind of sudden, agonizing pains in his chest that he had only pretended before to pressure his granddaughter into wedding Judd. Noble feared that the recent stress to which he had been subjected had taken its toll, that his heart was acting up as a result, though he had done his best to conceal his infirmity.

"All right, Judd," he growled at last. "We'll do it your way for now. Let's go home."

With difficulty the younger man repressed the triumphant smile that threatened to curve his lips. He had won the battle. Much as he longed to do so, there really was no point in rubbing it in and outraging Noble further—perhaps even goading him into changing his will yet again before he croaked, which would not suit Judd at all; for it had come to him these last several days that Noble was no longer an asset, but a liability. With Noble dead, Judd would not only inherit the High Sierra but could also divest himself without hindrance of his defiled wife. All he need do to bring about both objects was to bide his time and to wait for his chance to get rid of his decrepit godfather. It was a long way home, through hostile country. Anything could happen; anything could go wrong. Why, poor Noble might even lose his life.

Chapter Fourteen

The more she saw of Mexico, the more Araminta came to understand why the peasants had risen up in revolt against the dictatorial government; the wealthy *hacendados* who had claimed the best and richest land as far as the eye could see had left to the peons only terrain that was so harsh and inhospitable that even months of toil upon it seldom produced enough to fill all the hungry mouths of the poor families who eked out their existence there. Both the Mexican and Indian villages at which Rigo and the *bandoleros* stopped now and then for supplies were nothing more than a handful of crumbling adobe huts straggling along a lone, dry, dusty main road. At the center of each village square a single well provided water—sometimes not enough for all, and never enough for the meager crops stunted from thirst, withered from the unrelenting hot sun that parched the land. Everything that grew upon it was twisted and tortured by the elements; even the native trees and brush were sparse and scraggly, beaten and broken by the brutal wind and sand that scoured all in their path.

Only in the rolling foothills, the mammoth bluffs, and the solitary buttes, where the pines and the deciduous trees began to thicken, and, beyond these, in the massive mountains that cut a jagged oblique against the startlingly blue horizon, was there refuge from the interminable heat, the arid wind, the endless scrubland, the scorched prairie grass, the sweeping desert dunes. But in the rocky crags, there was no place to grow crops, though, occasionally, Araminta spied a handful of sheep or goats. These were as scrawny as the few cattle and pigs and chickens in the villages, animals as hungry as their masters and tough and stringy when butchered, but they were a feast all the same to those who knew no better, had nothing more. Araminta had never witnessed such poverty, such hopelessness, and, worst of all, such fear.

It was everywhere—in the wrinkled, weathered faces of the old men and women, who remembered Benito Juárez and another war, against the Emperor Maximilian; in the dark, solemn eyes of the children, who were still and silent when the desperadoes came. Of young men and women, there were but few. Most of the young men were dead, or gone as soldiers to one side or the other. The young women were in hiding, fearful of being discovered and dragged out and raped by all those who had, one way or another, taken their young men. Even the gaunt dogs did not bark at strangers, but whined and skulked away, their tails tucked between their legs. Only the chickens cackled loudly at interlopers, flapping their wings furiously, before they fluttered hastily from the path of trampling hooves.

Into these quiet, isolated villages Rigo and the *bandoleros* intruded, no one more aware than Araminta of the frightening picture they presented, bristling with weapons—rifles, carbines, shotguns, pistols, machetes, and knives—and with bullet-packed bandoliers crossed over their chests. She, herself, was an emblem of terror, mounted before Rigo on his prancing black stallion, her hair shining golden in the sun. It was obvious from her wrists, which he continued to keep tied while they traveled as a precaution against her running away, that she was his prisoner. But no one ever stepped forward to question him about her, much less to help her to escape. Instead, through the cracks and knotholes of tightly closed wooden shutters, unfamiliar dark eyes peered out at her flatly, with only an infrequent glimmer of curiosity. Such was the state of civil unrest in the country that even the capture of a *gringa* was little cause for comment. It was no doubt assumed, she thought, that she belonged to one of the vast, American-owned estates seized by the Revolutionaries and had been taken because she had committed some crime or simply because the desperadoes had desired some amusement. After all, was not this last the fate of poor Mexican and Indian women every day? Was this not why they must conceal themselves even from their own kind and in their own villages?

Unlike many men who came to the villages, Rigo at least paid for what he took—not in gold, which would have aroused suspicion if found in the villagers' possession, but in simple *reales* and *centavos*, which could be more easily explained. Wherever he went, he was known if not by sight, then by reputation. More than once, Araminta saw respect and a quickly masked flicker of fear in the eyes of the villagers when they learned his rank and name, General del Castillo; often, she heard him referred to as El Salvaje—the Savage One—perhaps reason enough for the villagers to ignore her plight. Still, although there was little chance of her escaping, she felt cheered whenever Rigo led the *bandoleros* into a village, for it meant that if nothing more, she would at least have a proper bath and a change of fresh clothes when he would borrow something from a peasant woman for Araminta to wear while she washed and dried her own riding habit. Sometimes they stayed for a few days in a village and she could rest from travel.

More than anything else about the hard life she now endured, Araminta hated the gritty red-gold dust that was a constant irritant, streaking her hair, smudging her skin, and coating her garments. Sometimes, she felt as though she would never be clean again, and she looked forward to the times when she could immerse her whole body in an old wooden washtub full of hot water. The fact that Rigo invariably watched her and touched her had ceased to matter. She hardly ever even fought him anymore, so accustomed had she grown to the feel of his eyes, his mouth, and his hands upon her, taunting and arousing her, despite herself—and leaving her maddened and unfulfilled. In some dim corner of her mind, she had accepted the fact that there was no escape for her from him or her fate, that, sooner or later, he would inevitably wear down her last vestiges of resistance and she would yield to him. Now, only her heart, yearning for some word of caring or tenderness, cried out in protest when he took her in his arms at night to teach her the lessons he would have her learn. Even so, Araminta knew that she would be glad in a way when he finally claimed her as his and this torturous game he played with her was ended.

At least then it would be over, and Rigo would let her go—but back to what, she did not know. She had had much time to think on her unexpected journey, and gradually, she had come to feel certain that Judd no longer wanted her—if he ever had. He did not love her, and he had far too much pride to take back a bride tarnished by another man. If he had even bothered to look for her, he must have long since given up the chase and returned home, writing her off as a lost cause—or dead. Judd had no real need of her now; doubtless it would be very convenient for him if she lay in her grave. He would be spared the embarrassment of a sullied wife and, still, having done as her grandfather had wished and married her, be assured of inheriting the High Sierra. No, even if Rigo released her, she could not go back to her husband, Araminta had miserably concluded. She must go away to someplace where she and the story of her scandalous abduction were unknown. Where she would go, how she would live, she did not know; so she tried not to think about her uncertain future, only of surviving until it came.

In those first few days after Rigo had kidnapped her, she had thought she would die; some part of her had *wanted* to die. Any other decent white woman in her situation would have killed herself, she knew, rather than submit to her shame. But another part of her that was even stronger than her longing for death had driven her to live, no matter what—and she drew courage from this inner well of strength and conviction. It was as though the Araminta who had existed before her abduction had vanished and another woman had taken her place.

Sometimes, gazing into a cracked, smoky mirror hanging on a wall in a village hut, she would need moments to recognize the woman staring back at her, to realize that this was her own reflection. She had grown thinner from the strenuous life upon the trail, eating on the run, camping out in the open. Her wide, slanted green eyes and high cheekbones were cast into relief by her loss of weight, giving her piquant face an earthy yet fey appearance, as though she were a wild gypsy. The wakened, wanton woman with her loose tangle of long, sun-gilded hair, her smoldering, sloe eyes, and her lush, provocative lips could not possibly be herself, she would think as though in a dream. And then she would spy Rigo standing behind her, a dark, predatory shadow in the mirror, that peculiar light in his eyes, a lazy, triumphant smile curving his mouth as his hands slid around her body to cradle her breasts possessively as he pressed his lips to that sensitive place where her nape joined her shoulder; and she would know, down to the very marrow of her bones, that the woman was no fantasy, but real, her own self, not only captured, but also inexplicably but undeniably enslaved by the man who held her prisoner in his arms.

Although he had kidnapped her and treated her as no gentleman would have, there were times when Araminta saw flashes of the man who had conversed with her on the creek bank, when, almost, she could close her eyes and let the sound of his smooth, seductive voice sweep over her and imagine that she was home again, had stolen away of an early morning dawn to meet him. Curious, how she ached so at those times that she felt like weeping, and how the strange closeness they shared then was so unbearable to her that she wished he were not kind to her in his own hard fashion, so it would have been easier to go on hating and defying him.

Her resolve to hold out against him nearly broke entirely the day he came to her, carrying a sketch pad, journal, and pencils, which he pressed into her hands, saying:

"You will draw. You will write what you see, Araminta—alias A. K. Munroe. And I will, in your pen name, dispatch your stories to Liam O'Grady at the *Record* in New York City. Ah, you are surprised that I know of your recent publications in that newspaper. But you see, *gringuita*, I have made it my business to know everything about you."

Of course, she had known that Rigo and his men had spied on her; he could not have planned her abduction so meticulously otherwise. But she had thought the sale of her first article, followed by others in the past months, a secret she had managed successfully to keep. That, even if he was motivated by his own reasons, Rigo actually wanted her to continue her career, she could not help but contrast with her grandfather's and then Judd's attitude about a woman's place. Soon, pictures of Rigo, the *bandoleros*, the villages, and their Mexican and Indian inhabitants began to fill her sketch pad, and words, her journal, as she detailed the story of the Mexican Revolution from a viewpoint that was both close up and personal, concentrating not so much on the war as on those fighting it.

"Full Circle" recounted the moving saga of an old man who, in his youth, had fought for freedom and Benito Juárez against the foreign Emperor Maximilian, and now had lived to see his country devastated yet again by a war in freedom's name. "A House Divided" told the tragic tale of a mother of two sons, one a member of the Federales, the other a Villista, neither knowing if he would someday meet his brother on a battlefield and be forced to kill him, the mother torn between her equally beloved sons. "What Price Freedom?" described the life of a little boy, Miguelito, orphaned when his father was killed by the *colorados* and his mother dragged away to serve as their whore. "Cry Havoc!" was a profound piece on Rigo himself and the men—the "dogs of war"—who followed him.

What Rigo thought of these articles and the charcoal sketches that accompanied them, Araminta did not ask; nor did he volunteer to tell her. He perused them mutely, his face impassive, then folded them up to be mailed, she presumed, to the *Record*. But never did his silent scrutiny persuade her to write other than the truth as she saw it, to slant her words, or to soften her pictures if they cast him or the Revolutionaries in a harsh, unflattering light. Nor, upon seeing this, did he demand that she edit her articles and censor her sketches to portray himself or his allies more favorably.

Araminta did not know if her stories and pictures even reached Liam O'Grady, much less if he published them, Mexico was in such a state of upheaval. But still, she wrote and drew almost feverishly, as though compelled by some unknown force to capture the Mexican Revolution and Rigo, as they had captured her. It was as though perhaps in this way, she could finally come to understand it—and him. For there were other sketches that she did not show him, pictures she drew when she felt confident that he was not aware of her studying him, images of him and self-portraits and pictures of them together that when she examined them more closely exposed to her aspects of their relationship that she did not wish to see. There were sketches of them mounted on Rigo's stallion, of them battling over a chessboard in the evenings, and of him teaching her by the light of a campfire to play the guitar he had bought from some peasant. One especially troubling portrait was of her own reflection in a mirror, with Rigo standing behind her, embracing her. They looked like lovers caught in an unguarded moment, Araminta thought when she inspected the picture later, and she shoved it beneath all the rest, her heart pounding queerly in her breast. The sketch was far too personal,

too revealing; she ought to destroy it, she told herself.
But for some unfathomable reason, she could not bring
herself to tear it up and throw it away.

After countless weeks they came at last to what
Araminta knew instinctively was Rigo's destination,
the hideout of the desperadoes. As her heart sank at
the sight, she realized that, incredibly, right up until
this moment, she had half hoped she might still somehow escape. But there would be no fleeing from this
place—even had she had somewhere to run.

They had ridden since dawn's early light, wending
their way from the inevitable scrubland into the high,
sprawling bluffs that rose in rich shades of ocher and
umber to the southwest, against the infinite turquoise
sky. They had followed a trail so narrow and steep as
it dipped and swelled that Araminta would have
guessed it impassable by even a mountain goat. Yet
somehow, they stuck to it, walking and leading the
horses when necessary through the towering walls of
rock that closed in on them from all sides, shutting
them off from the rest of the world. Eventually, the
stony, twisting track spilled suddenly into a surpris-
ingly wide canyon deep in the heart of the bluffs and
through which a stream lined with a few trees and
clumps of brush gurgled. Built into the naturally tiered
walls of the canyon were a series of adobe huts, with
small, rocky paths twining up to them. At one end was
a corral, in which several prime horses were penned,
and another narrow, serpentine trail snaking back into
the bluffs. Even Araminta could see what an easily
defensible place it was; a single man posted at either
end of the canyon could fend off numerous attackers.

At the approach of the *bandoleros*, other men and women and children came running to meet them. All the men, several clearly longtime friends, shouted out greetings and clapped one another on the back. Arms outstretched, husbands and wives and sweethearts openly kissed and embraced. Children squealed with delight and laughter as they were seized and hugged and hoisted onto their fathers' shoulders, while older youngsters skipped alongside, some proudly leading toward the corral the desperadoes' horses that had been entrusted to their care. As she watched the families' happy reunions, Araminta was struck by a sudden pang, a sense of wistfulness and isolation that she should be an onlooker instead of a participant in the joyful scene. This was the first time since Rigo had carried her into Mexico that she had witnessed the natural high spirits and expressiveness of the country's people, and she was drawn by it.

But after lifting her down from his saddle, Rigo led her not toward the others, but toward one of the adobe huts on the first tier above the canyon floor, not far from the arroyo. Inside, Araminta saw that the crude structure was small, consisting of only a single common room that served as kitchen, dining, and living room, and, to the rear, a bedroom visible beyond the rough curtain drawn to one side of the open doorway between the two cubicles. The furniture was simple and primitive, hewn of rough timber. In the eating area, there was a large plank table, with benches on either side, while the living area consisted of a settee, two chairs, a rocker, and a few smaller tables. Beyond, in the bedroom, were a rope-slung bed and night table;

a dresser with a mirror hanging above and, on the top, a basin and pitcher; and, in one corner, a chair. There was a modest fireplace in the kitchen, for cooking, and a larger hearth in the living area, for warmth. A mixture of woven Mexican and Indian rugs lay upon the adobe floors. Coarse curtains hung at the tiny, glassless windows with hinged wooden exterior shutters that could be drawn inward for closure against the elements—and gunfire. Although its occupant was General del Castillo, the hut was no more luxurious than the other similar buildings that Araminta had observed outside.

Still, it would be better than camping in the open and sleeping on the hard ground, she thought. Then she shivered as, of a sudden, it dawned on her that she would surely share this hut with Rigo, that here, for the first time since he had taken her from the High Sierra, she would be totally alone with him, without the other *bandoleros* sleeping just a few yards away, perhaps dissuading him from fully completing his loverlike assaults on her body and senses. The solitary bed abruptly loomed large and meaningful and threatening in her mind. Who would hear them now if, in that bed, Rigo chose to demand of her what she continued desperately to withhold from him? Who would hear her cries of fright—or, worse, of surrender? For how long could she go on deceiving herself, telling herself that she did not want him, when, in her heart, she knew that some part of her *did* want him? That only her sense of pride and a deep, as yet unacknowledged longing for more than what he offered had thus far prevented her capitulation?

At the thought, she bit her lower lip to still its sudden trembling, mutely holding out her bound wrists as she saw Rigo draw the knife at his waist and understood that he intended to cut the rope that hampered her hands' freedom of movement. The sharp steel sliced easily through the hemp; reflexively, she began to chafe her wrists to restore their circulation as he slid the blade back into its sheath.

"You will be glad to learn that it will no longer be necessary to keep you tied up." His voice was low, as smooth as warm molasses melting in her ears. Lingeringly, his dark-brown eyes swept over the length of her body, then met and held her own gaze intently, hypnotically. "There is no escape for you here, Araminta."

His softly spoken words, with their potent double meaning, seemed to hang in the suddenly highly charged air between them. Her green eyes widened. Her fair face drained of color, then gradually pinkened with the blush that slowly stained her cheeks. No longer able to go on meeting his stare, she glanced away, her thick, sooty lashes fluttering down like the wings of a butterfly to veil her gaze, to conceal her thoughts from him, who was so curiously adept at reading them.

"You will want to bathe, I know," he said. "I will see to the arrangements."

Rigo left her then, returning shortly afterward with two burly men, who lugged between them an old wooden washtub, such as was common in the villages she had seen. Rigo himself bore clean garments for her, a rough towel and washcloth, and a bar of coarse soap, which he laid on the dining table. After depositing the washtub on the floor of the kitchen, one of the two men who accompanied him began to build a fire in the kitchen hearth, while the other brought in buckets of water from the arroyo, pouring them into two cast-iron caldrons, for heating over the blaze. Then, having ascertained that Araminta had everything she needed, Rigo and the two men departed, Rigo informing her that he would be back later.

Once they had gone, she took closer stock of her surroundings. Rigo must somehow have sent word of their arrival to the canyon, she thought, for the kitchen was provisioned with fresh supplies, and the sheets on the bed, though worn and mended, had been recently laundered and smelled pleasantly of the hot summer sun in which they had dried. In Rigo's saddlebags Araminta located her hairbrush, which she carried with her back into the kitchen. Seeing that the water for her bath had started to boil, she found a potholder, with which she removed the two kettles from the fire, emptying their contents into the washtub, then pouring in the cold water that remained in the buckets, to bring her bath to an agreeably warm temperature. She closed the front door, drew the curtains at the windows, undressed, then slowly lowered herself into the washtub, sighing with enjoyment as the still faintly steaming water engulfed her. Reveling in the heavenly sensation of submerging and soaking her body in the water, its warmth penetrating and relieving her sore muscles, she laved herself leisurely with the bar of soap and scrubbed herself all over with the washcloth, then lathered and rinsed her hair. Only the lengthening shadows cast on the floor by the diffuse sunlight filtering in through the loosely woven curtains, warning her that the afternoon grew late, prompted her finally and reluctantly to step from the washtub.

She put on the peasant clothes—a loose, scooped-neck blouse with short, off-the-shoulder sleeves, and a full, ruffled skirt—that Rigo had left behind. Then she washed her own riding habit and, discovering some pegs in the wall by the fire, hung it up to dry. After that, she took up her brush and began patiently to work the snarls from her hair. She had completed her toilette not a moment too soon, she told herself, her heart pounding, as the front door swung slowly open to reveal Rigo standing there, a tall, dark silhouette against the setting sun.

It seemed that he, too, had bathed, for he was naked to the waist, his muscular bronze chest, matted with fine dark hair, still glistening from his ablutions. Living on the run, he had ceased to cut his hair, and now Araminta realized how long it had grown over the passing weeks, streaming back like the mane of a horse from his hawkish face to fall in shaggy, gleaming, jet-black waves to his shoulders. He looked like a savage, she thought, El Salvaje in truth, fierce, wild, and indisputably handsome. Padding on bare feet across the floor, he moved like some predatory animal to the bedroom, from where she heard the sounds of his hanging up his gun belt and sombrero and the rest of the garments that he carried, the thud against one wall as he pitched his boots into a corner.

Moments later, he reappeared, still clothed only in his black breeches. After tossing his gold cigarillo case onto the dining table, he strode silently to the kitchen's open shelves, from which he grabbed a bottle of wine and a pottery cup. Sitting down on the bench opposite her, he uncorked the bottle and poured its dark-red contents into the cup. Then, springing open the clasp on his cigarillo case, he withdrew a cheroot, which he lighted and dragged on, blowing a cloud of smoke into the air before speaking.

"Cook something for me, *niña*," he drawled arrogantly, his smoky-quartz eyes glittering beneath hooded lids, a lazy, mocking smile curving his mouth. "I'm hungry."

Araminta hated it when Rigo looked at her like that, hated the way it made her feel, all queer and trembling and mixed up inside and so weak in the knees that she always felt they would buckle beneath her. And the way he called her *niña*, as well, which was Spanish for "baby" and, in the context in which he employed it, a term of endearment for a lover, a mistress! For an instant, she yearned ardently to do him some violence; but she knew from experience that it would avail her nothing, that, laughing softly, he would only seize her and pin her arms behind her back and then kiss and touch her until, against her will, she melted against the length of his hard body. So instead, wordlessly, she rose to set about preparing supper, understanding that although it had not been before, this chore was now to be hers—as though she were indeed his lover, his mistress, even his wife, she thought, and was unable to stop herself from wondering what it would be like, in fact, to be married to him, to have him come home every night to her, and her alone.

That, with his demand that she cook for him, Rigo
had hoped and deliberately intended to foster precisely
this kind of thought in her mind, she did not know;
and while on some deep, subconscious level, he himself was aware of his motive, he did not care to examine it too closely. He knew only, as he watched her
moving about in the fiery glow of the sundown beyond
the windows, that feelings he had believed long dead
and that she had stirred again to life since he had
kidnapped her now burgeoned inside him. He wanted
her this way, he realized—though, even now, he did
not admit to himself why—wanted her in his house,
in his kitchen, in his bed. He wanted her just as he
had wanted Marisol, his wife, who had died and after
whose death, until now, he had wanted no other
woman. That there was nothing to prevent his having
Araminta in the way he desired, he knew, just as he
had known all along that he had never needed to do
so much as even kiss her to gain his revenge by ruining
her for Judd, that her abduction alone would have been
sufficient, for no one, least of all Judd, would have
believed her still a virgin afterward. Yet with this he
had not been content, Rigo recognized, because taking
vengeance on his enemy was no longer enough for
him.

Araminta did not know what dark thoughts preoccu-
pied him as he brooded and stared at her, wordlessly
smoking his cheroot and drinking his wine. She did
not want to know, she told herself, for she felt in her
heart that she would find out soon enough, and the
prospect both frightened her and filled her with a
strange giddying and unsettling excitement. The sun

had set swiftly while she cooked their simple meal, and now, as she carried the dishes to the table, where Rigo was lighting the oil lamps, she realized that the wind had cooled of a sudden and begun to rise, billowing the curtains inward, as though there were a sudden storm blowing up outside. A distant flash of lightning that illuminated the darkening sky confirmed her suspicion.

"Shall I—shall I close the shutters?" she asked.

"No." The word was low, unembellished.

But Araminta, who had come to know Rigo's many moods well, observed the muscle that throbbed in his cheek and recognized that tension brewed within him, as the storm brewed outside. Despite the wine that he had drunk, he was as tightly coiled as a panther preparing to spring, she thought uneasily as she sat down across from him, her own nerves stretched as tautly as thong. He splashed more wine into his cup and poured a cup for her, as well. She drank deeply, thinking that perhaps it would take the edge off her nerves. It was the first time since he had abducted her that they had truly been alone together. The thought preyed upon her mind. Did Rigo also think of it? she wondered. Was that why he was as restless as a caged animal? Since the night he had spurred his stallion up the grand staircase of the High Sierra to seize her in his grasp, they had been riding toward some tumultuous destiny. Would it be revealed tonight?

In silence, they ate by the flickering light of the oil lamps and the fire. Then Araminta cleared the table and put the dishes to soak, while Rigo carried a second bottle of wine and their cups into the living area, where he laid wood in the larger hearth, then ignited it to take from the night the chill born of the high altitude and the gusting mountain wind. Plucking a long, slender, burning twig from the kindling that blazed up quickly, he held it to the end of another thin black cigar, which he drew on deeply as he stretched out on one elbow upon the rug before the fire.

"Venga aqui," he demanded softly. Come here.

Not knowing what else to do, Araminta went. If she tried to run away, he could easily catch her—and who would discern her cries if she screamed? The others in the canyon were doubtless all snug in their huts, battened down against the fury of the approaching storm. And even if by chance someone *did* hear her, who would dare to invade the domain of General del Castillo, El Salvaje—the Savage One? But other than to hand her another cup of wine, he did not touch her. Instead, much to her surprise, he did nothing but lie there, smoking and drinking mutely as they listened to the wind that soughed and wailed like an eerie lament through the canyon. Finally, after a time, Rigo spoke.

"I want to tell you about Marisol," he stated quietly, his dark face abruptly twisted with an anguish that, even as Araminta wondered who or what Marisol was, aroused her pity and made her long strangely to comfort him, to stretch out one hand and smooth his black hair back from his face. But she did not, not knowing how he would interpret the gesture. "Marisol," he said again, his voice low with emotion, "my wife."

This, Araminta had not expected at all, and she was startled by the words. Her heart began to beat very fast. Now, at long last, she would learn the truth about his wife's death, whether Rigo had really murdered her, as people claimed, or whether he was innocent of the deed. Perhaps he would tell Araminta, as well, why he had kidnapped her and why he must revenge himself on Judd.

"It is a long tale," he continued, staring into the flames of the fire, his gaze distant, as though he were lost in his memories of another time, another place, and had forgotten her very existence. Still, when he again spoke, she knew that he had not. "But I want you to understand everything, Araminta . . . and we have time. . . ."

Chapter Fifteen

He was born just south of the border, in a village so small that it did not even have a name, really, although the villagers themselves called it Yermavilla—Desert Town. Like his place of birth, he had no name, really, although his mother called him Rigo and, at age fifteen, when he was old enough to be considered a man, he gave his own self a name, del Castillo—from the castle, because the imposing hacienda of the man who was his father had looked like one to him.

He was conceived one day when his father, a young, spoiled son and heir of a rich *hacendado*, rode—with a laughing, drunken group of other equally young and overindulged scions of Mexican estates—into Yermavilla to have a bit of sport and to sow their wild oats. If the women so "honored" by the young *cabal-*

leros were unwilling or belonged to other men, it did not matter. They could be dragged from their humble adobe huts, beaten, and raped by those who wielded the power in the land, and no one would lift a finger or speak a word in their defense. Such was life in Mexico. Such was the fate of Rigo's young, beautiful mother— to provide several hours of repeated amusement for a man who knew not even her name and whom she knew only by sight as the son of her lord and master, having seen him riding in the fields of wheat, wild lettuce, and beans, which were the primary crops in a province where the terrain would support little else. By this young man were her home and herself invaded. Afterward, he quickly forgot her.

She remembered him the rest of her life.

Nine months later, the unwanted seed planted in her womb bore fruit, a son who was nurtured on her pain and bitterness. Like her, he hated his father, who was totally ignorant of his existence and who, when by chance learning of it, gave him not a second thought. Early on, Rigo learned that his father had other, legitimate, blueblooded sons and so had no interest in or need of him, that his place in the world was one step short of hell and that he must never forget it. Forget, he did not. But because he learned it the hard way, he never accepted it; in his heart, he despised the ancient feudal system that had resulted in two classes in his country, the rich and the poor, with no way to ascend from the lower to the higher unless one became a general or a bandit—which quite often proved to be one and the same. With each passing year, as Rigo grew older, taller, and stronger, this harsh lesson was harder taught, that it should become even more deeply ingrained. He discovered what it was to be lashed with a whip or struck with the flat blade of a machete when he did not please the *hacendados*, and to be terrorized, as well, by their counterparts, the wild, reckless sons of the wealthy Texas cattle kings, who would sweep down from the north to raise hell and wreak havoc upon the border towns.

It was a raid such as this that had changed Rigo's life forever.

He had taken, that momentous summer, a bride by the name of Marisol, who, it was agreed by all, was the loveliest young woman in Yermavilla. He had also joined up with a band of renegades and outlaws, determined to claw his way up out of the muck in which Mexico would have seen him mired. It was while he was absent, rustling horses and cattle from across the border, for sale afterward in Mexico, that a bunch of young, bored Texas *gringos*, who, in line to inherit their fathers' cattle ranches and so having no challenges of their own in life, had swooped down into Yermavilla, drinking the local *cantina* dry, shooting up the town, bullying and terrifying the villagers, and, finally, abducting and raping Rigo's wife. As they had ventured south of the border to carry out their own offense of stealing horses and cattle from Mexico, for sale afterward in Texas, their spree lasted several days, during which time the *gringos* repeatedly took turns on Rigo's wife, whom they held captive, using her in every vile fashion imaginable. When they were finished, they tossed her a few coins and left her to make her own way on foot back to her village as best she could. This, Marisol, weak from her injuries and half out of her mind, somehow managed to do, thinking only that she must get help, that she must get home.

Since there are no secrets in a small town, everyone in Yermavilla knew, of course, of her shame. It was not the first time that such a terrible thing had happened to one of their young women, however, and it would not be the last. But the burden of her disgrace was to Marisol unbearable, especially when she realized that she carried the half-breed child of one of the *gringos* who had assaulted her. She was horrified by the thought that Rigo, whom she loved passionately, would be forever compelled to endure not only the stigma of a defiled wife, but also a child he had not fathered, a constant reminder of her ignominy. In a desperate attempt to rid herself of this evidence of her shame, Marisol swallowed an herbal decoction purported to force an unwanted fetus from its womb. But the combination of the poisonous mixture and the resulting abortion proved too much for her. His own raid ended, Rigo returned home at last, only to find her writhing in agony on the bed they had shared as young newlyweds.

She lived long enough to gasp out her tragic tale and the names of the *gringos* who had raped her, the name of their leader, who had used her most brutally of all—Judd Hobart—before she died in Rigo's arms. Stricken with grief and consumed with hate and anger, he spent the remainder of the long night washing and dressing her in her prettiest clothes, preparing her for burial. At dawn, he carried her body to the village church, where he laid her tenderly upon the altar and swore to avenge her cruel kidnapping, her savage dishonoring, and her torturous death. Rigo had always possessed a hot, ruthless temper, which was by now legendary in the Yermavilla, along with his proficiency at fisticuffs and his growing skill with a gun and knife. Unaware that Marisol had taken her own life (Rigo kept this fact a secret so that she might be buried in consecrated ground), the villagers uneasily concluded that he had killed her in a fit of jealous rage and shame over her disgrace.

That he had been branded a murderer by his own people, Rigo did not learn for some time afterward, for he was by then gone from Yermavilla to return to the band of renegades and outlaws with whom he was to ride for the next five years. Devoured by his burning desire for revenge, he soon proved himself the boldest, most daring, and most dangerous of all the *bandoleros* with whom he rode, and as a result, he shortly became their leader. Armed with the names that Marisol had whimpered, that were seared into his brain for all time, he started to make systematic attacks upon the Texas ranches across the border, stealing their horses and cattle, each time leaving behind a letter that told the tale of the heinous crime committed by Judd Hobart and his cohorts, and for which Rigo vowed to have vengeance.

He added to his list of adversaries the name of Noble Winthrop, Judd's godfather, when Noble proved powerful enough, along with the Hobarts, to succeed at hushing up the scandal of Judd's villainous deed. In the meantime, with the ill-gotten cash he made selling the stock he had stolen, Rigo began to build his fortune, which, determined to be something more than just a desperado all his life, he used to travel and educate himself about the world, eventually buying one ranch in Mexico and another in Texas, establishing himself on a par with the *hacendados* and Texas cattle kings. When the Revolution broke out in Mexico, he had more than enough money to run guns and other supplies across the border to the rebels, and more than enough intelligence and experience as a *bandolero* to lead his men, whom he had never disbanded, into guerrilla-style battles, ultimately earning for himself the rank of general.

And all the while, he plotted and planned and lived for the day when Judd Hobart took a bride.

"She was just a sixteen-year-old, my sweet, beautiful, gentle bride, Marisol," Rigo said with a quiet fierceness and bitterness that spoke volumes, "and Judd Hobart and his *amigos* murdered her as surely as though they themselves poured that poison down her throat. She was everything to me—and nothing to them, nothing but a Mexican girl they could use and abuse and forget."

Araminta, sitting beside him on the rug, did not answer. She could not speak for the tears that streamed silently down her cheeks at his story. It explained so much . . . everything . . . his life, the man himself, the scars upon his skin and upon his soul and why he had abducted her. She ached for him, for the pain he had suffered, for the loss he had endured. No wonder he hated Judd, had sworn to have his vengeance against him. Truly, her husband was a monster, she thought, shuddering as she remembered that Judd had assaulted her too, had attempted to rape her in the stables at the High Sierra, all the while describing in vulgar detail what he intended to do in bed to her once she was his wife. He had shocked and horrified her; still, she had seen no way out of the marriage and had tried to reassure herself that he was no worse than any other man. Now, Araminta knew that was not true. After kidnapping her, Rigo and his men could have treated her as viciously as Judd and his cronies had Marisol. Instead, Rigo had kept the others from her, and despite the liberties he had taken with her—and if she were honest with herself, Araminta must admit that these had been loverlike in nature, never unnatural, sadistic, or degrading—he had ultimately held himself in check, unable to carry out against her the violent crime that had been committed against both his mother and his bride.

Even had she been capable of speech, Araminta did not know what she might have said to him; she had no words to give him solace, no power to make up for all the years of deprivation and brutality, the adversity and sorrow that he had borne. How could he have behaved so charitably toward her? she wondered, for she did not think that she could have been so generous and merciful in his place but, rather, would have been bent on striking back furiously blow for blow, not caring whom she injured in the process. Even now, it was Rigo who comforted *her*, instead of the other way around, as he moved to take her in his arms and began tenderly to kiss the tears from her cheeks.

"Shhhhh. *Cállate, niña*," he crooned as he clasped her to him gently, rocking her as though she were a hurt child. "Hush, baby. It all happened a long time ago, and I did not mean to make you cry."

He was moved that Araminta should weep for him—he had not expected it—and for a time, he simply held her, kissing and stroking her quietly, smoothing her hair back from her face and caressing the long, silky strands, while she sobbed softly in his embrace, trembling with the force of her emotions, and buried her face against his broad, naked chest. How strong and muscular it was, she thought dimly; how wide and solid his shoulders were beneath her palms, powerful enough to bear the heavy burden of his own anguish and the pain she felt inside for him. Gradually, however, as she was consoled by his low, lilting Spanish voice, his gentle mouth and hands, she became more aware of him not just as a source of strength and consolation, but also as a man.

She could feel his warm breath, smelling pleasantly of wine and tobacco, against her skin, feel his chest move as he breathed. She could hear the steady, lulling beat of his heart against her ear, and the sound reassured her as it does a child in its mother's womb, making her feel safe and secure, comfortingly enveloped and protected as, outside, the wind, which had earlier died to a lull, now abruptly rose with a roar, whipping through the windows, billowing and buffeting the curtains and howling about the interior of the adobe hut, making the flames of the oil lamps and the fires blazing in the two hearths waver erratically and cast weird, dancing shadows upon the walls. With that warning, the storm that had for the past few hours been seething and churning and burgeoning in the heavens suddenly broke vehemently above the canyon. A ferocious bolt of lightning discharged so close to them, accompanied by such a deafening boom of thunder, that Araminta cringed and clutched Rigo tightly. Then the deluge burst tumultuously from the turgid black clouds massed and simmering in the night sky. The curtains at the unshuttered windows flogged again fiercely like sails in the shrieking wind, and with each chilly gust, the rain pelted inward, spattering as hard upon the adobe floor as it did upon the roof of the hut.

In that moment Rigo and Araminta seemed all alone in the canyon, all alone in the world, whirled by the storm into a place primeval, of endless darkness, of endless night, with only each other to hold on to. Without warning, as the firmament opened up to disgorge its contents, a delirious tide of sensation flowed through Araminta as strongly as the torrent the arroyo beyond the hut had become; she alternately flushed with fever and shook with chills. The feeling rushed through her entire body. Even her fingertips tingled, as though the lightning that had sizzled the heavens had also scorched her, unleashing inside her something as wild and atavistic as the storm. She had no thought of the future, or even of tomorrow, only of here and now as her hands, fingers tensed and spread wide, crept up to cradle Rigo's dark face. Her own was upturned to his, baring her swanlike throat in an age-old gesture of submission; her breasts rose and fell quickly with each shallow, ragged breath. Her green eyes were half closed and, in the lamplight and firelight, sparkled like uncut emeralds set amid the black-velvet sweep of her lashes; her dusky-pink lips were parted, an unfurling rose against her gilded face; and as she stared up at him, mesmerized, her veiled gaze darkened, pleaded with him mutely, and a soft, sighing whimper of entreaty, of surrender, rose from within her. She wanted him; she could no longer dispute that. He had made her want him—and then denied her. Surely, he would not now be so cruel.

"Por favor," she beseeched softly. Please.

At that, Rigo's fingers, wrapped in her unbound hair, tightened convulsively upon either side of her head, no longer gentle, but ruthlessly holding her captive now, making her acutely aware of his strength, of his power, of how easily he might crush her skull between his hands as he stared back at her fiercely, his eyes burning like twin coals in the dim, flickering light of the oil lamps and the fires in the hearths, setting her aflame, igniting her very soul. He was like some bronze pagan god kneeling over her, Araminta thought, or a devil, bent on conquering and claiming her, body and soul, and carrying her away to the dark, twisted maze of his hellish underworld. Beneath her palm, a muscle twitched in his set jaw; his breath came suddenly harsh and fast, hot against her face. Between them passed a current as highly charged as the electric storm that crackled and flashed through the windows; and then, with a groan, he fell upon her hungrily, seizing her mouth possessively with his own, determined, demanding, his tongue driving deep between her lips, weaving upon her its splendorous spell, taking her breath and her reason.

With every fiber of her being, Araminta met and gloried in his assault as, at his passionate, plundering kiss, something wild and barbarous leaped to full-blown life inside her, something that had hitherto been only a seed planted, a bud furled, sparingly nurtured, and that, now, given more than just mere sustenance, suddenly and explosively ripened and burst into dark, rapturous flower. Moaning, she clung to him ardently lest she be whirled aloft, hurtled into oblivion by the riotous storm that had caught them up in its madness and fury. Her heart raced faster than the wind, pounded harder than the rain; her blood roared like the swollen arroyo in her ears, singing a song as old as time's beginning. She was deaf, blind to everything but the man who crushed her to him savagely, as though he would not only bend her, but also break her, so she would never know another save him.

Again and again, he kissed her, boldly, insistently, his tongue ravaging her mouth, as though he could not get enough of her, would never get enough of her, and so meant to go on kissing her forever as he pressed her down feverishly upon the rug lying on the hard adobe floor before the fire and she felt the shock of his warm weight upon her as his body covered hers, his thighs imprisoning her own. Through her skirts, she could feel the hard evidence of his desire for her, and the hollow, scalding ache that erupted without warning at the secret heart of her in response was so agonizing as to be almost unbearable. Frenziedly, she kissed him back, her tongue twining with his, yielding to him and to inevitable fate, knowing that he was far stronger than she; and, like the wind that drove the rain hither and yon, heedlessly scattering it, she felt her inhibitions fecklessly strewn to the four corners of the earth, her ability to think swept from her mind into nothingness, so that she could only feel. Tightly, she clutched him as, in their feral, overwhelming hunger and need for each other, they tumbled and writhed upon the rug, her nails digging into his smooth, broad back, his hands everywhere upon her, tearing at her clothes, brutally ripping them and stripping them from her until she lay totally naked beneath him, her pale, creamy skin gleaming golden in the diffuse, dancing light.

Rigo inhaled sharply at the sight of her, for she was more beautiful even than he had ever imagined, and the understanding that, in moments, she would be his, only his, forever his, filled him with an awesome wonder and joy. She was his captive. Yet he, also, was surely hers, he thought, marveling that it should be so; for he had never in all these long, empty years dreamed of finding again what had been so cruelly taken from him when he was a young man in love. But now, when he had least expected it, here it was, in the shape of the woman Araminta, who had suddenly become as necessary to him as the air that he breathed, as vital as the storm that electrified the night. He would never be free of the enchantment that she had unwittingly worked upon him, and he did not want to be free of it; its bonds were sweeter than honey, sweeter than rich red summer wine and just as heady. It was as though all his hard life, he had ridden in search of her. Araminta. *Hado*. Fate. He could not deny it. He could no longer deny himself. Nor her.

As she sensed Rigo's dark-brown eyes upon her,

Araminta's own green ones flew open wide, startled and wondering, drugged with passion, and a flicker of fear. No man had ever before looked at her as Rigo did now, in his gaze a smoldering promise that he would possess her intimately, utterly, and she would belong to him irrevocably for the rest of her life. At the thought, her breath caught in her throat, for although she had offered herself to him, she had not known what to expect from him, did not know even now. She had not dreamed that what would happen between them would be such wildness, such madness consuming and devastating her, overpowering all her defenses, leaving her so exposed and vulnerable to him that even her heart and mind and soul were his for the taking. And these, he would have of her, as well as her body. For as she gazed up at him, she saw that his hands were at his belt, unbuckling it and then unfastening his breeches, and she knew that her time of waiting had come to an end, that tonight she would learn the full measure of her womanhood, and of him as a man. Araminta shivered at the realization, feeling suddenly fragile and helpless against him; and she wondered if, when the time came, he would hurt her very much—or if he would care.

Sensing her sudden apprehension, Rigo bent to kiss her again deeply, fervently, swallowing her breath and stilling any protest that she might have made as he shucked off his breeches and rolled naked atop her, the heat of him searing her to the marrow of her bones, like the blistering desert sun, melting her, turning her to quicksilver in his arms. She was fluid and boneless, his to mold and to shape as he willed—and did, his hands sweeping covetously over her body, his mouth lowering to taste the ambrosia of her throat and her swollen breasts crested with nipples taut and as rose-gold as the flaming sundown that had turned the sky wild and angry and presaged the puissant storm. She whimpered with delight and yearning as his teeth and tongue wreathed her nipples, as waves of exquisite pleasure, as sweet and sinuous as sprawling tendrils of white moonflowers, spiraled through her, enveloping and ensorcelling her, twined their vines about her throat and breasts. Rigo twisted his fingers in her hair and tangled it about the two of them, binding them together, inhaling deeply the scent of hot, desert sunlight that wafted from her tresses. The strands lifted and undulated, streaming in the wind, shimmering like liquid gold in the fiery light that enwrapped them with its scarlet glow.

He intoxicated her. Tiny pricks of light, like faraway stars, exploded in her mind, making her head reel; and within the fluttering lace mantilla of her hair that enfolded and ensnared them, she clasped Rigo to her frantically. The earth spun dizzyingly beneath her, seemed about to drop out from under her, sending her falling . . . falling into a black, whorling vortex. Her hands glided along his bronze flesh, slid down his back, feeling his powerful muscles ripple and quiver beneath her palms, the slick sheen of perspiration that coated his body. He was bathed in sweat, as was she, and misted with the rain that sheeted in through the windows, making their bodies glisten, one dark, one pale, each of them slippery as he moved across her, his hard, heavy sex both shocking and tantalizing her.

Surely, he would split her asunder with it. Yet even if all he brought her was pain, she felt it would be enough to satisfy them both. A kind of wild justice would be served upon the husband whom she now betrayed with every part of her and beneath whom she would have lain had not Rigo taken her from him, sparing her what Marisol had endured.

For that alone was Araminta grateful to Rigo, and more . . . breathless in his wake, discovering him as he discovered her, kissing and touching him everywhere she could reach, her lips and tongue tasting, licking the salt from his dark, smooth flesh, her hands exploring all the planes and angles of his hard, muscular body. She felt as though the infernal storm that clamored outside had snatched her up at last, carrying her away to a primitive place that was neither heaven nor hell, but somewhere in between, a place of peyote dreams and smoke and darkness garlanded with swirls of kaleidoscopic colors that danced and spun like chimes in the wailing wind, or the wild music in her mind, as fierce as a flamenco, its castanets the furious thrumming of her heart against Rigo's, its melody the tempestuous trill of the storm that whipped them to desperate frenzy.

As a thirsty desert rose opens to the rain, instinctively craving its life-giving moisture, so did Araminta open herself to him when he sought her, his hands and knees spreading her pale thighs wide, his fingers touching her where, during their nights upon the trail, he had dared to trespass before with quick, light strokes that had only heightened instead of easing the torment he had brought her. But now, as his hand found, snugly nested in its thicket of honey-gold curls, the dark, secret origin of her desire, Rigo lingeringly caressed the mellifluous, engorged nether lips that trembled and unfolded to him of their own avid, needy accord, his fingers slowly, torturously, dipping full length into the honeyed heart of her cinnabar petals dripping with nectar, then withdrawing to spread their dulcet elixir, only to plunge deep again and yet again. His tongue was in her mouth, mimicking the sweetly agonizing movements of his hand, the flicking of his thumb against the pulsing well of her passion, sharpening her desire for him to a keen, knife edge. Araminta moaned against his lips, gasping for breath, and strained fervidly against the lithe, corded length of him, knowing, now, that even this was not enough to satisfy, to quench the terrible, burning ache that he had kindled and stoked inside her. She wanted . . . wanted . . .

"*¿Me quieres?*" he muttered thickly, hoarsely, urgently, in her ear as his mouth left hers to scorch like a brand across her cheek to her temple, the strands of her hair, his breath a harsh gasp, a low groan against her heated skin. "*Dime, niña. ¿Me quieres?*" Tell me, baby. Do you want me?

"*Sí, te quiero,*" she whispered. "*Te quiero,* Rigo."

At her assent, her speaking at long last his name, the hard, questing blade of his manhood found her, stabbed swift and deep and true into the molten sheath of her, piercing her to its hilt, in a heart-stopping moment of shattering, white-hot pain that was ultimate domination, all invading and conquering. Until now, she had never really understood how absolute his incursion would be, how total her submission. At the shock of his sharp, stinging entry, the severing of her fragile, maidenly defense against him, she stiffened involuntarily beneath him, her back and hips arching wildly, uncontrollably, against him, obliviously aiding his penetration of her and intensifying his assault as he lifted and crushed her to him fiercely. She gasped, then cried out, a low wail of surrender that he smothered savagely with his triumphant mouth. Joined to her, accustoming her to the feel of him throbbing inside her, filling her to overflowing, he slowly pressed her back down upon the rug on which they lay. Withdrawing, he drove hard and deep again into her, his body taut with desire, quickening feverishly against her own as, blindly now, he began to move inside her, impaling her over and over, his head buried against her shoulder, his hands beneath her hips, sweeping her up to meet each strong, barbarous thrust, dark flesh melding urgently with pale, while the storm outside raged and the firelight within enveloped them in the glow of its flaring crimson flame, sealing them together now and for always.

As fragrant as the smoke-misted rain rose the sweet, musky scent of their primal mating as, with each bold, potent thrust of his manhood, the pain she had experienced at first evanesced into pleasure, heightening until, at last, lost to him, as he was to her, utterly and forever, she clung to him desperately, reaching, straining for some shadowy, unknown thing that she felt she must find or die. Headlong, she hastened with him down a high, wild wind, through dark, labyrinthine canyons that gave way to sweeping, soaring mesas, where a massive, atavistic sun blazed so hot and bright in the endless turquoise sky that, inexorably, it exploded, brutally, breathtakingly, bursting into an infinite spiral of scintillating conflagration, blasting and bathing the earth with a dazzling, utopian light that shimmered like a desert mirage, burned like a desert fire, making them cry out as it consumed them, glorified them, and then slowly charred them to cinders until, finally, there was naught save stillness and silence.

In that quiet after passion, Rigo held Araminta close, his warm embrace both protective and possessive as he cradled her head against his shoulder, feeling her crystal tears splash upon his chest and, knowing her now as he knew himself, down to the bone, needing no explanation for them. She was young, awed by and afraid of what had happened between them. She had welcomed and wondered at the violent beauty of it, and now she dreaded its repercussions to her, was stricken with fear and remorse, not yet grasping that, with her consummate response to his lovemaking, she had aroused within him a desire that bordered on obsession. He had known countless women, but never one such as she. What she thought was now ended between them, he knew was but its beginning, that his hunger for her had only been whetted, that he would never have enough of her, no matter how many times he took her. With her, as with no other woman, he had taken and given completely of himself, as she had taken from and given to him. She was all that he had ever wanted and dreamed of in a woman, the half that made him whole, the mate of his restless, seeking body and soul.

"Shhhh. *Cállate niña*," he murmured gently, as he had earlier when comforting her. "You have no cause for these tears."

"Do I not, Rigo?" Araminta asked tremulously, afraid and ashamed. What had she done? She had lain with him, yielded herself willingly to a man not her husband, a man who had used her to take his vengeance and now would have no need of her. "I have done what you wished. You have your revenge. You can send me back to Texas now, back to—back to my—my husband."

Cupping her chin tenderly, Rigo compelled her face up to his, his eyes searching hers intently, as though to ferret out the innermost secrets of her heart and mind and soul.

"Is this truly your desire, Araminta, that I return you to Judd Hobart?"

"It—it is what you intend, is it not?" she answered evasively, not daring to believe otherwise, not allowing the tiny seed of hope now planted within her to take root and grow.

"Before this night, *sí*," he agreed quietly. "But not now, *querida*. Not now! No, not even if I have to hold you prisoner here in Mexico for the rest of your life will I send you back to your *gringo* husband. You are mine now, Araminta. *Mine!*" he declared fiercely, savoring the taste of the word upon his tongue. "I will never let you go. *¡Bruja!* You have bewitched me, with your angel hair, your gypsy face, your sorcerous fire. *¡Te quiero! Te quiero, mi corazón, mi vida, mi* *alma.* . . .'' I want you! I love you, my heart, my life, my soul. . . .

Until this moment, Araminta had not known how badly she wanted to hear those words, how much she loved him in return, had loved him all along, since that very first day at the hotel in El Paso. Why else would she have gone on meeting him at the creek bank, would she have responded to the liberties he had taken with her while she was his captive, would she have given herself to him tonight, longing to take away his pain and, in a distorted attempt at retribution, to punish herself somehow for the anguish Marisol had suffered at Judd's cruel hands?

''Rigo, oh, Rigo, I love you, too!'' Araminta cried, her hands tightening upon him as though to reassure herself that he was real, that he was hers.

Her tears of sorrow became tears of joy, tasting sweet upon his lips as, his hands twining in her tresses, he once more found her mouth with his own. He rolled her over to press her down again upon the hard adobe floor, his naked body moving inexorably, urgently, to cover hers, while beyond the place where they lay, the storm gasped its dying breath and the arroyo spilled with a sigh into a quicksilver pool beneath the soft-glowing moon.

Book Three
The Villistas

Chapter Sixteen

Chihuahua, Mexico, 1913

At first when she awoke, Araminta did not know where she was, she had become so accustomed to sleeping on blankets spread upon the ground baked hard by the sun. As usual, Rigo lay beside her, one of his legs tossed intimately over hers, his arm encircling her body, his palm cupping her breast. But this morning, they were both naked. At the realization, the memory of last night came flooding back to her, and she recognized then that she lay in the adobe hut's rope-slung bed where Rigo had finally carried her after he had made love to her again upon the rug before the hearth. As she looked at his dark, handsome face, so strangely peaceful now in repose, Araminta wondered how she could ever have hated him, could ever have fought him. Now she knew it was only her unacknowledged fear of falling in love with a man who would never care for her and for whom she would never be anything more than the *gringa* bride of his enemy that had caused her to resist him. She marveled that Rigo should love her, that her own heart should overflow with all that she felt inside for him.

As though he sensed her gaze upon him, he stirred, drowsily opening his eyes and pulling her against him, in his touch, as he began to kiss and stroke her languorously, both seasoned skill and jubilation that she should be to him as his first woman, that he should know such joy at discovering her, mapping each line and every curve of her. His bronze face, in the luminous blush of the gilded pink dawn streaming in through the open window of the bedroom, looked younger than it was, softened by the knowledge that here, at least, he need not be on his guard. With Araminta, he need not be other than the man he was in his heart, for she alone knew his human fears and foibles—and loved him still. He should never have let her marry Judd Hobart, Rigo thought jealously, silently cursing himself and his revenge—though the taste of it had proved far sweeter than he had ever imagined. But in reality the fact that she was another man's wife had little meaning to him. It was he who possessed her—as no other man ever would—his lips and tongue and hands delighting and exciting her, as her own did him, her fingers tunneling through his glossy black hair to draw him even nearer as he drank deep of the wine of her rosebud mouth and grazed at her breasts, white-blooming lilies bursting with dusky-pink petals at their hearts. He planted his face in the valley between the flowering mounds, trailing a twisting path of erotic kisses down her taut, quivering belly to where the succulent, secret fruit of her swelled, berry juices sweet upon his honeyed tongue and velvet fingers. All he had charted in passion's hot, blinding fury, he now explored anew, lazily, reveling in her and the slow-burning, liquid heat that trickled through his body, stirring his loins as he embraced her, twined himself about her, dark skin enfolding pale, warm breath quickening against wandering lips and hands.

With her thumbs, Araminta traced the slant of his raven brows, the strongly chiseled bones of his hawkish Spanish face, the sensual curve of his mouth until he claimed her own again, tongue outlining her lips before compelling them to part in lush scarlet yielding. As fragile and sensitive as the flutter of a butterfly's wings, her own kisses lighted upon his thick-lashed eyelids and full, seductive mouth, the gleaming mane of his ebony hair. Her lips and hands touched upon the planes of his shoulders, mouth and palms gliding down his smooth, silky chest and broad back. Her tongue licked salty flesh, following the sleek line of hard muscles that flowed and rippled like quicksilver streams to the curve of his firm, narrow buttocks. All about him, her fairy tresses wove sweet enchantment and spun a gossamer web, ensnaring him as he drew the long, golden skeins across his lips and throat, inhaling deeply of their sun-washed perfume. The scent of her satin skin, smooth and flushed against his, was fragrant in his nostrils. Warning her of his fading patience, his dark eyes flared as her hand brushed, then captured the hard, seeking thorn of his manhood, deliberately teasing and stroking until his forbearance was ended and his weight covered hers, pressing her down upon the bed.

As soft as a dove, she lay beneath him, white wings opening, unfolding wide at the gentle but insistent pressure of his hands in silent demand. In a lazy, midsummer's dream, the two of them came together as one as, with a long, slow, hard thrust, he buried his sex deep in the mellifluous plum ripeness of her, splitting her and spreading moist, heated nectar. Again and again, the sweet, treacherous barb stung savagely, its seductive, serpentine venom seeping through her languid limbs and clouding her dazed mind until she arched blindly against its piercing, welcoming it, embracing it as it swept her down a rushing crystal river to a place as sylvan as Eden beneath a brilliant, sunburst sky, at its heart a glorious, timeless flame that seared and exalted her as he groaned, then cried out and, with a shudder that racked the entire length of his whipcord body, spilled himself inside her.

Afterward, as she lay wrapped in his arms, basking in the warm afterglow of his lovemaking, Araminta wanted to weep at the joy of it, at the bittersweet ache that filled her heart for him; for last night, Rigo had told her that before the Revolution, the peasants had been forced to make love in silence, for fear that they would be overheard and beaten by their lords and masters, who had grudged them even this closeness, this pleasure.

"¡Te amo!" she whispered fiercely, as though with

these words alone could she blot out his memories of his life before the war, when he had been less than a dog—and hold at bay the present and tomorrow, in which he was a dog of war. *"Te amo. . . ."* I love you. . . .

With his mouth, he stilled her words and gave them back to her. *Te quiero.* I love you/I want you, for to him, with his Spanish blood, they were one and the same, and in his language, the words meant both when spoken as he spoke them. It was enough she did not ask for more, not from a man who knew so much about lovemaking and yet had known so little love. There were scars worse than physical ones, scars that took a lifetime to heal. She understood this—as he had known that she would. A man such as he did not open his heart and soul to a woman who would despise them, nor a woman such as she herself to a man she did not love—and this, too, he had known.

Though she was there for less than a month, Araminta never forgot the adobe hut in the canyon, where Rigo first loved her and time stood still for a while, where they had lived as much like husband and wife as though they were indeed married, newlyweds, learning to know each other and making love together for hours on end. But inevitably, the wheel of time began to turn again, and the world, Mexico, and the Revolution intruded upon them, in the shape of a message from Francisco "Pancho" Villa, the general in chief of the División del Norte. A man who tarried in the bluffs, dallying with a *gringa*, while other *guerrilleros* fought the war for freedom, was a man that many would consider a traitor who deserved to be shot. Villa's meaning was clear: Treachery and desertion would not be tolerated. Officers who failed to follow orders would be executed, and Rigo was no exception to the rule.

Araminta's heart sank when she learned the news, for she felt certain that he would either leave her behind in the canyon or send her away to his estate in Mexico, Casa Grande, where she would be all alone until his return. But he informed her instead that she would be going with him to join the Villistas; that many Mexican women accompanied their husbands and sweethearts into battle. From the corral at the end of the canyon, he chose a pure white Arabian mare for her to ride, and, mounted on this, she traveled at his side. How different was this journey from their last!

Over the passing weeks, Rigo's band of desperadoes swelled from a handful to over five hundred or more as he dispatched men bearing his own messages to those under his command. How the *guerrilleros* knew how and where to find him, Araminta could only guess, for initially, the band moved rapidly and furtively, as it had before. Only as its ranks began to grow did it progress more slowly and openly, accompanied by cannons and supply wagons and horses for the rebel troops. Recognizing the brands of several Texas ranches, including both the H Bar S of the High Sierra and the Rafter C of the Chaparral, she realized that most of the stock was stolen, appropriated during Rigo's swift, stealthy raids across the border.

For the first time in days, Araminta thought of her

grandfather and Judd. By now, they must surely believe that she was dead. For the fact that they had never received any ransom note, that she had never been returned to them, there could be to them only one explanation: She was no longer alive, or if by some slim chance she was, she would be far better off dead. That she had fallen in love with Rigo, and he with her, they would never accept, would never believe, even if someone had offered them proof of it. But there would be none, for she would never, could never go back to Texas now, to Judd, not when she was Rigo's wife in all save name. Let them think that she had died; it was best that way. Judd was no doubt glad to think it, to have no evidence to the contrary; and even if her grandfather was not, Araminta thought that he would rather that she be lying in her grave than in Rigo's arms.

Earlier, when she had ridden bound and mounted before him on his bold black stallion—Rayo, meaning Thunderbolt, she had learned that the beast was called—there had been nothing for her, a captive, to do. When they had stopped to rest the horses or make camp for the night, she had sat mutely by, not trusted, lest she attempt to escape. Now Rigo taught her how to strip, rub down, and feed and water their horses; how to build a fire so she could start supper cooking, and how to unroll neatly the tent that he presently acquired, set it up and stake it down, and spread within it the blankets that they would share that night. In the beginning, it took her nearly two hours to do all these things, even though, usually, one or another of Rigo's men assisted her. Soon, she could perform these tasks in less than half that time. She grew strong from the heavy labor she endured. When the day arrived that she was able, without the least bit of struggle, to lift her saddle onto her mare, Araminta laughed to think that, once, she'd scarcely been able to drag it along the ground. As the ranks of Rigo's army gradually increased, however, there were eventually more than enough rebel soldiers to take care of this chore and others for their general and his woman; and Rigo's aide-de-camp, a young man by the name of Chico Morales, assigned various men to handle the more strenuous work.

From the women who came to follow the burgeoning army, Araminta learned how to recognize which plants and tubers were edible; to supplement their simple meals, she, along with the other women, picked wild berries and herbs and greens, and dug moist roots out of the hard earth, cutting the tops off as treats for the horses. Sometimes, she and the rest of the women dried and preserved their gatherings for eating later on, for villages were few and far between, fresh supplies not always available. Waste not, want not: That was the motto of the rebellious peasants who had learned its lesson only too well. She also discovered which plants were medicinal and could be used for healing, such as the one from which she made a paste to protect her skin against the drying and cracking effects of constant exposure to Mexico's harsh sun and arid wind. She discovered which plants were poisonous, that a knife dipped in a certain juice would bring instant death, that the powder of certain crushed leaves or dried berries sprinkled on food or in a drink would bring a slow, agonizing end. Rigo himself pointed out to her the peyote cactus, whose flowering fruit and juices would cause vomiting and hallucinations when eaten or drunk and that was used in special Indian rituals to open the way to the spirit world.

Fearful that despite all his precautions, Araminta might fall prey to the Federales, the Rurales, the *colorados*, Yaqui Indians, or worse, Rigo taught her, as well, how to defend herself with a blade, how to move and to feint, how to snap her body around like lightning and to hit the ground, rolling, and be back on her feet in seconds, how to drive the knife home into an assailant's throat or heart, twisting the blade to be certain that its grisly work was complete. Like many other women who accompanied his men, she carried concealed beneath her skirts the knife that he gave her, in a leather sheath strapped to her thigh. She could jerk the blade free at a moment's notice, a gypsy's or whore's trick, really, but one that might someday save her life in this wild, savage land torn by war. When Araminta least expected it, Rigo would sneak up on her, so her ears grew sharp, attuned to even the faintest rustle in the brush. She learned herself how to snake forward on her belly through the inhospitable terrain, pulling herself along with her elbows and not making a sound.

At night, she and Rigo continued the battles they had waged over the chessboard he carried always in his saddlebags, when she had been his prisoner and had sought to outwit him. She had never beaten him; nor did she win now. Chess was a game of pure intelligence and strategy, without a single element of

chance—other than the talent and resourcefulness of
one's adversary—and he was far too experienced a
military opponent for her to defeat him. Even as his
captive, Araminta had recognized his deviousness and
skill, had grown used to hearing him utter softly,
"Jaque," and then, shortly afterward, *"Jaque mate."*
Check. Checkmate. More than once, as though to a
child just learning the game, he had said, *"Jaque a la
reina"*—check to the queen—and his eyes had met
and locked intently with hers, his meaning plain: Look
to yourself, *gringuita*, for in the end, I will take you
just as I now take your queen. She had not dreamed
then that her surrender would be so willing, so loving—or that Rigo would come to care for her so
deeply, returning her love fullfold.

He went on instructing her to play the guitar, also.
On their ride to the hidden canyon in the bluffs, he
had bought the instrument from some peasant in a
village, and at night, when he had been certain that he
and his *bandoleros* were camped in a place where the
sound would not carry too far on the wind, he had
strummed it softly, producing beautiful Spanish music—sad ballads and slow waltzes, lively fandangos,
primitive *jarabes*, and wild flamencos. Observing that
Araminta had been captivated by the melodies, he had,
to amuse himself perhaps, decided to teach her how
to play; and because it was better than sitting with her
hands tied, the rope chafing her wrists and cutting off
her circulation, she had consented to learn. She was
proficient enough now to play several simple tunes,
though nothing like the highly intricate harmonies that
Rigo evoked from the guitar. Now, on nights when he

played, others joined in with their own instruments, and the men and women of his army sang and danced with unbridled, earthy abandon that was exhilarating, breathtaking to behold. The wind rang with the thrumming guitars, the jangling tambourines, the clicking castanets, and the hard ground shook with the staccato stamping of boots, their spurs' jingling. Those watching from beyond the flames of the campfires clapped their hands rhythmically to the music and yelled encouragement, which the dancers answered by whirling faster and faster.

One evening, several of the young women with whom Araminta had gradually become friends drew her into the circle to show her the elaborate steps. Shaking her head shyly, embarrassed, she tried to retreat. But when someone shouted "*¡La gringa! ¡La gringa!*" and others took up the cry, she began slowly to dance, imitating the rest of the women at first. But after a while, gaining confidence and fortified by the wine that she had drunk at supper, she abandoned herself to the primordial music, let it be her guide. The sensuous movements came naturally then, needing no thought or experience. Shutting her eyes, she allowed the rhythm of the wanton, throbbing beat to take hold of her, to pervade her very being. Her body undulated sinuously; her hips swayed. As graceful as a swan, she raised one arm, snapping her fingers and stamping her *guaraches* as she lifted one edge of her full, ruffled peasant skirt teasingly, displaying an enticing flash of leg, of thigh. The crowd roared its approval, urging her on as, one by one, the other dancers started to fall back to watch the beautiful young American woman, *la gringa*, who, if not for her golden hair and emerald eyes, might have been one of their own wild gypsies. Araminta was unaware that she danced alone now. The blood was pounding in her temples. She was lost in the pulsating music, dancing for Rigo, her lover, only for him, her arms imploring, taunting, promising, her head thrown back, her unbound hair tumbling down about her, her eyes closed, her lips parted and curved with an inviting half-smile. Sweat beaded her body, glistened on her skin in the moonlight and firelight as she spun, faster and faster, her skirts swirling high about her legs, the enthusiastic cries of "*¡olé!*" and "*¡la gringa!*" echoing in her ears before, catching her around the waist, Rigo swooped her up, his mouth hard and hungry on hers as, amid his men's lusty whoops of "*¡Arriba! ¡Arriba, General!*", he carried her off into the darkness, to his tent, where he pressed her down upon his blankets and took her fiercely, feverishly, without any preliminaries.

Araminta thought how different from Texas it was here, in Mexico, where she was admired and respected as Rigo's woman and no one cared that she was not his wife, where the people shrugged their shoulders at convention, understanding and accepting that such was love, such was life. *La gringa*, they called her, and *la mujer del general, la mujer del Salvaje*. The foreigner, the Yankee, the general's woman, the woman of the Savage One—the latter two enough to compel them to abide the former, she thought, not knowing that she herself daily, in countless ways, earned their esteem and won their hearts.

Her accent enchanted them when she spoke to them

in Spanish, gesturing a good deal to get her meaning across and making mistakes at first but gradually growing more and more fluent. At least *la gringa* tried to speak their own language, they acknowledged to one another, not expecting them to speak hers. She never shouted at them in English, as though they were slightly deaf and screaming would make them understand her foreign tongue. She worked as long and hard as their own women did, never demanding special treatment because she was the general's woman, the woman of El Salvaje. In the simple peasant garments she wore always now, she walked among the rebel soldiers after camp had been made for the night, shyly addressing this one or that, remembering the names of all, even their wives and sweethearts and children. No matter how harried and tired she was, she invariably had a ready smile for all, time to laugh at a joke, time to tell a group of children a story, time to clean and bandage a troublesome cut or scrape. Regardless of how her back ached, she stood half the evening over a fire, cooking hot *menudo* and *frijoles* and tortillas, ladling the meager but savory fare onto tin plates and making sure that they were distributed to every hungry mouth before she herself, carrying her own plate and Rigo's, found him and sat down beside him at last. The two of them ate only after everyone else had been fed, its being the duty of a general, Rigo insisted, to see to the welfare of his men before his own. Most nights, late into the wee hours of the morning, candles burned in the general's tent, where he conducted planning sessions with his highest-ranking officers, and Araminta recorded events in her journal and completed sketches she had roughed earlier for her articles about the Mexican Revolution.

She knew now from Rigo and his vast information network that Liam O'Grady had not only published her previous pieces in the *Record*, but also had made them front-page news, running them as an ongoing series under the heading "From the Front Line," and beneath, the smaller byline "by our correspondent in Mexico, A. K. Munroe." Except for politicians, few in America had paid much attention to what was happening south of the border, but Araminta's first few articles on the subject had sparked interest because of her previous work on life in the West. Women, especially, had been touched by "What Price Freedom?", the orphaned boy Miguelito's tale, and so by the time that "Cry Havoc!" had appeared, an audience had developed whose attention had been drawn to the war. These readers had been ready for Araminta's story about the Revolutionaries—and to start taking sides. According to word Rigo had received, the provocative piece had ignited fiery debates in the smoke-filled rooms of many of New York City's men's clubs and discussion of President Wilson's continuance of former President Taft's prohibition of arms sales to the rebels. For this reason, Rigo wished her to continue the articles, and she was happy to obey him. Perhaps in her own way, she could give back something to this country that was so unexpectedly offering so much to her. But, if she gained no more from it than Rigo alone, she would have more than she had ever dreamed would be hers when he had carried her across the Rio Grande.

Chapter Seventeen

Much to Judd's disgust, there had been no good opportunity during the return trip to Texas to ensure that Noble finished the journey—in a pine box. No matter how hard the younger man had tried to pretend that the moment when he had condemned Araminta, had hinted that he did not want her back as his bride, and had declared she would be better off dead had been a hideous aberration born of his shock and fear for her life at the hands of Rigo del Castillo, Noble had not been fooled one whit. While feigning acceptance of Judd's explanation, the older man had nevertheless been on his guard against him, too wary for Judd to make an attempt to kill him. The younger man knew that he must be successful, or the results would prove disastrous to his goal of inheriting the High

Sierra and ridding himself of his soiled dove of a wife—not that he had much doubt, now, that she was dead anyway.

There had been plenty of time for that son of a bitch Del Castillo to send a note demanding payment of an exorbitant ransom. Greaser pig or not, he was capable of writing a literate hand, as the letters that he had left behind during his horse and cattle raids on the Chaparral had demonstrated. Though they had not been signed, Judd had soon tracked down their author. He was the bandit husband of that cheap Mexican *puta* Judd and his cohorts had taken from Yermavilla to entertain them during their rustling spree south of the border that fateful summer. Marisol (though he and the rest of his buddies had called her Virgin Mari, not because she had been one, but because, whether performing or praying, she had always been on her knees, just like all good Catholics) had cried and screamed and fought like a wildcat at first. But Judd knew that in the end, she had wanted it, had liked it, had lusted for it—just as all women did after they had had some of the starch slapped out of them and their legs spread by a man who knew how to ram a woman every which way but loose. Despite all the rumors to the contrary, no doubt put about by Del Castillo himself to salve his Spanish pride and honor, Judd figured his enemy was a real namby-pamby in the bedroom; if he weren't, the dumb bastard might have been able to teach his wife a few tricks beforehand, and she wouldn't have been so damned stubborn and stupid and ignorant until Judd and his cronies had wised her up plenty. They had actually done her a real favor, showing her how a man expected to get his money's worth from a woman—especially from a hot-blooded Mexican slut who, for two bits, had probably bedded down with every greaser pig from the Rio Grande to Zacatecas anyway, in an attempt to satisfy what her husband hadn't!

It really was too bad, Judd thought sourly, that he hadn't had a chance to give his own bride a few of the lessons that he had taught Virgin Mari. He would have melted Araminta's icy exterior and heated up the fire beneath; she wouldn't have been so cool and haughty and touch-me-not then, but eager to open her mouth and her legs whenever he had ordered her to do so. Well, there was no sense in crying over spilled whiskey. The arrogant, prick-teasing bitch was doubtless cold in her grave by now, for since she had been so goddamned determined to make her own fiancé wait until their wedding night to bed her, Judd felt certain that Araminta had killed herself rather than submit to a pack of filthy Mexican *bandoleros*. If she had not, they surely must have murdered her themselves after using her up. It was the only explanation for why Del Castillo had made no ransom demand of Judd or Noble, nor delivered Araminta back to the High Sierra, deflowered and defiled.

He really didn't need to worry, Judd reassured himself for the umpteenth time, about those posters that Noble had, upon returning home, ordered printed and distributed all over Texas and even down in northern Mexico, offering a five-thousand-dollar reward for Araminta's safe recovery or for any information leading to her whereabouts and rescue. Nor ought the team of professional mercenaries that Noble had hired prove any cause for concern. That bandit who called himself Pancho Villa was on a rampage in Chihuahua, and with anti-American sentiment running so high in Mexico right now, no greaser pig worth his salt was going to hesitate to shoot four *gringo* gunslingers so foolish as to venture south of the border, in search of a *gringa* who was probably already dead anyway.

Following the course of the Rio Conchos nearly all the way, Rigo and his troops at last joined the three thousand rebel soldiers who formed the bulk of the Villistas in Ciudad Jiménez. There Araminta first glimpsed their general-in-chief, Francisco "Pancho" Villa, the infamous bandit and famous Revolutionary leader. Born Doroteo Arango, Villa was tall, as were many of the men of northern Mexico, though he was not so elegant and lithe as Rigo. Instead, Villa had the long arms, the long, stalwart, barrel body, and the short legs of the Indians with whom many of the original Spaniards and later, the Mexicans had intermarried over the years. His narrow eyes had the faintly Oriental cast of his Indian forebears' ancestors. His slightly receding black hair was cut short and matched the color of his bushy, handlebar *mustachios*. He looked every bit as hard and fierce as Araminta had heard that he was, for his smile—and he smiled often—seldom reached his dark, flat eyes, which were ever alert and watchful, masking a wealth of animal instinct and cunning, of innate shrewdness and raw intelligence.

Like Rigo and many others who were making their

mark in the Mexican Revolution, Villa had been an outlaw before the war. Also like Rigo, shortly after the outbreak of the fighting, Villa had appeared in El Paso to put himself, his knowledge, experience, and money, at the disposal of the Revolutionaries. People claimed that after twenty years as a *bandolero*, Villa had a fortune stashed under his mattress. But when he heard this tale, Rigo only laughed and told Araminta that Villa's "fortune" had, in reality, amounted to a mere 363 *pesos*, most of them so worn with age as to be as smooth as highly polished silver.

To the Mexican peasants, he was the equivalent of a latter-day Robin Hood. It was said that in times of famine, he had fed entire regions and seen to the welfare of whole villages evicted—under President Díaz's unfair land law—by the Federales. Privately, Araminta thought that it was as likely that Villa's lack of riches had stemmed more from his having wasted his ill-gotten gains on whiskey and women. Shocking though it was to Araminta, a common practice among the peons of Mexico was to have more than one wife. Villa had two, one a simple peasant woman who lived in El Paso and had been with him during all his years as a desperado, and one a slim young girl who kept the home fires burning in his house in Chihuahua City. Despite this, even Araminta was forced to admit that Villa was a genius in battle, for it was he who must be credited with the origin in Mexico of the guerrilla style of fighting that had served the Revolutionaries so well.

Perhaps it was because, being the son of peons, he

had never been to school, and so knew nothing of
the standard, accepted methods of waging war, and
because he had, before the Revolution, spent twenty-
two years of his life as a desperado, as well, that
he employed strategies more suited to bandits than
soldiers. He had been only a young boy of sixteen
when he had turned to crime. He had been delivering
milk on the streets of Chihuahua City when, in retribution for the rape of his sister, Villa always claimed
afterward, he had murdered the government official
who had violated her. This in itself would not have
caused him to be outlawed for long in Mexico, where
killings, especially crimes born of passion and black
Latin rages, were a common and accepted occurrence.
What had put the price on Villa's head was his subse-
quent rustling of cattle from the wealthy *hacendados*,
the powerful rulers of the land.

Soon, his very name had become, to the oppressed
peasants of his country, synonymous with rebellion
against the government, and his exploits legend. Eventually, nearly every murder or robbery in the whole of
northern Mexico was attributed to him. As his fame
had spread, poems and songs had been composed
about him, contributing to his notoriety. But although
he was uneducated, he possessed an inherent shrewdness, an inborn intelligence; and he had learned to stay
alive by trusting no one, not even his most faithful
companions, whom he had frequently ridden off and
left behind during the night, after they had made camp,
so even they had not known where he was to be found.
Even now, when his army settled in for the evening,
Villa would suddenly rise, fling a serape about him-

self, and head off alone for parts unknown, sometimes approaching the sentries he had assigned guard duty, to be certain that they were vigilant at their posts, and then reappearing, in the morning, from another direction entirely. Not even Villa's closest confidantes, the highest-ranking officers in his army, such as Rigo, were privy to his plans until he was ready to act on them. In this way he avoided defeat and capture.

Originally a captain in President Francisco Madero's army, Villa had been with General Victoriano Huerta when they were ordered north to battle the traitor General Pascual Orozco. Villa had been placed in charge of the garrison in Hidalgo del Parral and, with a lesser force but superior tactics, had decisively routed Orozco, doing the dangerous fighting of the campaign, while Huerta and his veteran troops had remained under the cover of their artillery. Later, claiming that he had wired an order to Villa in Hidalgo del Parral—which wire Villa maintained that he never received—Huerta had summoned Villa to Ciudad Jiménez to be court-martialed for insubordination. After a mere fifteen-minute trial, Villa had been condemned to be executed. President Madero himself had stayed the order, and Villa was incarcerated at Santiago Tlatelolco instead; so he had good cause to hate Huerta and had been only too happy to join the fight against him when Huerta had assassinated Madero and seized control of the reins of government.

In prison, Villa had passed the time by teaching himself to read and write; he was not even fluent in his native language, speaking only *pelado*, the crude Spanish of the peons, in which dialect Araminta had so often heard Rigo address his own men. But though, outwardly, Villa had appeared accepting of his fate, inwardly he had plotted how to regain his freedom. Eventually, with the assistance of Carlos Jaúregui, a young clerk in the military court, he had escaped from the Santiago Tlatelolco penitentiary in which he was held and made his way to El Paso, where he had renewed his friendship with Rigo. The two men had now and then ridden together as *bandoleros* in the past, drawn to each other by their common background, ingrained cleverness, and burning desire to better the lot of the Mexican peasants. When Villa had decided to return to Mexico to support the Revolutionaries, it was with Rigo, among others, that he had laid the first of his plans; and though the two men had each had faith that they would succeed, neither of them had dreamed that victory would come so surely and swiftly.

Both of them had sought recruits in the mountains near San Andres; Villa's fame was such that three thousand men had joined him within a month, to which number Rigo's own troops had added, becoming a special guerrilla detachment, running arms, ammunition, horses, cattle, and other supplies across the border. Two months later, Villa's army of largely peasant and untrained Revolutionaries had sent the Federales all over the province of Chihuahua fleeing for their lives back to Chihuahua City.

This was principally due to the Federales' being so rigid in troop structure, behavior, and deployment. Recognizing that his own army was composed of peons who had even less knowledge of military rules and regulations than he himself did, Villa did not care that he and his officers were rarely saluted or treated with formality. Lacking mathematical skills, he could not have begun to do the trigonometry necessary to calculate the trajectories of cannonballs or have figured the ratio of hits to misses of a hundred rounds of ammunition fired; nor did he grasp the fact that infantry, cavalry, and artillery should be positioned differently from one another to be effective, and so he was unencumbered by the theories about the best ways to make war.

In fact, when General Hugh L. Scott, the commander of Fort Bliss, had dispatched to Villa a booklet detailing the Rules of War as adopted by the Hague Conference, he had been bemused and spent hours reading it, after which he had declared that war was not a game, so why make up rules about it? He had been especially baffled by the regulation against lead bullets, because after all, he had said, they did the work, did they not? He had asked if he and another man got into a fight in a *cantina*, would they need to pull the booklet out of their pockets and read over the rules of conduct for such a situation? And then he had roared with laughter at the idea. But for quite a while afterward, he had delighted in badgering his officers about the booklet, inquiring if they knew what they were supposed to do in this circumstance or that, and shaking his head, pretending dismay but actually much amused when they were unable to answer correctly.

In one respect, however, Villa was far ahead of those who had developed the rules of what was humane or not in war—as though there were ever such a thing as a humane war: Villa's field hospital was spectacular. It consisted of forty boxcars, all of which were enameled inside and filled with operating tables and the newest surgical instruments. More than sixty doctors and nurses worked the boxcars, caring for the wounded who were shuttled by train from the front lines to the base hospitals he established at Ciudad Jiménez and Hidalgo del Parral, and eventually at Chihuahua City, as he advanced south through northern Mexico.

Now the march was on to take Torreón, which lay on the Rio Nazas, at the heart of Mexico, and so was of principal strategic military importance. The man who held Torreón could cut the country in half and push on to its capital, Ciudad de México. With the Zapatistas' attacking from the south, the Revolutionaries could crush the dictatorial government of Mexico between them, and the Constitutionalists, like Villa, who supported Don Venustiano Carranza, the governor of Coahuila, and his Plan of Guadalupe, could seize power. Already, there were those who proposed Villa as the next president of Mexico. But at this, he would merely shake his head, saying that he was a fighter, not a statesman, and not educated enough to be president. He was inexplicably, mulishly, wholeheartedly loyal to Carranza, whom he always referred to respectfully as *mi jefe*—my chief—despite Carranza's being an aristocrat, a grandee, and, although also a reformer, carefully avoiding any mention of restoring the land of Mexico to the peasants.

Now, as he spied Rigo striding toward him, Villa approached to kiss and embrace him in the Spanish fashion, as a fellow *bandolero* and freedom fighter, an old *compadre*.

"Rigo, *mi amigo. ¿Como estás?* At last, you choose to honor us with your presence, *compadre*, and not a moment too late! But now that I see the cause of your tarrying, it is understandable." His gaze appraised Araminta boldly, with the frank appreciation of a man who has an eye for both women and beauty. "So this is *la gringa* about whom I have heard so much. No wonder you chose to keep her, *mi amigo*, after stealing her away from *el esposo*, no? *¡Ay, caramba, General!* To possess the heart of a woman such as she . . . that is the true measure of a man, is it not?"

"*Sí, mi general.*"

The two men conversed in *pelado*, so Araminta could not understand them. Still, she did not need a translator to inform her that Villa found her attractive and approved of her for Rigo. No doubt this was due as much to the popularity of and controversy produced by the articles she had written about the Revolution as it was to her good looks, she deduced correctly, and was glad that Villa was apparently pleased with her work. Otherwise he might not have tolerated her presence in his camp and might have demanded that Rigo send her away, to his Mexican estate—or, worse, send her back to Texas, to Judd—for Villa had little love for *gringos*, whom he believed should not be meddling in affairs south of the border, but should mind their own business.

After the two men had finally completed their dialogue, Rigo led Araminta through the huge, sprawling camp filled with noise and confusion toward the railroad tracks that were the lifeline of the Revolution. Originating in Mexico, at the border, in Ciudad Juárez, the tracks bisected the entire country, running all the way south to the capital, Ciudad de México and linking all major points in between. For this reason, they were of such vital importance that every general in Mexico had a Superintendent of Railroads, whose job it was to defend and oversee every aspect of the trains responsible for hauling the men, the hospitals, the arms and ammunition, and the supplies that fueled the war. To carry out this critical task, Villa had delegated no less than his best friend and most trusted adviser, Mayor Fierro, whom he loved like a son and whose crimes, no matter how terrible, he always pardoned. That these offenses were so horrific, in fact, as to have earned Fierro the nickname "The Butcher" throughout the entire Revolutionary army, Villa curiously ignored, although he promptly executed any other rebel soldier guilty of wanton slayings.

Fierro was big and handsome and feared by all except Villa; for Fierro was a maniac, Rigo declared to Araminta as they walked along, and there was no one in the whole of the Revolutionary army, perhaps the whole of Mexico, who could outride or outfight him. After battle, he would literally, with his own revolver, shoot and kill hundreds of prisoners, pausing only long enough to reload.

"Take care to stay out of his way, *querida*," Rigo warned, "for if he wanted you, he would not hesitate to rape you, even though you are my woman; and even this, Villa would condone, protecting him as always."

Araminta shivered at the thought, glad that because of his high rank and riches, Rigo had his own private railroad car, an impressive Pullman-type painted a deep

russet, which he had somehow managed to have transported from El Paso to Ciudad Jiménez and to which
he now escorted her. Climbing the two steps to the
small platform at one end, he took a key from his
pocket and inserted it into the lock. The heavy door
swung inward, and he guided Araminta inside. She
stood still in the relative darkness of the stifling-hot
interior, while he moved to the heavy, green velvet
curtains, fringed and tasseled with gold, that hung at
each of the large windows lining either side of the
railroad car and began to draw them back, securing
them with gold satin braids to let the sunlight stream
in. Then he pushed up the window sashes one by one
to permit fresh air to dissipate the humid heat.

The railroad car was lavishly appointed, Araminta
saw as she inspected her surroundings. The parlor in
which she stood boasted dark-glowing, oak-paneled
walls and polished oak furniture upholstered in bro-
cades and velvets the rich desert shades of rose and
gold, turquoise and green; a plush wool carpet the
color of a saguaro cactus covered the floor. At the far
end of the room was a small pantry, bar, and kitchen
combined, behind and to one side of which was a
swinging oak door with an oval, beveled-glass inset,
which gave way to a short, narrow corridor and what
she initially assumed was a closet but that, when Rigo
slid back the pocket door, proved to be a washroom
fitted with oak-and-porcelain fixtures adorned with
gleaming brass taps. Running water! It seemed a lifetime since she had known that luxury, and she could
hardly wait to fill up the bathtub and immerse herself
in it! Down the hallway, beyond yet another swinging

door, this one of solid oak, lay the bedroom, which was as opulent as all the rest, furnished with a chair, an oak dresser, a chest of drawers, and two night tables, which flanked an elaborate brass bed covered with a plump, brilliant-turquoise satin comforter piled high with a multitude of desert-hued pillows. A second, heavy exterior door provided an alternative means of entering and exiting the railroad car.

Araminta had known, of course, that Rigo was perhaps as rich as her grandfather and Judd. But this was the first time that she had seen any real evidence of this fact, and she could not help but contrast the railroad car with the crude adobe hut they had so recently called home and marvel again at how easily her lover stepped from one world into the next. With a sudden flash of insight, as she recalled the modest little red caboose that Rigo had pointed out to her as the railroad car in which Pancho Villa always traveled, she realized that it was perhaps this very ability to transcend the classes that made Rigo so valuable to Villa.

Villa knew next to nothing about the *hacendados*, the power of the land, "the Spaniards," as he called them, except that, with one or two exceptions, he hated them and would see them all but those few driven from the boundaries of Mexico; for from the time of the Conquistadores, they had vanquished the Indians and enslaved them. In the veins of the peons flowed, among that of other tribes, the blood of the great Mayan and Aztecan empires, which had rivaled that of the Egyptians and had gone down to defeat at the hands of the Spaniards, their advanced knowledge and cultures lost, overthrown like their magnificent pyramids in the overgrown jungles of Mexico. This was the heritage of the peasants, as rich as that of the Spaniards; and perhaps Villa instinctively sought to reclaim at least a part of it. Maybe that was why he was smart enough to recognize that if the Revolution was to succeed, it would need men like Rigo, as well as men like himself. Maybe that was why he was so fiercely loyal to Carranza, also intuitively understanding that there was more than land worth taking from the grandees, things of beauty and harmony and grace, of which the peons had so little.

The more that she saw of this country, this wild Mexico that had begun to claim her heart as surely as Rigo himself had, the more that Araminta, too, came to understand what drove the leaders of the rebellion, what drove the man that she loved. Only in her arms did he forget for just a little while, she thought, find the inner peace that otherwise eluded him. This much—and more—she gave him when she opened herself to him and took him deep inside her, and she was glad, now, that it should be so.

"Do you like it?" Rigo's low, lilting voice intruded on her senses, startling her from her reverie. She blushed deeply at his question. Surely, he was a devil, in truth, to have read her mind and asked such a thing! Did she like it? As, unbidden, the image of Rigo's pressing her down, his mouth and tongue and hands moving on her body urgently, doing with her as they pleased and willed, rose in her mind, she flushed even more scarlet. "Do you like it?" he repeated, his tone now indicating his puzzlement at her lack of response. But then, as his gaze took in her downcast eyes, her rosy cheeks, the way in which her teeth nibbled at her vulnerable lower lip, a lazy, mocking note of amusement crept into his voice—"Araminta?"

Abruptly, she realized that Rigo had been referring to the railroad car, not his lovemaking at all, and that it was only her involuntary glance at the brass bed that dominated the room that had betrayed her thoughts to him. Stretching out one steely hand, he caught her wrist and drew her into the circle of his strong embrace. His hands slid slowly, sensuously, down her back, pulling her hips against his, so she could feel the hard heat of the sudden desire that flared inside him, quickening his loins, and made her own leap achingly in sweet, uncontrollable response. From beneath shuttered lids, his dark-brown eyes, smoldering now with passion, surveyed her intently, staring down into her own wide and tremulously consenting green ones. His mouth was inches from her own, his breath fanning her face, warm and exciting against her skin.

"*Do* you like it?" he deliberately asked yet a third time, his tone now as thick and husky as it was when he made love to her—and this time, Araminta knew that he did *not* mean the railroad car. "Answer me, *querida*," he demanded softly, giving her a small, rough shake. "The truth . . . I want to hear it. Do you?"

"Yes," she whispered helplessly. "Yes . . ."

For a timeless moment, Rigo gazed down at her, taking in the dishevelment of the blond tresses tumbling about her, damp with perspiration and wildly witchlike; her emerald eyes, like the quiet, rippling summer pools sometimes found in the shaded depths of a canyon; the dark, crescent smudges her long black lashes cast against her pinkened cheeks when she closed her eyes against his scrutiny; her finely chiseled retroussé nose, its nostrils flaring slightly with slowly awakening passion; her tremulously parted lips, the upper as sweetly curved as a cupid's bow and beaded with sweat, the lower full and generous; the small pulse that beat jerkily at the hollow of her slender throat; the swell of her ripe, round breasts above the low ruffled neck of the loose *camisa* she wore, rising and falling shallowly, straining against the thin cotton fabric. Then, overcome, he caught the long, shimmering cascade of her hair almost savagely and twisted her face up to his, his mouth closing over hers possessively with the assurance of a man who knew that this was his right and did not expect to be denied.

Beneath his own, Araminta's lips trembled vulnerably, soft and yielding before his assault, kissing him back fervently, her tongue meeting and welcoming his invasion, touching and tasting whorl for whorl as he conquered and plundered her mouth, searching out every hidden place within, leaving no part of its dark, moist cavity unexplored, unclaimed. Her head spun as he continued his slow onslaught upon her senses, and her belly shuddered for she knew now from sweetly tormenting experience that this was but a prelude to what would come, an exquisite, opening riff plucked upon the strings of her body and of her heart. In her ears, her blood sang, a melody as old as time itself. Her heart thrummed in her breast, pounding an ancient tattoo known to every woman who had ever loved a man. In his embrace she felt the hard-driving beat of the harmonious rhythm they composed between them, as wild and beautiful and pagan as a cabalistic chant, as heady as a drug-induced dream, its images vivid and tortured, swirling and pulsating with color.

With his mouth still locked on hers, Rigo bent her back slowly, deliberately, and her hands, twined about his neck, tightened, as though she were fearful of falling yet welcoming the plunge into a long, fathomless black void that whirled and eddied as it engulfed her. Her knees felt so weak that she knew that in moments they would buckle beneath her. Rigo knew it, too, and he suddenly dipped his arm beneath them, swooping her up as easily as he would have a child. But Araminta was no child. She was a woman aching with desire for him, needing what only he could give her.

In two long, powerful strides, he covered the distance to the bed; one knee, then two sank into the soft feather mattress as he descended upon it and lowered her down, the warm weight of his body sliding over hers, pressing her into the thick folds of the comforter. Against the turquoise satin, her gilded tresses spilled like sunlight across the endless desert sky, as bright and shining as a stream of gold coins that slipped through his fingers to scatter heedlessly amid the multitude of pillows spread like a Spanish fan beneath her. Her hair enchanted him, silken against his flesh, and so distinctive in color that even from far away, he could distinguish from the rest of the women who followed the army of Villistas the one who belonged to him—and him alone. *La mujer del general, la mujer del Salvaje*. So his people called her. So she would always be, for he would never let her go. Never! He would kill any man who tried to take her from him. She was his. *His!*

"Araminta . . ." he muttered her name, and again, "Araminta . . ."—so hoarsely and fiercely against her throat that she shivered and whimpered a little, both frightened and thrilled by the ferocity and depth of his love and desire for her. He was obsessed by her, filled with a raw, primitive, overwhelming male need to conquer, to dominate, and to possess her utterly. And of this, she was afraid, even as she exulted in her own female power to make him feel so, her ability to enthrall and surround and immure him, to hold him as much a prisoner as she. *"Ángela . . . gitana . . . bruja . . ."*

Angel . . . gypsy . . . witch . . . she was all of those things to him—and more, Rigo thought as his lips took hers again, his tongue tracing boldly, lingeringly, the delicate rosebud shape of her mouth before, with his teeth, he caught hold of her bottom lip, nibbling gently, reveling in the expression of unbearable longing so evident upon her face.

In his arms Araminta shuddered with a sudden fear that he should wield such power over her, that he should be so very certain of his dominion of her, should kiss and caress her so intimately, should know her down to her bones, down to her very soul, so that even if she were to protest against him, it would avail her naught. She had become his so totally, so absolutely, that he had only to look at her, and she would melt inside, all her bones dissolving, her loins turning to liquid fire, as they did now, burning for him to take her, to fill her to overflowing, to quench the agonizing flame of her want, her need.

As though he sensed her thoughts, Rigo's mouth roughened against the softness of her own, growing hard, exacting, crushing her lips, his teeth grazing the lower one, so she tasted blood, bittersweet upon her tongue. But she did not care. She was so caught up in the emotions he aroused in her that she could no longer think, could only feel as he went on kissing her forever, as though to drain every last ounce of strength from her body, leaving her weak and defenseless against him—and glad that she should be so. His mouth slashed like a Spanish bullwhip across her cheek to her temple, the strands of her hair, stinging, burning, as though he left raw wounds in his wake. He rained ardent kisses on her hair; his fingers weaving and ensnaring the tangled skeins, he buried his face in the heavy mass. He nuzzled her earlobe and licked her ear, sending a tingling charge surging through her body, from her neck clear down to the molten, secret heart of her, which quivered violently at the shock; and she involuntarily bucked against him, only to find herself further electrified by the brush of his sex against hers.

"*¡Jesús! ¡Qué te quiero!* How I want you!" Rigo rasped in her ear. A spate of Spanish followed, as though, in his passion, he had forgotten how to speak English—or perhaps it was just that his own language was so much more expressive of his feelings than hers was. "*Me quiero perder en tú, estar dentro de tú, te chingar, enamorar a tú, vez y otra vez. En tus brazos,* *me olvido todo pero tú . . . la guerra, los Federales, las Villistas, tu esposo . . . todo pero mi venganza, mi venganza dulce, más dulce que siempre soñaba, porque tú eres mío, solo mío, por siempre jamás mío, querida. Nunca te soltará, no . . . nunca. Contigo, soy completo, mi corazón, mi alma. . . .''*

Araminta did not understand all the words, but she intuited their meaning as he kissed her over and over, until her mouth was bruised and swollen, and her entire body grew so sensitive that his lightest touch was excruciating, like wildfire scorching her skin as his palms moved upon her shoulders, stroking them slowly, sensuously, for a moment. Then, all of a sudden, his eyes darkened with desire and his hands tightened—a brief warning of his intent—before gliding swiftly down her bare skin to jerk the short sleeves of her *camisa* down her arms to her wrists, imprisoning them at her sides and bunching her blouse around her slender waist. Freed, her burgeoning breasts burst from their filmy confines willfully, wantonly, exposing and flaunting themselves before his avid eyes, his covetous mouth, his fondling fingers. Eagerly he accepted the invitation, his palms grasping and squeezing the twin mounds, pressing them high for his lips. His mouth encompassed the tip of one breast and then the other, his tongue teasing the rosy crests into stiff, hard peaks that trembled and quaked with each new taunt, sending rapturous tremors coursing through her body. She moaned with pleasure at the sweet sensations, hungering for more.

Her captive wrists broke free of their bonds, and her hands swept up to Rigo's broad shoulders to tug off his bolero. Shaking, her fingers fumbled at the buttons of his shirt, struggling to unfasten them, a task made even more difficult by Rigo's catching her hands and kissing her palms before his lips found hers again, then traveled hotly down her throat to her breasts, her nipples. She would never get the remaining buttons undone, Araminta thought frantically, half crazy with wanting to feel his naked chest against hers, the fine mat of his dark hair like silk against her breasts. Her nails raked the partially revealed skin of his chest and she seized the opened edges of his shirt and yanked, popping the rest of the buttons and sending them flying. Neither she nor Rigo noticed or cared as they flung aside the last vestiges of their clothing.

Naked and gasping, they came together, rolling and tumbling across the bed, writhing and straining against each other until his hard, probing sex found her, drove into her so suddenly and violently and deeply that it took her breath away. She inhaled sharply, raggedly, her breath catching in a gasp, then freeing itself in a soft, low cry. She heard his sigh, his groan of pleasure at being inside of her, even as he aroused them both to a feverish pitch by deliberately, tantalizingly, withdrawing, then swiftly entering her again. His breath was hot against her throat and upon her breasts as his mouth devoured her, sucking her nipples greedily and laving them with his tongue. Frantically, she arched against him as he moved within her, spiraled down into her, each thrust stronger, harder, deeper than the last, until she was panting for air and clutching him to her wantonly, her legs locked tight around his, her nails furrowing the smooth, dark skin of his back as she reached for ecstasy and seized it with an intensity that matched his own.

A roaring tide of exhilaration washed over them then, enveloped them, churned inside and between them. Exquisite waves of sensual delight dipped and swelled within them, each one higher and stronger than the one before it, until the combers came so quickly and forcefully that they merged into a massive surge of unendurable sensation that swept away all before it and bore it aloft. Together, she and he rushed mindlessly along on its hurtling crest, clung to it desperately before, suddenly, it peaked and shattered, breaking, white-foamed, upon dark and golden sands misted with spindrift, casting the two of them up from the brine as, its fury spilled and spent, it gently ebbed and died.

When it was over, Araminta lay quietly in Rigo's arms, cradled against his hard, muscular chest as she waited for the railroad car to stop spinning, for her heart to slow to its normal pace. The sweat of him glistened on her skin, mingling with her own, and the sweet, musky scent of their lovemaking pervaded her nostrils. She and Rigo had mated like animals, she thought, slightly shocked; there was no other way to describe it. And she had enjoyed every second of it! Her cheeks stained crimson at the realization, flushing even more deeply as she observed the triumph and satisfaction in his drowsy dark eyes. Surely, he would *not* be so arrogant and audacious as to ask her yet again. . . .

"It *is* tempting, *querida*, I promise you," he

drawled impudently, reading her mind. "But what is the point . . . when I already know for certain the answer? Ah, that makes you blush even more, does it not, *mi gringuita?* In your country, a gentleman"— the word was faintly mocking—"does not speak of these things to a lady, *¿es verdad?* And a lady . . . she does not speak of them at all. *¡Ay, caramba!* Such *gringo* foolishness! I will never understand it. It is nothing to be ashamed of, Araminta . . . what is between us. It is the way of a man and a woman. In Mexico, we understand this. Here, *amor* is life; it is all, the one thing that the *hacendados* cannot take away from us. And no one can take you away from me. I would kill any man—even your husband, Judd Hobart, especially him—who dared to touch you. Do you understand this, *querida?*"

"Yes . . . yes," she murmured, shivering a little at the thought of Rigo's killing anyone, even Judd, at the realization now of how wholly she had given herself into his keeping, not only as his lover, but also as his possession. Even had she not fallen in love with him, he would have kept her as his captive anyway, after her surrender, she knew.

"Still, something troubles you, *niña, ¿sí?*"

"*Sí* . . . no . . . I mean— It's just that, sometimes, you make me feel so—so vulnerable and—and helpless against you, Rigo. . . ."

"As you are," he declared softly, his eyes gleaming as he deliberately rolled her over and pressed her down beneath his body. With one steely hand, he captured both of her slender wrists. "You see how weak and fragile you are compared to my strength? How easily

I make you my prisoner?'' Slowly, he lowered his mouth to her breasts, his teeth and his tongue making them flush and harden and grow taut with desire. When he lifted his head, an insolent smile curved his lips. ''How readily your body responds to my touch! That is the way that I want you to feel.'' His dark, handsome face sobered suddenly, and she knew he spoke in earnest now. ''That is the way that I will always make you feel—because I am sure that if I do not, you will grow dissatisfied and lose respect for me; and where there is no respect, there can be no love. This, you know in your heart, Araminta. A strong woman such as you needs an even stronger man; and if she does not have one, she will look elsewhere. I was young and careless once—riding away to become a bandit and leaving undefended what was mine—and I suffered for it. Now I am older and wiser—and I have become a very jealous man. What is mine, I keep and guard closely and let no man take away. But what I take from you, *querida*, I give back in full measure, because I love you, and because for that reason alone—though there are countless others—I would never deliberately hurt you. *¡Te quiero, niña! Dime . . . dime*. What more must I say?''

''Nothing,'' she whispered. ''Nothing at all.''

And when of her own volition, Araminta reached up and drew him down to her, he made love to her with a tenderness he had not shown her earlier, kissing her eyelids and her mouth gently as he slowly pressed himself inside her. Together they lay, breast to breast, thigh to thigh, so close that she did not know where she ended and he began. They were as one: no space between, no room in either's heart or mind for an-other—nor would there ever be. Like the night wind through the desert canyons, their bodies wound and quickened, lips, tongues, and hands engaged, while outside on the far horizon, the fiery sun began its slow descent against the bright and boundless turquoise sky.

Chapter Eighteen

Rigo had given her a child. Araminta knew in her heart that it was so, though she did not yet tell him, lest he send her away, for her own and the unborn child's protection, from the front lines of the war to Casa Grande, his estate in Mexico. He would never return her to Texas, not even to Casa Blanca, his own ranch there. Apparently her grandfather, at least, did not believe she was dead. According to the latest reports from Rigo's network of spies and informers, Noble Winthrop had caused to be printed and distributed all over Texas and northern Mexico posters offering a five-thousand-dollar reward for her safe return or any information leading to her whereabouts and recovery. He had further hired four professional mer-

cenaries, who were, even now, in search of her, somewhere in Mexico, Rigo assumed.

It would, of course, take her grandfather's hired
gunslingers time to track her down, especially with
Villa's army on the move and Rigo's having dispatched a handful of his own best rebel soldiers to find
the *gringos* and to put a halt to their ill-undertaken
quest. This, above all, was why he had made arrangements to have his private railroad car transported from
El Paso to Ciudad Jiménez and what had prompted
him to inquire whether Araminta liked it. For from the
moment she stepped inside it, she was confined to its
three rooms, given strict orders by Rigo that she was
not to set foot outside of it without his being at her side.
To ensure that she obeyed his command, he posted two
guards outside the railroad car, one on each platform
at either end to prevent her from exiting through either
door. As, in addition, each man stood to attention in
such a way that he had a clear view of one whole side
of the railroad car, it was impossible for her to climb
out of the large windows. Nor did Rigo overlook the
fact that she might in time become friendly with the
sentries and sweet-talk one or more of them into letting
her outside. Every four hours—except at night, when
he himself was with her and no one need be on duty—
the guards changed shifts and new faces assigned to
the task watched her. She had no real chance if she
decided she wanted to wander about a bit to persuade
any of them to act counter to Rigo's demands. Not
that any of the men would have, anyway, Araminta
thought, slightly piqued, for it had not escaped her
notice that they feared to cross him almost as much as

they did "The Butcher," Mayor Fierro. *He*, at least, for whatever unknown reason, did not bother her, a circumstance for which she could only be grateful.

Although she chafed at her enforced sequestering and, once after a particularly long and boring day, even cursed Rigo soundly for it, she nevertheless understood his insistence on her compliance and so, for the most part, grudgingly respected and accepted it. To relieve the tedium of her hours, she set herself a routine and followed it fairly regularly so she would always have something to do with her time.

Every morning, after Rigo made love to her, Araminta rose and cooked breakfast, while he read the newspapers, when available, and any reports from his men and messages from Villa. After they had eaten, Rigo bathed, dressed, and departed. When she was finished with her own toilette, she carried her journal, sketch pad, and pencils to the table and worked, writing and drawing until the siesta hour, when she ate lunch, either alone or, if he were able to snatch time away from his duties to join her, with Rigo.

After lunch, Araminta stripped down to her undergarments and took a long nap in the bedroom to try to escape from the worst heat of the day. Sometimes, Rigo was there and made love to her again, striding naked from the bedroom to the parlor or to the bathroom, to fetch wine to slake their thirst or a wet washcloth with which to cool their heated bodies. She watched him as he moved, admiring his lean, powerful, hard-muscled torso from beneath the sheet she drew up to cover herself modestly—much to his amusement. Then, if he were not pressed for time, his eyes bold and glittering with devilish intent, he would smile at her insolently and snatch the sheet from her grasp to hold her down and tickle her until, overcome with laughter and desire, she would beg for mercy— and more.

Following her nap, Araminta completed her work for the day and laid it aside for Rigo to inspect upon his return, which he did unfailingly, no matter how late it was or how tired he might be. She had supper with him if he had not dined with Villa and other officers, or, more usually, the troops. Afterward, if the night were young, she and Rigo played chess or the guitar, then went to bed—and made love yet again before drifting into slumber. If Rigo's appetite were at all typical, Araminta concluded, the girls at Miss Standish's Female Academy in upstate New York had not known what they were talking about when they had whispered that a wife need not worry about being "bothered" more than once a week by her husband— and that for the sole, dutiful aim of begetting an heir!

The only breaks in this routine were the times that Rigo fetched her from the railroad car to accompany him someplace or when she was visited by one of the friends she had made among the women. Unless Rigo were present, no men were permitted inside, of course. Sometimes, he took her to the cockpit, which Villa himself frequented most every afternoon at four o'clock, fighting his own birds and cheering them on with great enthusiasm. In the evenings, Villa and his *amigos* searched out some gaming hell, for while the general-in-chief did not smoke or drink, he did like to play faro. In the mornings, now and then, Villa would dispatch a swift messenger after Luis León, the famous bullfighter, and personally telephone the slaughter-house, to get a fierce bull. Then all rode to the nearest adobe corral, where after a group of *gauchos* had chopped the bull from the herd and sawed off its deadly, piercing horns, Villa, León, and any other dare-devil man who wanted to, Rigo included, would take up the matador's red capes and step into the arena. León, the professional among them, fought expertly and prudently, but Villa battled the bull so recklessly that Araminta, watching from the sidelines, began to think that he was as much a maniac as Fierro. When the beast, snorting and horns lowered, butted Villa from behind, literally driving him across the ring, Villa would finally turn and grasp the bull's head and attempt to wrestle the beast down before several of the others could rush into the arena to grab hold of the bull's tail and haul the bellowing, recalcitrant beast back. All the men, even Rigo, considered this great sport, but to Ar-aminta, it was sheer craziness, and she marveled that no one was killed. She started to think they were *all* mad, stark-raving *loco*, these wild and bold Latin men.

Villa loved to dance, as well. In fact, when the army had begun its march on Torreón, he had halted briefly at Ciudad Carmargo to act as the best man at the wedding of one of his old friends. According to rumors, he had danced without pause for two solid days and arrived at the front not yet having been to bed—which had no doubt partially accounted for his leniency in overlooking Rigo's own tardy arrival.

As Araminta had come to learn, Villa's behavior was just as unorthodox on the battlefield. Until now, no Mexican army had ever strayed far from its base of operations but had always remained near to the railroads and supply trains. Villa was the first general ever to think of temporarily leaving the women behind and pressing forward in a forced march of cavalry. This he did at Gómez Palacio, just outside of Torreón, terrorizing the enemy when he abandoned his base of operations and led his whole army on to the battlefield. As a result, Gómez Palacio was speedily taken and, shortly afterward, in September, Torreón fell. The victory was short-lived, however; for by this time, word had been received that Villa's old nemesis, General Pascual Orozco, had, with his own huge army, left Ciudad de México to proceed north, toward Torreón. In the face of this advancing threat, Villa was compelled to retreat. He did not go quietly, but paused over a month later and several hundred miles down the railroad tracks to attack Chihuahua City instead.

By now, Araminta was quite certain that she carried Rigo's child. She had missed her monthly flux yet a second time and then a third, and observed that her body was changing to accommodate the baby growing inside of her. She still had not yet told Rigo, but she thought that soon she must. He knew her body too well not to notice the slight swelling of her breasts, the faint darkening of her nipples, the small rounding of her stomach. She had to look closely at her reflection in the mirror in the bedroom to see these things; but a man so intimate with her, so accustomed to cupping her breasts possessively and covetously suckling her nipples, to sliding his hand slowly down her belly to her thighs, would surely notice much sooner than later.

Of morning sickness, she had experienced none, merely an incredible tiredness instead, so she slept even longer during the siesta hour, and her work suffered for it—though this she thought that Rigo did not suspect; she was a slow, careful writer, anyway, and it was sometimes days or even weeks before she finished an article and completed the sketches that accompanied it, not that he ever rushed her to produce. Araminta was for the first time glad that she traveled in the railroad car rather than by horseback, since she was able to lie down and rest when necessary, lulled into slumber by the rocking of the railroad car as Villa's train wended its way back north, cooled by the breeze that, stirred by the train's passing, wafted in through the windows of the bedroom in which she lay.

For five long days, the Villistas assaulted Chihuahua City, without success, so it must have seemed to Orozco that his dream of defeating his old enemy was nearly within his grasp. Araminta could only imagine his shock, then, when he woke up one morning to discover that Villa had outwitted him yet again by sneaking around the city, under the cover of darkness to attack by night. Because he lacked enough railroad cars to transport all his still-burgeoning troops, now nearly four thousand rebel soldiers strong, Villa had, at Terrazzas, surprised and seized a freight train of the Federales, which had been dispatched south by General Castro, the Federal commander in Ciudad Juárez. Then, upon realizing that he *still* hadn't enough

railroad cars for the job, Villa had brazenly telegraphed Castro, falsely informing him that the engine
had broken down at Moctezuma and requesting that
he send another engine and five more railroad cars.
Villa had signed to the wire the name of the colonel
in charge of the ambushed Federal freight train, and
the unsuspecting Castro had immediately dispatched a
new train. Thereupon, Villa had telegraphed him
again, this time untruthfully reporting to him that the
wires had been cut between the train's current location
and Chihuahua City, and, as a large army of Villistas
was now advancing from the south, asking what he
should do. The gulled Castro had wired back that
the supposed Federal colonel should return to Ciudad
Juárez at once. Villa had then swooped down upon the
relatively unguarded border town, impudently continuing to send deceptive telegrams all the way. Hearing
at last of Villa's arrival and realizing how cleverly and
shamelessly he had been duped, Castro had slinked
out of Ciudad Juárez, without even notifying his garrison of his departure; and after a swift, decisive battle,
Villa had captured the city, almost without firing a
single shot.

It was in Ciudad Juárez, so close to the border and
thus to El Paso, that the first attempt to wrest Araminta
from Rigo's grasp came without warning. It was now
November, and she had been gone from the High
Sierra for six months, with never a word to her grandfather. Knowing that he had been in ill health before
her marriage and increasingly gnawed by guilt over
how worried he must be about her, she begged Rigo

to permit her at least to let him know, via the telegraph system, that she was alive and well.

"Please, Rigo," she entreated earnestly, "do not refuse me this, especially when it is all that I have asked of you. He is an old man, and despite his pressuring me to wed Judd, I feel sure that in his heart, he does care for me and that he meant it for the best."

"This, I cannot believe, *niña*, although I suppose that it *is* possible that being Judd Hobart's godfather, and thus, one assumes, feeling some type of affection for him, your grandfather deliberately blinded himself to your husband's cruel, villainous nature. Very well, then. Since it appears to mean so much to you, and since no real harm can be caused by it—we march from Ciudad Juárez on to Tierra Blanca on the morrow, after all—I will permit it. But only this once, *querida*," he warned. "As I have told you before: What is mine, I keep—and will let no man, not even your grandfather, take away."

So Rigo escorted her to the telegraph station at the depot, where Araminta dictated her wire and he ordered the telegrapher on duty to send it. The telegram was not as long as she wished, for, his face stern and implacable, Rigo ruthlessly censored most of it, allowing only the briefest of messages to go out over the wire: "Grandfather, please do not worry about me. I am alive and well." To this, despite her objections, he deliberately added: "But I will remain so only if you withdraw the offer of reward money and call off the men you have hired to rescue me. Araminta."

"That is cruel and unnecessary!" she insisted, biting her lower lip to still its sudden trembling at this glimpse of Rigo as the hard, unyielding *bandolero*. And her independent spirit, which had been stifled by captivity and softened by love, began to rise in protest.

"No, it is not," he rejoined, a harsh edge to his voice. "Your grandfather must learn that he has no hope of recovering you, that you are irretrievably lost to him—forever! It is a kindness of the greatest magnitude, I assure you, that I permit him to know that you are alive at all! I have no love for Noble Winthrop, nor he for me."

"At least you can be sure of completely accomplishing your goal of gaining revenge on Judd," Araminta pointed out coolly, driven, by the hatred she had for this side of him, to goad him further, "for my grandfather will certainly tell him about me."

"You may be sure that that is the only reason why I indulge your request, *querida*," Rigo shot back just as icily, his eyes glittering as hard and narrow as they had when she was his captive.

"Oh!" she gasped, as stricken as though he had slapped her. All the love they had shared seemed reduced to an illusion, and Rigo became in her eyes an arrogant seducer who had beguiled her into submission. "Don't look at me that way—as though you owned me. Do you think my will and mind melt away when you touch me?"

"I do not think." Slowly, deliberately, he swept his eyes over her from head to toe before they riveted once more on her face flushed with mortification and anger. "I know, *gringuita*." He spoke the last word contemptuously, a sardonic smile twisting his mouth.

At that, Araminta was so incensed that before Rigo realized what she intended, she raced past him and stormed from the telegraph station, slamming the door behind her so furiously that it nearly shattered the inset glass window.

"Araminta!" he shouted, enraged, striding after her, knowing that he had pushed her too far. In his heart now he felt not only a terrible remorse but also a sudden, sharp stab of fear that she should be alone on the streets of Ciudad Juárez, which teemed with rebel soldiers, the vast majority of whom were not his own men. "Araminta!"

Behind her, she heard him calling her name and glanced back to see him chasing after her, roughly shouldering and knocking aside anyone in his path, such a murderous wrath transforming his face that it terrified her. At the thought of his unleashing upon her the full force and fury of his black Latin temper, perhaps even beating her for daring to argue with and defy him, she panicked and, hitching up her skirts, began to run wildly away from him. She had no clear idea of where she was going, only a vague, half-formed notion of reaching his private railroad car and locking herself in the bedroom until his anger cooled. But she had never before been in Ciudad Juárez and now, hopelessly scared, confused and lost, did not even remember the path they had taken to the telegraph station. Everywhere she looked, there seemed to be snaking railroad tracks and long, indistinguishable trains. All was chaos as the Villistas prepared to withdraw from the city to move on to conquer Tierra Blanca. Rebel soldiers were everywhere, loading into boxcars the guns and ammunition and the rest of the supplies that Villa, Rigo, and other experienced *bandoleros* had smuggled across the border from El Paso as well as leading nervously whinnying and snorting horses up ramps into the stock cars.

With relief, Araminta spied at last what she believed was Villa's little red caboose. Thinking that it would at least offer a temporary refuge, that, surely, Villa would defend her against Rigo, if only because the general-in-chief of the Villistas knew that her articles in the *Record* were helping to turn the tide against President Wilson's prohibition against the sale of arms to the Revolutionaries, she rushed blindly toward the caboose. She did not even see the gelding that bore down on her, ridden by one Ernesto Urbino, who had been one of her many guards until Rigo, disliking the way the man had looked at her, had curtly removed him from his post. Now, as Urbino, who had been watching her and waiting ever since for his chance to abduct her, bent from his mount to catch her up and throw her facedown over his saddle, Araminta screamed with fear. Her shrill, hoarse cry tore like the sharp talons of a falcon at Rigo's heart as he saw her carried helplessly away. There was little that she could do to save herself, dangling over the saddle as she was, the high Spanish pommel grinding painfully into her stomach and, with each rough jolt, her head banging defenselessly against Urbino's right stirrup.

"You, soldier! Get down off that horse at once!" Rigo demanded savagely as he raced toward the nearest mounted man in sight. "*¡Pronto! ¡Ándale, ándale!*" he yelled. Half demented, he commandeered the horse, practically jerking the poor, bewildered young man from the saddle before he flung himself into it.

"*S-s-í, General,*" the soldier stammered with fright, as he wondered what he had done to become the target of El Salvaje's infamous anger and then realized with great relief that it was directed at some other unfortunate soul. Rigo roweled his spurs mercilessly into the horse's flanks and tore out furiously after Urbino's gelding, now galloping wildly through Ciudad Juárez, causing people to shout, swear, and scatter hastily out of his way, lest they be trampled underfoot as first Urbino and then Rigo clattered through the narrow, twisting streets.

Within minutes, Urbino was clear of the city with Rigo hard on his heels, knowing with certainty that Urbino was headed for the border. If he managed to cross the Rio Grande into Texas, Araminta would be lost, delivered up unto her grandfather, Noble Winthrop, or, worse, to her husband, Judd Hobart, for the five-thousand-dollar reward that had been offered for her safe return. Rigo would kill her himself before he permitted that to happen! Abruptly hauling his appropriated mount up short and yanking from its scabbard on the saddle the young soldier's rifle, he swung the gun up to his shoulder, sighted careful aim down the barrel, pulled the trigger and fired. The bullet sped swift and true toward its intended goal, striking Urbino's gelding high on its left rear thigh. Screaming with agony, the horse bucked and then staggered wildly, lurching forward one step, two, and three before it fell and rolled heavily, pitching both Araminta and Urbino from its back. Still whinnying shrilly, it thrashed like a mad thing, hooves flailing, before, sides heaving and, with each labored breath, blowing its nostrils in anguish, it lay still.

Urbino himself stumbled to his feet in moments, having leaped clear from the saddle when he had realized that the gelding had been hit. But Araminta lay where she had fallen, dazed and whimpering, her head throbbing and the wind knocked from her by the force of the impact. In shock after the torturous, unreal ride and the collapse of the horse beneath her, she had no clear thought or even recognition of her own hurts. In some obscure corner of her befuddled mind, she prayed desperately as she lay there upon the hard desert ground that she would not miscarry the child nestled inside her womb. Dully, she felt Urbino's hand close painfully around one of her wrists, jerking her viciously to her feet. At that moment, rage overcame terror. A red mist formed before her eyes; a horrendous roaring sounded in her ears, and she seemed to lose all control of herself. As though the tiny part of her that was still sane had wrenched itself from her body, she suddenly went as berserk as a rabid dog, assaulting Urbino crazily, driven by fierce, blind, primitive maternal instinct to protect the child that she carried.

Such was her hysteria, her turmoil, that she did not even feel the blows when he slapped her face hard, first one side and then the other, snapping her head back and sending her reeling. She was only dimly aware of Urbino's drawing his pistol from his gun belt, and she attacked him again frenziedly, her madness vesting her with unnatural strength. Urbino, taken aback, was knocked off balance and fell, dragging Araminta down with him. She grabbed the revolver, inadvertently setting off a wild shot as the two of them tumbled and grappled across the sunbaked earth. Finally, with a cruel, ferocious shove, Urbino flung her aside, only to find himself the target of an even more murderous assailant as Rigo brought his lathered mount up short and launched himself from the saddle, kicking the gun from Urbino's hand and sending the weapon flying.

With the quick, cunning reflexes of an animal, Urbino sprang to his feet and drew the big Bowie knife at his waist. Just as rapidly, Rigo yanked from his own boot a wicked, double-ended knife. Each sharp, curved blade at either end of the slender bone handle flashed silver in the streaming sunlight as, with a flick of his wrist, he twirled the knife through his fingers before tossing it to the side and catching hold of it securely with his left hand. This technique, known as border shifting, alerted his opponent to how savage and deadly a man he had dared to cross.

"Is this your idea of loyalty to your commanding officer, Urbino?" Rigo snarled, his face dark with lethal intent. "Stealing his woman?"

"Five thousand *gringo* dollars cuts a lot of ties of allegiance, *General*," Urbino jeered in reply, but his wide, deceptive grin did not quite reach his flat black eyes.

"And this knife"—Rigo raised the diabolic knife he held in his hand—"has cut a lot of throats, Urbino. Say your prayers, and prepare to die, *amigo*."

Despite the sun that shone high in the sky, the blades seemed to gleam with their own cold fire as the two men began to circle each other warily. Bent forward slightly to protect his chest and belly from the other's knife, his arms outstretched as though for balance, each man danced on booted feet. Araminta reflected numbly, as she slowly began to rise from where she sprawled upon the ground, that they seemed to be performing a macabre parody of a ballet she had seen once at the theater. The weapons slashed through the air, making sharp, whooshing noises, like the sound of a lasso's or a bola's being cast, darting outward again and again in swift, cutting arcs. Already, Urbino's ugly, uneasy face was filmed with sweat, as well it might be, she thought, for Rigo resembled a devil as, with a lightning rapidity, he flicked and spun that fiendish knife and switched it back and forth between his hands, keeping his opponent guessing as to whether he would strike with the left or with the right. Araminta had seen Rigo practicing these skills now and then, but never at such a high rate of speed, and his incredible finesse seemed superhuman. She half expected the weapon to go flying from his fingers, but when it did not, Urbino's face began to tense with apprehension.

The cat-and-mouse game they played was getting on his nerves. He was anxious to get down to business before his courage failed him utterly. He wished, now, that his greed for the reward money had never proved greater than his fear of El Salvaje, that he had never dared to kidnap *la gringa*, the general's beautiful blond American woman. Plainly, the general was obsessed with her to the point of madness, and there was no telling what the *hombre macho y loco* would do! Now, not only was the fortune in *gringo* dollars lost, but perhaps Urbino's very life. He had to make his move quickly, before the crazy general closed in on him and it was too late!

Licking his dry lips, Urbino lunged forward, his knife sweeping out toward Rigo's belly. As lithely as a panther, Rigo sprang back, bouncing lightly on the balls of his feet; and as Urbino, unable to halt the impetus of his own forward movement, stumbled past him, Rigo sliced a long gash into him. Blood dripped from the thin wound in Urbino's side and from one of the blades of the double-ended knife. Urbino's hand dropped to his side, and he found to his astonishment that he had actually been cut. The sight of the blood on his fingers maddened him. Recklessly, he charged forward again; and Rigo scraped yet another narrow red weal of blood into Urbino's flesh. Over and over, Rigo slashed until it seemed as though his opponent's chest and his abdomen were a hatchwork of crimson soaking the peasant shirt he wore beneath the bullet-laden bandoliers crisscrossed over his torso.

Araminta had by now managed to wobble to her feet. Her head and stomach ached from being battered against Urbino's saddle; there were bruises on her wrist where he had grabbed her, and her face burned where he had slapped her so brutally. With trembling hands, she clutched the shreds of her torn *camisa* together, and prayed without words that Rigo would prevail. She watched as his satanic blade lifted once more. It glittered like a mirror in the sunlight, and then, suddenly, it fell, slitting Urbino's throat, severing his jugular vein. Blood sprayed warm and wet and sticky on Rigo's skin and garments, and a horrible, gurgling sound issued from Urbino's lips as he slowly crumpled to his knees, then toppled forward, face-down into the dirt, dead.

For a moment, Rigo stood there motionless, breathing hard, the knife still poised in his hand, blood trickling slowly down the handle. Then he knelt and, with quick strokes, wiped the weapon clean on the back of Urbino's shirt, then slipped the blade back into his own knee-high black leather boot. Rising, he strode toward Araminta and pulled her quivering figure into his arms, holding her close and gently stroking her hair as she sobbed quietly against his chest.

"Are you hurt? *Querida*, are you hurt? Let me see," he demanded when she shook her head mutely and would not look at him. Cupping her chin, he compelled her face up to his, swearing viciously in Spanish when he spied the swelling bruises that marred her skin. *"¡Sangre de Cristo! ¡Qué bastardo! ¡Qué hijo de la puta! ¡Maldito sea! ¡Maldito sea al diablo! ¡Espero que su alma miserable se pudra en infierno!"* Then his voice softened as he crooned, *"Ay, pobre niña. Lo siento, lo siento. Está bien, está bien. Él es muerto."* Tenderly, he kissed the tears from her cheeks, holding her in his arms until, at long last, she ceased to tremble. At that, Rigo's hand slid slowly down to her belly. *"¿El niño . . . está bien?"* The child . . . is it all right?

"You—you know about the baby?" Araminta whispered, half afraid he would be angry with her for not telling him of the child she carried. But when she looked up at him, met the dark eyes that gazed down into hers, she saw that they were alight with a curiously

gentle, brooding flame of desire and wonder and awe
that this, too, they had made between them.

"Did you truly think I would not know, *querida?* I
. . . who knows your body as well as my own? Many
nights now have I lain beside you and waited for you
to speak, to share with me this happy news. Why have
you kept silent instead? Can it be that although you
say you love me, there is a part of you even so that
hates me still? Can it be that you do not . . . you do
not want my child growing inside of you, Araminta?
Are you ashamed, *gringuita*, because it will be a half-
breed? An illegitimate, a bastard—like me?" The
thought of these things wounded him deeply; she could
tell by the sudden shadows that darkened his eyes.

"No, oh, no, Rigo. I have thought none of those terrible things, do you hear? Of course I love you! Of
course I want your child! *Our* child! How can you
think I don't? It's just that I—I was afraid that you—
that you would send me away . . . to Casa Grande—"

"Casa Grande? Is that what you thought? *¡Ay,
caramba!* My foolish *corazón*"—he smiled at her rue-
fully then, shaking his head—"why in the name of
God would I want to do such a thing as that? Because
I fight for the Revolution, the Federales seized Casa
Grande months ago and are even now, I am informed,
using it as one of their bases of operations. If not for
Casa Blanca, I would be as poor as the next man in
Mexico, I fear."

"Oh"—the word was small and surprised and
ashamed. "I—I didn't know. I'm sorry."

"*Sí*, I should think so, *niña*. Well, I confess I *was*
going to beat you for running away from the telegraph

station—'' As, at that, her eyes abruptly widened and her face paled—for she had, in truth, forgotten all about their quarrel earlier—Rigo broke off, frowning darkly. ''I was only joking, *querida*—although, now, I really *am* sorely tempted to beat you for your thinking that I ever would! Especially with your being *encinta!* I may be a lot of things—and not all of them pleasant—but I am not such a brute as that!

''*¡Dios mío!* How can you even think I would do such a thing? Never have I known such fear as I knew when I watched Urbino ride away with you flung over his saddle! But now, do you understand why you must never be so foolish as to run away from me again, no matter how angry or frightened you may be? I do not think I have ever truly given you any real reason to be afraid of me, and I tell you here and now that the only thing that would ever cause me to do so would be if I ever discovered that you were unfaithful to me. As for the telegram to your grandfather . . . well, do you not see now why I added what I did? It is for your own protection that I do these things, that I guard you so closely, Araminta. Urbino is not the only man in Mexico who might be tempted by the thought of a fortune in *gringo* dollars—and unless you have some secret burning desire to return to Judd Hobart, you will obey me in this matter, if not for yourself, then at least for the child. It is perhaps only by the grace of God that you did not lose it!''

''Yes, I know,'' she responded miserably, duly chastened and contrite, for in her heart, she knew that it had indeed been her own foolishness that had made possible Urbino's abduction of her.

"Then, come. The hour grows late, and we must return to camp."

So saying, Rigo walked over to Urbino's body, impassively scattering the buzzards that had already descended upon it. Hunkering down beside the corpse, he began to strip it of its weapons and ammunition, for these were like gold to the Villistas. Once he had finished taking what was of value, Rigo turned his attention to the fallen gelding, which was still lying quietly on the ground. Although stunned and in pain, the horse was not mortally wounded, and finally, he managed to coax it to its feet and tied its reins to the pommel of his own saddle. Then he lifted Araminta up onto his appropriated mount and swung up behind her. In silence, they rode toward Ciudad Juárez.

Chapter Nineteen

"She is still alive, and all this time, he has kept her."
Noble Winthrop spoke aloud in his empty study as he
stared down at the telegram that lay upon his desk.

"Grandfather, please do not worry about me. I am
alive and well. . . ." There was no doubt in Noble's
mind or heart that Araminta herself had, in truth, sent
the wire; for Del Castillo himself would surely not
have bothered with such a message. "But I will remain
so only if you withdraw the offer of reward money
and call off the men you have hired to rescue me."
Yes, in that part of the telegram, Noble could distinguish Del Castillo's hand. Although the wire in some
ways relieved Noble, in others, it disturbed him
deeply. Why not: "Forget the reward and call off your

men, or I'll kill your granddaughter"? That alone would have sufficed. No, the words in this telegram were those of a man who cared about Araminta, at least enough to permit her to set an old man's mind at rest, to give him the peace of knowing that she was still alive . . . and well. Those two words spoke volumes. Why not just: "I am alive"? *I am alive, Grandfather, but I would be better off dead, and so you must learn to think of me as thus.* "Please do not worry about me." *I am well; I am fine, Grandfather, and even though, yes, Rigo del Castillo has become my lover, he cares enough about me that he keeps me at his side and allows me to send this wire, to relieve your anxiety. My life here in Mexico is not so terrible. It is better than being dead, Grandfather; it is no worse than being the bride of Judd Hobart. This is why I haven't killed myself.* "But I will remain so only if you withdraw the offer of reward money and call off the men you have hired to rescue me." *Your granddaughter lies in my arms, old man, and because she pleases me, I do not intend to part with her just yet. Meanwhile, I can be kind to her—or not. It is up to you, old man. You decide.*

All this is what Noble Winthrop read into the contents of his granddaughter's telegram—delivered to him and not to Judd; and that, too, said much. . . .

My husband, I do not love you; I never did. I married you only because it was my grandfather's wish, and now, though I am still alive, I am dead to you. This, I understand.

My enemy, your bride is mine; the score is settled.

This, you know. It is enough. It is finished between us.

It is up to you, old man. You decide.

The wire had originated in Ciudad Juárez, just across the border, so near and yet so far away; and now, Araminta was gone, had slipped from his grasp, perhaps forever, swept away when, a mere week after taking the city, Villa's army had sallied forth from Ciudad Juárez to fall upon and slaughter with a vengeance the Federales at Tierra Blanca. Withdraw the reward offer, yes, Noble could certainly do that, and would. But to call off the team of professional mercenaries was another matter entirely. He did not even know where they were, those four hardened gunslingers he had hired to fetch back his granddaughter. He had paid them half their money up front, ten thousand dollars, twenty-five hundred per man; and they had provisioned themselves and set off across the border, knowing that it was no easy task they faced, except that if they located Del Castillo, they would undoubtedly find Araminta as well, if she was still alive. Why had it not occurred to Noble, to Judd, as it had to the professionals, that the obvious place to search for a general was in the midst of an army? Could four *gringos*, even if they *were* mercenaries, possibly hope to retrieve Araminta from among four thousand Mexicans? Their assignment was not now impossible, the gunslingers had reported, just more difficult. They would have to bide their time and wait for the right opportunity to present itself, but they would get the job done. That was the last word Noble had had from them. He had cried havoc and unleashed the dogs of war, and now there was no calling them back. *You decide*. No, Noble thought, it was up to fate now to decide.

A month after the fall of Ciudad Juárez to the Villistas, they had taken Chihuahua City and sent the last remnants of the Federales troops in Chihuahua, under the command of General Salvador Mercado, fleeing for the border town of Ojinaga, where he planned to cross over into Él Presidio, Texas, all roads to the south now being blocked by the Revolutionaries. In all the streets of Chihuahua City, the rebel soldiers and citizens were celebrating the victory of the Villistas over the entire province of Chihuahua; it was as though the whole city had joined in a huge fiesta. This was the best Christmas of the Revolution. The División del Norte and its general-in-chief Villa were triumphant; the Federales had been routed and sent packing. This was also the chance, for which the professional mercenaries hired by Noble Winthrop had been watching and waiting, to rescue Araminta; and in the end, their recovery of her was so simple that they almost could not believe it.

Now, there was in Chihuahua City a fashionable gaming hell known as Él Cosmopolita. It had used to be owned by Jacob La Touche, who was nicknamed "The Turk." An obese, shuffling man, he had come to Chihuahua City twenty-five years before, with no shoes on his feet and leading a dancing bear; and from this, he had risen to become a millionaire many times over and to own this foremost gambling establishment, El Cosmopolita. A magnificent mansion on Paseo Bolivar was his as well. It was called The Palace of Tears, because it had been built with the profits of the gaming hell, which had ruined many a family in Chihuahua City. But Villa's great victory was the defeat of the Turk, who, seeing the handwriting on the wall and valuing his life, thought it prudent to retreat with Mercado to Ojinaga. Upon entering Chihuahua City, Villa promptly confiscated both El Cosmopolita and The Palace of Tears. The mansion he presented to one of his generals as a Christmas gift; the gaming hell he seized for himself. It was here to El Cosmopolita that he went to celebrate his conquest of the Federales, cheerfully carting along with him several of his officers and men, including Rigo, to play roulette and poker.

"I won't be gone too long, *querida*," Rigo promised Araminta as he prepared to leave the railroad car, "for the roulette wheel is rigged; and for some unfathomable reason, we *Méxicanos* play poker without the sevens, eights, or nines, which does not make for as interesting a game as that played with an American deck of cards. When I come back, I'll bring a late supper from the Chinese bar—if that grizzled old Mongolian Chee Lee has cooked up anything worth eating! Meanwhile, you just rest. I know how hard this past month has been on you." His eyes darkened momentarily with concern as he kissed her mouth gently.

She was now in her fifth month of pregnancy; and

although she seemed to him more beautiful than ever, her face was pale from the toll all their hard traveling had taken on her, and mauve circles shadowed her eyes, reminding him of how she had looked that first day he had ever seen her, in the hotel in El Paso. Beneath the loose peasant gown that she wore, her belly now swelled softly but plainly with his child, and she appeared so like a madonna to him in the soft glow of the lamplight that his heart ached with love for her.

"I *am* tired." Araminta sighed, her eyes closing briefly. "I think I will just lie down and read awhile until you return. Have a good time, Rigo, and if I fall asleep, wake me up when you get back. I want to hear all about the festivities for the article I am working on, and how Villa celebrated his victory, and, most of all, whether you won or lost at poker."

Almost, Rigo changed his mind and stayed with her. But then she reminded him that it would be insulting to Villa if one of his most important generals failed to come to the fiesta, and finally she persuaded Rigo to go on. She heard him speak to the guards outside on duty and then, as his stallion was led up by his aide-de-camp, Chico Morales, mount up and ride off toward El Cosmopolita. She was, in truth, exhausted, and after reading a few pages of the newspapers, drifted into a slumber so deep that she did not hear the felling of the sentries who surrounded the railroad car nor the opening of her bedroom door. Yet even if she *had* heard the professional mercenaries silencing her guards and invading her domain, it would have availed her naught; for they had brought along a handkerchief soaked in chloroform, to silence her should she scream and bring the Villistas down upon them.

"Jesus Christ!" one of the gunslingers swore softly as he stared down at her lying on the bed so peacefully, her hair tumbled about her, gleaming like molten gold in the lamplight, her fair skin as luminous as a pearl dappled with roses, her breasts swelling and sinking softly beneath the translucent cotton of her gown. "Would you look at that! No wonder Del Castillo kept her for himself and didn't bother demanding a ransom!"

"Yeah, I'll say," the other man in the bedroom agreed as he bent to press the handkerchief over her nose and mouth. Untroubled, she breathed in the chloroform and drifted deeper into oblivion. "Check around, Cheyenne. See if she's got a shawl or something we can wrap her up in against the night wind— Son of a bitch!" he exclaimed quietly as he drew down the sheet that covered her body. "She's pregnant! Great. Just what we needed!"

"I concede it's a complication, but hell, Grant, what else'd you expect? Del Castillo kidnapped her, for Christ's sake! He's probably been at her day and night since the beginning. Here. Toss this poncho around her, then pick her up, and let's get out of here now."

Outside, a wagon driven by the other two men, Kiefer and Hondo, was waiting. Grant and Cheyenne loaded Araminta in back and covered her up, then climbed in beside her, their sombreros pulled down low over their faces. Pulling serapes about their shoulders, they sat pressed against the back of the seat, alert for any possible trouble as Hondo clucked to the team, and, wheels clattering gently over the road, the wagon rolled slowly out of Chihuahua City into the night.

Throughout the long journey to the border, the gunslingers were unfailingly polite. They addressed her as Mrs. Hobart, much to Araminta's annoyance, and did not harm her in any way, except that they refused to release her, even though she explained to them that she was in no danger from Rigo, that to the contrary, in fact, she was desirous of returning to him at once! They apologized but remained adamant, deaf to her pleas; the only way they could collect the rest of their money was to complete the mission they had undertaken. She had gone on imploring them endlessly, to no avail. Now she sat huddled in the back of the wagon in which she had ridden all the way from Chihuahua City—the folds of Rigo's poncho wrapped around her and an old *rebozo* covering and hiding her hair, Araminta was cast into the depths of despair. Soon, they would be at the border and then across the Rio Grande into Texas—

Oh, why had her grandfather sent these men after her? These mercenaries would do anything for money; they treated her courteously only because they wished to be paid and, under other circumstances, might just as readily have killed her. A dozen times or more, Araminta had thought of escaping from them; she still wore her knife strapped to her thigh, and if she was able to flee and to reach any village at all, she felt that Rigo's name would protect her. She knew enough Spanish by now to say, *"El Salvaje, soy la mujer del suyo."* The Savage One, I am his woman. Surely, hearing that, no one would dare to lay a finger on her! But still, encumbered by the child she carried, she would not be able to walk very far; and the gunslingers had watched her too closely thus far for her to make any bid for freedom. Yet if she did not try soon, her chance to do so at all would be irretrievably lost.

If only she could steal the wagon! If it were just Hondo guarding her, she could use her knife handle to hit him on the head from behind, then shove him off the seat and take his place. But the other three men, Cheyenne, Kiefer, and Grant, were on horseback; they could easily ride her down. Desperately, she glanced around at the high canyon walls that enclosed her. Once these bluffs were left behind, she would have no place to hide, even if she did somehow manage to gain her freedom. At least if she climbed up into the rocks, the professionals would have to leave their horses to come after her, and perhaps then she could circle around and take one.

This was a foolish, desperate plan, Araminta thought, but she could not think of another. Before she could act to carry out her scheme, however, Cheyenne called a halt, saying that it was time again to rest and to water the horses. Rigo, when he had abducted her, had never paused so often. But when he had stolen her away she had not been pregnant, easily tired, and compelled to answer more frequent calls of nature. Opening the wagon's tailgate, Cheyenne assisted her down and walked with her a short way down the canyon, where a jumble of boulders and rocks would provide a measure of privacy. Wordlessly, Araminta availed herself of it. She stared up at the serrated canyon wall, wondering whether she could, before Cheyenne realized what she was about, scramble up the narrow track that appeared to twine its way upward until it was lost in the bluffs. Surely, she must try.

It was hopeless; the ribbon of path was too steep and encrusted with a layer of small, loose rock that came away in her hands when she scrabbled for purchase, attempting to haul herself up, losing her *rebozo* in the process. Within moments, she was slipping, sliding backward to feel Cheyenne's arms close around her, lifting her and setting her firmly onto the canyon floor. Slowly he turned her about to face him, his hands on her arms, holding her prisoner.

"That was a foolish thing to do, Mrs. Hobart." His face, bearded with blond stubble, was etched with anger. "You might have been hurt; you might have fallen and injured your child. I can't permit that. Your grandfather's paying for your safe return. I'd be obliged if you wouldn't try anything like that again."

"And *I'd* be obliged if you'd take your hands off my wife!" a hard, cold voice growled unexpectedly, startling them.

My wife! Not *my woman*.

Dear God. It *was* Judd! Araminta saw when she turned toward the sound, cringing as her eyes confirmed what her ears had heard. This just couldn't be happening, she insisted to herself; this just couldn't be real. It must be a horrible nightmare—but its worst monster, Judd, her husband, mounted upon his favorite buckskin stallion, was just a few yards away. She shivered violently, knowing now what he had done to

Marisol, the cruelty of which he was capable, a cruelty
Araminta had only sensed before but instinctively had
feared. Understanding its full measure did not lessen
the horror, but, rather, increased it. She was no longer
a green girl. In Mexico, her eyes had been opened to
the world; and now they observed clearly the deep
lines of dissipation that grooved his coarsely handsome
face, the puffiness of his bloodshot eyes, the jaw already beginning to slacken from overindulgence in
food and drink, the brutal twist to his lips. Araminta
did not know how she could ever have married him,
not even for her grandfather's sake.

From crystal-blue eyes narrowed and as hard as
flint, Judd stared back at her, feeling as though someone had slugged him powerfully in the groin, doubling
him over. Christ! She was beautiful, more beautiful
than he had remembered, an ice maiden melted to
release her pure-burning flame. He had never seen her
hair down before, never realized how long it was,
tumbling past her waist, a waterfall of liquid fire in
the sunlight. In the depths of her raw-emerald eyes
smoldered the sensuous knowledge of a new-wakened
bride; her lush, dusty-rose mouth begged for a man's
hard, hungry kisses—and had received them, Judd
knew as his gaze dropped to her belly swollen with
the half-breed bastard brat that Del Castillo had
pumped into it! No wonder the greaser pig had not
ransomed or returned her. He had got her with child—
and, from the looks of her, almost right from the start.
He must have been quite sure that the bastard was his
to have kept her; he had not shared her, then, but had
made her his alone. Well, that would change soon

enough, once Judd got his hands on her. She was too soiled for the role of his wife, but the part of a whore would suit just fine before he finished with her.

"Step away," he directed to Cheyenne. "You've done your job—and, for all I know, maybe then some—and now, it's over. Here's your money." Judd hefted from around his pommel a pair of saddlebags and tossed them on the ground. Much as he hated to part with their contents, he did not want to tangle with the mercenaries, and the one standing before him looked as though he might be willing to come to Araminta's assistance. "Take it and go."

"No! Please," she beseeched, laying an imploring hand upon Cheyenne's arm. "Please don't leave me alone here with him."

"He *is* your husband, Mrs. Hobart—whether you like it or not," the gunslinger stated flatly, determinedly shaking her off, bending to retrieve the saddlebags and slinging them over one shoulder. "And just like he said: I've done my job—and only my job, for whatever it's worth—and now it's over." Then, his face stoic, he strode, without a backward glance, toward the rest of his crew. In moments, they had mounted up and departed from the canyon, heedless that they had destroyed her life.

Slowly, Judd swung down from his saddle and began to stalk her, taking a perverse delight in how, her eyes wide with fear, her face blanching, she backed away from him until she was pressed up against a solid boulder, trapped like a cornered animal, and there was no place left to run. Brutally, he seized her then, hauling her up against him so she could feel the hard bulge in his breeches, his hand grabbing her hair and jerking her head back as though to snap her neck in half. He wanted her still, and hated her for that, for daring to survive and give to another what had belonged to him, her husband. For that, he intended to make her pay; she could see it in his eyes as, for a long, tension-fraught moment, he leered down at her, his foul breath reeking of stale whiskey. And then, to Araminta's utter horror and revulsion, he spread his hand across her rounded belly and asked derisively:

"Did you like it?"

Do you like it?

Yes . . .

She closed her eyes hard at the memory of what she had shared with Rigo, trying to blot it out so it would not be besmirched by her husband. Tears trickled from the corners of her lashes, seeping into the hair at her temples; trying to gather her courage, she forced herself to blink the droplets away. When she did not respond, Judd gave her a vicious shake.

"Answer me, you goddamned slut! You Mexican's whore! Or I swear I'll break your proud, frigging neck! Did you like it?"

She knew then that he expected, that he *wanted* her to cower from him, to grovel at his feet, to beg for mercy, to deny what he asked of her; and so, resolutely stiffening her spine against him, Araminta did none of those things.

"Yes," she replied quietly, steadily somehow— and the taste of Rigo's revenge was sweet upon her tongue. "The answer is yes; he didn't even have to force me." Judd hit her then, with his beefy fist, backhanding her so hard across the face that she reeled and staggered and sprawled backward upon the earth, her head ringing from the impact. Blood spurted from her cut lip as she looked up at him so savagely through the snarled curtain of her hair that he felt a momentary twinge of uneasiness. "Rigo will kill you for that," she said softly, with certainty, so that despite himself, Judd laughed nervously—with the bravado of a coward, she thought scornfully.

"Or maybe I'll kill him instead—just as I killed your grandfather, you bitch! Yes, I did, right before I came here," he boasted, shocking and anguishing her with the unmistakable ring of truth in his words. "Do you know? I actually believe that old fool was going to carry out his threat of having you divorce me, of dragging my good name through the courts, and of disinheriting me, of cheating me of the High Sierra! He knew I didn't want you back, you see—at least, not as my wife. But Noble couldn't let it rest! Nooo! He had to print up those damned reward posters, hire those frigging mercenaries.

"It was Noble who was supposed to show up here today, not I. He had grown supicious of me, you see, didn't trust me anymore, knowing what all I had to gain by getting rid of you and him both. So he didn't even bother telling me you were alive, that the mercenaries had found you and were bringing you back. If I hadn't just happened to drop by the ranch this morning, I wouldn't even have known about the telegram they sent him, arranging this meeting. Lucky for me that Teresa was so overjoyed by the news—and expected that I would be, too—that she ignorantly blabbed the whole, was even obliging enough to show me the wire. The stupid cow! She signed Noble's death warrant.

"I set out after him at once. He had a head start, but since he was so old and ill, that didn't matter. I caught up with him quick enough, and when he tried to drive me off with his cane, I grabbed it and bashed him over the head with it. Whooee! You should have seen that old fool! He toppled like a poleaxed steer out of his saddle, probably never even knew what hit him! Then I lifted his saddlebags and came on. He's buzzard meat, I tell you—and so will that son of a bitch Del Castillo be if he has nerve enough to show his greaser pig face around here!

"And now, I'm tired of all this talk . . . *wife,*" he sneered, his eyes raking her body in a way that made Araminta's skin crawl, made her want to vomit. He was mad, a maniac! "I think it's about high time we celebrated our wedding night, don't you?" With those words, Judd reached down with both hands and caught the round neck of her poncho, brutishly jerking her upright and tearing it in half, exposing her thin, translucent cotton gown to his hideous gaze, crazed with mania and lust. Knowing she had no hope of fighting him, Araminta prayed for death. As though he had read her mind, Judd jeered, "And all the while I'm rutting on top of you, you think about this, you cheap little *puta:* When I'm done with you, I'm going to kill you, too—along with that abomination you let that bastard Del Castillo spew into your belly!"

"You know, somehow, *amigo,* I don't think so."

Araminta's heart leaped. Stunned disbelief and inconceivable joy flooded her when she heard that low, mocking drawl, that lilting Spanish voice she would know anywhere. Wrenching away from Judd, she cried out, "Rigo!", and then the two men became a blur as all the pent-up hatred and emotion they felt toward each other for over a decade was now unbridled and given full, furious rein. Rigo flung himself at Judd, and they went down in a sickening thrash of limbs, rolling and tumbling, pummeling and pounding each other brutally, viciously, murder in their hearts. Their terrible, even gleeful ferocity was horrifying, yet Araminta was morbidly enthralled by it, unable to tear her eyes away. She still half feared that Rigo was just a desert mirage. Yet in her heart, she had known that he would come for her, that he would find her wherever she might be, though he must search the earth to its ends for her with Hell standing in his way. He bashed and battered Judd unmercifully, blackening his eye and bloodying his nose before Judd butted him powerfully, knocking him back.

His hand shooting to his holster, Judd drew his pistol. But catching hold of Judd's wrist, Rigo beat it ruthlessly against the ground, again and again, until Judd was forced to let go of the revolver and it went skidding away, just out of reach. Wildly tearing free of each other, both men sprang to their feet, their faces now marred by cuts and bruises and covered with blood. Their hard, virile bodies strained with effort, they stood toe to toe, each slugging the other, grunting and groaning, wincing with pain. A loud, sharp crack testified to a broken rib; Judd grimaced, positioning one arm to shield the vulnerable spot. Rigo's smile was diabolic as he homed in, his fists hammering Judd's face and belly unmercifully, then landing a hard uppercut on the chin, sending Judd sprawling. Then Rigo launched himself upon his fallen opponent and Judd's legs came up, kicking him squarely in the groin, hurling him back, making him stumble and double over. Suddenly, each was on the ground again and at the other's throat, choking, strangling. Gurgling, trying to gulp air, Judd mashed his splayed hand hard against Rigo's face, flattening his nose in a desperate attempt to force him off, while Rigo beat Judd's head violently against the ground until, in a underhanded trick, stretching out his arm, Judd grabbed up a handful of desert sand and threw it straight into Rigo's eyes, blinding him. Rolling over, Judd snatched up his lost gun and staggered to his feet, raising the pistol, pointing it straight at Rigo's heart.

"No! I won't let you! I won't let you!" Araminta screamed, sobbing, flinging herself into Judd's path, her hands clawing like a wild thing at his face until he seized her around the waist and, yanking her to him, jammed the barrel of the revolver hard against her temple.

"Say *'Vaya con Dios,'* you bitch," he snarled as he cocked the hammer; and her eyes widened with helpless terror and met Rigo's own horrificd, stricken glance in a desperate, silent, emotional outpouring of all the words there was not time to speak before a terrible, roaring explosion deafened her ears and a merciful blackness swirled up to engulf her.

Lovers Entwine, and Hearts Enfold

Chapter Twenty

Chihuahua, Mexico, 1914

"I had to shoot. He would have killed her, just as he tried to kill me." Slowly, Noble lowered the rifle he held in his hands and stared at the grotesque corpse of his godson, Judd, sprawled in a heap upon the ground. Noble's voice held a kind of wonderment as he spoke, as though he still could not believe that Judd had so viciously attacked him with the malacca cane, smashing him over the head with it and, when he had collapsed and plummeted from his saddle, had galloped off and left him for dead. "You should have finished what you started, boy!" he said suddenly, speaking so sharply that for a moment, Rigo thought that the old *gringo* was talking to him, and he glanced up swiftly, his dark eyes flashing like the blades of his double-ended knife, from where he knelt upon the earth, Araminta's unconscious figure cradled tenderly against his breast. "Didn't I always tell you, Judd: Finish what you start, boy . . . *didn't I?* If you had, none of us would be here now."

It just didn't seem right to Noble that Judd was dead and that Rigo was alive . . . still alive, damn him, the infernal bandit! Such was the potency of the thought that for an instant, Noble was half tempted to shoot him, too. Convulsively, Noble's hands tightened on the stock of his rifle, itching to pull the trigger. But then he saw something he had not seen for a very long time, and as he watched it, damned, foolish old man's tears that would not be held back stung his eyes, and, without his even being aware that he did so, he slowly shoved his rifle into its scabbard.

His son, Preston, and daughter-in-law, Katherine, had looked at each other like that, as Rigo and Araminta were looking at each other now that her eyelids had fluttered open at last. They were oblivious to all save each other, their faces naked with love, with longing, with so much emotion that no words were necessary. Her arms were twined about his neck, and now, he was embracing her and kissing her deeply, feverishly—and she was clinging to him and kissing him back shamelessly, damn it, tears silently streaking her cheeks. With his lips, Rigo brushed them away gently; and then he did speak, muttering to her in that incomprehensible foreign tongue of his—except that Araminta seemed to understand and to hang on every word, her heart in her eyes, her hand laid tenderly against his cheek for a moment before she clasped his own hand in hers and pressed it to her belly, where their child grew within her.

A child. Noble closed his eyes tightly at the realization, a hard lump rising in his throat at the sudden, painful, unbidden knowledge that he was an empty, embittered, lonely old man, who had driven away his own child, his only son; and with all his heart, he begrudged and envied Rigo that hand on Araminta's belly, that life that, born of Rigo's seed, grew within her.

Ah, young man, young man so much wiser than I, once I, too, knew what it was to be young and in love . . . so long ago that for so many years now, until this moment, I had almost forgotten. . . .

A terrible and unexpected anguish rose within Noble at the realization, of what he had lost, of what he had so carelessly thrown away, all of it gone now, even Araminta and the child she carried within her, the child that should have been conceived of her marriage to Judd Hobart, but that, conceived out of love instead, was Rigo del Castillo's. That he, Noble, should live to see the day when the blood of his enemies should mingle with his; for was it not his own blood in Araminta's veins, and in that of the child she would bear to this handsome, hot-blooded Spaniard, this proud, strong young stallion of a man, with a world of knowledge and wisdom in his dark eyes?

Oh, proud, stubborn old fool of a man! What wouldn't you give to have it all to do over again!

Noble thought, cursing himself and his blindness until now, when it was too late. His head spinning, his heart aching, he slowly toppled from his saddle.

"Grandfather! Grandfather!" Araminta cried, springing to her feet and rushing to his side, her face etched with concern as she bent over him, half raising him and loosening his collar. "Is it the pain in your chest again?"

No, the pain in my heart.

"Oh, Rigo." Araminta glanced up at him, anguished, as she cradled her grandfather against her shoulder. "Help me get him up, get him to a doctor. I think he's dying."

But instead of doing as she asked, Rigo hunkered down beside her, studying her grandfather dispassionately from beneath hooded lids.

"Well, if that is the case, I must say, old *gringo*, that I am surprised," he drawled mockingly, causing Noble's eyes abruptly to fly open wide and meet his own fiercely.

Why, how dare this brazen young Mexican deride him? Noble asked himself, incensed.

"What I mean is," Rigo continued, "what a disappointment it must be to a big, strong man like yourself . . . to survive such a crack on your skull—which would no doubt have staggered even the hugest of bulls—and then—¡caramba!—somehow to manage to ride all this long way to rescue your granddaughter, only to die here in the desert, in Chihuahua, south of the border. Well, I am surprised, that's all. Were I in your shoes, old *gringo*, I should want to die in my own country, in my bed, and I should do everything in my power to cheat death, to live to see my grandchildren.'' Rigo shrugged indifferently. ''But then, what do I know? A poor Mexican peasant like me, eh? Still, that is what I myself should want, what I myself should do, old *gringo*, were *I* in your shoes.''

A strained little silence fell at that, but Rigo appeared not to notice.

''You know, Araminta, *querida*,'' he went on casually, as though the thought had just occurred to him, ''I am thinking of selling Casa Blanca. Now that the Federales have been sent packing from Chihuahua, I can reclaim my land here, and our child can be born at Casa Grande.''

''Araminta, get me up!'' Noble growled suddenly through gritted teeth, discovering, strangely, that the dizziness in his head and the pains in his chest had begun to dissipate at the insidious challenge that had been issued him. He would show this arrogant bandit, this impudent desperado, the stuff of which Noble Winthrop was made! But he was a big man, and Araminta was not strong enough to lift him to his feet.

For a very long minute, Noble stared at the bronze hand outstretched to him, the hand that had, at the last moment, dauntlessly knocked aside the gun barrel pressed to Araminta's temple, even as Noble had fired into Judd's body, so that the bullet from Judd's own pistol discharged at the impact of Noble's shot had spent itself harmlessly, sparing Araminta's life, and that of her unborn child.

''Well, old *gringo*, have you made up your mind yet today about whether you're going to live or die? It is your decision. So, you decide.''

You decide. In those two words lay a second chance, a chance not to repeat the mistakes of the past, a chance to get it right this time.

"Today . . . today, young man, I'm going to live," the old man said, taking the outstretched hand.

"A wise decision, old *gringo*," the young man said, helping the old man to rise.

The young woman was silent, her head cocked a trifle, listening intently to the sweet Spanish love song boldly plucked on the strings of her heart.

Author's Note

Dear Reader:

I wish I could tell you that *Desperado* is a work
of total fiction, born wholly of my imagination, and
that I made up all the horrible things that the
hacendados, both Spanish and American, did to the
common people of Mexico. But I can't, for
unfortunately, they happened and were all too real,
the direct cause of the Mexican Revolution, which
began in 1910 and may be said to have lasted until
1917, when Venustiano Carranza became president;
or 1920, when Alvaro Obregón became president;
or 1929, when Pascual Ortiz Rubio became
president; or 1940, when Manuel Avila Camacho
became president; or even that in its own way, it
continues even now. All of these years were marked

by turmoil and violence, with the last important rebellions happening in 1938, when Saturnino Cedillo was defeated.

Mexico is in many respects a wild, savage, and beautiful country. I have visited it many times; and I continue to be amazed that while our sister south of the border knows so much about us, we know comparatively little about her—and this despite our own country's large Hispanic population. Truly, this is an oversight in dire need of correction! Like Canada to the north, Mexico to the south is our closest neighbor. I have, in the character of General Rigo del Castillo, attempted to bring alive for you, the reader, not only the spirit of the diverse Mexican culture itself, but also the tender and romantic side that is too often overlooked or forgotten in our fascination with *el hombre machísimo*. Neither General Rigo del Castillo nor *la gringa*, Araminta Winthrop, ever really existed outside of my imagination. The "ballad" at the beginning of the book is my own—though I would like to think the Villistas would have sung it had they only known it, for it is in keeping with many of their own. It may, by the way, be sung to the tune of "Mr. Froggie Went A-Courtin' ".

In portraying the notorious Pancho Villa, I have tried to rely primarily on first-hand accounts written by those who actually knew him personally. I am especially indebted to *Insurgent Mexico*, by John Reed, a noted journalist and also the author of *Ten Days That Shook the World*, his classic reportage on the Socialist Revolution, which established him as the founder of the modern school of creative journalism. John Reed reported from Mexico during the Revolution and traveled with the Revolutionary armies, among them, the Villistas. He knew Pancho Villa personally, and many of the anecdotes I have related in *Desperado* about both Villa and the Villistas are from Reed's work, although the few liberties I have taken, for plot purposes, with a small portion of the material, or any errors I may have inadvertently made, are my own. The two Mexican songs quoted in Chapter Thirteen are recorded by John Reed in *Insurgent Mexico* (New York: International Publishers, 1969), pages 67 and 158, respectively. Corrections to the Spanish and to the English translation are mine.

Although from much of what has been recorded about him, we can probably safely conclude that Mayor Fierro was indeed a maniac, I do not know that the same can be said about Villa. Studying him, I personally formed the opinion that had he been a traveled, educated man, he would have proved a great leader. His grasp of what ought to have been beyond his reach, both intellectually and academically, appears to have been uncanny, his major difficulty the fact that he was, as he himself realized, a peasant, not a politician (although I daresay he would have been right at home with many of those in our own Congress today!). Whether Villa was a good man or a bad one, I cannot say. I suspect that he was indeed ruthless when it served his purpose; but I also believe that like our own Billy the Kid, Jesse James, and Butch

Cassidy, much of the real man has been lost amid
the legend, both heroic and infamous deeds blown
wholly out of proportion, with little consideration
given to the fact that, like much of today's troubled
youth, Villa was a product of both his times and his
society, being just sixteen when he first killed a
man—and that, he always insisted, for raping his
sister. Had the Villistas ever been able to come to
terms with the Zapatistas, they could doubtless have
crushed Mexico's dictatorial government between
them. Unfortunately, the Mexican armies, both
Federales and Revolutionaries, have a history of too
many generals and not enough rank-and-file
privates. After their second victory in 1914, over
Torreón, the Villistas, like so many of their ilk,
gradually devolved into chaos and disintegration.
Villa himself died in 1923, at the age of 45, when,
despite that by then, he lived relatively quietly, he
was ambushed and assassinated in Hidalgo de
Parral, 200 miles south of Chihuahua City. His
1919 Dodge, riddled with bullet holes, may be seen
at Quinta Luz, his former 30-room mansion and
now a museum in Chihuahua City. Grave robbers
exhumed his body in 1925 and cut off his head,
which is still lost; the rest is buried in Mexico City.
But ¡Viva Villa! is a cry that is not forgotten. The
U.S. prohibition against arms sales to the
Revolutionaries south of the border was lifted in
1914.

   I would like to acknowledge and thank my editor
and friend Fredda Isaacson, for standing by me
through thick and thin during my writing of

Desperado, at a cost of long hours and general
inconvenience to herself, I know. Despite this, she
listened, sympathized, advised, and offered words
of praise and encouragement, so invaluable to
writers, who work alone day in and day out and
have so precious-few outlets for venting stress and
frustration, and so few resources for garnering a
word of appreciation and a pat on the back for a job
well done. A mere thanks is insufficient to express
my deep gratitude because Fredda somehow always
manages to do both, dole out criticism in kind doses
and compliments in genuine ones. I do not know
what more a writer could ask from her editor—and
can only hope that the reverse also holds true.

Last but never least, I come to you, the reader,
for without you to buy and read and enjoy my
books, there would be no point in my writing them.
Having begun writing my first novel, *No Gentle
Love*, in 1976, I have been in this business now for
well over a decade. If I have not said it before, it is
time to say it now: I do thank you. *Desperado* is
dedicated to you, for your caring and support
through the years, for your wonderful letters, for
the fact that when you read my books, people who
exist nowhere beyond my imagination come alive in
your own, as well, making you laugh and cry as
much as they do me. They are my special friends,
as are each and every one of you. I hope that Rigo
and Araminta entertained you as much as they did
me. If you would like to write to me or to receive a
copy of my free, semiannual newsletter, you may
send your letter or request, along with a legal-sized,

stamped, self-addressed envelope, to me in care of Warner Books, Inc., 1271 Avenue of the Americas, New York, New York 10020. I read each and every one of your letters personally; they are my "little bit of Christmas" all year round. Till next time, good health, good fortune, and good reading, *mis amigos!*

Rebecca Brandewyne